THE BODY
UNDER THE
BRIDGE

·················· ··················

*"Paul McCusker weaves threads of the natural,
unnatural, and supernatural into a darkly tangled mystery for his detective-
turned-priest Father Louis Gilbert, to unravel."*
– BRIAN SIBLEY, *author of* Shadowlands

*"Paul is a truly accomplished writer. His plot construction is masterly…
Father Gilbert is a great creation."*
– ADRIAN PLASS, *writer and speaker*

"If you like mysteries you will love The Body Under
the Bridge *– but it's more than that; beyond the plot twists you will find
deeply spiritual themes about good, evil, the family, and the consequences of
our choices. An incredible mixture of chills and thoughtfulness."*
– ROB PARSONS, OBE

*"Paul McCusker is a master at telling a good mystery
that keeps you wondering what the next page holds. McCusker has
a great gift and you, the reader, are the recipient."*
– GLENN T. STANTON, *author, speaker and researcher for*
Focus on the Family

*"Beautifully written… Paul McCusker joins the likes of
G.K. Chesterton and Dorothy L. Sayers with his wise and witty
creation, Father Gilbert."*
– PHILIP GLA

OTHER WORKS BY THE AUTHOR

The Mill House

A Season of Shadows

Time Scene Investigators: The Gabon Virus
(with Dr. Walt Larimore)

Time Scene Investigators: The Influenza Bomb
(with Dr Walt Larimore)

Time Thriller Trilogy:
Ripple Effect
Out of Time
Memory's Gate

Adventures in Odyssey *(12 novels)*

Passages *(6 novels)*

The Imagination Station Series *(18 novels)*

The Colossal Book of Quick Skits

ORIGINAL AUDIO DRAMAS

The Father Gilbert Mysteries: Investigations of Another Kind

C.S. Lewis at War: The Dramatic Story Behind Mere Christianity

The Life of Jesus: Eyewitness Accounts from The Luke Reports

Bonhoeffer: The Cost of Freedom

Amazing Grace: The Inspiration Stories of John Newton,
Olaudah Equiano and William Wilberforce *(with Dave Arnold)*

NON-FICTION

C.S. Lewis & Mere Christianity: The Crisis That Created a Classic

Screwtape Letters: The Annotated Edition

THE BODY UNDER THE BRIDGE

PAUL MCCUSKER

LION FICTION

Published by Lion Fiction
an imprint of
Lion Hudson plc
Wilkinson House, Jordan Hill Road
Oxford OX2 8DR, England
www.lionhudson.com/fiction

ISBN 978 1 78264 107 0
e-ISBN 978 1 78264 108 7

First edition 2015

A catalogue record for this book is available from the British Library

Printed and bound in the UK, October 2015, LH26

To Adrian & Bridget, whose ongoing friendship and love have been a source of inspiration and comfort for many years.

ACKNOWLEDGMENTS

With gratitude to Tony Collins and his team at Lion Hudson for their input and help throughout the writing process. Thanks to my wife Elizabeth, who graciously reads, re-reads, corrects and suggests. Fr John Bartunek gave spiritual guidance and advice. Rev. Andrew Montgomery was always on my mind, whether he knew it or not. To Janet Kobobel-Grant for her advice and friendship. And Tommy and Ellie McCusker often provided inspiration and distraction, each as needed.

I'm thankful, too, for the many fans of the *Father Gilbert Mysteries* audio dramas who have contacted me over the years. Their encouragement means a lot.

CHAPTER 1

The feeling had come upon Father Louis Gilbert suddenly. Cold slimy fingers caressed the back of his neck. His eyes burned and a taste like old nicotine filled his mouth and the back of his throat. An acrid smell of ammonia assailed his nostrils.

He sat perfectly still at his desk. The pen in his hand held steady two inches above the notepaper. He waited for the feeling to pass. It didn't. He carefully lowered the pen and took off his round, gold-rimmed reading glasses. His eyes turned to the closed door.

Something had changed just outside of his office. Mrs Mayhew, the secretary for St Mark's since time began, had stopped typing on her computer keyboard. Her chair scraped across the hardwood floor as she pushed back from her desk. In his mind's eye, Father Gilbert saw her stand up, responding to the rapidly approaching footsteps.

He braced himself. The feeling meant his adversary was nearby – one he'd known as a Scotland Yard detective. It had often sneered at him from the shadows and taunted him out of the corner of his eye. It was Death.

Father Gilbert rose to greet it.

Mr Urquhart, the church sexton, burst in. His face was red, his bald head dripping with sweat. "Father," he spoke in a deep Scottish accent. "Come quickly. There's a man on the tower. He says he's going to jump."

* * *

"Please phone the police, Mrs Mayhew," Father Gilbert said as he rushed past her desk.

"Of course, Father."

Father Gilbert hurried after Mr Urquhart down the hall leading to the nave of St Mark's. "How did he get up to the tower?" The door was usually locked.

"I was cleaning the vestibule," Mr Urquhart called over his shoulder. His voice came in gasps. "I had moved some hymnals into the closet just inside the staircase. He must have slipped in when my back was turned."

Reaching the nave, the two men broke into a run – a straight race between the neat rows of polished pews. They reached the vestibule where the door to the church tower stood open.

"I saw him just as he rounded the first turn in the stairs," Mr Urquhart said. "I chased him up to the belfry. He told me to stay away or he'd jump."

At the bottom stair, Father Gilbert paused, remembering what a long climb it would be. "Please wait here for the police."

"Yes, Father."

A large man, barrel-chested and broad-shouldered, Father Gilbert reached out and grabbed at the railing – a rope, actually, that had been threaded through strategically placed eyelets. He propelled himself upwards.

The stairs circled up and up, winding like a coiled spring inside a square box. He couldn't remember the measurements – how many stairs, how tall the Normanesque tower was. What he *did* remember was that he hadn't been to the gym in weeks.

He could feel the sweat on his scalp under his thick and dishevelled hair. Damp formed at the back of his grey clerical shirt. His stiff white dog collar was cutting into his throat.

Reaching the door to the belfry, he hesitated. The air was thick and musty, relieved only by a ribbon of fresh air coming from the open hatch above. The formidable iron bell hung still and alone, the ropes dangling down all the way to the bottom of the tower. He followed the planking along the wall to the opposite side where an iron ladder stretched up. Grabbing the ladder, he climbed upwards towards the square patch of blue sky above. The ladder shivered under his weight.

He reached the top rung and grabbed the two handles that allowed him to heave his body onto the sun-baked tar. The cool breeze of a beautiful late spring day chilled the hot moisture on his face. Fumbling to his feet, he squinted against the bright sun.

The church tower was square and framed on all four sides by waist-high parapets. Directly opposite from the hatch, a man stood with his back to the priest. Shaggy sun-bleached hair felt onto broad shoulders, the top of a Y-shaped torso – a lean and muscular body shown off by a tight T-shirt. The man wore faded denims, the back pockets torn. His well-worn boots were splattered with mud, cement, and plaster. Presumably he was a builder.

The man reached over and placed a hand on one of the parapets. He seemed to be admiring the view of the town of Stonebridge below.

Father Gilbert took a step forward. His shoe scuffed the gravel. The man spun around to face him.

Father Gilbert held up his hands in a gesture of submission. "This is my church. I'm Father Gilbert."

The man's face was prematurely aged from too much time in the sun. There were deep lines on his forehead and around his eyes, blond stubble on his cheeks and chin. He might have been in his thirties but looked older. Rivulets of tears had smeared the dust on the man's cheeks. Father Gilbert saw something dark in his eyes, a terrible despair. This man would not come quietly down the stairs.

Somewhere behind the normal sounds of Stonebridge's traffic, a police siren wailed.

The man's eyes darted in the direction of the sound. He looked at the priest in accusation.

"It's standard procedure when a man threatens to jump from my tower." Father Gilbert attempted a casual step forward.

The man took a step back, pressing himself against the parapet. With a grace that matched his body, he pulled himself upwards onto one of the embrasures.

"Don't!" Father Gilbert said sharply. He raised his hand, as if he could pull the man back with sheer force of will.

"There's nothing you can do," the man said.

"Then you have nothing to lose by telling me who you are and why you're up here."

The man shook his head.

"Don't I have a right to know why you want to throw yourself off of my tower?" Father Gilbert kept his hand outstretched.

The sirens were below them now. Father Gilbert wished the police had shown better sense. Then came the slamming car doors and urgent shouts. The man glanced over the side. Wiping the back of his hand across his eyes, he let out a small whimper.

"What's your name?" Father Gilbert asked. "I've told you mine. It's common courtesy to give me yours." And it was police procedure to establish a rapport as soon as possible. Something as simple as an exchange of names sometimes brought a would-be suicide back to humanity.

"It's all in my wallet. The police will find it when they collect my body." His voice was a painful rasp.

"Then tell me why you're here."

With a sudden sob, the man lowered his head. "I don't have a choice."

"Of course you do."

He shook his head. "It's the only way to stop them."

"Them?"

"Before they make me do things." His tears fell freely. "It's not fair." He faltered, his words lost in his sobs. He muttered to himself. Father Gilbert couldn't make out what he was saying.

"Look at me," Father Gilbert said. "Keep your eyes on mine. Whatever you're thinking and feeling right now will pass. But, go over that wall and your situation will become permanent."

The man tilted his head as if listening to something. Then he said, "It shouldn't have been found."

"What?"

He reached into his pocket and pulled out a gold chain. He held it up. A large medallion, the size of a drinks coaster, dangled in the light.

"What is it?" Father Gilbert wanted to get the man's focus on something other than dying.

"A curse."

"What does that mean?" Father Gilbert moved a step closer.

"Are you a holy man? Maybe if I leave it with you…"

Voices and footfalls echoed up from the hatch to the belfry.

The man's eyes darted towards the sound. "Before this is over, there are a few people who'll wish they did what I'm doing now."

"Whatever the trouble is—" Father Gilbert began to say.

The man cut him off. "Staying alive is too painful." He spoke with a voice choked by a deep anguish.

"Tell me what you mean," Father Gilbert said. "We'll talk it through."

The man shook his head. His face contorted as he fought back more tears. "I don't want to be an angel."

"An angel? What kind of angel?" Father Gilbert hoped the questions might keep the man engaged.

The capped head of a police officer appeared at the hatchway.

The man looked at the medallion, still dangling from his hand. "I'll leave this with you."

Father Gilbert took another step forward. "Listen to me, you don't—"

"*Take it,*" the man snapped and tossed the medallion at the priest, the disc spinning and the chain spiralling in the air.

Father Gilbert instinctively reached out to catch the medallion and knew he'd been duped. The man brought up his free arm. In his hand was a Stanley knife. The blade was out.

"Stop!" Father Gilbert shouted and threw himself at the man.

With a firm stroke, the man slashed the blade right across his throat. Blood pumped out of the gash, a warm spray in the wind that hit Father Gilbert's face.

Like a diver pushing off from the side of a boat, the man thrust himself backwards and disappeared over the edge of the tower.

Father Gilbert cried out as he rushed to the parapet.

He leaned over the edge, harbouring the unlikely hope that the man was clinging to the side of the tower. The man was not there. Nor was he lying on the bed of flowers that bloomed directly below.

Mr Urquhart stood next to a wheelbarrow filled with pulled weeds. He looked up at the priest, shielding his eyes with a dirty hand. "Father? What are you doing up there?"

"Where did he go?" Father Gilbert shouted. His voice was a strangled croak. "Did you see him?"

The old Scot looked around, then up again. "See who?"

"The man! He was up here in the tower and..." Father Gilbert's

13

voice trailed off. There were no police cars in the car park, nor any sirens. He glanced over at the hatch to the belfry. No one was there. Everything was perfectly normal.

He felt sick.

"I'm sorry, Father, but I don't know what you are talking about!" Mr Urquhart shouted up.

"Never mind." Father Gilbert stepped back. Leaning heavily against the stone, he gazed at the roof and replayed the scene in his mind. It was as vivid as anything he'd ever experienced.

He looked down at his shaking hands. He was clutching the gold medallion.

CHAPTER 2

Father Gilbert wasn't on mind-altering medication. He didn't suffer from delusions. He wasn't prone to hallucinations, trances, or visions, in the ecstatic religious sense of Jesus or Mary appearing before him. He was cautious about those kinds of experiences.

From time to time, however, he had unexplainable encounters that were similar to those chronicled by saints and mystics: vivid scenes that he perceived as real, as real as anything his senses could perceive. Usually these encounters were relevant to events that were about to unfold. He wouldn't call them premonitions, since they didn't directly foretell anything. They offered no instructions.

Among the many certainties of his faith, he allowed for a candid *I don't know*. He was never afraid of not knowing. Mystery was an inherent part of faith; it filled the gap between the limited understanding of Man and the limitless knowledge of God. The spiritual world had many dark corners that were filled with its own secrets and rules. He was often drawn to those places. *Why?* That seemed to be God's business. Mostly he was left feeling like an actor in a play he hadn't rehearsed for, working from a script he'd never seen.

He rarely spoke of these encounters to others. He knew people would think he was mad. And he feared he would be branded as the sort of American hyper-televangelist showman he disdained.

Mr Urquhart deserved an explanation. Mrs Mayhew, too – though she was a dyed-in-the-wool traditional Anglican who looked askance at anything unduly sensational. He couldn't miss the way they looked at each other – and at him – as he detailed what he'd experienced. They accepted it in silence. No questions, no suggestions that he should go immediately to the nearest mental hospital. A nod, and it was back to work.

Did he know what the encounter in the tower meant? No. He didn't recognize the man. He couldn't explain the gold medallion.

Nausea welled up within him. The encounter wasn't real, apart from the extraordinary physical evidence he now clasped in his hand. And he couldn't shake the harsh sting of failure. He hadn't stopped the man from throwing himself over the side.

Father Gilbert now paced the grounds around the church, his eyes moving back and forth from the well-tended grass and brick pavements to St Mark's Church itself – its large, rough, grey stones and arches, the stained-glass windows. He occasionally glanced up at the tower. It was a formidable-looking Norman structure. Strong and beautiful, but not elegant. Local legend asserted that when the tower was added to the original church, its design was based on the Magdalen College tower in Oxford.

He wondered how many people had used that tower for the purpose of suicide in the church's thousand-year history.

He drifted into "The Garden of Peace" – an area enclosed on three sides by tall hedges. It contained a stone statue of St Mark standing in a small bed of flowers, and a couple of benches meant for sitting and reflecting. The garden was meant to suggest seclusion, though how secluded a person might feel when surrounded by the traffic and shops and offices no more than fifty yards away, was a good question.

St Mark's was an anomaly, a funny little island in the middle of Stonebridge. The grounds had once spread out on all sides for a full six acres. Then came the inevitable sell-off of land as the church needed money to pay its bills. The bustling High Street of modern shops stretched past the front of the church, on the west side. A shopping centre with its vast car park appeared within a stone's throw on the north side. A two-storey office building loomed on the east side. The only patch of land held back from commercial use was the graveyard on the south side, enclosed by a tall wrought-iron fence with spear-tipped posts evocative of many classic horror films. Father Gilbert once asked in a homily if the fence was meant to keep people out or keep them in. For that he received a polite chuckle publicly and a few complaints about bad taste privately.

Father Gilbert sat down on one of the benches, hunched over, and rested his arms on his knees, the medallion still held tightly in his hand. Through the entrance to the Garden of Peace, he could see the flowerbed at the base of the tower. That's where the man would have fallen. He imagined the body jammed between the rough grey stones of the church wall and Mr Urquhart's daffodils.

Father Gilbert lifted the medallion for a better look. The gold was tarnished and flecked with mud. A lozenge-shaped red jewel sat in the centre. On the bottom, near the edge, was the head of a bird – at least, Father Gilbert assumed it was a bird – with branches moving up from the head to encircle the gem. The shoots of the branches sprouted round leaves. There were specks of white within the gold and he wondered if they might be small diamonds.

He turned the medallion over. The image on the back was upside down from the image on the front. To the left of the jewel was a man hanging on a cross – presumably Jesus – and to the right was an inscription that was too worn to make out. He frowned and turned the medallion around, then back and forth.

A voice called from the other side of the hedge. "Father?"

"I'm here," he said to the voice.

Father Hugh Benson, the new curate at St Mark's, rounded the wall of green. The young priest wore an anxious expression on his normally cheerful face. Clearly he had spoken to Mr Urquhart or Mrs Mayhew. Father Gilbert had forgotten that the young priest would also need an explanation.

Benson stopped in front of Father Gilbert. "Are you all right?"

"Who did you talk to – Mr Urquhart or Mrs Mayhew?" he asked.

"Both, actually." He sat down on the opposite end of the bench. "Mrs Mayhew said you had walked out of your office looking terribly worried. She asked you a question, but you didn't answer. You went up to the tower, for no apparent reason, and then shouted down at Mr Urquhart. Something about a man killing himself."

Father Gilbert shook his head. It certainly sounded absurd.

"Was it a dream? You fell asleep at your desk?" Benson frowned, his jet-black eyebrows forming a straight line over his grey eyes. "Were you sleepwalking? It's a bit frightening to think of you in a somnambulistic state on the church tower. You could have fallen."

"I've never been a sleepwalker," Father Gilbert said.

Benson scrutinized him. "Mrs Mayhew is afraid that you haven't fully recovered," he said – a reference to Father Gilbert's recent extended time away in a monastery.

"I was away on a *sabbatical*, not rehab."

"They said the Bishop sent you away to the monastery because of burn-out." Benson hesitated. "You were dealing with the death of your mother – and other things."

"This has nothing to do with that."

Benson fell silent as if to concede that the argument wasn't his to have. Then he said, "There is one thing, though. Mr Urquhart was wondering how you got through the door. He said the tower door is always locked and you didn't use your key."

"He puts the extra hymnals away in the closet there after every service. There's every chance he'd left it unlocked." As he spoke, Father Gilbert also realized that it was then possible for someone – anyone – to access the tower without being noticed. That might explain how the medallion got there.

Benson nodded towards the gold disc in Father Gilbert's hand. "Is that it? The one from the roof?"

Father Gilbert nodded.

"May I see?" Benson asked.

Father Gilbert handed it over. Benson studied each side for a moment, then turned it back and forth. "When the front image is right-side up, the back is upside down. Do you think it's a mistake?"

"It's a terrible mistake if it is," Father Gilbert said. "To put Jesus and the cross upside-down is extremely sacrilegious."

"Maybe it was meant to be flipped, like a coin."

"A medallion this size?" Father Gilbert countered. "The chain suggests that it's meant to be worn around the neck."

"Or hung somewhere as a decoration." Benson examined the chain. "Are these bits of cloth?"

Father Gilbert took back the medallion and put on his glasses to look more closely. Fragments of brown cloth were stuck to the gold chain, easily mistaken for dirt.

"What do you make of the symbols?" Benson asked.

Father Gilbert lifted the medallion to catch the daylight better. "Well, the image of Jesus on the cross is ordinary enough – unless it was meant to be upside-down. I can't make out the inscription."

The younger priest pointed. "What's that thing on the other side? The head of a bird? Are those branches and leaves? Do they mean anything?"

Father Gilbert held the medallion at one angle and then another, a realization dawning on him. "Those aren't branches and leaves. They're tail feathers. We're looking at a peacock and its plumage."

"Symbolizing what?"

Father Gilbert thought for a moment. "Peacocks have a variety of meanings in English history. Renewal, status, wealth. Early Christians thought they symbolized eternal life. Others considered them bad luck – because the ends of the feathers looked like eyes. Some called them 'evil eyes'."

"So you had some kind of dream or a vision that manifested itself in a solid object." Benson's tone wasn't sarcastic or even sceptical. It was just a statement.

"The man in the tower said it wasn't meant to be found," Father Gilbert said. "He called it a curse. He seemed to think that leaving it with a priest might undo the curse."

Benson shook his head. "Whatever you experienced up there was certainly vivid. Are you sure you're not on medication?" He eyed Father Gilbert with a playful smile.

Mrs Mayhew stepped through the entrance to the garden. "Father? Bill Drake is on the phone for you," she said.

Father Gilbert looked at his watch.

"No, you're not late for lunch," she said, anticipating his thought. "But he says it's urgent."

* * *

Father Gilbert went into his office and picked up the receiver. "Good morning, Bill."

"I'm phoning as a fellow member of the Stonebridge Historical Trust and a friend of the current Lord Haysham. Your presence is required at the Haysham estate immediately." Father Gilbert thought that if a voice could sound as if it was winking playfully, Bill Drake's did. He wondered if Drake was setting him up for a prank.

"Why?" Father Gilbert asked.

"They found *something*," Drake said.

"Don't be so cryptic, Bill. Who are *they* and what's the *something*?"

"*They* would be the workers who've been crawling all over the estate for the past few weeks – the ones who found the bridge," he said.

"Oh. *Them*." Lord Haysham had come up with a controversial plan to turn a section of his estate into commercial property. He'd had workers in to drain a marsh as part of his extensive landscaping efforts. In the marsh they had unearthed an old stone bridge, possibly the original bridge after which the town had been named.

"And they found what?" Father Gilbert asked. "The original village that went with the bridge?"

"No. They found a body."

Father Gilbert tensed. "A body?"

Benson, who had been lingering outside by Mrs Mayhew's desk, now stepped to the door.

"Actually, they found a *foot*," Drake said. "They assume the foot is attached to a body. It's under the peat and they don't want to touch it until the police arrive. Lord Haysham wants you to come right away. Maybe your presence will calm the hordes. We've got the makings of a riot here."

"A riot?" Father Gilbert asked, then groaned. "Is David Todd there?"

"Of course."

Father Gilbert sighed.

"Hurry. You don't want to miss the fun." Drake hung up.

Father Gilbert put the receiver down. He placed the gold medallion on the desk.

Benson remained in the doorway, watching him.

Father Gilbert came around his desk. "You drive."

CHAPTER 3

Father Gilbert squeezed his large frame into the passenger seat of Benson's Mini Cooper. "I don't know how you can drive something the size of a pencil sharpener."

"Then let's take your car."

"It's in the garage."

"It's *always* in the garage. In the two weeks I've been here I've never actually seen your car."

They drove out of the church car park and took the one-way system down the High Street of Stonebridge. The town was quintessentially English, with a mix of tea, pastry, and gift shops tucked between the more modern grocery, hardware, and clothes stores. Past and present, vintage and contemporary – England to its very core.

Father Gilbert gazed out of the passenger window and considered how much Stonebridge had changed in the few years since he'd arrived. The outward spread of London commuters had reached this far south. The train from nearby Polegate made it a fairly easy ninety-minute journey to Victoria station. Those commuters needed homes to live in. And with those homes came the demand for shopping centres, cinemas, and all the other modern amenities. What was the town to do? Some people were all for development, others vehemently against it.

"Anything I should know before we get there?" Benson asked.

Father Gilbert adjusted his position in the seat. He looked at the younger priest. A handsome face, wavy black hair – he could have been an actor or a model. The girls in the parish had done nothing but swoon since his arrival. The church youth group had doubled in a fortnight.

"The town council is in a civil war over the issue of land development. And Lord Haysham is at the centre of the current battle. He's rather progressive in his views about how to manage his property."

"Progressive – how?"

"Hundreds of acres of land to the south of Stonebridge belong to him," said Father Gilbert. "Last summer rumours sprang up that he was going to sell off parcels to developers. The environmentalists complained. Haysham was coy, neither confirming nor denying their suspicions. People took sides. To those who want jobs and commerce in the area, Lord Haysham is a visionary. To those who want the land unspoiled, he is a villain."

"Which side are you on?"

Father Gilbert ignored the question. He wasn't interested in taking sides. "A few weeks ago landscapers and workers showed up at the estate, allegedly to drain a marsh. The environmentalists protested. Then the workers unearthed an old bridge."

"An entire bridge was in the marsh – and no one knew?" said Benson.

Father Gilbert rested a hand on the dashboard. "Time and tide covered it well. And it was a *stone* bridge and perfectly positioned to be the original stone bridge the town was named after."

"That's an incredible find," Benson said.

"The environmentalists went apoplectic," Father Gilbert continued. "The area had to be preserved for environmental *and* historical reasons. They demanded the work should stop."

"And now they've discovered a body," Benson said.

"Actually, they found a foot."

"Oh." A pause. "Whose foot? Lord Haysham's? Had he lost one?"

"We'll find out together," said Father Gilbert.

A silence. Then Benson said, "Do you think this is connected to your vision?"

"We'll find that out together, too." But Father Gilbert had a nagging feeling the events were linked somehow.

* * *

They drove out of Stonebridge proper and took a stretch of straight road that cut south between rolling green hills of farmland and forest. The late-morning sun washed the view in a white haze.

Father Gilbert pointed. "The driveway for the Manor is just ahead, on the left. But go past that to the Old Stonebridge Road."

As they passed the turn-in for Haysham Manor, Father Gilbert could see the driveway stretch a hundred yards or so along an open lawn to the front of a Georgian-style mansion.

Benson gave a low whistle. "That's impressive. It must cost a mint to maintain."

"I would imagine so."

"Does Lord Haysham *need* to sell his land?" Benson asked.

Father Gilbert shrugged. "We've never discussed his finances." Old Stonebridge Road came up. He gestured. "There."

Benson signalled and turned onto a one-lane country road, lined with hedgerows on one side and a forest on the other. Then it angled to the left and snaked deeper into the forest. The sun all but disappeared behind a thick canopy of trees, the speckled light turning a murky grey with green hues.

"Where the road ends there's a clearing where you can park."

The clearing was hardly clear. Benson wove the Mini through a dozen cars that weren't really parked as much as haphazardly abandoned.

"What's going on here?" Benson asked. "This can't be about the body. Not already."

He found a spot between an elm tree and a rusted Range Rover covered with environmentalist stickers. Father Gilbert suspected the stickers were holding the car together.

The two priests got out and walked beyond the clutter of cars to a path.

A fresh-faced police constable with a wisp of post-adolescent moustache stepped from behind a tree. He was dressed in the standard white shirt with a black compact radio mic on the shoulder, a utility belt, and dark trousers.

"Hello, Ian," Father Gilbert said.

"Hi, Father."

"Keeping everything under control?"

"The natives are more restless than usual." He glanced at Benson as if he might be one of the restless natives.

"I'm the new guy," Benson said.

"So you are." He turned his attention back to Father Gilbert and said with significance, "Lord Haysham is here."

"Is he?" Father Gilbert hoped to sound reasonably impressed. "Is that unusual?"

A nod. "He must've come because of that body found in the marsh. Not that anyone would tell me." He grinned. "They just called me in to stand around and look tough."

"You're doing a fine job." Father Gilbert moved on.

They followed the path through the woods. In the distance, Father Gilbert could hear the low growl of an engine – the pumps to drain the marsh, he suspected. The forest opened to a small meadow. A crowd was gathered. A few placards were held up with scrawled slogans like *Stop The Destruction* and *Save Our Heritage*. From the clothes and styles of hair, Father Gilbert assumed most of the participants had skipped their university classes to be here. Voices rose in a heated argument.

Father Gilbert circled around the crowd. Two men stood in the centre, both shouting, neither listening, and the crowd stood watching as if the encounter might come to blows. Yet there was something about it all that seemed well practised.

Benson seemed to have the same feeling and asked in a low voice, "What are we watching? It reminds me of a pro-wrestling match on the telly."

Father Gilbert tipped his head towards the first contender, a stocky round-faced man with carefully styled curly brown hair, in his forties. "That's David Todd. You may remember him. He was on the church committee that interviewed you for your job."

Todd always had the look and energy of a man who had an agenda for his life – and he had fallen behind somehow. Every day was a struggle to catch up. He always walked like a man who had somewhere better he needed to be.

Father Gilbert nodded towards the other man – tall and slender with strawberry-blond hair and a classically pale English complexion. He was wearing high leather boots over his trousers and a white shirt under a waterproof jacket. "And that's the current Lord Haysham."

David Todd was shouting. "The bridge is of great historical importance. You can't simply destroy it as if—"

"I've said nothing about destroying the bridge," Lord Haysham shouted back. "Why do you assume that I—"

"Your entire record in the area of conservation and preservation is atrocious. It's immoral and unethical that you—"

"I haven't done anything that—"

"It's been your family's legacy to disregard the needs of the people around you—"

And so it went.

Father Gilbert noticed a man standing off to one side with a small digital voice-recorder to catch the action. Tim Patrick, with the local newspaper. Next to him was a photographer, also with the paper, snapping photos of the encounter.

Benson leaned to Father Gilbert and asked, "Is this real or for show?"

Father Gilbert shrugged. "Who knows any more? *They* probably don't. Their families have been feuding for at least three centuries."

"About this land?"

"About everything that strikes their fancy." Father Gilbert tapped Benson's arm. "There's Bill Drake."

The meadow sloped upwards to a ridge. At the top a man stood half-turned to them. His hands were clasped behind his back. He looked intently towards a small valley that had once been a river but was now a patchwork of fields and marshes. On the opposite ridge of the valley, a couple of hundred yards away, Haysham Manor sat on what would have been the far bank of the river, its back to them. Father Gilbert imagined that, had the river survived, the house would have sported a small dock and a boat or two. Now, the land sloped down to the builders who were busying themselves around the old stone bridge at the far end of the marsh. Earth-moving tractors and other pieces of large equipment sat silent near the mouth of the bridge. A concentration of men in wading boots had formed around the bridge's base. Presumably that was where the body had been found.

"Ah! Gilbert!" Bill Drake called out as they drew close.

A retired solicitor, Drake had become one of Father Gilbert's best friends in Stonebridge. The sight of him always made Father Gilbert smile. "Hello, Bill."

Drake was an egg-shaped man, dressed in traditional English tweed. He had a wild crop of white hair on his head and a white goatee. His round face was free of wrinkles and his eyes had a youthful sparkle to them. He could have been a drawing in a book by Dickens. Someone from *Pickwick*.

Drake put out his hand to Benson. "And you must be—"

"Hugh Benson," the priest said and shook Drake's hand.

"Gilbert's new chauffeur." Drake smiled.

"His car is in the garage."

Drake laughed. "His car's been in the garage for years."

"Why did you summon me?" Father Gilbert asked.

Drake took a pipe from his jacket pocket. "Early this morning the workers found a wooden crate at the base of the stone bridge."

"A crate of what?" asked Father Gilbert.

"Cannonballs."

"I thought they found a *foot*," Benson said.

"They did – later," Drake said. He put the pipe in his mouth, lit it, and gave it a few decisive draws. "You see, there was a chain attached to the crate. The chain disappeared into the peat. So the men dug it out. That's when they found the foot. The chain was attached to the ankle."

"Sounds like a Mafia hit," Benson said.

"Two corpses in one morning – eh, Gilbert?" said Drake. "Business as usual for you."

Father Gilbert frowned. Drake had heard about the tower, probably from Mrs Mayhew. His eye caught two men in suits among the workers by the bridge. One held a video camera. "Are the police there?"

Drake pointed with the mouth piece of his pipe. "That would be our own Sherlock Holmes and Dr Watson. Though we never know which is which. DS Sanders, and DC Adams is the one with the video camera."

"Well, I hope that's over with," a voice said from behind them.

They turned. Lord Haysham came close, reaching a hand out to Father Gilbert, who shook it politely.

"Good afternoon, my Lord," Father Gilbert said.

"Please," Lord Haysham protested. "I've asked you before. *Michael* is my name." He smiled and the lines around his face and mouth seemed deeper and more defined than usual.

Father Gilbert gestured to Benson. "Michael, this is Hugh Benson, our new curate. Hugh, this is Michael Haysham. Or *Viscount* Haysham, to put it formally."

Lord Haysham shook the young priest's hand. "Glad to meet a younger priest. Not enough young people in the church these days."

"A pleasure, sir," said Benson, looking unsure about whether he should bow.

"You've had your share of trouble today," Father Gilbert commented. He peered back at the protesters. They were huddled around David Todd. The reporter and photographer continued to chronicle the event.

"No worse than usual," Haysham answered wearily. "Todd is making the most of it. He always does when the press are involved."

"It sells papers." Drake took another drag on his pipe.

"And you know *that* will sell papers," Haysham said, turning his attention to the crew next to the bridge. "A *foot* attached to a crate of cannonballs. God save us!"

"Presumably the foot is attached to a body," Father Gilbert said.

"I hope so," said Haysham. "If the thing is in pieces, I'll never get the marsh done. It was bad enough finding that bridge."

"Does anyone know how old the bridge is?" Benson asked.

"I've got researchers trying to find out. Local maps and documents – that sort of thing," Haysham said. "The foreman on the job thought it might be seventeenth century."

From behind them, a protester began a chant of "Save the land!" A few joined in, but it gained no momentum and petered out to an embarrassing mutter.

A walkie-talkie crackled to life on Haysham's belt. He fumbled with the catch, then lifted it up. "What is it, Dennis?"

"The police would like you to come right away," Dennis said. "The foot is definitely attached to a body."

In any context, it was a comedic declaration.

"Right." Lord Haysham waved to the three men. "Come along, gentlemen. I'd like you to witness this."

Chapter 4

Father Gilbert and Benson trailed Drake and Haysham down to a well-worn path that cut across a higher section of the drainage area. The earth was soft and damp. They circled around to the worksite.

Haysham barked instructions to the foreman, who arranged waders for everyone.

As they dressed, the two police detectives walked over. The first was Detective Sergeant Sanders, middle-aged, with short-cropped hair and a narrow face. Detective Constable Adams was younger and boyish-looking. They were the Scenes of Crime Officers, or SOCO, as they were better known.

DS Sanders said to Haysham, "The coroner should be here any minute."

Haysham gave a quick nod and moved off.

Bill Drake introduced the two priests to the detectives.

"Father Gilbert," DS Sanders said. "What's the word from Scotland Yard these days? Or have they stopped phoning?"

"They stopped phoning. They don't like how I dress."

Once the waders were put on, Father Gilbert and the rest moved close enough to see the crate of cannonballs, and the chain leading to a shackle clasped firmly around a brown, leathery-looking ankle and foot. The lower part of the leg was visible as well and Father Gilbert could see what looked like the bottom of a pair of breeches. *Eighteenth century,* he guessed. The leg disappeared into a thick, dark, reddish peat.

"Why don't you dig out the rest of it?" Haysham asked impatiently.

"That's the coroner's job," DS Sanders said. "We don't want to mess up the crime scene."

Lord Haysham leaned in closer. "Well, it's not a *recent* crime. That thing has been there for quite a while."

Father Gilbert gazed at the exposed leg, then allowed his eyes to trace the shape and position of the rest of the body. He moved close to DS Sanders. "Someone has already been digging here," he said softly.

"What do you mean?" DS Sanders asked.

He pointed. "There, where the head might be. It looks like someone dug up the peat and then pressed it back into place."

DS Sanders squinted. "There've been men walking all over this place."

"It's not just trampled."

There was a stir of activity further up the hill. A middle-aged woman with dark hair streaked with grey made her way towards them. She wore a blouse of no fixed colouring and corduroy trousers that had faded from too many washings. She had donned the hip-high waders – which made her look twice her size.

"Who is that?" Benson asked.

"Carol Grant from the coroner's office," DC Adams replied.

The two detectives walked off to greet the woman.

"So," Benson said. "I know how they do it on television, but how does it work in real life? What, exactly, is a coroner? Is she a doctor – forensics expert – or what?"

"The 'or what?' may be more accurate," Drake said. "You should explain, Gilbert. You have more experience with this than I do."

"That was years ago. I don't know how they've changed the process," Father Gilbert said. But Drake's attention had already shifted away. Father Gilbert explained to Benson: "The coroner may or may not be a doctor or forensics expert at all. Often, the coroner is merely a legal officer, the equivalent to a judge, whose job is to take responsibility for the body and remove it to the morgue or a laboratory, depending on its condition or apparent cause of death. And, often, the coroner doesn't come at all, but sends an underling to handle the case."

Carol Grant moved past them, with the two detectives following behind her. A messenger-style case was slung over her shoulder. She didn't greet anyone, but went directly to the shackled leg.

"She's a bit mature to be an underling," Drake said quietly to Gilbert.

"Good Lord, it's a bog body!" Grant exclaimed.

There was muttering from the assembled crowd, as if she'd just used a rude euphemism.

She pointed and said, "You see how the skin looks like wrinkled leather. That's what happens to bodies found in peat. The peat mummifies them."

More mutterings, though Father Gilbert couldn't tell if they were impressed or confused.

"There was a case near Manchester," DC Adams offered, looking pleased with himself. "Pieces of a body they found in a bog up there. They called it the Ludlow something-or-other."

"The Lindow Man," Grant corrected him.

Father Gilbert remembered the case. At first the Manchester police thought it was the body of a local woman – murdered and chopped up by her husband. It turned out to be the pieces of a man from the Iron Age.

"Will you remove it, please?" Haysham asked.

Grant shook her head. "We can't simply dig it out. We need an expert to help us."

"What – a *bog* expert?" Haysham asked. "Where are we going to find one of those?" His tone suggested he anticipated further delays.

"Professor Ben Braddock will know what to do. He's at the University of Southaven." She patted the sides of the waders. "May I borrow someone's mobile phone? Mine's in the car."

DS Sanders gave her his phone and, clenching it between her shoulder and cheek, she used her free hands to pull a square of plastic from the bag on her shoulder. She covered the exposed leg, foot, and ankle. "This is to prevent any further contamination. The exposure to the air could accelerate decomposition."

From the protesters on the opposite ridge came a distant chant. From an echo, Father Gilbert could make out that they were shouting, "Haysham, vandal! Haysham, vandal!"

"Oh, spare me!" Lord Haysham cried out. Tossing up his arms, he walked away towards a group of workmen near the bridge.

"What happens now?" Benson asked, his eyes still on the corpse.

Father Gilbert wondered if this was the first time Benson had seen a dead body. "Normally it'd be taken to a laboratory where they'd have to determine the cause of death. If the cause proved to be unnatural, then the case would be handed over to a forensic pathologist, probably sent from the Home Office in London. He or she would conduct a full post-mortem and determine the exact cause of death. A team of Criminal Investigation Detectives would then be assembled to find the guilty party, if possible. Since, however, this really is a 'bog body', I assume this professor Braddock will take charge. I'm not sure what his procedure will be."

Drake was at Father Gilbert's elbow. "My theory is that the victim had intended to shoot himself from a cannon and fell off the bridge instead."

"You should suggest that to Carol Grant right away," Father Gilbert said. "I'm sure she'll appreciate your solving the case so quickly."

They waited. Father Gilbert remembered how much he disliked this part of dealing with corpses – the tagging and labelling as if the body was a product being inventoried. This was the inevitable end of all men, he knew, but the indignity still bothered him. This bog body had been a person – someone with a life and family, and hopes and dreams that were now lost to the ages. He wondered how many people would live their lives differently if they thought they'd end up like this: buried in peat with a lot of strangers gawking at them.

"This will make the news," said Benson.

"They'll probably call it *The Haysham Man*," Father Gilbert said.

DS Sanders' walkie-talkie gave a burst of static. Then a panicked voice – Father Gilbert assumed it was young Constable Ian – said, "Sorry to bother you, sir, but the protesters are demanding to be allowed to come to the bridge."

DS Sanders punched the button on the device. "Tell them no. This is a crime scene. If they try, arrest them. Understood?"

"Yes, sir."

Father Gilbert looked in the direction of the protesters. They were now beyond the ridge of the other side of the valley and out of sight. A movement caught his eye and he saw a single tree further along the ridge. It stood alone, silhouetted against the sky, billowing up in the shape of a mushroom cloud after an atomic explosion. At the bottom of the plume, a body hung at the end of a rope, jerking and swaying from a low branch.

Father Gilbert breathed in sharply and took a few steps forward. "Good heavens," he said.

"What's wrong?" Benson asked.

"That tree," Father Gilbert said. The body was in silhouette, the legs kicking spasmodically.

Benson looked. "What about it?"

"Don't you see it?"

Benson looked again. "No."

Nausea hit Father Gilbert's stomach and rose to his throat. He swallowed hard. He wanted to run to the tree. If there was any chance of saving the man…

"What do *you* see?" Benson asked.

Father Gilbert watched the hanging man. A final kick of the legs and then the distant shadow was still and lifeless.

He turned to Benson, who was staring at him.

"What's wrong?" Benson asked carefully.

Father Gilbert took a deep breath. His heart was banging around in his chest. "I thought I saw something."

Benson's eyes narrowed. "Like you saw the man in the tower?"

Father Gilbert glanced back at the tree. The hanging man was gone.

A large crow landed on a nearby fence post and squawked a stern warning. About what, Father Gilbert didn't know.

CHAPTER 5

Professor Braddock arrived half an hour later. He fitted the part, with shoulder-length grey hair and a bushy moustache that looked like a holdover from a seventies sitcom. He completed the look with a corduroy jacket that had leather patches on the elbows, faded jeans, and cowboy boots. He dismissed the offer of waders, choosing instead to go straight to the body through the muck. No doubt the mud would give authenticity to the pre-washed jeans.

He took a quick look at the shackled limb and then shouted, "Who tampered with this?"

The crowd shuffled, but no one stepped forward with an answer.

"What do you mean?" Haysham asked. "No one has touched anything."

"You're wrong," snapped Braddock, then pointed to the area of peat that Father Gilbert had noticed earlier. "Someone has already been digging here."

DS Sanders shot a look at Father Gilbert.

"Who discovered the body?" Braddock demanded.

The foreman standing next to Haysham said, "Erskine."

One of the workers raised his hand like a schoolboy. "Actually, I reported it after Colin told me."

"Colin who?" Haysham asked.

"Colin Doyle. He was here first thing. He usually gets here before the rest of us. He told me he'd found the crate and the chain… and the leg, obviously."

"Where is Doyle now?" Grant asked.

"We don't know," Erskine said. "He left. On family business, I think he said."

"He found a body and then *left*?" Grant was incredulous.

"Well, *find* him," Haysham said to the foreman.

The professor turned back to the bog body. "Carol, do you mind if I examine it?" he asked as he put on a pair of spectacles he'd nabbed from one pocket, then produced a pair of surgical gloves from another.

"Not at all," Grant said, appreciating the professional courtesy of being asked.

He carefully crouched down and removed the plastic wrap she had placed around the foot and leg. He bent his face closer, then followed the leg up to where it disappeared into the peat. Reaching into an inner pocket of his jacket, he brought out a small brush. He used the wooden end to push away a small section of peat, revealing more of the cloth. "Eighteenth century," he said.

"Do we investigate cases from the eighteenth century?" DC Adams asked DS Sanders.

"How do you want to remove the body, Professor?" Carol Grant asked.

Braddock stood up and perused the men and equipment. "We need to isolate this entire section of peat – ten feet around, I'd say – so as not to hack up the body. For all we know, there are others down there. We have to be very careful. And move that crate simultaneously with the body. I don't want the skin or leg ripped off."

The foreman stepped forward. "May we use the digger?"

"Shovels."

Groans from the crew.

"Where do you want to take it, Carol? I have no room at the University," Braddock said.

"The Southaven mortuary has space. We can work there."

"What will you do with it?" Haysham asked the professor.

Braddock took off his glasses and shoved them into his shirt pocket. "First we'll have to get the body out of the peat and give it a good clean. Then, depending on how well it's preserved, we'll run some tests and get a few specialists involved to find out the make of this chain and crate, for example. And the clothes. Sometimes these bog people are perfectly preserved, down to the buttons on their sleeves and what they ate right before they died."

Father Gilbert touched Benson's arm. "Let's go," he said softly.

Benson nodded. They moved out of the mud and back towards solid land.

As they removed the waders, Father Gilbert said, "The chain on the medallion had brown fibres stuck in the links. It may be the same cloth as the breeches on that bog body."

Benson's eyes widened. "If that's true, then…"

Father Gilbert nodded.

"But how did the medallion get from here to the church tower?"

"They're missing a man," Father Gilbert reminded him.

"Colin Doyle?" It took a moment to register. "Was he the apparition you saw?"

There was no way to answer until Father Gilbert saw Colin Doyle himself.

He looked over at DS Sanders, who was busy taking a statement from Erskine.

He dreaded doing what he knew he had to do. It would push credulity to tell the detective about the encounter in the tower – and the arrival of the medallion there. But Father Gilbert knew he had no choice.

* * *

The office for the building site was a small trailer propped up on breeze blocks. The foreman – a man with deep furrows of worry on his brow – flipped through files in a dented metal cabinet.

Father Gilbert leaned against a scarred metal desk. His back hurt. The run up the tower stairs, the walk across Haysham's estate, and the marching around in waders had done him no favours.

DS Sanders, who had accepted Father Gilbert's story with more tolerance than the priest expected, stood in the centre of the office. "Tell me about Doyle. Is he a good worker? Reliable? Trustworthy?"

"Yes," the foreman said. "I'm surprised he left early. He's usually the first one here and the last one to go."

Sanders' eyes went to Father Gilbert.

"Here it is," the foreman said. He pulled out a folder, dropped it on the desk, and sorted through the paperwork. A small photo fell to one side. He grabbed it and held it up for the detective and priest to see. "This is Colin Doyle."

Father Gilbert knew the face immediately. Colin Doyle was the man on the tower.

DS Sanders took the photo from the foreman. "I assume this was a photo you took for security purposes."

"And for the insurance. That's why we have the gate set up with the scanner."

"Gate?" Father Gilbert asked.

"A makeshift security gate, as you come around the drive from the house," the foreman explained. "Only authorized workers come through. And it keeps the protesters at bay. Lord Haysham is afraid one of those idiots will try to sabotage our work."

"What keeps them from coming across the marsh?" Father Gilbert asked.

The foreman shrugged. "They don't want to get their clothes dirty?"

"Is there a log of everyone who comes and goes?" asked the detective.

"Names and times. It's all computerized."

"I want to see the log."

"I'll have to get it from the security company."

"Please do." DS Sanders turned to Father Gilbert. "Well?"

"It's him."

"You know Colin?" the foreman asked.

"Not really. But I've seen him."

"This is beyond belief." DS Sanders shook his head. "I'll come back to your church to get a statement – and to bag that medallion."

"Medallion?" the foreman asked.

"Just phone the security company, will you?" Sanders snapped.

The foreman held up his hands to make peace. He went around the desk to the phone.

Father Gilbert's eyes returned to the photo of Colin Doyle. It was a head-shot, the kind enshrined on most photo IDs. Colin gazed at the camera with eyes that showed none of the despair the priest had seen earlier that morning.

He offered a prayer for the missing man. Dead or alive, he would need it.

CHAPTER 6

Benson was quiet as he drove Father Gilbert back to Stonebridge. Every now and then, he glanced quickly at his passenger. Then a tell-tale sigh.

Father Gilbert broke the silence. "Is there something you want to say?"

Benson tightened his grip on the steering wheel and squirmed in the seat. "I'm trying to get my mind around the idea that you've *never* seen Colin Doyle before."

"Not that I'm aware."

"But you saw him this morning in a dream, or as an apparition, and he gave you a medallion." His knuckles turned white against the steering wheel. "And it turns out he's the same man from the building site where a body has been found. And now he's missing."

Father Gilbert waited.

"Don't you find it unnerving?"

"Yes," Father Gilbert said. "Not because it happened, but because I don't know what it means."

"Does it have to mean something?"

"*Everything* has meaning," said Father Gilbert. "It's just a question of digging hard enough."

They pulled into the church car park.

* * *

Father Gilbert dragged two guest chairs together in the middle of his office, then wheeled his leather-backed chair around the desk. DS Sanders and DC Adams arrived just as Benson dashed off to handle a hospital visit. Mrs Mayhew provided a tray of coffee and tea.

"We look like a therapy group," said DC Adams, who sat a briefcase on the floor next to his chair.

DS Sanders asked Father Gilbert to repeat exactly what had happened on the tower and what the man – Colin Doyle – had said.

Father Gilbert went through the scene again with a calmness in his voice he didn't feel. DC Adams recorded the statement on a digital recording device and scribbled notes. Vacating the proffered chair, DS Sanders paced the office.

DC Adams stared at Father Gilbert. "You know this sounds insane, right? You're describing something that didn't actually happen. Colin Doyle wasn't physically here."

"He may have been here at some point," Father Gilbert said. "How else can I explain the medallion?"

DC Adams looked at DS Sanders.

"May I see it?" DS Sanders asked.

Father Gilbert lifted it with two fingers by the chain. DS Sanders produced a clear plastic evidence bag. Father Gilbert dropped it in. DS Sanders sealed it, then looked at it more carefully through the plastic.

"Does it mean anything to you?" he asked the priest.

Father Gilbert detailed his thoughts about the design on the front and back – the upside-down crucifix, the peacock, and anything else he could think to mention. He then pointed out the brown fibres in the chain.

"We'll check it for prints, then get it to the professor," DS Sanders said and handed the evidence bag to DC Adams. "It may be connected to the bog body – or not."

Adams turned the bag over and over, a mystified look on his face.

DS Sanders flipped open a notepad and said, "Colin Doyle's address is in Southaven. I'm almost certain he's a member of the builder family."

"*Those* Doyles?" Father Gilbert asked. The Doyle name appeared on signs at a variety of building sites. They were wealthy – and notorious. They'd lived in the Southaven area for generations and were officially in the building business. Unofficially, Jack Doyle had his fingers in a lot of dubious enterprises around the area: the black market, maybe drugs and prostitution. It was an open secret that he was connected to the London underworld, but the police could never build a case against him. Father Gilbert also remembered hearing about Doyle's various philanthropic efforts – money to various charities and museums. He thought he'd heard that they attended the Cathedral in Southaven, at least on important occasions.

Father Gilbert asked, "Is the job at Lord Haysham's a Doyle operation?"

"No," said DS Sanders. "I'm curious about that. Why would a Doyle work for a competing company?"

"Maybe he got tired of all the corruption in the family business," DC Adams said.

Father Gilbert mused, "The Colin I saw on the tower was in despair and extreme emotional distress. He said he didn't have a choice but to kill himself. It was the only way to stop 'them'."

"What 'them'?" DS Sanders asked.

"I don't know," Father Gilbert answered. "He then said they found something that shouldn't have been found. The medallion."

DC Adams lifted the evidence bag again. "There. But now it's here."

Father Gilbert continued, "Colin said staying alive was too painful. 'They' would make him do things. He said there were a few people who would wish they'd killed themselves before this whole business was over."

"What was that stuff about being an angel?" DS Sanders asked.

"He said he didn't want to become one."

"But then he cut his own throat and threw himself over the side," DC Adams said. "A funny way to avoid being an angel."

Father Gilbert smiled at the detective's mistake. "Angels aren't humans who've died. We don't go to some cloud in the sky, sprout wings, and play harps for eternity. Angels are distinct from us."

DC Adams shrugged at the difference. "Then what did he mean?"

Father Gilbert shook his head. "He didn't explain."

DS Sanders said, "I like ghost stories as much as anyone, Father. But I don't know what to make of this."

"There's nothing to make of it," DC Adams said sourly.

The detective sergeant turned to his co-worker. "Put Father Gilbert's 'vision' aside for a moment. The medallion is a *physical* fact. If it's linked to that body – which is part of a crime scene – then we have to take every piece of evidence seriously."

DC Adams lowered his eyes. "It's a load of rubbish."

DS Sanders' mobile phone rang. "Pardon me." He picked it up and moved to the far side of the office with his back to them.

"I know how you feel," Father Gilbert said to DC Adams. "The whole situation seems beyond plausibility."

DC Adams grunted.

A tap on the door sounded and Mrs Mayhew stepped in. "Father, should we adjust the church schedule? Is there anything I ought to cancel?"

He thought for a moment, then shook his head. "No. Leave my schedule as it is. I believe we're almost finished here."

"Yes, Father." She took the tea tray and left.

DS Sanders shoved the mobile phone into his pocket. He turned and looked at them with a grim expression. "They found Colin Doyle."

"Where was he?"

"He hanged himself in his garage."

Father Gilbert groaned.

DC Adams uttered a profanity, and then said quickly to the priest, "Sorry, Father."

DS Sanders' eyes were fixed on Father Gilbert. "His wife found a note. Colin wrote he'd found the medallion and had no choice. Dying was the only way to stop the pain. He didn't want to be an angel, he wrote. The same words you claim he said to you in your dream, Father."

DC Adams' eyes darted to Father Gilbert. "How do you explain that?"

"I can't."

The two police officers gazed at him. For lack of a plausible explanation, Father Gilbert was now a suspect. And so he should be, if they were any good at their jobs. He'd admitted to seeing Colin Doyle earlier. He had the medallion in his possession – a medallion mentioned in a suicide note that Doyle might have truly written, or might have been coerced to write, or which might have been forged by the priest. Doyle's hanging could have been staged to look like a suicide.

Those were only a few of the possibilities the detectives should now be considering. That Father Gilbert's motives were unknown to them didn't make any difference at this point. Motives would be sorted out later.

DS Sanders moved towards the door. "Don't leave the area, Father."

CHAPTER 7

"**Y**ou're a suspect?" Benson asked when he returned to Father Gilbert's office.

"Not officially," Father Gilbert said, "but they'll be back with more questions. The obvious one being how I came into possession of that medallion."

"You told them—"

"An unbelievable story," Father Gilbert said. "The likely scenario is that Colin Doyle took the medallion from the Haysham site and brought it to me."

"Why?"

"For money, perhaps. The black-market antiques trade can be lucrative. And the Doyles are known for dabbling in it."

"But you're not connected to—"

"I'm telling you what the police are probably thinking," Father Gilbert reminded him.

"And then – what? You met him at his garage and murdered him in a way that makes it look like a suicide?"

"Possibly."

"You don't have a car."

"It's easy enough to make people *believe* I don't have a car. There are plenty of ways to get around."

Benson thought for a moment. "How do you get off the suspect list?"

"It depends on the timing of when Colin Doyle left the worksite and when the coroner determines he died in his garage." Father Gilbert wanted to inject some hope into the conversation, though he wasn't sure if it was for Benson's sake or his own. "If it's a window of time when I was here, then Mrs Mayhew and Mr Urquhart are my alibi. And the five people who attended the 7 a.m. service."

Benson fell silent.

Father Gilbert went to his bookcase and found Crockford's

annual directory for the Church of England. "The Doyles have some connection to the Cathedral in Southaven. I know Sean Fisher. He's the Canon there."

A knock at the door and Mrs Mayhew peeked in. "David Todd wants to see you before the meeting," she said.

"Meeting?"

"The building committee," she said. "You instructed me not to change the schedule."

"Right."

Benson raised an enquiring eyebrow.

"We're discussing how to raise money for the bell tower," Father Gilbert explained. "Mr Urquhart insists that it's in danger of falling over if we don't do repairs."

"Shall I allow David Todd to come in?" Mrs Mayhew asked.

"Of course."

Benson stood up to relinquish his chair as David Todd entered. His curly hair was wet and he wore a casual outfit of jeans with a polo shirt under a jacket. Father Gilbert assumed he'd had a quick shower before coming to the church.

"Hello, Father."

"Hello, David. What happened with your protest?"

"The police broke us up. It was Haysham's doing, I'm sure." He put his hand out to Benson. "David Todd, in case you don't remember me."

Benson shook his hand. "Of course."

"So, what are they going to do with the body?" Todd asked, trying to sound casual, without success.

"They've taken it in for examination," said Father Gilbert.

"I heard it might be a couple of centuries old."

"Possibly."

"Too bad for Lord Haysham, then."

"Why?" Benson asked.

A smug smile was on David Todd's lips. "If it has historical significance, then his land can't be used for development. It'll have to be explored and excavated."

"Perhaps," Father Gilbert said, thinking, *Don't get your hopes up.*

"I heard the police were here," Todd said. "Why did they want to talk to you?"

"Oh, the usual. They wanted the benefit of my skills as a former detective with the Yard."

Todd eyed him. "You're not going to tell me what's really going on, are you?"

Father Gilbert smiled back at him as an answer in and of itself.

"All right, then. I'll see you at the meeting," Todd said. He nodded to Benson, then stepped out of the office.

"I don't know what to make of him," Benson said.

"You're going to see a lot of David Todd around St Mark's. His family's relationship with the church goes back a long way. As does Lord Haysham's."

"Will Lord Haysham be here for the meeting?"

"He's on this particular committee, yes."

"Isn't that trouble?"

Father Gilbert nodded. "Fortunately, they don't often argue when they're at St Mark's. It's supposed to be neutral ground."

Benson shook his head. "Isn't it hypocritical for them to pretend to worship together and still hate each other?"

Father Gilbert gazed at the young priest. "Is the church for people who are changed by their faith or for those who are still changing?"

"If you're going to get all spiritual about it, I withdraw the question." Benson feigned a look of contrition and moved to the door. He lingered there.

"Something else?"

"Just for the record: we don't believe in curses, do we?"

"Curses?"

"Colin Doyle said he was cursed."

"I can't spell out the official Anglican position," Father Gilbert said. "Not sure we have one. I suppose it depends on the curse. Though, in this case, it's not whether *we* believe in them or not. It's whether others believe."

"Why others?"

"People who truly believe in curses are apt to do stupid things."

CHAPTER 8

Alone for a few moments before the committee meeting, Father Gilbert phoned Canon Sean Fisher at Southaven Cathedral. He left a message on the voicemail system. He then leaned back in his chair, pressed his fingers together, and closed his eyes. His current co-workers would have assumed he was praying. His former co-workers at Scotland Yard would have known he was going over the facts of the case in his mind.

Colin Doyle had been working at Lord Haysham's and found the medallion on the bog body that morning. Had it caught his eye or was there something about the body that had caused him to look for the medallion? If the latter was the case, then was it right to think he had taken the job at Haysham's because he knew the discovery of the bridge would also lead to the discovery of the body? (*When* did Doyle take the job at Haysham's?)

Having grabbed the medallion, Doyle then delivered it to the church tower. Somehow. For some reason.

Then he went to his garage, composed a suicide note that was uncannily similar to an imaginary discussion with Father Gilbert, and killed himself.

Father Gilbert sighed deeply. Finding the medallion had pushed Doyle to the ultimate act of self-absorption. How could a piece of jewellery lead to that level of despair?

The priest lowered his head and said a prayer for the soul of Colin Doyle.

* * *

Father Gilbert walked down a narrow hallway past a couple of rooms designated for children's education. The walls were adorned with boards filled with drawings and posters with cute Christian sayings, usually accompanied by fuzzy kittens. He reached a meeting room that doubled as the church library. Bookshelves covered the walls while a rectangular table sat in the centre. Half a dozen chairs lined each side of the table. With the care of a hostess setting the table for Sunday dinner guests, Mrs Mayhew had placed the committee agenda at each chair.

He sat at the chair at the head of the table. As the committee members filed in, he glanced over the brief agenda. Old business: the tower. New business: Mr Urquhart wanted to say a few words about the ongoing flooding in the crypt.

Father Gilbert directed Benson to sit at his right. Mrs Mayhew sat down to his left, placed the notepad squarely in front of her, and then quickly checked her collar and blouse to be sure they hadn't gone askew.

David Todd took a chair at the opposite end of the table. Lord Haysham arrived late, ignored the chairs closest to David Todd, and sat down near to Mrs Mayhew. Haysham had changed from his tweeds into a black cardigan, grey trousers, and an open-necked white shirt.

Father Gilbert said nothing about the bog body at Lord Haysham's estate, nor did he bring up Colin Doyle's suicide. He began with a brief prayer and then led them in the well-worn discussion about the tower, including a budget for repairs, fund-raising, and the process for finding the contractor to do the job – the sorts of things that left everyone but Henry Locksmoor, the church accountant, glassy-eyed and slack-jawed.

Mr Urquhart then talked about the flooding of the crypt, which truly was old business, but had come around again for its annual revisit. Mr Urquhart was now convinced that the tower might be subsiding because of water damage below the ground.

David Todd had been attentive and polite during the meeting. But the mention of the flooding brought out the fire in him again. "Has anyone investigated whether or not the flooding in the crypt may be due to *someone* draining his land and saturating the surrounding area with water?"

Lord Haysham was unperturbed. "There's no evidence that the work on my land is affecting the church or any other building in Stonebridge."

Todd ignored Haysham and said to Father Gilbert, "Look at the pond down by the common. Or the path along the stream. You can hardly cycle there for all the mud. Ask Jack Ramsey. His farm has suffered because of it."

"Unsubstantiated," Haysham said coolly.

"For you," Todd said. "The entire town could disappear into a sinkhole and you wouldn't notice because of your greed."

"David, please," Father Gilbert said. He suddenly felt a weariness deep in his bones.

Mr Urquhart said, "It's likely the water damage is due to all the rain we've had this spring."

"There you are," Lord Haysham said.

Todd snorted. "It doesn't let you off the hook. Your selfish pursuit of—"

"David!" Father Gilbert snapped. "*Sanctuary*, please! None of that kind of ranting here."

Todd looked at Father Gilbert for a moment. Then, with an affected calmness and formality, he said: "As a member of this church, I have to insist that Lord Haysham instructs his engineers to divert the marsh-water in a manner less detrimental to our church and community."

Haysham folded his arms and let out a *harrumph*.

"You can have that conversation somewhere else," Father Gilbert said with finality.

The meeting ended after a discussion about how to properly assess the crypt's flooding. David Todd left quickly. The others chatted as they drifted out.

Lord Haysham lingered long enough for the room to clear.

"I don't know what I'm going to do with the two of you," Father Gilbert said.

"He started it," Haysham replied, with a boyish smirk. Then he leaned in close and said, "Would you like to see the bog body up close?"

CHAPTER 9

As he walked to Benson's Mini Cooper, Father Gilbert glanced to the far end of the church car park. Lord Haysham had parked under the shade of an oak tree and was nearing his car when David Todd stepped out from behind the tree. He said something to Haysham. Haysham stopped at the driver's door, but didn't open it. He responded. Todd came closer. Their postures and hand-gestures as they talked suggested something other than their usual tension.

Benson also saw the two men and asked, "Should you intervene?"

Father Gilbert reached for the passenger door. "Let them work it out," he said. But he kept his eye on them as Benson navigated the car out onto the road. There was something about the expressions on the men's faces that told Father Gilbert they weren't discussing land development or property management. It was a worried conversation between two men who had a common problem they weren't sure how to solve. *Conspiratorial*, was the word Father Gilbert would have used to describe the scene.

"What does David Todd actually do?" Benson asked.

"He sells houses and land," Father Gilbert said. "Like an estate agent at times, but more like an investor or a broker or something like that. It's always been fuzzy to me."

"Wouldn't that make him more agreeable to land development?"

"One would think," Father Gilbert said. "But that would imply a certain reasonableness behind his thinking. The argument between the Todds and the Haysham family goes back too far for reasonableness."

Father Gilbert fought his growing irritation with both men. Each grated on his nerves in one way or another. Haysham's attitude exuded a certain smugness, the superiority of the wealthy over the ignorant poor. Todd's attitude, on the other hand, conveyed a working-class arrogance, militant and belligerent as he spouted outdated phrases from a book on social justice he'd probably read at college.

Ironically, both men presented a false front. Haysham privately suggested a loathing for his inherited wealth and the snobbery of his peers. There were times when Father Gilbert was certain he would have enjoyed an entirely different life. And David Todd was not working-class at all, having been raised in an upper-middle-class family. His hatred for Haysham seemed more like an addiction than a conviction. If Father Gilbert had believed in reincarnation, he could easily imagine the two men as souls replaying the same battle over and over again throughout time.

Benson drove them south to Southaven – a modest city on the south coast. Its glory days had been centred around shipbuilding and shipping, the docks busy with incoming and outgoing goods. Now the docks contained office buildings and luxury flats. The ships were mostly gone, apart from a renovated eighteenth-century warship for the tourists. Ferries now catered for people travelling across to France.

The coroner's office and mortuary were tucked in an industrial complex that had been taken over by local law enforcement. Father Gilbert and Benson signed in at a glass-enclosed front desk. A young assistant, who couldn't take her eyes off their clerical collars, led them back to a small meeting room. On one wall was a wide window looking into a room of fluorescent lighting and stainless steel – a lab for post-mortems.

The standard surgical instruments were there. Long, sharp, functional. And the drills, both electrical and manual. Father Gilbert shuddered. He had seen his fair share of autopsies without an incident of vomiting or fainting. But the drills, their noises, and their purposes had brought him close.

The bog body lay on a steel gurney surrounded by trays of small brushes, scrapers, and bottles labelled as distilled water. Father Gilbert remembered seeing a documentary on television about the process. The distilled water was used to spray the peat from the body. The small brushes and scrapers were then used to clear other sections of the corpse. It was a painstaking process. He assumed the body would have to be carefully scrutinized on the outside before they cut it open to see what was inside.

Father Gilbert stepped closer to the window. Brown and shrivelled, the corpse faced him, drawn up into a foetal position. It was dressed in a collarless shirt, an overcoat, and breeches with corroded buckles just below the knee. One wrinkled leg was covered with a riding boot. The other leg showed exposed leather-like skin down to the shackle. The ankle was so thin, it was a wonder the shackle hadn't slid off. The rusted chain that had attached the leg to the crate of cannonballs was now free of both and sat on a smaller table. The crate wasn't to be seen. There was something about the position of the corpse – the way the hip lay – that struck Father Gilbert as odd, as if the victim had a deformity.

The features of the face were shockingly distinct. It was stretched in that grotesque way mummified faces often are: the eyes closed and the mouth constricted in a permanent scream. The nose was slightly pressed down and angled to one side. Father Gilbert could see the eyebrows, even the crow's feet around the eyes. The hair was matted and chocolate-coloured, probably stained by the peat.

Father Gilbert eyed the corpse from head to toe. He stopped at the exposed foot and wondered where the second boot had gone.

A woman in a white lab coat entered the autopsy room and, without looking at them, sat down on a stool next to a counter. She typed quickly on a laptop, then pressed her eyes against a microscope.

The door to the meeting room opened. Professor Braddock entered, carrying a battered leather briefcase. He eyed the two priests with obvious disappointment. "I thought Lord Haysham was here," he said.

"He's on his way," Father Gilbert said.

The professor looked them over again. "Haven't I seen you before? You were at the site where the body was found."

"That's right." Father Gilbert made introductions.

Braddock briefly shook their hands, then gave Father Gilbert a fresh look. "You found the medallion, too, I heard. At the church."

"On the roof of the tower."

"That's a confounded thing," Braddock said. "How did it get from the site to your church?"

"That's a very good question." Father Gilbert gestured towards the corpse in the other room. "Have you had much success?"

"I'll save my preliminary findings for Lord Haysham and the Chief Constable," he said and moved to an empty bulletin board covering part of the wall. The professor retrieved papers and photos from the briefcase and began pinning them to the board.

"May I look?" Father Gilbert asked.

"They may not make any sense to you," the professor said.

"Oh, go on. Give me a try." Father Gilbert stepped over to the board. Benson joined him.

The photos showed the bog body from various angles, with close-ups of the skull. A long slender gash was visible on the left side of the head, just below the crown and above the ear.

"Tell me, Professor: how is it possible for bodies to be preserved in peat?" Benson asked. "Wouldn't peat speed up decomposition rather than hinder it?"

"There've been several theories about that," Braddock began, clicking into teacher mode. "The key ingredient in peat is a moss called *sphagnum*. It dies and releases other substances which eventually get turned into humic acid."

"What does humic acid do?" Benson asked.

"All sorts of strange things. It makes the bones go soft so that they bend, stretch, break, or even flatten under the weight of the bog. That's why they sometimes look distorted. And the humic acids also mess around with the skin, slowing down the decaying process and turning it brown. Something to do with the nitrogen in the flesh. But there remains the question of why some bodies are almost perfectly preserved while others are badly decayed."

Benson rubbed his chin thoughtfully, clearly playing the role of the inquisitive student. "I remember reading an article about that. Two sixteen-year-old Irish girls—"

"Oh yes. *Them*," said Braddock, not to be outdone by a layman. "They were interested in the Lindow Man. You know about the Lindow Man, I assume."

"A little," Benson said.

Braddock nodded, as if that was enough to proceed. "Most experts thought he was probably a sacrifice victim – part of a Druidic rite. Like everyone else, the two Irish girls wondered why he was so well preserved when other bodies found in the vicinity weren't. So they tried an experiment using stillborn pigs from a local farm. The girls picked several bog sites that had the same chemical make-up for preservation – low oxygen, antiseptic properties – and dropped the pigs in. They waited, I think, six or seven months and then dug the pigs up. They clearly had too much time on their hands."

"What did they find – besides bacon?" Benson asked.

Braddock looked at the priest with disdain. "Some of the pigs were very well preserved while some of the others had decayed. So the two girls went further. They experimented to account for the differences. What they figured out, over time, was that the state of preservation was directly related to the length of time between the death of the pigs and their burial. In other words, if the body was dumped in the bog immediately after the subject died, then it would probably be well preserved. If, however, there was more time for decay *before* the body was put in the bog, then it would have greater degrees of decay in the peat."

Benson gave an *aha* expression. "The peat works as a preservative in one instance and an accelerator in the other."

Braddock nodded. "The girls won several awards. And archaeologists and forensic experts are still following up on their work."

"I'm sure those girls were a lot of fun on a date," Benson said.

Braddock gave a thin smile. "At sixteen I was trying to figure out how to kiss Diana Hamilton, not discover the secrets of decaying bodies. That came later."

"The kiss or discovering secrets?" Benson asked.

Braddock snorted.

Father Gilbert thought about what he was doing at the age of sixteen. Obsessing about becoming a detective and dating Katherine Donovan, he recalled. The thought of Katherine and how their relationship had played out made him frown. He pushed the memory aside.

The professor pinned up photos of the medallion. The close-ups brought out the details. Some of the dirt had been removed. The engraved inscription was still worn, but clearer than it had been.

Benson moved in close and read, *"Rex regum et Dominus universorum."*

"Roughly translated: *King of Kings, Lord of the Universe,"* Braddock announced.

"Or 'Lord of Lords'," Benson said.

Just then Lord Haysham walked in with Carol Grant, looking every bit as frumpy as she had earlier in the day, even without the waders. Chief Constable James Macaulay, a tall, white-haired, square-jawed man in police uniform, followed her. A younger man in a plain suit trailed behind them both. He wore a stony expression, all business.

"Sorry we're late," Lord Haysham said. He offered introductions around the room. The younger man, whom Father Gilbert had met on some unremembered occasion, was Detective Inspector Alexander Wilton. He was related to a parishioner of St Mark's.

The Chief Constable turned to Braddock. "We were told you have preliminary findings from the so-called bog body." His cavernous voice boomed in the small meeting room.

"Only the most basic information," Braddock said. "It will take some time to do all we need to do with that corpse."

"But you are moving quickly," Lord Haysham prodded.

Father Gilbert noted the look between Haysham and Braddock. Delays with draining the marsh – and the subsequent development of the land – could cost Haysham a lot of money. He wondered if Lord Haysham had offered Braddock a substantial grant or a donation to the University to hurry things along.

"So, what do you have?" Macaulay asked.

Braddock stepped over to the board of photographs. He pointed to the various images as he spoke. "The body, at least as much as we've uncovered, appears to be perfectly mummified. Eighteenth century, based on the clothes. I'd guess his age to be around thirty-five years at the time of death."

"How did he die?" Lord Haysham asked.

"A blow to the head." Braddock pointed to the close-up of the gash.

"Weapon?" asked DI Wilton, taking down details in a notepad.

"We can't say for certain," Carol Grant interjected, as if she thought she ought to say something. "Something sharp-edged."

"Probably a sword," Braddock added. Then he swung his hand as if brandishing the weapon. "Swung by a right-handed man. My current theory is that the victim was struck in the head, chained to a crate of cannonballs, and dropped in the river."

"You know for certain he died from a blow to the head?" Father Gilbert asked. "Have you checked the lungs? If he was still alive when he was thrown in—"

"Yes, yes, we will certainly check," Braddock said irritably.

Carol Grant explained, "A pathologist and forensics expert will come down from London on Monday. Professor Braddock has invited various specialists in to examine the corpse: chemists, microbiologists, entomologists, botanists, metallurgists, and textile experts."

Braddock continued, "Then, I will send samples of the victim's tissues to various geneticists and blood-typing specialists. I have yet to do proper X-rays, CT scans, and DNA sampling. We may ask a medical artist to create a representation of the face."

"Can you guess *when* the murder took place?" Benson asked.

"Specific to date, hour, or time? Not yet. But we'll get fairly close."

"What about the medallion?" Haysham asked.

"I'm bringing in an expert on antique jewels and artefacts," Grant said. "Mary Aston. She's good, if somewhat unorthodox."

"I believe I met her at an event in London," Haysham said. "An auction or something of the sort. Attractive." The last sentence was said in a way that suggested he thought of her as more than merely attractive.

"There is little doubt that the medallion was stolen from the site by Colin Doyle," DI Wilton said. He let his gaze fall on Father Gilbert. "How it got from there to Father Gilbert remains a mystery."

"Are there any clues as to *why* Doyle took the medallion?" Father Gilbert asked.

"Part of his DNA, probably," DI Wilton said.

"You know for a fact that Colin Doyle is a member of Jack Doyle's family?" Father Gilbert asked.

"Colin Doyle was the oldest son of Jack and Colleen Doyle," said DI Wilton.

"DI Wilton is leading the investigation now," Macaulay stated, answering the unspoken question about this new member of the team.

"What about DS Sanders?" Father Gilbert asked.

"Reassigned," Macaulay said quickly. He gestured to DI Wilton. "Go on, Alex."

Wilton flipped a couple of pages in his notepad. "According to the security system, Doyle scanned his badge at the site at 5:57 a.m. He was always on the job by six. One of the workers was there when Doyle found the foot and chain in the mud."

"What time was that?" asked Father Gilbert.

"Around half-six. Doyle had been checking the pumps around the old bridge. He found the chain first, then followed it to the foot."

"Did he call out immediately?" asked Father Gilbert.

DI Wilton looked perturbed by the interruptions. "No. His co-worker came on the scene first."

"That would be unusual, right?" Benson asked.

"Yes," Haysham said. "Anything out of the ordinary is supposed to be reported right away."

DI Wilton went on: "According to Doyle's co-worker, part of the upper torso of the corpse was exposed. Perhaps the peat had shifted because of the drainage. Anyway, it was hard to tell what he was looking at, but he remembers seeing something shiny there."

"Likely the medallion was worn around the victim's neck," Braddock said.

"The co-worker left Doyle alone with the body while he ran to get the site foreman," DI Wilton said.

"Don't they have walkie-talkies?" Father Gilbert asked.

"Neither man did then. They had forgotten them, or they were being recharged in the office – I'm unclear about that." DI Wilton tapped the notepad with his pencil. "We assume the medallion looked valuable to Doyle, so he took it. Maybe he assumed he could make some money from it."

Father Gilbert bristled at the easy conclusion. "Is that a wise assumption? Greed may not have been his motivation."

DI Wilton folded his arms. "Is it wise to assume he was motivated by anything else?"

"I wouldn't exclude greed, nor other possibilities," Father Gilbert said.

"*Father*, you may rest assured that we know our jobs and will consider all possibilities," Macaulay said. "Go on, Wilton."

"The security system logs Doyle as departing the site at 6:48. We know from Doyle's mobile phone that he placed several phone calls from 6:59 to 7:12 – all of them to the same number."

"Who did he call?" Haysham asked.

"His father," Wilton replied. "Which, we now know, was unusual."

"Why?" asked Father Gilbert.

"According to Colin's wife, he'd had a falling out with his father a year ago and walked away from the family."

"And their fortune," Macaulay added. "Which may explain why he was working as a builder for another company – and why he nabbed the medallion."

"What did his father say about the calls?" Father Gilbert asked.

"Allegedly Jack Doyle is so distraught by his son's suicide that he's unable to speak to us," DI Wilton said.

"Allegedly?" Benson asked, indignant. "His son is *dead*."

Wilton ignored Benson and looked down at his pad again. "The first five calls were unsuccessful attempts to reach his father. The sixth attempt got through at 7:12 for six minutes."

"So they *did* talk," Carol Grant said.

"Or he left a long message on his father's voicemail. We don't know yet," Wilton said. "We don't know yet where Doyle was between 7:20 and 8:30. Though the drive back to his house would have taken at least twenty minutes, depending on traffic."

Enough time to take the medallion to St Mark's, Father Gilbert thought.

DI Wilton nodded to Carol Grant.

She took a step forward for no specific reason. "We believe he died sometime between 8:30 and 9:00," she said. "Cause of death: a broken neck and asphyxiation by hanging."

"He hanged himself in his detached garage, using a rope tied to the rafters," Wilton added. "He used a stepladder to climb up, then kicked it away."

Father Gilbert and Benson exchanged glances. This let Father Gilbert off the hook as a suspect, since he had solid alibis for his whereabouts from 7:00 until 9:00.

Wilton said, "Doyle's wife Amanda arrived home around 9:00 from a morning meeting at their kids' school. She was surprised to see Colin's car in the driveway. She thought he'd forgotten something. She checked the house. When she didn't find him there, she went to the garage. The suicide note was taped to a pane of glass on the inside of the door, which was closed but not locked. She entered the garage and saw him hanging. From all appearances, he was dead. She panicked. At first, she tried to lift him by his legs, thinking to relieve the tension of the rope in case he was alive. She didn't have the strength for it. So she searched for something sharp enough to cut through the rope. Nothing was immediately to hand."

Father Gilbert winced as he imagined the poor woman coping with the initial shock of seeing her husband and then desperately trying to save him.

"She phoned for the ambulance at 9:06," DI Wilton continued. "They arrived at 9:17. Doyle exhibited no vital signs nor was there any change, in spite of their best efforts. Doyle was officially pronounced dead at Southaven Hospital at 9:58. Apart from the note, which had been written in pencil on a yellow pad Doyle kept on his workbench, there was nothing unusual in the garage or house. No sign of a struggle. Amanda Doyle confirmed that the handwriting on the note was Colin's, including one word that he typically misspelled."

"Which word?" Father Gilbert asked.

"*Medallion*," DI Wilton answered. "Amanda said he often got the spelling of words confused if they had double *L*s. He left one of the *L*s out."

Father Gilbert nodded, appreciating that whoever had interviewed Amanda Doyle had had the presence of mind to be that detailed.

"What else do you know about Doyle?" Haysham asked.

DI Wilton gave a slight shrug. "He was a quiet man, a hard worker. Married for seventeen years to Amanda. They were sweethearts from school. They have a twelve-year-old son and a ten-year-old daughter. No police record, apart from a parking ticket ten months ago."

"Is there anything to explain why he killed himself?" Father Gilbert asked.

DI Wilton shook his head. "No history of drugs, mental illness, or depression. His wife is devastated, as you'd expect, and she's mystified. He seemed all right when he left the house earlier this morning." He closed his notepad.

"Good work," Macaulay said.

Father Gilbert thought through the timetable of Colin Doyle's activities. There was plenty of opportunity for Doyle to have driven to St Mark's and left the medallion – even going up to the top of the tower and down again. He could have done it during the 7 a.m. service. That had started on time and finished at 7:45, including the usual post-service socializing with the handful that had shown up. Mr Urquhart would have unlocked the tower door to retrieve the small prayer books they used for the shorter service. If it had been left unlocked, then there was no mystery about how Doyle got in. The *why* was the perplexing part.

Father Gilbert also remembered that his encounter with Doyle had happened around 8:45. That fitted the time if he had hanged himself between 8:30 and 9:00. Though the notion that such a bizarre encounter could actually *fit* with the harsh reality of a suicide struck Father Gilbert as nothing less than astonishing. How had he come to a place in his life where he accepted it so readily? What if he had been dreaming or was simply delusional? Without the existence of the medallion, it would be easy to think so.

Father Gilbert's eyes went back to the bog body beyond the viewing window. The glass reflected the room behind him. A blurred image of Professor Braddock gesturing to the photographs pinned to the bulletin board faded from view. Instead, he saw two men on the old stone bridge.

It is night. Moonlight illuminates the edges of the thick clouds above and offers cold light to the bridge and the ribbon of river underneath. One man wears a long overcoat and carries a staff he uses for walks along the country lanes. The other man wears a cape – typical of the time – which he wraps around himself as if he's cold. These two men know each other well. They argue like familiar enemies. Eventually the man with the staff gives a sharp gesture to the other as a punctuation mark. They are finished. He turns to walk away. And then the second man throws his cape aside. He unsheathes a sword. It comes up, catching a flash of moonlight. The first man begins to turn as the sword comes down swiftly. He flinches, his eyes closed as the edge of the sword slices into his skull. His legs buckle. He falls to the ground.

The man in the cape nudges the victim with the toe of his boot. Then, with great difficulty, he grabs the man under the arms and drags him to the end of the bridge. There is a horse and cart there. Clumsily he hoists his victim onto the back of the cart – the upper torso first, then the legs. The man in the cape climbs onto the back of the cart and goes to a heavy crate in the front corner. He is not a strong man, not used to this kind of labour, but he manages to push the crate back to the victim. He wipes his brow; his hair has come loose from its ponytail, hanging long around his face. Something catches his attention. He looks around quickly, then goes to the front of the cart and produces a short chain from beneath a horse-blanket. He kneels next to his victim and removes a boot. He shackles the chain tightly to the fallen man's ankle. Holding up the boot for a moment, he is unsure of what to do with it. He hastily shoves it under the victim's coat.

He tugs at the chain until he's satisfied with the security of the shackle on the victim's leg. He attaches the other end of the chain to an iron ring on the side of the crate. Then he climbs into the driver's seat and drives the horse and cart to the centre of the bridge. He pulls at the reins to coax the horse to back up, angling the rear of the cart against the stone wall of the bridge.

Climbing back into the cart, he pushes the crate to the edge. He checks its position – looking at the crate, then over the side of the bridge, then the crate again. He positions his victim next to the crate. Again, he checks and double-checks the trajectory. He pauses. His head tilts as if to listen. He looks around and stops – he stares at Father Gilbert as if he knows he's there. Then he kneels down next to the crate and pushes. The crate teeters and finally tips off the back of the cart, narrowly missing the top of the stone wall, and plummets towards the river. Even before the crate has fallen past the top of the wall, the connecting chain jerks the dead man – if he is dead – off the cart. The body is grotesquely limp as it follows the crate. The shackled leg is pulled straight, while the other leg briefly catches on the edge of the cart, stretching it at an unnatural angle, probably dislocating the hip. The weight of the crate yanks the leg free and the torso slides off. The back of the head glances against the wall as the body follows the crate into the dark water.

The moon runs from this terrible scene, rushing behind fat clouds that now cry large tears of rain on the man in the cape. He stares down at the river for a few moments. After a while, he returns to the driver's seat and slaps the reins. As if it knows what has just happened, the horse moves across the bridge slowly, its head down as if it is pulling a funeral carriage. The scene fades from Father Gilbert's view as the sky unleashes a dark-grey curtain of rain that falls upon the stage.

A hand fell on Father Gilbert's shoulder. "Father?" It was Benson.

Father Gilbert turned. All eyes were on him, amused expressions playing on their faces.

"Daydreaming, Father Gilbert?" Haysham smiled.

"The hip is probably dislocated," said Father Gilbert.

"What?" Braddock asked.

"And the missing boot," Father Gilbert said. "Has the victim's second boot been found?"

Professor Braddock's eyes lit up. "Funny about that. We found it under the victim's coat."

CHAPTER 10

Going back to Haysham Manor for drinks wasn't high on the list of things Father Gilbert wanted to do that day. But Haysham invited them as they left the coroner's office and Father Gilbert saw from Benson's eager expression that he should accept.

Benson was excited as he drove them back towards Stonebridge. He squirmed in his seat, drummed his fingers on the steering wheel, and then finally asked, "Are you going to tell me what's *really* going on?"

Father Gilbert gazed at the young priest. "*Really* going on?"

"The encounter on the tower was one thing. And your expression when you were looking at that tree on Haysham's land was another. And then you mentally left the room back at the coroner's. What are you seeing?"

Father Gilbert took a deep breath. "I'll let you know when I have something sensible to say."

The finger-drumming stopped. "You must be relieved, though. The timing of Colin Doyle's death puts you in the clear. And it corresponds with your vision on the tower."

"It would seem so."

The finger-drumming started again for a moment, then stopped. "I assume you've heard of astral projection."

Father Gilbert nodded. Astral projection was the idea that a spirit could leave a body and travel to other places, even appearing to people in the physical realm. It was often associated with near-death experiences. Father Gilbert knew about it from personal experience.

"Do you believe in it?" Benson asked.

"To some degree." Father Gilbert didn't want to explain to what degree. To do so would raise more questions than he could answer, and require him to talk about the death of his mother and the events that had ultimately led to his sabbatical. "Christian mystics reported out-of-body experiences that transported them to other people and places. But the church frowns upon astral projection if a person attempts it to meet with other spirits."

"Allowing that it happens, then Colin Doyle could have put the medallion up in the tower and then 'returned' when he died," Benson said, then laughed nervously and shook his head. "Just saying it out loud sounds mad."

Father Gilbert was beyond worrying about how it sounded. "Why return in spirit? Why not give it to me in person?"

"You weren't available," Benson said. "Or he was determined to kill himself and thought you might interfere. Maybe he intended to throw himself from the tower and changed his mind. Or… or…" He groaned.

Father Gilbert looked off to a green field. They were trying to apply rational human thinking to a situation that went beyond rational human thinking.

Benson turned onto the driveway leading up to Haysham Manor. The tyres pushed over the mix of gravel and stone, sounding like one very long throat-clearing. He brought the car to a sliding halt behind an official-looking black saloon. Probably Macaulay's.

Stepping under the arched entrance, Father Gilbert crossed the small enclosed porch to the large wooden door and pushed the doorbell.

"It's less impressive than it looks from the road," Benson said.

Seen close up, the manor was certainly showing its age and need of repair. The paint on the door was chipped and the wood along the bottom was warped and scuffed. Untended ivy crawled over the archway, giving a home to all manner of insects that buzzed around their heads. A massive spider's web stretched from the inside corner of the archway to an iron chandelier above them. Dead moths and an assortment of bugs dangled like old clothes on a line.

"Should we knock?" Benson asked as he swung a hand at something small with wings.

"Let's wait a moment."

An unlocking sounded from somewhere inside. The door opened to reveal an attractive woman with long blonde hair that she'd tied back to highlight her bright, friendly eyes. She wore a bulky beige sweater over black leggings and, for a moment, she looked young enough to be Lord Haysham's daughter; she was, in fact, his wife.

"Hello, Father," she said with a practised smile. A small dimple to the right of her mouth appeared in the perfectly smooth complexion of her face.

"Hello, Lady Haysham," Father Gilbert answered warmly.

"Stop that. If you don't call me Rosalyn, you're no longer welcome here."

Father Gilbert introduced Hugh Benson. She shook his hand and then waved for them to enter.

"They're in the study," she said. "Come in."

The front hall was spacious with a sizeable decorative table in the centre. The table was cluttered with folded newspapers, mail, keys on rings, and an enormous vase with faded silk flowers. A wide staircase faced them with books and shoes sitting on the bottom steps, as if they'd tried to make the climb but simply couldn't do it. To the left was a room with ornate furniture and paintings, all very French-looking and strategically placed as if for a magazine photo-op. Father Gilbert remembered being told at a Christmas party there that the room was only used for tours and special occasions.

Lady Haysham guided them down a hall beyond the stairs. She opened a door on the right and they entered a modest room that, unlike the first he'd seen, looked as if it had been stolen from the front of a semi-detached house in a middle-class part of town. The walls contained family photos and the tables were overrun with the real clutter from the people who really lived there. The only reminder of the room's true location was the massive marble fireplace that took up a quarter of the opposite wall.

Lord Haysham stood with Chief Constable Macaulay in front of the fireplace. The charred remains of the logs and ashes of past fires were piled high and spilled onto the hearth at their feet. Both men had glasses in their hands.

Bill Drake sat in a wing-backed chair near double French windows leading out to a patio. He was sipping something red in a small glass. He lifted the glass in a salute. "Gilbert."

"This is so much better than that ghastly morgue," Lord Haysham said. He offered them drinks from a wide assortment of bottles on a table on the opposite side of the room.

"We have Evensong in an hour," Father Gilbert said. "A cup of tea for me, please."

"The same for me," said Benson.

Haysham looked at his wife, raising an eyebrow. Rosalyn took the signal, smiled at him, and left. He waved at the two priests to sit down.

Books and magazines were randomly stacked around the chairs and sofa. Father Gilbert stepped carefully to avoid kicking them over. More magazines and empty mugs littered the coffee table. The Oriental rug, which covered the central section of the hardwood floor, was worn and faded.

Once they were seated, Lord Haysham said, "Well, what do we make of it all? Speak candidly."

"I hope Professor Braddock won't allow speed to affect his work," Father Gilbert said.

"One can work fast, but still be thorough," Macaulay stated. "Especially someone with Professor Braddock's experience."

"And DI Wilton? Is he experienced enough to handle this case?" Father Gilbert asked.

"Without question. I have every confidence in him." End of discussion.

Drake fished in his pocket, presumably for his pipe. "Tell me about the medallion. Any prevailing theories about how it wound up at the church?"

"None at the moment." Macaulay took a sip of his drink. "Any light from you, Father Gilbert?"

"Only Colin Doyle can answer that question," Father Gilbert said.

"May he rest in peace," Drake said and lifted his glass.

"His family background certainly puts a question on his motives," said Haysham.

"Let's put his family background aside for a moment," Drake said. "Take me through the possible scenarios."

"Well, in any scenario, Doyle finds the body," Macaulay began slowly.

Drake toyed with his pipe. "We assume that Doyle couldn't have expected such a find. Is that correct?"

"There's no evidence he was a treasure hunter, if that's what you mean," Macaulay replied. "That is to say, we don't think he took the job here because he believed they'd unearth anything valuable."

Drake nodded.

Macaulay continued, "Doyle sees the medallion. Perhaps he picks it up for a closer look. In one scenario, he sees that it's valuable, so he steals it and runs off."

"But why run off?" Father Gilbert asked. "He could have pocketed the medallion – or hid it somewhere. He must've known that running off would draw suspicion to him."

"He left to phone his estranged father," Benson said. He was sitting on the edge of the chair, his body tense with repressed energy.

"Why *leave* to do that?" Drake asked. "He could have used his mobile phone anywhere on the site and had privacy."

"Is there an adequate signal here?" To answer his own question, Benson took out his mobile phone and held it up to check the connection. "It's pretty good inside the house. Is it the same down by the bridge?"

"I've had no problems," Haysham said. "But why call his father? They were estranged."

Any answer was delayed as Lord Haysham's wife arrived with the tray of tea. She poured for the two priests, even remembering that Father Gilbert took his with milk and sugar.

After she left again, Macaulay said, "Maybe he felt compelled to tell his father about the medallion because of its potential value on the black market."

"Or perhaps the medallion had a special significance for his father." Drake lit his pipe.

Sipping his tea, Father Gilbert thought about Colin Doyle's actions between leaving the site and hanging himself. "Maybe he left because he was panicked."

"Panicked?" asked Drake.

"Discovering that body and the medallion caused Doyle to panic."

Drake puffed at the pipe, tamped the tobacco, and puffed again. "Is that what you saw in your vision? He was panicked?" That twinkle was in his eye.

"I'd say he was dealing with panic that had turned to despair," Father Gilbert said. "What if that's why he called his father?"

"Or he knew then he was going to kill himself and wanted to have a few last words with his father," Haysham offered.

"Or his father said something to drive him to suicide," Benson said.

Drake laughed. "Good God. It's like playing *Cluedo*."

"His suicide note was specific about the medallion," Father Gilbert said, trying to keep them on track. "Finding it may have been a surprise, but his knowledge of it wasn't. He knew what it was when he found it. And he panicked."

"That's *your* version," Drake said. "You're merging the facts with your vision."

Father Gilbert shrugged.

"We have to stay with the material evidence," Macaulay said.

"Besides, how could he possibly know anything about such an obscure medallion – or be panicked enough to kill himself over it?" Haysham asked.

"Mentally unstable," Macaulay said. "Didn't he say the medallion was cursed?"

"Whatever Doyle felt, it was enough for him to contact his father," Benson said. He got to his feet and began to pace. "It was also enough for him to drive to the church. It's possible he made it up to the church tower through the door one of us had left open or had unlocked. Maybe he thought about killing himself there and decided against it."

Drake examined his pipe. "Suicides don't usually run from place to place. To the church – then home to his garage. His behaviour was more helter-skelter than one would expect."

"Which would also suggest panic rather than premeditated action." Father Gilbert took a gulp of his tea. Not enough sugar.

"Why leave the medallion at the church?" Haysham asked. "Surely he couldn't have assumed that anyone would find it there – not quickly, at least. How often does anyone go up to the tower?"

"Not often," Father Gilbert said.

"Perhaps he didn't want it to be found," Drake suggested. "He left it there believing no one would find it for a long time. And, if someone did, there'd be no reason to connect it to the body – or to him."

"There are a lot of easier places to hide a medallion," Haysham countered. "He wouldn't have had to go to the top of the tower."

Macaulay frowned. "This is endless. There are any number of reasons why he behaved as he did."

Benson stopped pacing. He looked disappointed. "Isn't this the fun part of an investigation?"

"With some cases, perhaps." Macaulay upended his drink into his mouth. "This one annoys me."

"Here's what I think," Bill Drake announced. "Colin Doyle found the medallion, thought it was worth a lot of money as a religious artefact, and raced over to Father Gilbert to find out how much he could get for it. Father Gilbert saw its value and schemed to *murder* Colin Doyle to get the medallion. Thinking fast, Gilbert followed Doyle back to his house, coerced him to write a fake suicide note, and then strung him up in the garage. He then took the medallion back to the church where he hoped to sell it for a small fortune."

"Very funny, Bill," Father Gilbert said. "I'm sure you're a laugh-riot at will-readings."

Macaulay eyed his empty glass and said with no hint of humour, "We considered that scenario. But his secretary and sexton have given him alibis."

"They're in on it," Drake said.

Father Gilbert could hardly believe what he was hearing. "You considered that scenario!" he said to Macaulay.

Macaulay looked impassive. "Didn't you say not to exclude any possibilities?"

"But why would Father Gilbert tell the police about the medallion?" Benson asked.

"Because Gilbert knew he might get caught when he tried to sell it on the black market," Drake said. "So he made up the whole ludicrous story about having a vision of Colin Doyle and finding the medallion on the church tower. As a former detective, he knew it would throw the police a wobbly."

"You're a big help, Bill," said Father Gilbert.

"Does the medallion have any religious significance?" Haysham asked.

"The symbols suggest that it might. But I can't say for certain," Father Gilbert replied.

Macaulay placed his glass on the coffee table. "I'd like you to stay close to this investigation, Father Gilbert. As a former detective, you'll have helpful insights."

"But I'm a suspect."

"*I* don't consider you a suspect," Macaulay said. "But I can't deny that your connection to the bog body, the medallion, and Colin Doyle's death is curious. Though visions won't hold up as evidence in a court of law."

Father Gilbert drained the last of his tea from the cup. "Evensong," he said to Benson. "Thank you for the hospitality, Lord Haysham."

Following Father Gilbert to the door, Benson said to Macaulay in a stage whisper, "Don't worry, Sheriff. I'll make sure the varmint doesn't skip town."

Chapter 11

Father Gilbert had hoped the Evensong celebration would give him a sense of calm – of peace. The aesthetic beauty of St Mark's often took the priest out of the world and into the dominion of God. The stone columns rose up to the vaulted roof, pointing to heaven. The stained-glass representations of the miracles of Christ reminded him of the healing God offered. The marble altar and ornate screen, filled with statues of St Peter, St Paul, St John, and St Mary, told him that he wasn't alone; the Spirit and the people of God were with him. The polished brown pews and the ever-present fragrance of flowers and candles took him away from the concrete and car exhaust outside. The words of the Book of Common Prayer, with all the elegance and poetry of Shakespeare's time, whispered to him that not all of life was raw flesh and bone.

However, this mystery of the medallion made it difficult to shake off the temporal world for the spiritual one – because it involved both. One encroached on the other. Rather than hoping for peace, he prayed for wisdom.

Father Gilbert and Father Benson had dinner at The Mill House, a charming old pub on the outskirts of Stonebridge. Father Gilbert enjoyed the roast lamb. Benson opted for the shepherd's pie. The younger priest must have sensed Father Gilbert's mood and did not press him about the subject that was on both their minds. Their conversation wandered from a comparison of local restaurants to the ongoing conflicts in the Church of England between progressive and traditional forces.

At one point Benson lamented the number of Anglo-Catholics who had given up their allegiance to the Archbishop of Canterbury for the Bishop of Rome. "No matter how bad it gets, it can't be *that* bad," he said. "It's abandonment."

"Have they abandoned the Church of England or has the Church of England abandoned them?"

"Touch not the unclean thing," said Benson with a smile. "I'm the sixth generation of Anglican ministers in my family. I was raised to be loyal to *our* church, no matter what."

Father Gilbert wasn't sure if he admired that kind of loyalty or found it alarming. There were no ministers of any denomination in his family background. He knew of only one relative, his grandmother – his mother's mother – who had been devout about her faith. All of his other relatives subscribed to the traditional English practice of attending church for weddings, baptisms, funerals, and maybe Easter and Christmas. Later in life his mother had embraced an evangelical form of Christianity. They had rarely discussed it, which was also in keeping with English tradition. After she passed away, he often wished they had.

The two priests left The Mill House and parted company. Benson was staying in a small flat the church had purchased years ago above a newsagent's shop. Father Gilbert returned to the vicarage, a free-standing house nestled between rows of semi-detached houses that had been built on the property later. He put on the kettle for a cup of tea, checked his phone messages, then opted for a hot bath. There were few things better than a good soak in a bath the size of a canoe.

Sinking into the steaming water, he thought about Colin Doyle on the tower, recalling the adrenal surge he had felt when Doyle had slashed his throat and pushed himself over the side. As appalled as Father Gilbert was by the evil he saw as a detective, he couldn't deny the addictive nature of the work. Any crime, no matter how bad, was a mystery to be solved. There were times when he actually forgot to react the way a normal human should when faced with the horror of a violent death.

The tap dripped. He pushed his big toe into the mouth. The water was cold. The metal of the tap reminded him of the Stanley knife Colin Doyle had suddenly produced from nowhere.

Why did Doyle cut his throat? If the encounter had been real, it was easy to assume Doyle wanted to guarantee his death, in case the fall didn't kill him. Or, in the land of visions, it represented the ritualistic killing of a sacrificial lamb, the shedding of innocent blood. A criminal profiler could argue that cutting a victim's throat was a means to ensure silence, much like cutting out the tongue.

He shuddered. There was every chance the encounter said more about his own psychological state than Doyle's.

What about the body hanging from the distant tree? Was it a precognition of Doyle's death by hanging in his garage? And then there was the vivid scene of the two men on the stone bridge. Was it a speculative imagining of what might have happened? But then, how did he know about the boot being tucked under the coat? It couldn't be coincidence.

It was unusual for so many encounters to come to him in rapid succession. He couldn't escape a feeling of dread, that worse things were about to happen, that a formidable evil was at work.

He climbed out of the bath and paced as he said his nightly prayers. Crawling into bed, he picked up a novel from the nightstand. He put it down again and turned off the light. The darkness was definitive. He lay back and listened to the ticking clock. It took him back to the hours he had spent sitting at his wife's bedside as she lay dying of cancer – the contradictory feelings about the passing of time and how he dreaded losing her, yet yearned for her to be free of her pain.

"You're more impatient for my suffering to end than I am," she'd said. "Do you want it to end for my sake or yours?"

Mine, he realized.

"But God is more real to me in my pain than at any other time in my life," she'd said.

"That's not much of a testimony about God."

"Don't be such a baby," she'd said to him. "It always gets worse before it gets better."

One night as he sat next to her and listened to the clock, she suddenly opened her eyes and said, "You know, when it gets better, it'll be the best it can ever be."

He yearned to believe her. It was a long time later that he began to understand what she meant. Her grace while dealing with cancer was an initial nudge towards a faith that had eluded him. Ironically, it was death, his great nemesis, that pointed him to life.

Now, as he fell asleep, he saw the shrivelled face of his dying wife transformed into the healthy and vibrant face of the woman he had first married.

It'll get worse before it gets better, he thought before plunging into a dreamless sleep.

CHAPTER 12

"Mary Aston is here," Mrs Mayhew half-whispered in the phone.

It was a little after eight in the morning. Father Gilbert had taken the 7 a.m. service at the church again and, afterwards, had slipped away to a nearby café for breakfast.

"I'll be back in a few minutes, if she doesn't mind waiting," he said. He hadn't ordered yet and threw money on the table to cover the cost of the tea.

Mary Aston was sitting in the small reception area next to Mrs Mayhew's desk. She stood up when Father Gilbert walked in and extended a hand. "Father Gilbert," she said.

She shook his hand with the confidence of a woman who knew exactly what she wanted and how to get it. He instantly understood why Lord Haysham had spoken about her as he had. She was stunningly beautiful. She had a slender face with ivory skin and wide brown eyes that pinned him with intense interest, as if nothing else could possibly be more interesting to her than what he might say. She had an aquiline nose perfectly placed over a set of full lips that spread easily into a smile. Her brown hair was loosely pulled back at her nape, in a way that set off an elegant neck. She wore a pale-blue blouse under a fitted navy-blue suit that set off her slender but shapely figure. She exuded professionalism and sensuality at the same time. Father Gilbert's collar suddenly seemed rather tight. He couldn't remember the last time he'd met a woman as beautiful.

"Miss Aston." He greeted her with what he hoped was priestly politeness.

"*Mary*," she corrected him.

He guessed that she was in her early to mid thirties. She didn't wear a wedding ring.

"Would you like some tea?" he asked.

"No, thank you."

Father Gilbert invited her into his office. He stepped aside as she entered. He glanced at Mrs Mayhew and caught a disapproving look. Making sure to leave the door open – priestly protocol, he told himself – he gestured to a chair. Mary sat down.

She carried a black portfolio case. Placing it on her knees, she pushed a gold button and the clasp popped free. She pulled out a thick stack of papers and files. Several photos slipped out and fell to the floor. Father Gilbert moved quickly to retrieve them for her, noticing that they were copies of the same photos he'd seen at the coroner's – the bog body and the medallion. He wondered if Braddock or Macaulay or Wilton had shared them with her.

"Have you had a chance to examine the medallion?" he asked.

"Before I came here," she said.

"And?"

She held up a photo of the medallion. "It's called the Woodrich medallion and was part of a set that included a ring and a sword." She glanced at Father Gilbert. "The suicide victim didn't say anything about those, did he?"

"He didn't mention it in his note."

Her eyes fixed on him. "I wasn't talking about his note. I meant your conversation with him on the tower."

Father Gilbert restrained an impulse to swear.

She gave him a wry smile. "It was in the police report."

"Professor Braddock believes a sword may have been used to kill the bog person," he said.

Mary checked the portfolio and produced a drawing of a sword. "This is the Woodrich sword."

The drawing showed a wide sword with an engraving of flowers on the flat of the blade. The hilt had a grip carved in a swirling design and the cross guard had a curved extension to the bottom of the hilt that looked custom-made for the user's knuckles. Father Gilbert's eye went to the two edges of the blade itself. A quarter of the way down from the pointed tip, the smooth edges suddenly became serrated for several inches, and then went smooth again all the way to the hilt.

"Is that normal?" Father Gilbert asked, pointing to the serrated edges.

"It shows up on a few swords of the time," she said. "The saw-tooth style guaranteed more damage when thrust in and pulled back out of the opponent."

Father Gilbert studied the artwork. He tried to remember if this was the same sword he'd seen used on the bridge. Finally, he said: "The victim was struck in the head rather than run through. An odd choice, if death was intended."

"Maybe the murderer wasn't a very good swordsman," Mary suggested.

Father Gilbert handed the drawing back to her.

"I've asked the police to check the area around where the body was found," she said. "But I'm not hopeful the sword'll be there."

"Is the Woodrich Set significant?"

"Historically, yes." Her brown eyes were suddenly alight. "The pieces go back to the time of Henry VIII. Thomas Cromwell, the King's hatchet-man, gave the medallion, sword, and ring to Jeremy Woodrich of London."

"Should I know that name?" Father Gilbert said.

She shook her head. "Woodrich was a staunch Catholic but did what Thomas More refused to do – he supported the King in the argument over the divorces and Papal authority, which is why he was well liked by Thomas Cromwell. Cromwell gave him the Set by way of thanks."

Father Gilbert pointed to a photo of the medallion. "A man of Cromwell's religious sensibilities would have known better than to render Christ and the cross upside-down."

"I'm surprised that, as an ardent Protestant, he commissioned a crucifix at all." She examined the photos again. "Maybe it's not the cross that's upside down, but it's the back of the medallion that was designed the wrong way around. The inscription is positioned so it works either way."

"If Woodrich lived in London, how did the Set wind up in this area?" Father Gilbert asked.

"It moved with the Woodrich family as they suffered various changes in fortunes. One generation of Woodriches reclaimed their Roman Catholicism during the reign of Queen Elizabeth and suffered greatly for it. Another generation supported the Pilgrims and went to America. For a hundred years, the Woodrich family was divided between America and Britain and it was anyone's guess where the Set was – here or there. Then, somehow, one of the Woodrich daughters wound up with it. She married a vicar who eventually became the Bishop of Lewes here in Sussex."

"You wouldn't have a flow chart of all this, would you?"

She smiled – a captivating smile. "The entire Set disappeared in the late 1700s."

"Lost or stolen?" Father Gilbert asked.

She gave a slight shrug and Father Gilbert was again aware of the way her body moved. She said, "At the time there was a rumour that Joshua Todd had it."

"Joshua *Todd*?"

"Yes." Mary seemed pleased that he was surprised. "A direct ancestor of David Todd."

Her look of pleasure distracted him. He wished she wasn't so beguiling. He didn't usually have this much trouble concentrating even with a pretty woman nearby, but something exceptional was happening here. "Why would Joshua Todd have the Set?"

"The Todds were tradesmen then. Joshua Todd claimed that the Bishop of Lewes had promised the Set to him in payment for extensive work the Todds had done on the Bishop's home. Then the Bishop's family claimed after his death that Joshua Todd had stolen the Set. There was no paperwork to prove either side."

"But Joshua Todd had the Set?"

"No. I've found no evidence that he ever did. He argued that he should have been given the Set, not that he actually had it."

So the Todds' propensity to argue goes back several generations, Father Gilbert thought.

"The truth is complicated by the fact that the Bishop of Lewes was a scoundrel who often made promises he never kept. And Joshua Todd was a belligerent man who despised the wealthy and the powerful."

And that hasn't changed either, Father Gilbert thought. "The Bishop of Lewes wasn't a member of the Haysham family, was he?"

Mary nodded. "He was. How did you guess?"

"It seemed inevitable somehow." He thought again about the Todds and the Hayshams locked in a battle that would replay itself generation after generation.

"Joshua Todd disappeared sometime in 1792," Mary said, referring to her notes. "The assumption was that he'd taken the Set with him. But here we are, over two centuries later, and the medallion shows up on an unidentified body. Professor Braddock is now taking bets that our corpse is Joshua Todd."

"That seems likely."

"I'm intrigued that the medallion wound up here at St Mark's," she said, her eyes on him again. "It's as if it came home."

Father Gilbert frowned. "You make it sound like something from *The Lord of the Rings*, as if the medallion had a *will* to return. And how is St Mark's its home?"

She placed her hands on the portfolio. Her fingernails were painted in a light blue, perfectly manicured. "I have a copy of a letter from Joshua Todd's grandson Francis. Francis was the minister of this church from 1874 to 1890." She pulled out a photocopy of the letter and gave it to Father Gilbert.

"Did you get this from David Todd?" he asked.

"Yes," she said coolly. "I met with him last evening."

"You don't waste any time."

Another shrug, another shift in her blouse. "I was in Brighton for a conference. It's not far."

The letter was written in broad cursive and dated *17th of August, 1889*. The salutation was to *D*. Father Gilbert scanned it, looking for the reference to the Woodrich Set. He found it near the end. *The Woodrich blade and jewel are not to be a source of anxiety for you,* the letter stated. *The church is a perfectly safe place in which to keep them. Yrs, Francis.*

"How did David Todd get possession of a letter written to someone else?" Father Gilbert asked.

"He doesn't know. It was in his family records. He has an entire attic filled with boxes of letters and documents."

Father Gilbert wondered if David Todd had said so, or had she been to his house – in the attic or somewhere else upstairs? He repented of the thought. "Does Todd know who *D* was?"

"No. But the fact that Francis Todd was a vicar here and the sword and jewel were being kept safe somewhere on the church premises made me think of you."

"I'm not as familiar with St Mark's history as I should be," said Father Gilbert. "But one of our parishioners, Margaret Clarke, is. She's made a hobby of it."

"Is she credible?" asked Mary.

"She's well into her eighties and has attended here her entire life. That seems credible to me."

She gathered up her papers. "Would it be all right if I spoke to her?"

Father Gilbert thought about the last time he'd been to visit Margaret. She was on the eccentric, even reclusive, side. "She may not be comfortable with a stranger. I should go with you."

"Thank you." Her hand touched his arm lightly, quickly, then retreated. "Would now be too soon?"

"She's not the sort of woman who likes to be surprised by visitors," he said. "I'll have Mrs Mayhew arrange an appropriate time."

A few minutes later Mrs Mayhew confirmed that Mrs Clarke would expect them for tea at 4:00.

"Tea at four. How old-fashioned," Mary said, smiling.

"It's how things used to be done," Mrs Mayhew said sharply as she walked out.

With the business finished, Mary gathered her things and moved for the door. She lingered, as if she had something she wanted to ask or say but, after a moment, she announced that she was overdue to meet with Professor Braddock. She stood and handed her business card to Father Gilbert. "That's my mobile phone. Just in case you need to reach me."

He had his fingers on the card, but she didn't release it.

"For anything," she added and her eyes were on his.

He turned away as if something had caught his attention on the desk. *Good heavens,* he thought, *she knows exactly the effect she has on men.*

"Thank you, Father."

"Happy hunting," he said and felt foolish. He glanced in her direction again, and then moved to the other side of his desk. He feared he would watch her exit too closely.

Mrs Mayhew would have blocked his view anyway, as she stepped into the doorway. "I don't trust her," she stated. Then she asked pleasantly, "Tea?"

Father Gilbert nodded. "Yes, please."

"I assume you know that Margaret Clarke is a great-aunt to Detective Inspector Wilton," Mrs Mayhew said. "He's investigating this case, isn't he?"

"Yes, he is. Thank you, I didn't realize."

She left and he closed the door.

He couldn't imagine what was wrong with him. Attractive women didn't usually affect him so strongly. He recognized the way Mary Aston used her charms, but he didn't like the way he was succumbing to them.

He turned to the nearest bookcase and looked over the spines of the books. He had a collection of prayers by Thomas Aquinas. There was a prayer about fighting temptation he hoped to find, quickly.

CHAPTER 13

Sean Fisher, the Canon at Southaven Cathedral, returned Father Gilbert's call. Father Gilbert pictured him as they spoke – a short, thin man whose entire demeanour exuded the same precision as the cut of his silver hair. The Canon confirmed that the Doyles had attended the Cathedral infrequently over the years but not to the extent that any of the clergy were on intimate terms with them. The Dean of the Cathedral had gone to the house to offer his pastoral help that morning but was thanked and dismissed within five minutes.

"What about Colin Doyle's family?"

"They aren't members of the Cathedral," Fisher said. "They attend All Souls' Church. You'll want to talk to Desmond Singh. He's the vicar there."

Father Gilbert looked online and found a website for All Souls' Church. It seemed to be a lively Evangelical assembly with a variety of meetings and clubs and Bible studies. He navigated to a brief biography of the Reverend Desmond Singh, born and raised in Hyderabad, India, but educated at Wycliffe Hall in Oxford. The designation of "Reverend" pointed to Singh's Protestant sensibilities, as a contrast to the more traditional and Anglo-Catholic "Father". Father Gilbert dialled the number on the website.

"This is Reverend Singh," a gentle voice said in English, but with a distinct Indian accent.

"Reverend Singh, this is Father Gilbert at St Mark's in Stonebridge."

"Ah, Father. I was hoping to hear from you. We need to talk."

* * *

Father Gilbert met Reverend Singh at a pub halfway between their respective towns. Mr Urquhart had provided the transport, dropping Father Gilbert off on his way to a garden centre further along the road. The pub had been bought by a corporate chain and converted into a family eatery, complete with a play area for small children. Video games and fruit machines lined a far wall, flashing and occasionally trumpeting bad synthesizer sounds to draw attention to themselves. The rows of bottles behind the bar were lit up, their colours luminous like Christmas lights. A man sat at the bar, cradling a drink in his hands, staring ahead at nothing. In another time, he would have had a cigarette in front of him. He wore a beige mac. His hair was greasy, sticking out in tufts. He was loneliness incarnate.

"Colin wasn't the suicidal type," Reverend Singh said. "Until now, I would have said he was as engaged in his life as a man could be."

"So you're genuinely surprised by what happened."

Reverend Singh nodded. He was a dark-skinned man with wide eyes and radiant white teeth. His jet-black hair was combed back and held in place with gel. He stirred a straw around his glass of fruit juice. "He was making plans for a holiday in Spain with his family. He and his wife were house-hunting for a larger home. They also purchased a new car a few weeks ago. *Not* the behaviour of a man who was planning to kill himself."

"Then his decision was impulsive." Father Gilbert lifted a mug of hot tea to his lips.

"What would trigger such a sudden impulse?" It was a tough question. Reverend Singh looked truly bewildered. "He was a faithful parishioner. A good man, I'd say."

Father Gilbert wished that being a faithful parishioner and being a good man always went hand in hand.

A thoughtful pause with more stirring. The ice rattled in the glass. "The detective suggested that Colin had stolen a piece of jewellery from the body they dug up. That doesn't fit with the man I knew. He was no thief."

"Was he well off? Do builders make good money these days?"

"I can't say for certain, but I suspect they do."

"Enough to go on holiday while buying a new car and looking for a larger house?"

"Are you suggesting he was supplementing his income illegally?"

"I'm not suggesting anything," Father Gilbert said. He was pushing hard, perhaps too hard.

"The reputation of being a Doyle followed him, no matter where he went," Singh said.

"I heard he and his father had a falling out."

Another nod from Reverend Singh.

"Do you know what it was about?"

"I asked him once," Singh said. "He made it clear he didn't want to discuss it."

No doubt privacy was part of the family code, Father Gilbert thought. It was often the code within dysfunctional families.

"The Dean of the Cathedral told me he went to Jack Doyle's house," said Singh. "He was summarily dismissed."

"By Jack Doyle?" asked Father Gilbert.

"Yes. Though Colin's mother attempted to be cordial." Singh finally took a drink of his juice, not using the straw. Then he said, "The Dean said he felt a strong emotion at work in the house."

"That can't be a surprise, all things considered."

"It wasn't grief," Singh said. "He said it was something else."

"What?"

"Fear." Singh levelled his gaze at Father Gilbert.

Father Gilbert waited. There was more Singh wanted to say.

"I feel it, too. It has been present with me since yesterday morning, even before I heard about Colin's death. Fear." He went back to stirring the ice.

"Fear of what?"

"Evil, perhaps." Singh lifted his drink but didn't put it to his lips. He spoke quietly. "What do you think of dreams, Father Gilbert?"

"What kind of dreams?"

"Dreams that, when we awake, we suspect mean something?"

"All dreams mean something," Father Gilbert said. "But I think most dreams are our attempts to sort through the clutter in our minds – all the fragments of thoughts, ideas, memories, experiences, sensations. We're trying to process them, but without a conscious will or sensible order to the effort."

"The Bible speaks of dreams. God used dreams as a way to communicate with men." Singh gazed at Father Gilbert again. "Do you think He does that now?"

"It's not for me to say what God will or will not do. But I see no reason for Him not to use dreams now, if He thinks it's the best way to communicate to us." Father Gilbert was intrigued by where this conversation was heading. "What were your dreams?"

"They're a bit fuzzy to my conscious mind now," he said. "Yesterday morning, right before awakening, I dreamt that Colin Doyle was standing on a church tower."

Father Gilbert pressed his lips together, if only to keep his mouth from falling open.

Singh continued, "My impression was that he intended to kill himself. But there was something he was determined to do first. He paced around the tower. In one hand he was holding a... a gold necklace of some sort. In the other hand, he had a knife, the kind one uses to open boxes. He was agitated. Then I saw a flock of winged creatures – bat-like but human-sized, fanged, terrible demons – suddenly descend upon him. It was as if they were after the jewel in his hand. He fought them off. Then, just as suddenly, they flew away as if startled. Then I saw a man coming up through the hatch."

"Who was it?"

"My dream ended before I could see. Though my impression was that the man was you." He shook his head slowly. "I woke up with my heart racing. I felt a very palpable fear."

Father Gilbert hardly knew what to say. He realized his fingers were intertwined so tightly that his knuckles had turned white. "Has anyone mentioned to you about Colin going to the tower at St Mark's?"

"No." Singh's dark-brown eyes suddenly grew wide. "Did he?"

"We don't know for sure. He may have, before he killed himself."

A sharp exhale from Singh. "That is a remarkable coincidence, then."

"More than you know," Father Gilbert said. "At the same time Colin was in his garage, I had a dream – for lack of a better word – about Colin on the tower."

Singh leaned back in his chair. He placed his palms down on the table as if steadying himself.

Father Gilbert detailed his encounter with Colin on the tower.

Singh pulled his hands back and clasped them as if in prayer. "This is unbelievable," Singh said after a long pause.

"It is."

"Has this ever happened to you before?"

"Once or twice." The door to the pub opened. A family came in. Two children raced to the play area.

Singh spoke in a hushed tone, "In India, we are taught to take dreams very seriously. This raises in me a fear I haven't felt since I was a child, before I became a Christian."

Father Gilbert considered telling him about seeing the body hanging from the tree, and the assault on the bridge, but it seemed like too much at this moment.

Singh returned to the straw in his drink. He stirred with greater energy. The ice had nearly melted into the orange liquid. "There is more at work here than what we know, Father. Something evil."

"Without question."

"We must be vigilant."

"You said you had fearful *dreams*. More than the one?"

"Yes – a second dream, though it was more perplexing." Singh nudged the glass aside. "It involved a fight between two men. One had a sword. They were on an ancient bridge."

CHAPTER 14

Father Gilbert didn't believe that the seemingly random convergence of mundane events often labelled by people as "coincidence" was random at all. The world was a vast tangle of interwoven webs and intricate patterns of cause and effect that, at its core, reflected a spiritual reality. We, as humans, were constantly being nudged towards a heavenly or a diabolical realm. Nothing was random. Even the mundane was filled with significance. How else to explain, for example, a man who ties his shoes every day of his life and then one day, while bending to accomplish that simple task, his back seizes up and puts him in hospital for several days? There he meets another patient with whom he talks – and that talk changes his perspective about the existence of God. He investigates further and discovers what it means to have a relationship with Jesus Christ. The man's eternal destiny changes because he bent to tie his shoes. And, by coincidence, he met another man in the ward who impacted his life in the most profound way.

Explainable? Yes. But what explanation could anyone offer for the so-called coincidence of the dreams Father Gilbert had shared with Reverend Singh? It was unnerving.

No, he thought, none of what had happened in the past thirty-six hours was mere coincidence. Nor was it a coincidence that he and Father Benson had lunch at The Countryman Café, a stone's throw from St Mark's, and David Todd happened to drop by.

All the tables were filled, so Todd slid onto a chair next to Benson. "May I join you?" he asked, without waiting for an answer. "The best sausage sandwiches in the area. Have you ordered?"

"A few minutes ago," Father Gilbert said.

Todd signalled the harried waitress. She came over, took his order for the sausage special, then left again. Todd produced the local paper, which had been tucked under his arm. He spread it out in front of them. The main headline on the front page announced that a body had been found under "Haysham's bridge". There was a photo of Lord Haysham and David Todd arguing in the centre of a crowd.

"Nice photo," Father Gilbert said.

"This will slow him down," Todd said.

"Is there anything about Colin Doyle?" Benson asked.

"Page three," Todd said. "Just a paragraph about a possible suicide and so on. It's a terrible thing."

"Did you know Colin Doyle?" Father Gilbert asked.

"Why would I know him?" Todd countered.

"No reason." Father Gilbert noticed that Todd's question wasn't an answer.

There was a brief silence, but Todd was looking at Father Gilbert.

"All right, David, what else?" Father Gilbert finally asked.

Benson looked at Father Gilbert as if he'd missed something.

Todd pushed the cutlery aside and leaned both elbows on the table. He moved in close. "Guess what I did only an hour ago?"

"Took a vow of poverty to become a monk?" asked Father Gilbert.

Benson chuckled.

Todd didn't. "I gave a swab of my cheek-lining to the police. Apparently they think the body from the bridge is a relative of mine. They want to compare our DNA."

"Joshua Todd," Father Gilbert said.

"You've heard about him?"

"From Mary Aston."

Todd smiled. It was on the edge of being lascivious. "Gorgeous, isn't she?"

Father Gilbert nodded. He felt Benson's eyes on him. They hadn't talked about Mary Aston's visit yet. But Father Gilbert had no doubt that Mrs Mayhew had mentioned it – and Mary – to Benson.

"She's a remarkable woman. I've met her at various antique auctions," Todd said.

"I didn't know you collected antiques."

"I don't. I was selling some items." He didn't elaborate. "I've promised to help her find the rest of the Woodrich Set, if I can. I've told her she's welcome to look over my family documents."

Father Gilbert suspected Todd would welcome her to do more than that, given the chance. He immediately repented of the thought.

"You have to admit, this raises a number of questions," Todd said. He began to rearrange the tabletop – the salt and pepper moving to the left, the sauces to the right. Nervous energy, much like Reverend Singh's habit with the straw.

"What questions?" Benson asked.

"About Joshua Todd's death. Who murdered him, the ownership of the Woodrich medallion…" The café door opened and something outside caught the afternoon sun. It flickered, hitting Todd's face. He raised his hand to shield his eyes and squinted at Father Gilbert. "That hurts."

The flickering light went away and he lowered his hand.

"You know about the Woodrich Set, right?" Todd asked.

"Miss Aston gave me a brief history. But Father Benson hasn't heard."

Todd's mobile phone rang and he fished it out of his pocket. "Sorry," he said and glanced at the screen. His facial expression changed and his eyes widened with alarm. Then, quickly, he caught himself and forced a smile at the two priests. Punching the button, he shoved the phone back into his pocket. "Blasted phones. They're a nuisance."

"If you need to take the call…" Father Gilbert began.

Todd waved him off. "It was nothing important. What were we talking about?"

"The Woodrich Set," Benson reminded him.

"Oh. Right." He picked up his water glass and took a drink. The ice trembled. "The legend of the Woodrich Set has been in my family for years. More whispered than openly talked about, like a skeleton in the family closet."

"An interesting choice of expression," said Father Gilbert.

"The discovery of the body on the Haysham estate confirms what I've always believed: Joshua Todd was murdered by the man who was then Lord Haysham."

"You can't know that," Father Gilbert said.

"The bridge is on his property, isn't it?"

"The bridge was on one of the main public roads into Stonebridge," said Father Gilbert. "It skirted the Haysham property then. Everyone used it."

Benson held up a hand. "Why would Lord Haysham want to kill Joshua Todd?"

"Rope," Todd said.

"Rope?" Benson repeated.

Todd nodded. "In the early eighteenth century, my family were tradesmen who eventually became masters in different kinds of industry. You'll find Todds in the North who became captains of the mercantile world – cotton and weaving. The Todds here were successful in rope manufacturing, supplying the ships in the docks of Southaven. It became one of the mainstays of Stonebridge's business interests."

"Isn't Stonebridge awfully far inland to serve the docks in Southaven?" Benson asked.

"The Mill River once cut through Stonebridge and extended to Southaven and the sea," Todd explained. "Though the Hayshams owned most of the land along the river. It was their way of controlling the business in the area, to get their percentage of it. They would not allow anyone to use that land commercially."

Father Gilbert was surprised. "They owned that much land – all the way from Stonebridge to Southaven?"

"They did then, yes." Todd scowled. "They'd have claimed ownership of the river itself if they could have got away with it."

"I still don't understand why Haysham would want to kill Joshua Todd," Benson said.

Todd continued, "My family's rope-making business was hugely successful. Even the Hayshams had to buy from us. They saw the profits and wanted control of it. I have letters suggesting subtle coercion to outright intimidation. But Joshua Todd refused. Then he developed a faster and more efficient way of making the rope – ahead of his time, I think. Suddenly the Todds were in the upper class. The Hayshams didn't like it. It was offensive for the Todds to take their place with the ruling class. So Haysham put a spy into our family business. They stole our method of rope-making. Within a few years, Joshua Todd was driven out of business and nearly wound up on the streets."

"Surely he'd saved enough of his fortune to live comfortably," Benson said.

"He lost his money on bad investments, some connected to the Hayshams," Todd said. He moved the shakers and bottles to one end of the table, then idly swiped at some crumbs with the palm of his hand. His expression was sour. "You see, the Hayshams have done their best to destroy the Todds at every opportunity. Joshua Todd went from wealth to poverty in only a few years."

"Is that why he served as a handyman for the Bishop of Lewes?" Father Gilbert asked.

Todd looked impressed. "He took work where he could get it."

"What about the rest of the Woodrich Set? Is there anything in your family legend about that? I mean, apart from the letter Francis Todd wrote to his parishioner about the sword and ring being at St Mark's."

Benson was surprised. "St Mark's?"

Father Gilbert gave him an I'll-explain-later look.

"I'm going to check our archives to see what else I can learn about that Set." Todd leaned back from the table as the waitress arrived with their food.

The conversation turned to normal chat as they ate. Benson asked Todd about the local housing and land market. Todd gave a full report about how much things were likely to improve in the area, in spite of financial downturns elsewhere.

Father Gilbert watched David Todd. He was enthusiastic and confident as he spoke, but there was something in his eyes that betrayed a deep anxiety. Father Gilbert suspected it wasn't related to the conversation, but something else. He thought about the earlier phone call.

As they finished lunch, Father Gilbert's mobile phone rang.

Todd jumped at the sound, then laughed. "I don't know why I'm so jittery."

Father Gilbert pressed the phone to his ear. "Hello?"

"Lord Haysham's wife phoned and has asked you to come to the house right away," Mrs Mayhew said.

"Why?"

"She didn't say. But she was distressed."

"All right. Thank you, Mrs Mayhew." Father Gilbert turned to Benson. "We have to go."

Benson took a last bite of toast. "I'll drive," he said, as if he had a choice.

Todd tossed his serviette onto his plate and looked at Father Gilbert. "No trouble, I hope," he said, as if he knew exactly what the call was about.

* * *

Lord Haysham paced his family room, brandishing a golf club like a weapon. His face was red. "It's nothing short of corporate espionage," he raged.

Fathers Gilbert and Benson stood by the door, having just refused an offer of tea from a worried-looking Lady Haysham.

"What's wrong?" asked Father Gilbert. He'd never seen Lord Haysham so agitated. Benson moved to the wing-back chair, standing behind it as if using it for cover.

"What's wrong?" Haysham asked, pacing in heavy-footed strides. "I have it from the police—"

"DI Wilton?"

"It doesn't matter," Haysham snapped. "This Doyle fellow was a *spy* for David Todd."

"What makes them think so?" Father Gilbert asked.

Haysham fumed. "Todd's number was on Doyle's mobile phone. Repeated calls, *after* Doyle began working on my property. There were texts about money. Doyle's bank records show deposits from David Todd's company paid into his personal account. The sums were significant."

Father Gilbert thought of Doyle's new car and the forthcoming holiday. He was also impressed by the speed with which the police had found the phone numbers and accessed the bank records. He was less impressed that the information was shared with Haysham.

"Why would David Todd pay Doyle to spy on you?" Benson asked.

"To report to Todd everything that happens at the site, with the intention of putting a stop to it. Any misstep. Any find. Todd would use it all to sabotage me." He snorted.

Father Gilbert shook his head. He was tempted to ask what Haysham expected, considering the animosity between the Hayshams and Todds.

Lord Haysham lifted the golf club. "Now I understand how Todd and his protesters arrived so quickly after that body was found." He looked at the club as if only just realizing he had it in his hand. He smashed it down onto a cushion. Dust blew up into the shaft of sunlight coming through the window.

"You have to relax, my lord," said Father Gilbert. "Put down the club."

Haysham tossed it onto the couch and went to the French windows. He looked out at the stone patio, or somewhere beyond. "I'm losing money with every delay," he said. "Discovering the bridge was bad enough. If that body turns out to be Todd's ancestor, he'll make the most of it to delay me further. No doubt he'll blame *my* ancestor for the murder."

Fathers Gilbert and Benson exchanged looks.

"I wish my ancestor *had* killed Todd's," Haysham said softly. "It's what I'd like to do to him now. I'd like to wring his neck."

Father Gilbert stepped towards him. "Stop it. That kind of talk will get you in trouble."

Lord Haysham turned. He took a deep breath and exhaled slowly. "Yes, of course. You're right. There's no point in lowering myself to his level."

At that moment, a phone on a small table began to ring. Lord Haysham jerked his head and looked at it. Father Gilbert saw in his expression something familiar, and thought of David Todd's expression when his mobile phone had rung at lunch. Was it fear?

"My wife will get that," Haysham said. But he kept his eye on the receiver as it continued to ring.

"She must be busy," Father Gilbert said.

His wife appeared in the doorway and looked anxiously at her husband. "Michael?"

"Don't bother with it," he said.

She stepped out again. The three men were silent as the phone rang a few more times, then stopped. Haysham relaxed.

"Why didn't you answer it?" Father Gilbert asked.

"The press," he said without conviction. "They won't leave me alone."

"Really?" Father Gilbert asked.

Lord Haysham saw his expression. "To be honest, I've been receiving crank calls ever since that body was found. Probably Todd's fanatics. They have my wife worried."

"You too, from the looks of it," Father Gilbert said.

Benson moved out from behind the chair and to the phone. "There's a number you can dial to get the caller ID."

"I tried. The number was blocked."

Benson lingered, as if he might try for himself, then moved back to the chair.

"What can we do for you?" Father Gilbert asked.

Haysham picked up the golf club, then dropped himself onto the couch. "Tell Todd to leave me alone. Surely you can do that, as his vicar."

"As the vicar, I'd rather arbitrate a meeting between the two of you to work out how to live with each other for the long term," Father Gilbert said.

Haysham shook his head. "He's irrational whenever I'm around."

Father Gilbert thought for a moment, then said, "Have you ever researched the conflict between your families?"

"Why would I?"

"The root of your problem could be found there. Besides, the best defence is a good offence," Father Gilbert said. "The Todd family maintains that somehow the Hayshams robbed them of money or opportunity or intellectual property. If you can establish the facts from your family papers, then you can argue against any potential scandal Todd puts out to the public. And if you determine that your ancestors actually *did* rob the Todds, then you can offer some sort of restitution to make peace."

Haysham was affronted. "*Pay* him?"

"Why not?"

Haysham muttered a colourful profanity.

Benson blushed slightly and looked away.

"Do you know where your family papers are?" Father Gilbert asked.

"My father hired Adrian Scott to serve as our family archivist. He has everything I know about."

"We'll start there," Father Gilbert said. "I'll donate Father Benson's time to the effort."

Benson cringed. "What?"

"Anything to bring peace to our parish," Father Gilbert added.

Benson nodded.

Haysham groaned. "It's a waste of time. But you have my permission, if you think it'll help. Tell Scott to show you everything we have."

There was nothing else to be said, so the two priests moved towards the door. Haysham trailed behind them.

"Look," Haysham said, "I'm dreadfully sorry about my tantrum. Finding this body has undone me. I'm not a superstitious man, but the body and Doyle's suicide seem like bad omens."

"Surely you don't believe in omens," Father Gilbert said.

"I didn't used to."

CHAPTER 15

"Am I supposed to thank you for that assignment?" Benson asked Father Gilbert as they climbed into the Mini.

"You can if you like," Father Gilbert said with a half-smile. "I meant what I said about keeping the peace. If you can find anything in the archives that'll help defuse this situation, then your time will be well spent."

Benson headed the car towards Stonebridge. "What if I find that Lord Haysham's ancestor really killed Todd?"

"Then we'll use that information to find another way to peace."

"Are you that much of an optimist?"

"Not at all." *Especially not in this case,* Father Gilbert thought. "But the truth is bound to help us more than accusation or speculation."

"How do I find Adrian Scott?"

"Scott's Second-Hand Bookshop is in the centre of the town, down the High Street on the corner across from the large furniture store."

Benson glanced at the clock on the dashboard. "It's almost three. Will it wait until tomorrow?"

Father Gilbert scratched at his chin. "I suppose two centuries of fighting can wait to be resolved for one day. As it is, we're due at Mrs Clarke's at four."

There was a long pause. Benson came to a small roundabout, entering it too fast. The tyres squealed. Father Gilbert grabbed the dashboard to keep from sliding over to the driver's side.

"Is everything all right?" Father Gilbert asked once they were righted.

"Sorry," Benson said. "This isn't how I expected my first few weeks in this parish to go."

Father Gilbert looked at the young priest. He wished he could say that this was the first time anything like this had ever happened in his experience, and that probably nothing like it would ever happen again. But he couldn't.

* * *

Mrs Clarke's bungalow was one of many on The Avenue, an upmarket part of Stonebridge. The houses themselves were modest when they were built after World War II, but had now gained character and prestige with age. The Tudor-style dark beams stretched out horizontally, vertically, and diagonally against the white stucco. The windows were leaded with a diamond pattern in their centres and Father Gilbert could make out the blurred colours of flowers in vases inside each diamond. Just as they reached the door, a car pulled up to the kerb. Mary Aston got out. She smiled and waved.

"Mary Aston?" Benson said.

"That's her."

"Good heavens," Benson whispered.

Father Gilbert glanced at the curate, then at Mary as she approached them. He was acutely aware of her good looks and noticed the very graceful way she walked, as if she was on a fashion runway rather than a stony pavement. He wondered if her poise and confidence came with instinct or with training.

"Am I late?" she asked. She pushed a lock of hair away from her face.

"You're not." Father Gilbert nodded to Father Benson. "This is—"

Benson held out his hand. "Father Benson."

"A pleasure," she said.

Benson had a slight blush in his cheeks. Father Gilbert held back a smile. Her beauty was undeniable, he thought. Even the slight wrinkles around her eyes added character. As did the tiny scar just above the right side of her mouth.

Suddenly the front door was pulled open from the inside. Mrs Clarke gazed at them. "I was beginning to wonder if you intended to knock or if we should have our tea here by the front door."

She was thin, with a milk-white face and deep lines in her forehead and around her mouth. She had sharp blue eyes, but they were red-rimmed and pinched, as if she spent a lot of time squinting – or worrying. Her grey hair was meticulously styled.

"I'm sorry, Mrs Clarke," Father Gilbert said. He introduced Father Benson, whom she had met at church but might have forgotten, and then Mary Aston.

"Well, aren't you a pretty thing," she said to Mary as she took Father Gilbert's arm and drew him into the house. "We mustn't dawdle. The tea will get cold."

They entered a short entrance hall and turned right into the front room. It was decorated with cherry-wood furniture and coloured fabrics – a lot of creamy pinks, rosy pinks, bright pinks, and those kinds of pinks that look more purple than pink. Father Gilbert felt as if he'd stepped inside a ball of candyfloss. Small shelves held dozens of porcelain figurines of cats and dogs of varying breeds. They reminded him of the many figurines in his mother's house in Tunbridge Wells – though hers were of men and women dressed in Regency-era clothes, reflecting her insatiable enjoyment of Dorothy Sayers novels. He also remembered what a chore it had been selling them all after she'd died.

A marble coffee table sat in the centre of four chairs. A teapot under a cosy, cups and saucers, and small sandwich plates were assembled along with an assortment of scones, jam, cream, and finger sandwiches of cucumber and salmon – with the crust trimmed from the bread, of course. Mrs Clarke indicated where each should sit, then sat down herself and poured the tea.

Father Gilbert thanked her for going to such trouble for them. There was the obligatory chit-chat about Mary's work in antiques, which Mrs Clarke said must be fascinating, and then quickly changed the subject to the weather and the condition of the garden and then a scandal in Parliament that Father Gilbert had missed on the news – all followed by an awkward silence.

"You must be wondering why we're here," Father Gilbert finally said.

"Mrs Mayhew said it has to do with the history of St Mark's."

"Yes."

"Is it because of that ghastly business at Lord Haysham's? A corpse under the bridge? My nephew told me a bit about it. Well, rather, he's my *great*-nephew." She looked at Father Gilbert with anxious eyes. "Is that it?"

"Have you ever heard of the Woodrich Set?" asked Mary.

Mrs Clarke was putting a spoonful of sugar into her tea and Father Gilbert thought he saw a slight hesitation in the action.

Mary continued, "It's a medallion, sword, and ring."

As Mrs Clarke picked up the cup, it rattled against the saucer in a way it hadn't before. "I've heard of them," she said. "Though no one's spoken of them since I was a young girl."

"Why did someone speak of them then?" Mary asked.

"My father – Tom Wilton – was a police constable in Stonebridge. He was also a regular member of St Mark's. There's a stained-glass window dedicated to him – the one with Jesus and the children on the north side of the nave."

Father Gilbert remembered it. "The craftsmanship is excellent."

"I'll be sure to look for it," Mary said with an endearing smile. "What can you tell us about the Set?"

Mrs Clarke looked distracted, her eyes fixed on her cup of tea, but seeing something else. "It was a long time ago. 1938. So I can't promise factual accuracy. I was eight years old at the time."

"Understood." Mary leaned forward, as if nothing should distract them from what Mrs Clarke had to say.

"There was a sword – the Woodrich sword – discovered in the cellar of the church—"

"The crypt?" Father Gilbert asked.

"No, in the other section, the one with the plumbing and pipes. I believe workers were putting in a new boiler or some such thing. I was never clear about that. They had to dig up the ground in a corner and found the sword wrapped in old oilcloth." She paused as if she was unsure about continuing, then said, "They found it with a skeleton."

There was a rattle as Benson almost spilled his tea. Mary sat up straight.

Father Gilbert leaned forward. "A *human* skeleton?"

Mrs Clarke nodded. "The sword was placed in its arms, like you see in those brass rubbings of knights in ancient cathedrals." She glanced around at them. "More tea?"

Without waiting for a reply, she poured tea into their cups.

"The police were called in, of course, which is how my father got involved," she said. "Detectives from Scotland Yard also came from London to assist in the case."

"Did they ever learn who the skeleton was?" Mary asked.

"I don't believe the body was ever identified. They speculated that it had been there for over a hundred years."

"The letter written by Francis Todd," Mary said softly to Father Gilbert. "He said the sword was safe at the church."

"That was 1889. The body had been there all that time?" asked Father Gilbert.

Father Benson looked puzzled. Father Gilbert gave him a quick nod, yet another I'll-explain-later look.

"You'll have to speak up," said Mrs Clarke.

"I'm sorry," said Father Gilbert. "Please continue."

She put her saucer and cup down. "I heard my father say one night that whoever it was had probably been killed by the sword and then buried with it. Apparently there was a tell-tale mark on one of the bones in the ribcage where the sword had nicked it."

"The victim had been stabbed in the chest?" Mary asked.

Mrs Clarke gave a small shrug. "I don't know. Though I remember they said it was missing a front tooth. Isn't that a peculiar thing to remember? It made me think of a boy I knew at school who was missing a front tooth. He could spit further than anyone else, as if that was any sort of accomplishment."

"Was there a ring?" Mary asked.

Mrs Clarke looked puzzled.

Mary held out her hand and spread her fingers, to offer an example. "Maybe a ring on one of the skeleton's fingers?"

"No one said so in my presence," Mrs Clarke said. "I would have remembered that. But the *sword* – that was the topic of a lot of conversations."

"No doubt people were curious," Father Gilbert said.

She glanced around. The lines of worry around her eyes seemed to deepen. "It was more than that. People began to speak as if the sword was cursed. Even people with good sense, who didn't believe in such things."

Father Gilbert's eyes went to Mary and then Father Benson. Both were watching his reaction.

"Why would people talk about a curse?" he asked.

"Because bad things happened after that sword was found," she said in a hushed tone.

Benson said, "I'm sure anything that happened could be explained rationally."

"Perhaps. But it was very strange." Mrs Clarke used both hands to spread her skirt, then folded them on her knees. "A young man was scalded by a puncture in one of the boiler's pipes only an hour after the sword was found. Then the sword was taken to the local police station and kept there – until the building burnt to the ground."

"Is this fact or the musings of an eight-year-old girl?" Father Gilbert asked.

Mrs Clarke looked at him earnestly. "I saw the sword for myself, Father. There was something about it that made me uneasy, as if I was in the presence of…" Her voice trailed off.

"You saw the sword?" Mary asked.

"We kept it at our house for a short while, after the incident at the police station. My father was a constable, as I said. It was evidence. Then odd things happened to *us*. Our cat disappeared. We had an infestation of bats in our attic. I remember there was tension in the house, as if we were all on edge and didn't know why. No one wanted to say it was because of the sword, but we all thought it was. I sneaked a peek at it one day when my parents weren't home. I was surprised."

"Why?" asked Father Gilbert.

"When the police station burned down, everything had been destroyed. Even the guns they kept in a safe were damaged by the intensity of the heat. But not the sword. There wasn't a mark on it."

"How did they explain that?" Benson asked.

"They couldn't," she said, then clasped her arms around herself as if she'd become chilled. "It gave me nightmares – and seemed to change every time I dreamed about it. Longer, brighter, more colourful, more gems, more dangerous. And I imagined it in the clutches of that skeleton."

"Can you describe the sword for me?" asked Mary.

"I wouldn't vouch for my description, not after all these years and all those dreams," she said. "It's all mixed up in my mind now."

"If I showed you a drawing?"

Mrs Clarke shook her head. "Oh, I wouldn't want that. I might have nightmares again."

"It left that much of an impression on you," Father Gilbert said.

"Yes," she said. "Especially since my mother didn't like having it in the house. She and my father had rows. She demanded that he get rid of it."

"Did he?" asked Mary.

A nod.

"What did he do with it?" she asked.

"He gave it to the Vicar of St Mark's. They reasoned that, by rights, it was the church's property, because it was found there."

"Didn't anyone realize what it was? Why didn't they contact a museum in London or an expert?" Mary sounded exasperated.

"An expert came, I think," Mrs Clarke said. "He specialized in swords."

"A metallurgist?" Benson offered.

"He didn't know what to make of it. Even Scotland Yard thought it was just an unusual find. We got the impression that no one could be bothered with it. We were a nation headed for war with Germany. A sword like that seemed unimportant."

"Surely the Todds were here at the time. And the Hayshams. Even the Woodrich family would have said something, had they been told," Mary said.

"It wasn't the age of mass communication, my dear girl," Mrs Clarke said politely. "We were a small town and had no internet or mobile phones like you do. And it wasn't important enough to put on the radio. The local newspaper may have done an article."

"Still—" Mary began.

"I won't attempt to explain the actions of the people of the time," Mrs Clarke said firmly.

Mary nodded.

Mrs Clarke chuckled and looked at Father Gilbert. "We didn't even have regular use of telephones then. It was a simpler time."

Father Gilbert remembered visiting his grandfather in one of the villages outside of Bristol. No telephones, no indoor toilets, a coal-fired stove. It was indeed a simpler time, but not necessarily easier.

Mary asked, "What became of the sword after it went to St Mark's?"

"The Vicar of St Mark's – John Ainsley – kept it at the vicarage until they'd had enough of it."

"Enough of what?" Benson asked.

"The curse, of course," she said. "That was tragic. Adam, the oldest son, drowned in a pond. He was only twelve years old. Then Mrs Ainsley miscarried her unborn child, possibly from her grief. And John Ainsley – who was a vibrant middle-aged man – had a stroke and lost all mobility on his right side, including his ability to speak clearly. All of this happened in the three months the sword was in the house. Mrs Ainsley demanded that the church leadership take the sword away."

"Did they?" Mary asked.

"Yes." Mrs Clarke's brow furrowed. "I don't know who took it or where it went. My memory can only go so far. That I remember as much as I do is a miracle in itself."

"I'm grateful," Mary said. "What you've told us fills in a large gap in the story of the Set."

"It doesn't seem like much of a Set," Benson stated. "It sounds like the medallion, sword, and ring haven't been all in one place for a couple of centuries."

"Think of the value if they were reunited," said Mary.

Mrs Clarke shivered. "I wouldn't want to think of that at all."

"Why not?"

"If the sword alone is cursed with so much evil, what about the other items? What would happen to the poor owner?"

Father Gilbert's gaze went to Mary. Her eyes were on Mrs Clarke. Her expression suggested that she was imagining the Set being together in one place again – and she didn't consider it a curse at all.

Aware of being looked at, she turned to Father Gilbert. He looked away quickly.

"I wonder if we might turn to more pleasant subjects," Mrs Clarke said and picked up the plate of sandwiches to pass around. "Tell me about your plans for restoring the tower, Father."

* * *

"I don't believe she told us everything," Mary said once they were outside and moving to their cars.

"Why do you think that?" Father Benson asked.

"Years in this business have given me an instinct about people."

"Meaning that you've learned not to trust anyone," Father Gilbert said.

She shot him a look, but didn't respond.

"This doesn't put you any closer to the sword," Benson said.

"I'll take whatever information I can get. I'll search for the Ainsleys. Someone in that family may know where the sword went." She reached the driver's door of her car. Both men had followed her.

"Maybe it's in the church records," Benson offered.

"I'll ask Mrs Mayhew to search our files," Father Gilbert said. "I'm sure she'll be overjoyed to do it."

* * *

From his office, Father Gilbert could hear Mrs Mayhew slamming filing-cabinet drawers. He had known she wouldn't be happy about the assignment, but he hadn't expected outright hostility from her.

He thought about Mary again. He had noticed that she'd made it a point to shake his hand before she got in her car, grasping it for a moment longer than was customary. "I'll be in touch," she'd said.

"She didn't shake *my* hand like that," Father Benson complained as they drove back to the church.

"You're too young for her," Father Gilbert said.

"Aren't you too old?" he countered.

"Women like that appreciate maturity."

Benson laughed. "I'll bet she appreciates more than maturity," he said.

"Behave yourself."

Father Gilbert thought about Mrs Clarke's account of the sword. Finding the sword with the skeleton in the cellar had certainly triggered tragic events. If it was cursed, if it truly carried some kind of evil within it, then finding it now could be hazardous. And her logic that uniting the three pieces of the Set might empower evil all the more wasn't such a ludicrous idea.

Mr Urquhart stepped into the doorway. "You wanted to see me, Father?"

"Is the boiler room locked?"

"No, Father."

"I'd like to have a look at it."

"Any particular reason?"

"I want to see where the body was found."

The fuzzy eyebrows lifted high.

CHAPTER 16

Father Gilbert explained to Mr Urquhart about the discovery of the body in 1938. He took the news in his stride.

"Strange things are always happening around St Mark's," the Scot said.

"What do you mean?"

"Items out of place, strange noises coming from nowhere. I was working in the crypt early today and found some red-coloured clay on the ground."

"Is that unusual?"

"You won't find clay that colour anywhere in our crypt, or even around the church. It was tracked in by someone."

"Who?"

Mr Urquhart shrugged.

"We lock the crypt, don't we?" Father Gilbert asked.

"From time to time, because of the rain. The water seeps in there from the Lord knows where. I wouldn't want guests to make a mess," he said. "I've kept it locked since that Doyle fellow killed himself."

"Why the crypt? I'd have thought it was the tower we'd want locked," Father Gilbert said.

Mr Urquhart hesitated, then said: "I think he went down into the crypt before he went up to the tower."

"What makes you think so?"

"That red-coloured clay is all over the Haysham estate. I've often seen it on Lord Haysham's boots."

Mr Urquhart's workroom was tucked away in the far corner of the church. There he kept his workbench and tools, gardening implements, and other handyman gear. An old door stood to the side of the workbench. He wrenched it open. Just then Father Benson rounded a corner, looking red-faced.

"Taking the tour without me?" he asked, slightly miffed.

Mr Urquhart flipped a switch and a bare bulb lit up over

a wooden staircase. Down they went on the rickety steps to an uneven cement floor. A narrow passageway took them further into the recesses of the church. Pipes and wiring criss-crossed over their heads, thanks to years of renovation and restoration. Water-stained boxes and crates stretched out along the stone walls. Old Christmas wreaths and other seasonal church decorations hung from hooks. As cluttered as it all looked, there was a sense of Mr Urquhart's organization.

They came to another room and Mr Urquhart found the light switch and turned it on. The room contained the mechanics of the church: a furnace, an electrical panel, various gauges and dials, large water pipes with pressure valves and handles.

He led them around the furnace. A torch appeared in his hand as if by magic. "This is where the old boiler sat," he said, pointing to an empty concrete slab tucked away in a dark corner. "I assume your body was found back there."

The three of them squeezed between the furnace and its various appendages, and the wall. There was an open space on the other side of the furnace. It was certainly large enough to accommodate the burial of a body. The cement floor stopped there and dirt stretched on into darkness.

"May I use that?" Father Gilbert asked. Mr Urquhart handed over the torch. He shone the light on the ground and the shadows scattered like rats. He almost expected to see the outline of a grave in the dirt, but it was brown and undisturbed.

Father Benson shivered. "Am I the only one feeling a draught?"

"It's always cold and damp down here," Urquhart said.

Father Gilbert moved the light along the ground, then a few inches up on the wall. "What's that?" he asked and stepped across the dirt. "Something is scratched into the stone."

He moved in closer and knelt down, the light intensifying the dark lines. It was a circle with an inverted star inside.

"What is it?" Mr Urquhart asked.

"A pentagram."

"I've never noticed it before," Mr Urquhart said.

"Have you been back here much?"

"No. I pulled out some old boxes a few years ago," Mr Urquhart said. "But I would've noticed *that*. I'll sand-blast it out, first chance I get."

Father Gilbert reached out to touch it, but stopped a fraction of an inch short. The symbol, though it had become something of a cliché in pop culture, still had power. "I'd say it's been here for a long time."

Father Gilbert stood up and turned off the torch. The shadows gathered again. He had a strong desire to get out of that corner, to flee the darkness of the cellar.

Mr Urquhart suddenly announced: "It gives me the creeps. I'm not staying."

Father Benson nodded and moved quickly around the furnace.

Mr Urquhart waited for Father Gilbert to move. He waved his hands as if shooing the priest out.

As they ascended the stairs, Father Gilbert decided to talk to the Bishop about a rite or ritual they might use to reconsecrate that part of the building.

* * *

"A pentagram," Benson said once they were back in Father Gilbert's office. "Isn't that something out of horror B-movies?"

"And heavy metal bands," Father Gilbert added. Apart from anything to do with curses, he wondered if satanic symbols were connected to the sword, ring, and medallion somehow.

Benson seemed to be thinking along the same lines. "Does it have anything to do with the body and the sword?" Benson asked.

"Mary Aston will have to answer that question," Father Gilbert said.

Benson paused, and then asked, "Do you trust her?"

"I'm prepared to give her the benefit of the doubt."

"Is that because she's especially attractive?" he asked.

"Her being attractive makes me *less* inclined to give her the benefit of the doubt," Father Gilbert said.

"That's uncharitable."

"Mary strikes me as a woman who has learned to use her looks and the force of her personality to get what she wants," Father Gilbert said. "We have to be careful."

Mrs Mayhew stepped in with a file of papers. "I've found something for you."

* * *

Mrs Mayhew had made a copy of the typed minutes from a church vestry meeting held on 31 October 1938 – Halloween, of all days. She pointed to a single paragraph in which the verger, Albert Challoner, informed the vestry that Mrs Rachel Ainsley wanted the "Cellar Sword" removed from her household. Mr Challoner proposed that he should reclaim the sword and place it in the vault for safekeeping.

"What vault?" Benson asked.

"It may be a bank vault," Mrs Mayhew said. "The church kept certain valuables in it during World War II. But we've inventoried everything in it. No sword."

Father Gilbert knew of another vault, of sorts, in the cellar of the old vicarage. It had been bombed out during the War. A few years ago, while searching for other missing antiques, he had retrieved the few items inadvertently left in it. No sword there, either.

"Are there vaults in the crypt?" Benson asked.

"Not the kind one would use for safe-keeping a valuable antique," Father Gilbert said.

"May I hold onto this?" Father Gilbert asked Mrs Mayhew.

"It's your copy," she replied. "Though I don't know what use it is."

"I'll show it to Mary Aston," Father Gilbert said.

Mrs Mayhew frowned.

Father Gilbert asked: "Do you know anything about the Challoners?"

She shook her head. "It will be my life's goal to find out," she said.

* * *

Father Gilbert took a stroll around the church grounds. Ostensibly, he wanted some fresh air. In fact, he wanted to call Mary without worrying about Mrs Mayhew or Father Benson eavesdropping. He didn't expect to say anything worth overhearing but, if he wanted to be truly honest, he felt embarrassed about talking to her in front of anyone else.

Standing on the graveyard side of the church, he took out his wallet and retrieved Mary's card.

He felt an adolescent sense of anticipation. It was ridiculous, he knew. But her actions, even if he misinterpreted them as flirtations, gave him a feeling he hadn't felt since school. Perhaps it was his ego, flattered to have a beautiful woman give him a second glance. Or maybe it was sheer loneliness. Whatever the reason, he told himself that his actions and motives were pure. He wanted to pass on information. That was all. He dialled her number on his mobile phone.

Be careful, he heard himself say to Father Benson.

A movement in the graveyard caught his eye – actually, an impression of movement more than a clear visual. He looked up. For a moment there was nothing. Then a boy appeared from behind a headstone, running in a crouch, and dashed behind another, as if he was in a game of hide-and-seek. But there were no other children around.

It struck Father Gilbert as curious – something about the way the boy was dressed – but he'd only caught a glimpse. The boy didn't appear again. He thought about walking over to look, but the phone suddenly rang in his ear. He'd forgotten he had dialled. The chirps went on several more times before Mary's voicemail picked up. "Gilbert here. Come to Evensong," he said after the beep. "I have a piece of the puzzle for you. Or we can meet afterwards."

Meet afterwards? Why didn't he simply give her the information in the message? There was no need to meet.

He was being reckless. He admitted it.

She won't come to Evensong anyway. She won't meet me afterwards, he assured himself – and felt disappointed.

* * *

It wasn't Mary who showed up after Evensong, but Detective Sergeant Sanders. Standing next to the door with his arms folded, he looked like an overdressed homeless man. His skin was pale, and heavy bags had gathered under his narrow brown eyes. From the frumpiness of his dark suit, Father Gilbert guessed he'd slept in it – or not slept at all.

"A word, if you don't mind," he said to the priest after the obligatory hellos.

The congregation had gone, so they sat down on a back pew.

"I'm following a few leads," Sanders said.

"I thought Alex Wilton was in charge of the investigation."

"I'm doing this on my own initiative," he said sourly. "I don't have time for their politics."

"Politics? Is that why you were taken off the case?"

"As a former cop, you should know the answer to that question."

"As a former cop, I also know it's a bad idea for a detective to continue working a case from which he's been removed." Father Gilbert eyed him. "Does DI Wilton know?"

"No, and I'm not telling him." Sanders' look at Father Gilbert suggested that *he* shouldn't mention it either. "DI Wilton is in Lord Haysham's pocket. Haysham and the Chief Constable are golfing pals. You've seen how quickly things are getting done." He snorted. "Haysham knows more about the case than I do."

Father Gilbert nodded. "What leads are you following?"

Sanders glanced around the nave, making sure they were alone. He said in a low voice, "We could start with David Todd and his various relationships."

"Why David Todd?"

He gave the priest a coy look. "You already know that Colin Doyle was on Todd's payroll."

"Do you know why?"

"Todd was paying Doyle to spy on the work at Lord Haysham's estate."

"Corporate espionage? Is that what this is about?" Father Gilbert asked.

"It's about the *truth*, Father. I spent two hours with Colin Doyle's grieving widow. Something drove him to suicide. This business with Todd is connected. I promised her I'd find out what happened to her husband."

"It's never a good idea to make promises to the victim's family."

Sanders gave him a cold look.

Father Gilbert said, "So, what does David Todd say about paying Doyle?"

"He won't talk to me without a solicitor, which says a lot all by itself."

"David Todd is good at watching his back," Father Gilbert said, and wondered if the same could be said of DS Sanders.

"I'm checking into that medallion, too."

"Isn't that Mary Aston's job?"

"She doesn't care about the investigation," he said. "She cares only about the medallion and that sword and ring."

Father Gilbert made a non-committal "Hmm."

Sanders kept his eyes on Father Gilbert. "She's had a romantic relationship with David Todd."

Father Gilbert restrained his surprise. "*Had?*"

"A couple of years ago. The affair may have ended his marriage," Sanders said.

"Speculation," Father Gilbert said. He didn't know the specifics of why Todd's wife had left him. Todd had never discussed it directly, though Father Gilbert had offered to counsel them both. Todd claimed his wife didn't want help – and he made it clear he wouldn't have agreed anyway.

"I don't care about Todd's love life – or hers," Sanders said. "But it complicates things because of Haysham."

"How so?"

Sanders' expression skirted an outright *you-don't-know?* smirk. "David Todd stole Mary Aston away from Lord Haysham."

Father Gilbert clenched his teeth. He knew the two men were competitive but, if true, this was ridiculous. "Is that gossip or do you know it as a fact?"

"Fact. She was sleeping with Haysham, but Todd must have made her a better offer."

Father Gilbert took a deep breath. Hearing this kind of sordid news was bad enough, but the feeling that Sanders was playing him somehow made it worse. "Why are you telling me all of this?" he asked.

"You're part of this investigation. Don't you think it's important to know the backgrounds of everyone involved? Motives?"

Father Gilbert conceded the point with a nod.

"Mary Aston was with you when you met with Margaret Clarke, right?"

"How do you know that?"

"Mrs Clarke told Wilton. We sit opposite each other at the station. I overheard his side of their phone conversation."

"And?"

"I'd like to know what you talked about."

"There's nothing confidential in it," Father Gilbert said, as if to assure himself that he wasn't betraying anyone. He then explained to DS Sanders about the events from 1938, including the discovery of the body and what Mrs Mayhew found in the church records about the sword being moved to an unknown vault.

DS Sanders tapped his finger against his chin. "1938? I'll check our records for any information about that."

"Don't be surprised if DI Wilton already has," Father Gilbert said.

A smug look. "Wilton wouldn't know where to begin to look. I do."

CHAPTER 17

Father Gilbert bought some fish and chips and ate it at home. He washed it down with a pint of ale and thought about the rivalry between Lord Haysham and David Todd. He wondered if he should do more to bring an end to it. He was their vicar, after all. And for both Haysham and Todd to bed the same woman while married to others was beyond the pale.

He tidied up after his meal and stood at the kitchen sink to rinse the dishes. It seemed like a lonely act: a place setting for one, nothing to do next except check emails or go through some paperwork. The house threw echoes back at him. He prayed, hoping to unburden himself of a mixture of self-pity and – what? Jealousy? Was he jealous that Haysham and Todd had slept with Mary? Or was it envy that they both felt free enough from moral constraints to do such a thing?

He thought about Mary. In times long past men talked about being bewitched by women. He'd always dismissed the idea. But the irrationality of his thoughts and feelings made him wonder.

The dishes were dried and put away when the doorbell chimed. He glanced at the clock – it was a little before eight. He went to the front door and opened it, expecting to see Father Benson there on church business. Mary Aston stood in the shadows of the porch.

"I'm so sorry," she said, not sorry at all. "I only got your phone message fifteen minutes ago. I hope I'm not bothering you."

"Not at all," he said. There was a pause, the moment when he was supposed to invite her in. He didn't.

She waited, then gave him a verbal nudge. "You said you found something?"

"That's right." His brain began to function again. "A reference to the sword. In the minutes from a 1938 vestry meeting." He realized he had left the copy in his jacket and turned to get it.

She stepped inside. "May I come in?"

Men never really grow up, Father Gilbert thought in the millisecond after her question. At heart, they remain the same boys they were in school: glandular, testosterone-saturated, with a stunted and very adolescent view of women and sexuality. His first thought was, *Yes, of course, come in.* And drinks would be poured and their guards would be down and something interesting would happen between them, without commitment, without guilt, without consequences of any sort.

Concurrent with the first thought was a second: *Yes, of course, come in. I'll put on the kettle,* because he was a priest and his motivation would be one of hospitality and pastoral care. And they'd drink tea and talk, and nothing would happen between them whatsoever except that she'd be impressed with his strength of character and he'd be all the stronger for it.

A third thought came to him and it was the one he acted upon. Rather clumsily and in a voice that sounded to his ears like it came from a pimply teenager, he said, "Actually, there's a pub just down the street, if you'll wait here while I get my wallet. I'll be right back."

He didn't wait for her to respond. He didn't even look at her. Clutching his jacket, he went off in search of his wallet and keys, embarrassed that she stood at the open door for such a long time. He moved from the front hall to the kitchen and around to the sitting room, frantically searching. There was a noise behind him, and he turned quickly. Mary stood there with the keys and wallet in her hand.

"They were on the table by the front door."

"Ah." It was where he always put them.

"A drink here would be comfortable," she said, gliding into the room. She put the wallet and keys down on a side table. "Surely you must have something. You Anglican vicars don't abstain from everything."

"Hardly."

She placed a hand on the top of the table, her forefinger lightly caressing the wood at the edge. "We are mature adults, aren't we?"

The fear of embarrassment can often be stronger than any other emotion, even survival, Father Gilbert thought. He felt a powerful urge to prove that he was indeed a mature adult and that it was petty to worry about having a drink with this woman in his house.

Her eyes were on him. He sensed her anticipation.

"It would be better if we went to the pub," he said without conviction.

She took a step closer. "It'd be more comfortable here."

He saw in her eyes an eagerness that he suddenly realized had nothing to do with him. Perhaps she was eager to please herself or to claim a victory over a supposed man of God or to exploit anything that happened between them for her own ends. Perhaps it was only about finding the sword.

Reaching past her, he grabbed his wallet and keys from the side table. She was so very close. He caught a hint of her perfume. He thought she might reach for him. "The pub has a better selection of drinks," he said quickly and moved into the hall.

She lingered.

He reached the front door. *When had she closed it?*

She entered the hall, but remained by the doorway into the sitting room.

He opened the door. "Shall we?" It wasn't a question.

Her expression as she pressed past him suggested that she was a woman who did not like to be refused.

* * *

The George had everything Father Gilbert loved about pubs – dark wood, dim golden light, paintings of assorted artistic styles hung randomly on the walls by the various owners over the past hundred years. He loved the sound of low voices and the clinking of pint glasses.

They settled into a corner table and ordered drinks. Father Gilbert looked at Mary Aston across the table. The battery-operated candle cast a warm glow on her face. She was beautiful, there was no denying it. To have that face gaze back, with something akin to a loving expression, would be an enjoyable experience for any man.

There would be no loving expression from her now. "The minutes?" she asked impatiently.

He took the page out of his jacket pocket, unfolded it, and handed it over. "This confirms what Mrs Clarke told us. The sword was moved at the request of Rachel Ainsley."

She read over the paragraph, then pointed to the top of the page. "What are these names?"

He looked at the list. "They're members of the vestry."

"All dead by now, I assume," she said.

"More than likely."

She kept her eyes on the page. "They may have children or grandchildren in the area."

"Possibly," he said.

She reached into a bag – more like a stylish backpack – she'd brought in with her. "Do they have Wi-Fi in this pub?"

"Yes." He knew only because there was a sign for it by the front door.

Mary pulled a small laptop computer from her bag. She sat it on the table and turned it on.

"You're efficient," Father Gilbert said.

"Force of habit." She angled the laptop so he could see the screen, then moved closer to him. Then she taunted him. "This won't scandalize anyone, will it?"

"Only me," he said.

Mary navigated the pointer to a website that purported to find anyone in the world in fifteen seconds or less. She typed the first name from the vestry minutes, narrowing the search field to England and then narrowing it further by indicating a fifty-mile radius around the postal code for Stonebridge. Of the eight names, only one had a hit: Clive Challoner.

"That must be him."

"It could be a different Challoner."

"How many Challoners have you ever met?" she asked.

"Not many. None, in fact." Father Gilbert pointed to the screen. "He lives in Summerhill."

"Where is that?"

"Between Stonebridge and Southaven."

She looked at her watch, as if considering whether or not it was too late to contact him. "Tomorrow morning," she concluded.

The drinks arrived. Father Gilbert had a pint of ale, Mary had ordered an exotic drink with a name evoking sun-drenched beaches.

He lifted his glass in a toast. "To your good health."

"Thank you."

They drank.

"I mean, thank you for helping me." She rubbed her fingers around the edge of the glass. "I know this isn't really your concern."

"Well, apart from my curiosity, it *is* my concern."

"Why?"

He thought the answer was obvious, all things considered, but he said, "It involves my church, which involves me."

"Oh," she said with a small pout. "I thought you might be doing it for me."

She's regrouping, he thought. *She's going back to her flirtations.*

"That goes without saying," Father Gilbert said, willing to play along now that he had no interest in allowing her to succeed.

The screen on her laptop screen flickered. A screen saver program kicked in and the image of a pentagram, red against a black background, appeared.

He pointed. "A pentagram?"

Mary looked at it as if trying to remember why it was there. "I was researching religious symbols on my last job. This screen saver program downloaded from one of the websites I used. I've been meaning to get rid of it, but haven't taken the time. Why?"

Father Gilbert told her about the pentagram carved into the wall of the church cellar. "Has that symbol ever been associated with the Woodrich Set?" he asked.

"Not specifically," she said, punching a button to make the screen saver disappear. "I know people think of it as a symbol of evil. But, historically, it was often the opposite – used to ward off evil rather than invite it."

"I didn't know that."

She nodded. "As symbols go, it wasn't one of the more popular ones around. A German magician used it during the Renaissance. It appears in Goethe's story of Faust. And there was a French occultist who put it back into the spotlight late in the nineteenth century. Aleister Crowley used it as part of his Thelemite cult. Then, in the past half-century or so, Anton LaVey and his Church of Satan nabbed it. That's how it has become known more recently. Heavy metal bands and other wannabes started using it."

He took another drink. "What does the symbol mean?"

"That depends on who's using it and when."

"Give me the overview."

She took out a piece of paper and a pen and drew a pentagram as she talked. "Well, the pentagram, or *pentacle*, was thought to have power because it can be made without lifting the pen off the page."

"I remember that from grammar school."

"You – and a lot of kids throughout history. That's one reason some scholars believe it shows up as often as it does in ancient settings. Kids are simply trying to show off their dexterity by making something fancy out of a continuous line. And it's also found in nature – the starfish and creatures like that. In fact, the five points were thought to represent the five elements of nature: air, light, wind, fire, and water – with a parallel to our five-fingered hands. Pythagoras and his disciples said it was a sacred symbol representing the harmony of mind and body."

"Nothing diabolical in that," Father Gilbert observed.

"A few historians believe the pentacle was used by the early Christians to represent the five stigmata of Jesus. Or that the continuous, unending line symbolized the coming together of the beginning and the end."

"The Alpha and the Omega."

"In the Middle Ages, it was used to ward off evil," she said. She shifted in her seat to face him. He was aware of the way her leg brushed against his. "Though, from the church's point of view, I could understand why it fell into disfavour. The Gnostics used it, as did the Manichaeans and lots of other heretical sects. It was also connected to alchemy. It became popular with the Freemasons, too."

Father Gilbert remembered some of these details from theological college and from a few BBC documentaries. "The Freemasons called it the 'blazing star'—"

"With the *G* in the middle." She draw a capital *G* in the centre of her pentagram. "To remind everyone of the blessings that light and life have given to everyone on earth."

He looked at her drawing. "The 'G' meant...?"

"'God' or 'gnosis' or 'geometry'," she said. "Or 'glory' – which is how some Satanists use it, representing the glory and power of the individual, the ego."

Father Gilbert mused on this as he gazed at the pentagram. "There was some significance to the star being upright or pointed down. I get that confused."

"Pointed up, it's a representation of white magic. Down is associated with black magic." She pointed to the symbol. "You see, when it's pointed down, the shape resembles a goat's head. Goats are an important symbol in satanic rites, a corruption of God's sacrificial lamb. And there's the separation of sheep from goats at the last judgment."

"And it's your screen saver?" Father Gilbert asked, teasing.

She smiled. "It's either protecting my computer, or bewitching whoever uses it. What have I got to lose?"

"Maybe your soul," Father Gilbert said. He meant to sound playful, but it didn't come out that way.

She glanced at him very seriously and closed her laptop. She tucked it back into her bag. She crumpled up the paper and took another sip of her drink. "Care to join me for my drive to Summerhill tomorrow?"

"I would, but I'd have to check with my boss first."

"The Bishop – or Mrs Mayhew?"

"The latter."

They finished their drinks and slid out from behind the table.

Mary sighed. "I'm staying at the Traveller's Inn – or whatever it's called. It's boring. No character."

Her eyes met with his again. He was supposed to make her a better offer.

"I'll walk you back to your car," he said.

Mary had parked across the street from the vicarage. She thanked Father Gilbert again for his help. There was no lingering this time, no further suggestion of anything that might happen between them. He watched her drive away until the red brake lights had disappeared around the corner at the bottom of the street. Turning to go inside, he caught sight of a car a few doors away. A four-door saloon. In the half-glow of the streetlamp, he saw the silhouette of a man sitting in the driver's seat.

He stepped through his front door and closed it. Without turning on any lights, he went to the window of the front room and peered out.

The saloon drifted by without its headlights on, the driver hidden by shadow and a reflection of light on the door window. As it passed under a streetlamp, Father Gilbert saw that the car was red.

* * *

He paced as he went through his nightly examination of conscience – an ancient spiritual exercise that was meant to expose any obvious sins of the day and to tease out those that may have been buried.

He thought about temptation. It is far better to avoid temptation, one of the saints wrote, than to try to control it. It is far better to resist it at once than to try to reason with it.

Good advice when temptation is an outside force to be reckoned with. But when it was intertwined with one's own rationalizations, that was something different. The line between temptation and action was razor thin and easily passed over without resistance, control, or reasoning.

Deliver us from evil… that I so readily embrace.

That night Father Gilbert dreamt of goats' heads and druids cavorting around a bonfire in a moonlit field. One druid, with a thick beard and a heavy brown robe, wielded the Woodrich sword and struck down another man. He then knelt and, like a dog at a brook, lapped at the man's flowing blood. The image jolted Father Gilbert awake.

He lay in a cold sweat. It occurred to him that the Woodrich Set hadn't been made by Thomas Cromwell for Jeremy Woodrich in the time of Henry VIII, but may have existed further back in history. And he wondered if Cromwell had given the Set to Woodrich not as a gift but to get rid of it.

Climbing out of bed, he went to the sink in the bathroom to get a drink of water. He didn't turn on the light, not wanting to blind himself. He fumbled for the glass. It was normally to the right of the sink next to his toothbrush holder. Why wasn't it where he'd left it? He moved his hand further along the counter and brushed the side of the glass. It tumbled over the edge and smashed on the tiled floor. He stepped back, worried about his bare feet. Reaching around the doorframe, he found the light switch and turned it on. The light dazzled his eyes. He waited for them to adjust, then looked down at the mess. Shards of glass glittered brightly in the space between the sink and the bath. He knelt, picking up the largest pieces and tossing them in the bin. He'd have to get the dustpan and brush from the kitchen. He stood up.

Out of the corner of his eye, he registered that something wasn't right about the mirror. He blinked, trying to focus on what he was seeing. A pentagram, in red, was drawn on the surface of the mirror with what might have been blood.

As he stared at the symbol, he saw a movement in the reflection.

A man, dressed in a red eighteenth-century uniform, stood behind him, a sword raised.

Father Gilbert spun around as the blade sliced through the air.

CHAPTER 18

The story goes that J. B. Phillips, an Anglican clergyman and the translator of a popular edition of the New Testament, suffered from deep depression later in his life. Phillips was bedridden from the illness. The famous writer C. S. Lewis arrived on two occasions to say a few words that were particularly meaningful to Phillips at that time.

Phillips was comforted.

The only problem was that Lewis had died a few days before.

Puzzled by this appearance of a dead man – who looked radiant with good health – Phillips confided the encounter with a retired Bishop who lived nearby. The Bishop said simply: "This sort of thing is happening all the time."

Father Gilbert thought of this story as he sat at his desk the next morning. His head hurt. There was a piercing pain just over his right eye, precisely where the blade of the sword might have hit, had the swordsman not disappeared right before the blade should have made contact.

"Are you all right?" Father Benson asked. He stood in the doorway, a mug in his hand. "You look tired."

"I didn't sleep very well," Father Gilbert said. He took a bottle of paracetamol from his desk drawer, spilled out three tablets, and downed them with his tea.

"Any reason for your lack of sleep?" Benson asked as he sat in the guest chair.

He'd spent most of the night awake. He prayed, read from his Bible, and thought through the meaning of the encounter. As with the others, he couldn't think of a single rational reason for it. Had it been nothing but a dream, he would have chalked it up to a nightmare caused by the day's events. He had no intention of mentioning any of this to Father Benson. He shrugged.

"Mary Aston?"

Father Gilbert looked up at Benson. "What about her?"

Benson smiled. "Have you heard from her?"

Was he suggesting something?

"We talked," he said simply, then told him about their conversation.

Benson nodded, impressed. "It was clever of her to search the internet for the names of the vestry members."

"Mrs Mayhew," Father Gilbert called out and regretted it as someone stuck a needle into his right eye.

Mrs Mayhew appeared at the door. "Yes, Father?"

"Clive Challoner?" he asked.

"The verger's son?"

He was impressed with her instant recall. "I assume so. Does he live in Summerhill?"

"Yes, if he hasn't moved in the past twenty years. That's where he lived when he was a parishioner here."

"He hasn't attended since I arrived."

"He stopped coming just then," she said.

"Because of me?"

"He didn't say." She looked troubled. "Is this about that sword?"

"He might know something about it."

"Would you like me to phone him?"

"Mary Aston is going to speak to him," Father Gilbert said.

She frowned. "Then you may want to pay him a visit to undo the damage. I'll find him for you."

"Damage?" Father Gilbert asked.

Benson managed a small smile. "Apparently Mrs Mayhew and Mrs Clarke had a chat on the phone after our tea yesterday. Both women think Mary is… well…"

"Aggressive?" Father Gilbert offered. His experience with her the night before certainly proved it.

"Not the word they used, but a suitable one." He lifted the mug to his lips. It was red, with faded lettering on the side for some long-forgotten event.

Father Gilbert thought about the red car parked in front of his house the night before. "Do we know anyone who drives a red saloon?"

"A lot of people do. Why?"

"There was one parked near my house – with someone in it. I got the impression I was being watched. Or someone was watching Mary Aston."

"Mary Aston was at your house?" A look and tone of immediate disapproval.

"Don't get yourself worked up," Father Gilbert said. "She came to the house first, then we went down to the pub. Her car was parked in front of the house. When we came back I noticed a red saloon sitting a few houses up. Someone was in it. After she drove away, the red car followed."

Benson shrugged. "Considering the impression Mary Aston gives, it could have been any one of a dozen men in that car."

Father Gilbert couldn't disagree – and left it alone at that. He invited Benson to sit down so they could go over the day's schedule – hospital visits, home visits, a meeting with a bank official, and an evening Bible study at the Stonebridge police station.

An inquisitive look from Benson.

"It's for ex-convicts on probation," Father Gilbert explained.

"I don't see much time for my visit with Adrian Scott," Benson said.

Father Gilbert knew it was unfair to throw Father Benson, a stranger, at Adrian Scott. Especially in this situation. "Squeeze it in somewhere. I'll go with you, if there's time. Just don't wait for me. Use Haysham's authority to get him to cooperate."

Mrs Mayhew returned. "Well."

"Well what?"

"I just phoned Clive Challoner's house," she said. "I spoke with his daughter and she said she'd intended to call you. She needs to see you immediately."

"Oh dear. Has Mary Aston already caused that much damage?" he asked.

"No. She wants to discuss funeral arrangements."

"Whose funeral?"

"Clive Challoner's. He died last night. A sudden heart attack." Mrs Mayhew handed him a slip of paper. "Here's the address."

* * *

Father Benson drove them both to the village of Summerhill, which was little more than a pub and a post office with a handful of houses scattered around them. Number 15, Summerhill Road, was a bungalow only a stone's throw from a pleasant river that pushed itself alongside the main road. A man was walking a Labrador on the opposite side. The trees on the bank were turning green with fresh leaves. Father Gilbert wanted to stop, stretch on the grass, close his eyes, and put his face to the sun. His headache had subsided, but he still felt tired.

Lynn Challoner was a middle-aged woman with wiry copper-coloured hair and red-rimmed blue eyes. She greeted the priests at the front door and burst into tears while thanking them for coming so quickly. Sympathies were offered and a round of tea was prepared in a cramped kitchen that smelled of cleaning chemicals. The dutiful daughter had been tidying up her father's house. Routines, no matter how mundane, defied death's attempts to take comfort and consistency away.

Once they were settled at the kitchen table, she explained, "I come up from Southaven every morning to spend time with him. This morning he didn't answer the doorbell, so I used my key and let myself in. I nearly tripped over him. He was lying on the floor of the front hallway."

"Did he have a heart condition?" Father Gilbert asked.

"He had one of those angioplasty procedures a few years ago and has been on daily medication since, but I didn't believe a heart attack was imminent," she said. She pressed a tissue to her nose. "He was in good health. He should have had more time."

Her eyes flooded and she dabbed at them with the tissue.

"Why the front hall?" Father Benson asked.

She looked at him, startled, as if he'd suddenly appeared. "I don't know. I talked to him on the phone at 9:30 last night and he was about to go to bed. He was often in bed before ten."

"Where is the phone?" asked Father Gilbert.

"There's one in the kitchen and another one on his nightstand."

"Maybe someone came to the door," Benson suggested.

"At that time of night? Anyone who knows him wouldn't think of dropping by that late."

"Maybe it was someone who didn't know him," Father Gilbert said, thinking of Mary Aston.

"A salesman? At that hour?"

Father Gilbert shook his head. "No." He knew he couldn't go further without suggesting more than he knew.

"Why are you asking so many questions?" she asked. "Do you think there's something suspicious about his death?"

"Not at all," Father Gilbert said. "We don't mean to alarm you. It's only that we were going to contact your father about something that's come up at the church."

A flicker of memory came to her. "Oh – that's why your secretary called. Yes, it was providential, I told her. But why did you want to talk to my father? He hasn't attended your church in years."

"It's not about him. It has more to do with *his* father, when he was the verger at St Mark's," said Father Gilbert.

"My grandfather?" she asked, and her brows knitted together. "What kinds of questions could you possibly have about him? Did he run off with the church funds?"

Father Gilbert chuckled. He wished it was as simple as that. "Did your father ever mention the Woodrich sword?"

She shook her head. "What is it?"

"It's part of an antique collection. There was a sword, a ring, and a medallion. Your grandfather saw the sword in 1938. Maybe your father did, too."

"1938! Good heavens, you're going far back. My father would have been only three years old then. Why are you asking about it now?"

"The medallion has been found and now we're searching for the sword," Father Gilbert replied. "Our church records indicate that your grandfather had it moved to a vault of some sort, but we don't know what vault."

"Vault?" She tilted her head back and lightly touched her throat. "The only vault that comes to mind would be the mausoleum at the cemetery."

"You have a family mausoleum?" Father Gilbert asked. He couldn't imagine that the Challoners were that wealthy.

"It's a shared mausoleum," she said. "Other families are buried in it, too."

"Which cemetery?" Father Gilbert asked.

"Sussex Memorial Gardens. It's where my father will be interred."

* * *

Back on the road to Stonebridge, Father Gilbert thought about Clive Challoner's death. That he'd died now was troubling enough. But he wondered if Mary Aston had gone to visit him after she'd left the pub. She was determined enough to do it. But, he reasoned, even if she had visited him, it wasn't as if she had the ability to induce a heart attack – unless she'd tried to seduce the poor man. He frowned at the corruption of his thoughts.

"Clive Challoner died of a heart attack, right?" Father Benson suddenly asked. "You're not thinking he was murdered."

Anything was possible. "There'd have to be an autopsy to determine the cause of death."

"Lynn Challoner didn't say anything about an autopsy," Benson said. "Are you going to suggest it?"

"I'd like to," he replied, then closed his eyes and sighed. "But I won't."

Benson glanced at him. "What's wrong?"

"Did you see what was scratched into the wood next to the front door?" Father Gilbert asked.

"No."

"A pentagram, like the one at the church."

"*What?*" Benson gripped the steering wheel as if he was afraid he might drive them off the road.

"To the left of the door-post." Father Gilbert had seen it on the way out. It was a fresh cutting, too. Probably done by whoever had visited Clive Challoner. He thought of the wall in the church cellar – and his mirror.

"Should we go back?"

"And do what?" Father Gilbert didn't want to distress Lynn Challoner more than he had to. Not after she'd lost her father.

"Should we call the police?" Benson asked.

"I'll tell DI Wilton."

Benson hummed to himself, or it might have been a groan. "Do you trust Wilton after what DS Sanders told you?"

"I don't trust anyone at this point," Father Gilbert said bluntly. "But Wilton is in charge of the investigation. I have to speak to him if I'm going to speak to anyone."

"Spoken like a former policeman. Follow procedure." He may have been jabbing at Father Gilbert, or simply acknowledging reality. Father Gilbert didn't know or care. His mind went back to Mary Aston. Had she gone to see Challoner after she'd left him? Did she see the pentagram? Or had she scratched it into the wood herself – and, if so, why? If not, then who did?

"Is there any way we can look inside the mausoleum?" Benson asked. "The sword may be there. And if it's all connected…"

Father Gilbert had already thought about that. "We have to make arrangements for Clive Challoner's burial anyway," he said, as if an added excuse was needed.

"This is getting messy," Benson said.

Father Gilbert looked out of the passenger window. It was beyond messy now – and every instinct in his being said it would get messier.

CHAPTER 19

Father Gilbert tried to reach DI Wilton but didn't get an answer on his mobile phone. He then called the office number and wound up with DS Sanders. Sanders took the news about Challoner's death in his stride, declaring it another unfortunate coincidence in this very bizarre case. He offered to contact the Southaven Police – they had jurisdiction over Summerhill – to see if an autopsy was legally warranted. He doubted it would be.

Throughout the afternoon, Father Gilbert and Father Benson went about their various parish duties, dividing responsibilities between them to make up for their lost time in the morning. Benson officiated at the noon service and then visited three parishioners at the hospital.

Reverend Singh phoned to say that Colin Doyle's body had been released by the coroner. There'd be a funeral in a few days, though no one but immediate family would be allowed to attend. Father Gilbert hadn't been sure it would be appropriate for him to attend, but this put the question to rest.

Father Gilbert took the Evensong service with the hope that Father Benson would use the free time to talk to Adrian Scott, Haysham's archivist.

Father Gilbert thought about the mausoleum holding the Challoner graves. And he was determined to find out if Mary had visited Clive Challoner last night. But she didn't answer her phone at the odd times he called during the day, nor did she return his messages.

A little before eight that evening he walked over to the Stonebridge police station – a plain brick building that looked like a community hall. DI Wilton was in the reception area when Father Gilbert arrived. Just as Father Gilbert started to ask if he'd talked to DS Sanders about Clive Challoner, Father Benson came in, looking like a man who thought he was late.

"Perfect timing," Father Gilbert said.

Benson looked relieved.

"This way," DI Wilton said and led them past the sign-in area, through an electronically locked door, and into a room containing a haphazard collection of desks, chairs, and filing cabinets that looked like boats washed into a cove after a hurricane. A handful of uniformed and plain-clothes officers were still at work, only glancing at the priests. One wall contained a line of closed doors that led to other offices and the holding cells in the back. Set into the far wall was a rectangular window giving a clear view of the conference room where the Bible study would take place.

Father Gilbert had created the Bible study a few years before as a help to convicted criminals placed on probation. He'd reasoned that, since the convicts had to check in with the local probation officer there, a study and discussion time might be useful. Most of the convicts were white-collar or low-risk criminals whose crimes hadn't warranted much time in jail. An average of six men attended.

Father Gilbert and Father Benson adjusted the chairs and placed the Bibles and the evening's printed handouts on the scarred wooden table.

DI Wilton watched them for a moment, then said, "I heard from Sanders about the latest fatality in our case."

"Do you think it's connected?" Father Gilbert asked. "DS Sanders seemed to think it was a coincidence."

"A strange coincidence, then," Wilton said. "Though it would have been helpful if you'd called me directly rather than DS Sanders. I'm head of the investigation, you'll remember."

Father Gilbert noted the rebuke and said, "I tried to reach you first, but you didn't answer your mobile. I called here and Sanders picked up your phone."

"Try harder to get me next time," DI Wilton said and walked out.

Father Benson watched him go. "He's getting rather feisty."

"Police work is a competitive business," Father Gilbert said, remembering well the inter-office politics and endless manoeuvring for promotions or recognition. *A lot like the Church of England,* he thought.

The Bible study attendees drifted in, stopping by the parole officer's cubicle, then wandering into the meeting room. Father Gilbert greeted each one warmly as he introduced Father Benson. Father Gilbert could tell from the priest's eyes that he was unaccustomed to dealing with the criminal classes. He seemed to peruse each one, as if trying to figure out by how they dressed what crime each had committed. Father Gilbert knew that one could never tell by looking. These men looked and dressed very average and middle-class – more likely to get in trouble for stealing pens from banks rather than embezzlement of the high-finance kind or, in one man's case, sex with a minor he'd met on the internet.

The evening's study integrated passages from the Bible with Francis de Sales' *Introduction to the Devout Life*. Father Gilbert had a particular affection for de Sales, a sixteenth-century priest, later declared a saint, who was dedicated to helping the average person practise holiness. He brought de Sales' writings, together with the words of St Paul and St Peter, to get the group beyond any "pie in the sky" piety. These were men who needed down-to-earth and unflinching Christianity.

The study itself lasted only half an hour. The rest of the time was dedicated to a sort of group therapy, as each man unloaded about trouble at home, the social embarrassment of being convicted, difficulties finding jobs, trying to hold onto some semblance of normal life. Father Gilbert effectively discouraged any self-pity or excuses from the men. Practical holiness, he reminded them, was about being honest about oneself.

The meeting ended a little after nine. As the two priests tidied up the room, Father Benson commended Father Gilbert for his leadership in the meeting.

"Thank you," Father Gilbert said. "I look forward to seeing what you do with the meeting next week."

"What *I'll* do?" Benson frowned.

"The purpose for you being here was to meet the men and watch how we conducted the group so you could take over from me occasionally."

"But I don't know anything about the lives of convicts."

"You know about *men*, don't you?"

Benson shrugged, then nodded.

"By the way, any chance you got in touch with Adrian Scott?" Father Gilbert asked.

"Not yet. I drove over to—"

His statement was cut off by a commotion from the main room. There was a shout, and a chair was knocked over with a crash. Father Gilbert looked out through the glass and saw Lord Haysham struggling against DS Sanders at one of the desks.

"Please, just sit down!" DS Sanders shouted.

"I will *not* sit down," Lord Haysham said. There was a slur in his voice.

Father Gilbert drifted to the doorway of the meeting room, still moving as if he was picking up papers. Benson did the same – very close by.

A side door flew open and DI Wilton burst in. He stormed over to Sanders' desk. "What's going on here?"

"Lord Haysham is about to get thrown into a holding cell if he doesn't *sit down*," DS Sanders said. He righted the chair and stood it next to Haysham, who glared and swayed unsteadily.

"I want my solicitor," Haysham snarled as he dropped down onto the edge of the chair.

DS Sanders sat down at his desk and opened a file drawer. He pulled out a handful of forms.

"Well?" DI Wilton asked, stepping between Sanders and Haysham.

"I was on my way home when I saw Lord Haysham driving in an erratic manner. I pulled him over. He's well over the drink limit."

"Since when are you on traffic duty?"

"I'm always on traffic duty when people drink too much and drive."

"I had *one* drink," Lord Haysham said. "Ask anyone at The Mill House."

"It must have been a very large drink," DS Sanders said.

"Leave this to me," Wilton said to Sanders.

"So you can let him off? I don't think so."

Wilton glowered at Sanders, then adopted a more reasonable tone. "Come on, Steve. Leave him to me."

It was the first time Father Gilbert had heard Sanders' first name.

Sanders shook his head. "Just because he's rich – and your *pal* – doesn't mean he can ignore the law."

"One drink is not breaking the law," Haysham said.

"Be quiet," Sanders snapped at him.

"You can't speak to me that way." Haysham looked as if he might stand, but Wilton put a hand on his shoulder.

"*Do* something," Haysham said to Wilton.

Wilton said to Sanders, "Let's talk."

Sanders shook his head. "Not interested."

"I outrank you. Come into the other room. Now."

Sanders wouldn't look at Wilton. He stared at the top of his desk.

"Think about what you're doing," Wilton said more gently.

Sanders frowned, then slumped ever so slightly. He abruptly pushed his chair away from the desk and stood up. "Don't move an inch," Sanders ordered Haysham.

The two detectives disappeared into one of the side rooms.

Haysham let his gaze drift around the room. He saw Father Gilbert. "Ah!" he cried out. "A friend!"

Father Gilbert made his way out of the conference room. "Just one drink?" Father Gilbert asked.

"That's as much as he needs to know." Haysham hooked a thumb at the closed door. "He's got the brains of a turnip. How embarrassing for him."

"For him?" Father Gilbert asked, thinking it was Haysham who ought to be embarrassed.

"The dressing down he'll get." He leaned towards Father Gilbert, nearly fell over, recovered, then affected a stage whisper. "He was following me, you know. The sneak. The whole thing was a set-up. He probably works for David Todd."

The door opened and DI Wilton came out alone. "M'Lord, I'm sorry for the misunderstanding. I'll be happy to drive you home."

"Not necessary, Alex. I'll make my own way, if it's all the same."

"I wouldn't drive again, if I were you."

"You're not me."

"I'll phone your wife."

"You will not!"

"A taxi, then."

"Suit yourself."

Haysham struggled to his feet and Wilton escorted him through the security door to the front of the station.

Father Gilbert and Father Benson exchanged looks.

"This is unusual," Father Gilbert said. "He's not a heavy drinker."

"Obviously not," Benson said.

Father Gilbert decided to check his schedule for tomorrow, to find time to pay Haysham a visit.

DS Sanders emerged from the side room and, with only a quick glance in Father Gilbert's direction, went to his desk, grabbed his car keys, and then marched out through the rear exit.

The two priests finished packing up the study materials and made their way out. They reached the kerb in time to see Lord Haysham ride away in a cab. DI Wilton stood with his hands in his pockets.

"Goodnight," Father Gilbert said to him.

"Not really," DI Wilton said. He spun around and went back inside.

It began to rain.

* * *

Father Gilbert checked the bath and was tempted to peek in the wardrobe and even under the bed to make sure nothing was lurking there. He never knew if or when he'd have another encounter.

The sound of the rain helped lull him into a deep sleep – until the shrill ringing of the phone jolted him awake. He grabbed for the receiver as, blurry-eyed, he checked the red digits on the alarm clock. 5:57 in the morning. His mind flitted through the darkest possibilities in the few seconds it took to get the phone to his ear.

"Hello?" he asked. His voice sounded drunk to his own ears.

"I'm sorry to bother you, Gilbert." It was Bill Drake.

"What's wrong?"

"Lord Haysham has been murdered."

Father Gilbert sat up in bed. "*What?*"

"David Todd has been arrested. He's being held at the Stonebridge station."

Rain splashed lightly against the window. Father Gilbert struggled to clear the cobwebs in his head. "Did he do it?"

"I don't know the details yet. Todd is refusing to talk to the police. He said he'll talk only to you."

"Why me?"

"He wouldn't say."

"Are you representing him?"

"You know I've been on retainer with the Haysham family for years."

"Yes, yes," Father Gilbert said, impatient that he was so slow in waking up. "How is Lady Haysham?"

"Medicated," Drake said.

Father Gilbert groaned.

"Do you need a lift?"

"I'll walk. It'll wake me up." He also needed time to get a grip on his feelings. He'd known Haysham for a few years, even considered him a friend. But the thought of murder made him feel sick – just as he'd felt before the encounter on the tower. Death had come, to be sure, and wasn't finished with any of them yet.

CHAPTER 20

The rain had stopped by the time he reached Stonebridge's police station. Inside, it was far more active than when he'd left it a few hours before. Chief Constable Macaulay, looking fit and sharp as if he'd just come from a dress parade, and DI Wilton, looking less so, met him in the reception area. Father Gilbert was taken through to the meeting room where they'd had the study group. He noticed a detective talking to a baggy-eyed man at one of the desks. A similar interview was playing out at another desk, with one detective talking to two sharply dressed men. Father Gilbert recognized them from The Mill House restaurant.

Once seated at the conference table, Macaulay folded his hands on the top and shook his head slowly. "This is a bad business."

"It certainly is," said Father Gilbert. He wished he had called Father Benson to come with him. A second set of eyes and ears would have been helpful. "What are the details?"

Macaulay nodded to DI Wilton. "Go on, Alex."

Wilton took out his notepad and flipped it open. "We know that Lord Haysham and David Todd met at The Mill House at 7:00 p.m."

"Why?"

"To talk about recent events at the Haysham estate."

"Who called the meeting?" Father Gilbert asked.

"We don't know yet. In any event, they met and both men drank quite a bit. The conversation got heated. Threats were made, according to both the waiter and the manager." He gestured to the window and the two men being interviewed by the detectives. "They're giving their statements now."

"What kinds of threats?" Father Gilbert asked. "Who threatened who?"

"Allegedly Haysham said that he was going to 'bring Todd down' and Todd said he was going to 'destroy Haysham'."

"They've talked like that for as long as I've been here," Father Gilbert said.

"They parted company a little before nine and, shortly after, DS Sanders brought Lord Haysham here, as you know."

"He left in a taxi," Father Gilbert said. He looked through the window to the baggy-eyed man and suspected he was the cab driver.

"It took ten minutes to get to the Haysham estate. According to the cab driver, whom you saw coming in, Lord Haysham insisted on being dropped off at the end of the drive."

"It was raining. Why did he want to be dropped there?"

"The cabbie said that Lord Haysham wanted to walk the rest of the way so he'd get a chance to sober up a little. He didn't want his wife to see him 'in his cups'." Wilton flipped a page. "The cab driver got a call for a passenger pick-up south of Stonebridge, so he pulled to the edge of the drive at the road. He waited while another car came from the direction of Stonebridge. It pulled into Haysham's drive. He thought, but couldn't be sure, that it was a red saloon of some sort."

"A red saloon?" Father Gilbert asked.

Macaulay looked at the priest. "Is that significant?"

"Maybe," said Father Gilbert. "Though I don't think David Todd drives a red saloon. I thought he had one of those small, white, fuel-efficient things."

"He has two cars. One white, one red," said Macaulay.

"Any chance of getting moulds of the tyres in the driveway?" asked Father Gilbert.

"We can. But it won't do much good. The rain has washed out everything," Wilton said. His gaze went back to the notepad. "The cabbie was curious and looked in his rear-view mirror. He saw Haysham approach the driver's side. Then he walked around and got in the passenger side. The car turned around in the drive and came back to the road. It turned right out of the drive."

"Towards Stonebridge?" Father Gilbert asked.

"Correct. The cabbie turned left to go to his next fare."

"Then what?"

"Nothing until 4:00 a.m., when a jogger came upon Lord Haysham's body on the bike path that runs along the canal from the centre of town."

"The path eventually goes past his estate," Father Gilbert said. "Who would jog in the rain at four in the morning?"

"This man, apparently," Macaulay said.

"He's local. No record," added Wilton. "Just a fanatical fitness type."

"Why was Lord Haysham on that path?" Macaulay mused.

"He may have been taken there and murdered – or murdered in a different location and the body deposited there," Wilton said. "With so much rain and mud, it's hard to know. I hope the autopsy will give us a clue."

Father Gilbert thought of when he'd last seen Lord Haysham: drunk and belligerent, scowling as he got into the cab. If Wilton had given him a ride, or if Father Gilbert had offered a lift in Benson's car, who knew how differently things might have turned out?

"Cause of death?" Macaulay asked.

"A head wound," Wilton said. "A long gash, very deep. Probably cracked the skull."

"From what?" Father Gilbert asked, guessing the answer.

"Initial guess is that it was the thin edge of something sharp and heavy," said Wilton.

"A sword," said Father Gilbert.

"Possibly. Though it could have been something *like* a sword. The coroner will have to determine that."

Macaulay drummed his fingers on the tabletop. "Crime scene?"

Wilton shook his head. "Nothing so far. As I said, the rain has washed everything away. Our SOCO team is still there."

Wilton hesitated – a telling look, as if he wasn't sure he should continue.

"What?" Father Gilbert asked.

"It may be nothing."

"It may be something," Macaulay said.

"There was a small piece of wood near the body. It had a symbol carved into it."

"What symbol?" Macaulay asked.

Father Gilbert already knew the answer.

Wilton fixed his eyes on his notepad. "A pentagram."

"How strange," Macaulay said. "Isn't that a symbol of the occult? Are you saying Haysham was the victim of a nut-job from a cult?"

"No, sir," Wilton said – and nothing more.

"Pentagrams seem to be showing up a lot lately," Father Gilbert said.

"Where?" Macaulay asked.

Father Gilbert told Macaulay about the church cellar and Clive Challoner's house.

Macaulay rubbed his face. "Are you saying there's a connection between a body found in the church cellar decades ago, Challoner's heart attack, and Lord Haysham's murder? This is preposterous."

Father Gilbert turned to Wilton again. "What kind of wood was it?"

"A plank, like a slat from a fence. The wood looked weather-worn but the carving was fresh. I suspect it came from the fence that borders that part of the path."

"The killer took the time to carve the pentagram there at the scene?" Macaulay asked. "Like the mark of Zorro?"

Wilton shrugged.

"Why did you arrest David Todd?" Father Gilbert asked.

"Why wouldn't we?" Wilton asked, a challenge. "A heated exchange with Haysham at The Mill House. Threats. A red car. That's more than enough to bring him in for questioning."

Father Gilbert nodded as a concession. "Why did Todd insist on talking to me?"

"He didn't say," said Wilton. "He's been uncooperative since we brought him in. He's said only that he didn't murder Haysham and that he wanted to talk to you."

"Then I ought to have a word with him," Father Gilbert said as he stood up.

* * *

The observation room was a small, dark box with a small desk, a computer, and a few folding chairs. A video camera stood on a tripod with wires stretching to the computer. The camera faced a large two-way mirror that allowed the observers to see into a brightly lit interrogation room, padded with white panels to cushion the sound. David Todd sat at a rectangular brown table, a half-finished cup of coffee in front of him. His face was set in a frown, his red-rimmed eyes fixed on the tabletop. He had an angry bruise on his left cheek and a split lip.

Macaulay stood to Father Gilbert's right. "I never thought Todd would go as far as murder."

"Maybe he didn't do it," Father Gilbert suggested.

Macaulay gave the priest a condescending look.

Wilton stepped in. He went to the computer and typed in an instruction that triggered a green light on the camera. He checked a few more settings. Then he signalled Father Gilbert to follow him.

They walked the few steps to the interrogation room. Wilton held up a hand for Father Gilbert to wait, then opened the door. Father Gilbert could see Todd over Wilton's shoulder. He slowly looked up at them.

"As you requested," Wilton said and moved aside for Father Gilbert to enter.

Father Gilbert went to the table. "Hello, David."

"Father." A low, mournful tone.

Father Gilbert sat down across from Todd, his back to the mirror. Wilton slipped out and closed the door behind him.

"Are they treating you all right?" Father Gilbert asked.

Todd shrugged, then tipped his head in the direction of the mirror. "You should have asked them yourself." He turned his face to the mirror and spoke to the men on the other side. "Do *you* think you're treating me all right?"

"How did you get those?" Father Gilbert gestured to the bruise and cut lip.

"I fell when I got home. I guess I had more to drink than I thought."

Father Gilbert sighed. "It looks bad, David. You should be getting legal advice."

"Later." He winced as he touched the split lip. He pumped his right leg up and down impatiently. "There are things my solicitor won't understand. You will."

"Like what?"

"The presence of evil."

"What kind of evil?"

"The kind that kills people." He screwed his face up a little as if he'd experienced a sudden pain somewhere.

Father Gilbert watched him. "David, are you talking about an external evil or something you feel inside?"

He leaned forward. "Help me," he whispered.

A chill went up and down Father Gilbert's spine. Todd's voice was filled with despair, much like Colin Doyle's had been. "How can I help you?"

Suddenly, Todd straightened up and looked at the mirror again. His eyes were wide, then he narrowed them, as if concentrating on something in the mirror or beyond it.

Father Gilbert was tempted to turn and look.

Todd relaxed, his gaze on Father Gilbert again. "I didn't kill Lord Haysham. He was angry and tipsy when he left me at The Mill House. You know what a mean drunk he can be."

"Actually, I *don't* know that," said Father Gilbert, noting the way Todd referenced Haysham in the present tense.

"He is. And if you're looking for people who hated him enough to kill him, you'd have to question half the town."

"Unfortunately, you were the one last seen with him."

Todd shook his head.

"You didn't pick him up on the driveway to his estate?" Father Gilbert asked. "That wasn't your white car the cabbie saw?"

"I was driving my red Peugeot last night."

"Oh. Right. Sorry." It was an old interrogation trick – and Father Gilbert felt a slight disappointment that Todd had fallen for it.

Todd spread his arms. "I don't know what happened to Haysham after he left me. Cabbies. A car on his drive. They don't mean anything to me. I was home."

"There are witnesses who've said you argued at The Mill House. What did you argue about?"

Todd snorted. "The same thing we've been arguing about ever since he started developing his land."

"Then why meet with him? You already knew his position."

Todd shrugged.

"Did you talk about Colin Doyle?"

"What about him?"

"You paid him to spy on Haysham for you."

"Business, that's all."

"Environmental business? To thwart Haysham's development of his land?"

Todd gave a wry smile.

"If it wasn't because of your protests, then…" Father Gilbert paused to think. He ventured to say, "Colin Doyle wasn't spying to thwart Haysham because of the environment, but to get a step ahead of any possible deals with the land. Knowing the inside track would allow you to invest in the investors."

"Now you're thinking," Todd said.

"You're connected to the Doyle family," Father Gilbert said, realizing. "Jack Doyle told you to enlist Colin, to exploit any business opportunities the Doyles might want to grab."

Todd's smile remained. But he said nothing.

"Did Colin know you were working with his father? Or were you the means for Jack Doyle to keep an eye on Colin?"

Again, Todd didn't reply.

"Is that what you and Haysham argued about?" Father Gilbert asked.

Todd sighed. "We argued about the body found under the bridge. And what happened between our ancestors."

"You think he owes you something for that."

Todd sat up straight. "He certainly does," he said sternly. "But it's in his DNA to fudge on his commitments."

"What commitments?" Father Gilbert asked.

Todd's lips twisted into a sneer. "That's between us."

Father Gilbert flinched. He had never seen that expression on Todd's face. "Whatever the topic, he didn't agree with you."

"No. He left and that was the last I saw of him." Todd put his hands on the table and stretched his fingers apart.

"Where did you go after you left The Mill House?"

"Questions, questions, questions," Todd said impatiently. "Are you here as a priest or a detective?"

"You're the one who asked me to come. I'm simply trying to understand what happened."

Todd closed his eyes tightly, as if in pain. "I went home. I *stayed* home."

"Can anyone—?"

"No, there's no one to corroborate my story." He opened his eyes again. "I'm alone. And I doubt that my neighbours saw me come home."

"What about Mary Aston?" asked Father Gilbert.

"What about her?"

"She said she's going through your family archives to find the Woodrich sword."

"Yes, she is."

"She wasn't with you at all last night?" Father Gilbert asked.

A groan. "As a matter of fact, we were going to meet up at my house, but she didn't show."

"Do you know why?"

"I haven't spoken with her."

Father Gilbert didn't know where this conversation was supposed to go. Any detective could interrogate Todd better than this. Why had Todd asked for him? "All right, so you didn't kill Lord Haysham and you spent the night at home alone."

"That's right."

"Then why am I here? What's all this nonsense about evil?"

Todd looked confused for a moment, as if he didn't know what Father Gilbert was talking about. Then he bit his lower lip until a thin line of blood showed. He arched his fingers into a claw and scraped his nails across the table.

"David," Father Gilbert said.

Todd pulled his hands to his lap. Sucking in his lower lip, he licked at it. "Sometime after 9:30," he suddenly continued, "a note was shoved through the letterbox. It said, 'Take your place.' And I've been receiving telephone calls with a voice whispering that same message. 'Take your place.' It chills me to the very bone."

Father Gilbert remembered Todd's reaction to a phone call at lunch. "What does it mean?" Father Gilbert asked.

"Something terrible."

"Be more specific."

"I can't!" Todd's voice took on a childish whine. "Don't you see? I can't!"

Father Gilbert stayed calm. "Did you show the note to the police?"

Todd shook his head. "I didn't get a chance. Wilton and his thugs were rather forceful when they came for me." A glance at the mirror again.

"Where is the note now?" asked Father Gilbert.

"I left it on the kitchen table. You have my permission to go to the house to look at it. You know where the key is."

"All right, I will," Father Gilbert said. "Though, a note won't prove anything."

"I'm not telling you to prove anything to *them*," Todd said as he hooked a thumb at the mirror. "They're idiots. But *you* can make sense of it."

Father Gilbert imagined Wilton's reaction to this scene. It wouldn't have surprised him if a chair crashed through the mirror from the other side.

"There's something evil going on here, Father Gilbert. Even beyond Haysham's murder." Todd leaned forward and whispered again, "There's more to this than they know, Father. It's not about Haysham's land, it's about the Woodrich Set."

"What do you mean?"

"The *Set* is evil. The medallion, the sword, the ring…" his voice trailed off. He looked down at the table.

"David, you have to be more specific. *How* are they evil? What makes you think so?"

"That's all I can say." He looked at the mirror again, then back to Father Gilbert. "I won't say any more in front of *them*."

Father Gilbert put his hands on the table. "What do you want me to do for you?"

He thought for a moment. "Call my solicitor. I left the information with Wilton," Todd said softly.

Father Gilbert waited. "Is that all?"

Todd looked up at the priest with newly wet eyes. "Do you know what it's like to wander so far that you think you'll never find your way back again?"

"I know the feeling."

Todd lowered his head. "Use your instincts, Father. Follow the evil and you'll find out what's really going on here."

* * *

"Rubbish!" DI Wilton said with a few accompanying euphemisms after Father Gilbert had joined him in the observation room. "It's a trick to distract us."

"Or he's playing the insanity card," Macaulay said. "Lining up his defence."

"Or he's telling the truth," Father Gilbert said.

Wilton groaned. "You're not taking him seriously! An evil note? Evil phone calls?"

"Lord Haysham was receiving crank phone calls, too," Father Gilbert said.

"How do you know that?" Macaulay asked.

"He got one while I was at his house."

Macaulay was surprised. Wilton shook his head.

"He told us he'd been getting them since the body was found," Father Gilbert continued. "He assumed they were Todd's people trying to harass him. But David got one when we had lunch with him."

"I'll check the log on his mobile phone," Wilton said. "But I still think it's rubbish."

Macaulay folded his arms. "Todd's connection to the Doyle family was unexpected. It makes sense, though, if Jack Doyle wants in on any development deals."

"Why not talk to Lord Haysham directly?" Wilton asked.

"Perhaps he did and Lord Haysham rejected his participation," Macaulay said. "Lord Haysham was sensitive to Doyle's reputation. He wouldn't have knowingly crawled into bed with that sort."

That sort, Father Gilbert thought. He thought unkindly about what *sort* Haysham had crawled into bed with. He repented.

Wilton pointed towards the glass. "You see? It's all about business. *Not* this spiritual nonsense."

Father Gilbert nodded towards the video equipment. "I'd like to see the video of our interview. There are a couple of things that have me puzzled."

Wilton frowned. "Unfortunately, the video stopped working halfway through the interview. Some kind of glitch."

Father Gilbert thought of the moment in the interrogation room when Todd's expression had changed as he stared at the mirror. He wondered if that was when the glitch happened.

"What do you know about the car?" Macaulay asked.

"I met with Mary Aston last night and someone in a red car was watching us. It pulled away from my street when she left."

"She was at your house?" Wilton asked. He tried to sound casual and failed.

"She stopped by my house. We walked to The George down the street."

Wilton's eyes narrowed.

"I'd better phone Todd's solicitor," Father Gilbert said. "Do you have that information handy, DI Wilton?"

Wilton scowled as he left the room.

Macaulay said to Father Gilbert, "I'm going out to visit Rosalyn after I make sure things are set here. Would you care to join me?"

"Yes, I would." He thought about his various duties at the church. The normal routines would have to be changed because of the murder. "I need to ring the church first."

"I'll meet you out front." Macaulay went to the door. His hand on the knob, he asked Father Gilbert, "What do you really make of the note at Todd's house?"

"I assume you would want to consider everything related to this case," Father Gilbert replied. "Are you getting a warrant to search his house?"

"That will take a few hours, all things considered." Macaulay opened the door. "He gave *you* permission to look inside. But I strongly recommend that you don't tamper with anything."

Father Gilbert nodded. Macaulay left.

Stepping over to the video camera, Father Gilbert looked at the small monitor jutting from its side. The screen was black except for the digital counter in the upper right-hand corner. A sequence of digits and nonsensical symbols flickered randomly, as if it couldn't fix itself on a specific point. Then the screen came to life. The now-empty interview room appeared in the viewfinder, with the table and chairs under the harsh light.

The screen jumped to an image of David Todd sitting at the table with Father Gilbert, whose back was to the camera. The digital counter indicated the time from several minutes before. Todd was speaking to Father Gilbert, then suddenly turned his head and glared directly at the camera. How he knew precisely where it was beyond the two-way mirror was an unnerving question.

Todd's face suddenly stretched and distorted into an elongated mask with hollow black circles where his eyes had been, the nose an open wound of thick red blood, the mouth unnaturally drawn down into a jaw-breaking scream. The image seemed to move, pixilating, then broke into a pool of squirming maggots that pushed through the screen and onto the table and floor below the camera.

Father Gilbert jumped back, banging against the wall.

The maggots writhed, as if dropped onto a hot surface, then seemed to dissolve into the woodwork and carpet.

The screen went black.

CHAPTER 21

Father Gilbert and Chief Constable Macaulay drove in silence to the Haysham estate. The gun-metal grey sky threatened more rain.

Father Gilbert thought about his experience at the police station. Evil was as real as anything Good. He had no doubts about that. He had seen Evil in many forms, some truly supernatural. And just when he thought he had a grasp on how it operated, something happened to confound his conclusions. The ongoing visions – or glimpses – he'd been witnessing unnerved him. He assumed that was their purpose. Something, or someone, wanted to throw him off.

And what was he to make of David Todd's behaviour? Was it an act to cover the murder of Haysham? Or maybe David was truly psychotic. Or was it the manifestation of demonic possession?

There was a legend that, during his murder trial, Charles Manson stared at the prosecuting attorney with his penetrating eyes and the attorney's watch suddenly stopped. A small trick, maybe. Yet true demonic possession often involved the physical world being manipulated – furniture moved or thrown, electronic equipment working in bizarre ways, beds levitating, walls and ceilings cracking. The images in the viewfinder and the appearance of the maggots fitted the profile.

None of these things would impress the police. The facts for them were far simpler: David Todd had the opportunity and the motive to kill Lord Haysham.

He felt a twinge in his chest. Lord Haysham was dead. He'd hardly had time to think about it. A man with whom he'd had countless meetings, shared a few drinks, enjoyed or endured a variety of social events, had discussions about church doctrine and even the length of sermons, was gone from mortal perception. Lord Haysham was now simply Michael Haysham again, a man in the hands of God.

He glanced at Macaulay, who was intently watching the road.

There was a mystery to be solved. A suicide and a murder. What was his role in the unfolding tragedy? He had been drawn into it – but for what purpose?

He looked out of the passenger window, the distant fields and flocks of sheep spread out under a filtered light.

That's it, he thought. *For now, I have to think as the shepherd of a member of my flock.*

He had never felt less equipped for the job.

* * *

Lady Haysham knelt next to a small garden adjoining the stone patio just outside Haysham's study. The garden was an unattended collection of jagged stalks that had once been flowers and shrubs. Lady Haysham stabbed at the muddy earth with a trowel.

"Rosalyn," Macaulay said.

She jerked around to see who had spoken, nearly losing her balance. "You sounded like—"

She stopped herself and got to her feet, dusting at her clothes with gloved hands. The effort only spread mud on her blue jeans. Her hair was tied back in a scarf. She wore a light-blue coat and brown boots – all splattered with mud. Father Gilbert saw from the dull look in her eyes that she was indeed medicated.

She gestured apologetically. "I've been wanting to deal with this flower bed for, oh, I can't remember how long. We've been so busy."

"Rosalyn, we're terribly sorry—" Macaulay began.

She held up a gloved hand. "No, don't. I can't abide sympathy. I want you to catch my husband's killer." She spoke calmly.

"Oh, you can be sure we will," Macaulay said firmly.

"Is there anything I can do for you?" Father Gilbert asked.

"Our solicitor is taking care of everything."

"Bill Drake," Father Gilbert said.

She looked at him first with an expression of *Do you know him?* followed quickly by a *Silly me, of course you do* look. "The children will be here this afternoon."

The children were a son and a daughter, both at university. Father Gilbert assumed the son, Philip, would receive the hereditary title and take charge of the Haysham estate. A daunting task for someone in his early twenties. But he remembered Philip as a sharp and intelligent young man, a version of his father before time had softened the edges.

Rosalyn frowned, as if fighting back the tears. "Telling them was so hard. Such a shock. One never expects a loved one to die this way. We were supposed to grow old together." She waved the trowel as if shooing away her emotions. "I won't be maudlin. I hate maudlin women."

Father Gilbert remembered a meeting for a Southaven charity to help single mothers financially. One single mum began to complain about her dismal lot in life – a husband who'd abandoned her, leaving her with three small children. While Father Gilbert had tried to respond to the woman with comfort and encouragement, Rosalyn had stepped up and told her to stop whinging. "You're capable of so much more than that," she said. "Get over your husband, stop brooding about your difficulty, and let's figure out how to sort out the mess you're in."

Somehow, Rosalyn got away with it. The woman wasn't offended at all, but worked with Rosalyn on a plan of action. Had *he* spoken to her in that way, he'd have been summoned before the Bishop and disciplined. Apparently, brutal truth was a woman's prerogative.

Looking at her now, he wondered if she was having a similar conversation in her head. *No whinging. No self-pity. You're capable of so much more than that. Pull yourself up by your bootstraps and get on with it.*

He'd have to keep an eye on her. The strong ones often fell the hardest.

Rosalyn waved the two men towards a set of iron patio furniture. "Sit down. I'll see about tea."

"No thank you," Macaulay said.

"Something stronger?" She looked from one face to the other.

"Not for me, thanks." Father Gilbert held a chair for her to sit down. After she did, he sat next to her.

Macaulay pulled a chair out. It scraped against the stone with a loud screech. He nodded by way of apology and sat down on the other side of her. "What can you tell us about last night?" he asked.

Father Gilbert had wondered how long it would take the Chief Constable to ask. Compassion was one thing, but a murder case was getting older by the minute. And he knew how the memory would play tricks. Incidental details might be lost, or held onto and hardened into unfounded conclusions. If Rosalyn believed David Todd had murdered her husband, she might remember only those things that might prove it.

"Last night," she said it distantly, as if it had been years ago. "Michael went out to meet with David Todd," she said. Saying Todd's name brought her lips into a hard line.

"Did he say why he was meeting with David?" Macaulay asked.

"David Todd *killed* Michael," she said suddenly. "If he's saying otherwise, he's lying."

"We'll need more evidence to prove it in court," Macaulay said. "Why did they meet?"

"Michael didn't say specifically. I assume he wanted to find a solution to their problem."

"Which problem?"

"The body under the bridge, I assume," she said. She eyed the trowel in her hand as if she wondered how it had got there. She put it down on the patio table. "Michael was anxious about resuming work on our property."

A cool breeze moved across the patio. Macaulay folded his arms against it. "Did you ever witness David Todd threatening your husband?"

"Apart from the usual slurs, no," she said. "Though I wondered about the crank phone calls."

"Did your husband say they were from David Todd?"

She shook her head. "But he knew the caller. I could tell. And he found them distressing."

"We'll have all the phone records checked," said Macaulay.

"And there was the letter," she said.

"What letter?"

"It was on the doormat in the front hall, but he wouldn't let me read it. Later, I found it on his desk and sneaked a peek. It was handwritten, in an old style of penmanship. Very flowery."

"What did it say?" asked Macaulay.

"Something like 'Take your place.' That's all."

"Take his place? What does that mean?" Macaulay asked.

She shrugged. "Michael walked in and caught me reading it. He grabbed it, tore it up, and threw it in the fireplace. It burnt up."

Father Gilbert asked, "What about your husband's overall frame of mind?"

"He was uncharacteristically irritable," she said. Then, more softly, "Maybe afraid."

"Of what?"

She rubbed the back of her gloved hand across her forehead, leaving a muddy line. She didn't notice. "I don't know. But he told me more than once that it wouldn't surprise him if David Todd would arrange to have him killed, or do it himself."

* * *

Mrs Mayhew sat at her desk and dabbed her tear-filled eyes with a tissue. "It's terrible," she said. "I know he had his flaws, but he was a good man."

Father Gilbert stood on the opposite side of her desk. He felt badly for not remembering how Haysham's death would impact people like Mrs Mayhew. It was unusual to see her cry. She tended to avoid overt shows of emotion or anything else that smacked of sentimentality.

Father Benson sat in the visitor's chair next to the desk, leaning forward on an elbow as if he might reach out to pat her hand, but thought better of it. "Did you know him well? I mean, apart from his attending church here?"

"I've known that family my entire life. My grandmother did the washing for his grandmother."

"So you and Lord Haysham were friends," Father Benson said.

"People these days are far too cavalier about the word 'friends'," she said sharply. "We were *acquaintances*, on very cordial terms. I believe that gives me the right to grieve."

"I'm very sorry," he said.

She dabbed at her eyes again, then looked up at Father Gilbert. "I can't believe David Todd would do such a thing. I know the two men disagreed, but to resort to murder…"

"Did Lord Haysham have other enemies – anyone else who might want to harm him?" Father Gilbert asked. He thought, from her vantage point as the church secretary, she'd know more than he would.

"In my experience, men of wealth and power always generate an unreasonable resentment in some people. And there are enough sick-minded people out there who'd take violent action," she said.

Father Gilbert was about to re-ask the question, hoping she might think of someone specific, when he saw her expression change. Her eyes went cold as they saw something behind him. Or someone.

Father Benson saw the same thing and turned to see what had triggered the change.

Father Gilbert smelled the perfume and knew the reason.

"I'm sorry to interrupt," Mary Aston said. She stepped into Father Gilbert's line of sight.

Father Benson stood up. "Good morning."

"May we help you?" Mrs Mayhew asked in a frosty tone.

Mary kept her eyes on Father Gilbert. "I'd like to talk to you – privately."

Father Gilbert waved a hand towards his office. "Of course. Come in."

With a stone-like stare, Mrs Mayhew watched as Father Gilbert allowed Mary to pass through. Father Benson gave him a cautionary nod.

The instant he closed the door, Mary fell into his arms and buried her face in his chest. Her sobs were quiet and her shoulders gently shook.

He put his arms up in a gesture of comfort, but didn't draw her close.

"I can't believe the news about Lord Haysham," she said when she had composed herself. She stepped away from him and moved to the chair. A tissue appeared from nowhere. She touched it to her cheeks and nose. "Who would do such a thing?"

"The police suspect David Todd."

She spun around. "No!" then "He wouldn't!" then "Would he?"

"You know him better than I do."

"Why do you think that?" she asked.

He shrugged. "An impression I picked up somewhere."

She sat down and wrapped her arms around her handbag. She looked small somehow, almost vulnerable. "We were close because of my investigation."

"The Woodrich Set brought you together?" Father Gilbert asked.

A sharp look. "You could say that."

"The police will want to talk to you."

"Why?"

"Where've you been for the past day?"

"In London."

"Can you prove that?"

She looked concerned. "Do they consider *me* a suspect, as well?"

He leaned against his desk. "Should they?"

She frowned at him. "For a priest, you have a strange way of comforting people."

"Are you here for comfort?" He knew he sounded ill-tempered. He wasn't sure why he was being so hard on her.

"Do *you* suspect me of something?" she asked.

"Did you visit Clive Challoner after you left me?"

"At that hour? No. Why?"

"He died of a heart attack that night."

A shadow moved across her face. "That's why no one answered my calls."

"There was a pentagram scratched in the wood just next to his front door," he said.

She stood up. Her face was a picture of indignation. "You think there's a connection to me because I had that pentagram on my computer?"

"I don't know what to think."

Her cheeks turned red and her nostrils flared. An unattractive look for some women, but not her. She really was a magnificent creature. "I'm capable of a lot of things, Father, but inducing heart attacks isn't on my list of talents."

He was unmoved by her indignation. "Do you know of anyone who might follow you around in a red car?"

"I have several acquaintances with red cars. Red cars are common enough." Her perfectly formed eyebrows lifted. "I'm being followed?"

"When you left my house the other night."

"Why didn't you tell me?"

"I tried to ring you."

"My mobile is useless," she said. She opened her handbag and dropped the tissue in. She exhaled loudly, exasperated. "I'm obviously on *your* list of suspects, so it's probably best that I go. I'll grieve somewhere else."

Her peevishness annoyed him. Even if her emotions were real, they seemed like a tool she was using to play him.

When he didn't respond, she made as if to go past him to the door. For all the room she had in which to move, she steered very close to him. She was giving him a last chance.

"Wait." He lightly touched her arm. "I don't like the feeling of being played. I'm not sure who to trust."

Her expression softened. "There are ways to earn trust."

Father Gilbert understood her meaning, then removed his hand and took a step back. Was she sincere or was it an instinctive form of manipulation? He didn't want to find out. Moving away from her, he said, "Clive Challoner's daughter mentioned a vault."

The significance registered in her eyes. "What vault?"

"It's in a mausoleum at the Sussex Memorial Gardens near Southaven."

"Did she say anything about the sword?"

"She didn't know anything about it."

"Maybe it's there. Maybe it was put there for some reason." She slung her handbag onto her shoulder. "I want to see the vault."

"*We'll* see the vault," Father Gilbert said.

CHAPTER 22

As it turned out, the young woman in the Memorial Gardens office didn't care that Father Gilbert was a priest or why he was there. She had the look of a goth girl, a pale face set off by dyed jet-black hair, heavy black eyeliner, and a diamond stud in her nose. She politely showed them a map of the grounds and where the mausoleum was located. The phone rang and she turned away.

The cemetery was vast, with a maze of stone paths stretching out to different sections. The tombstones ranged from modest squares and rectangles to long slabs and ornate sculptures of angels and crosses. Many of the markers seemed to have their own personal style, as if it was the last chance for the dead to look unique rather than as they really were: dust and bone.

The ground was a sodden cushion from the earlier rain. The sun hadn't emerged with enough force to dry anything. They reached the mausoleum – a plain grey stone structure with an arched roof and a matching archway above a black iron gate, straight out of a Hammer horror film. They stepped across a puddle in front of a single step to the gate. Father Gilbert grabbed the latch to the gate and pulled. It opened on rusty hinges.

"How clichéd," Mary said.

Father Gilbert led the way into a damp room. The ceiling was probably seven feet high. The cement floor was uneven. The walls contained columns of square markers, four in each column, lopsided and tilted, as if each new coffin was slotted in however it might fit best. Everything was shrouded in a bleak grey light, with black shadows sprayed here and there like paint. Father Gilbert half-expected Peter Cushing or Christopher Lee to step out. He wished he'd brought a torch.

"I shudder to think of the condition of that sword if they put it in here," Mary said. "What were they thinking? How could they *not* know its value?"

"If they thought it was cursed, they may have hoped the grave would eat it up."

"Superstition." Mary drifted to one wall.

"It was enough to drive Rachel Ainsley to demand that the vestry remove that sword from her house," Father Gilbert said as he moved to look at another wall. "Albert Challoner took her seriously enough to agree."

"Do vergers usually believe in curses?" she asked.

Father Gilbert tried to come up with a glib response and failed.

At a glance, he saw that the dates on the various markers in front of him went back to the early eighteenth century. Each vault was sealed up tight. If the sword had been placed in one of these chambers, he'd have a hard time knowing which one.

They moved along the walls, stepping past the many other family remains represented there.

"Here's Albert Challoner," Mary said, her voice a damp echo. "He died in 1947."

Father Gilbert joined her to look. Albert's final resting place was second down from the roof of the mausoleum. The bottom of the marker was partially obscured by a thick moss that had spread over a large portion of that column of markers.

"I assume they didn't put the sword with him," she said. "It must be with someone who'd died prior to or in 1938."

"Or in an empty chamber," Father Gilbert suggested. "If it's here at all."

"How do we get past this moss?" she asked.

He looked around for anything hard and found a jagged piece of concrete. He used it to scrape downwards from Albert Challoner's name. The moss came away in smeared chunks – and a section fell away to reveal a symbol ornately engraved into the lower part of the marker. A pentagram.

"That's interesting," Mary exclaimed.

Father Gilbert stepped back to look at the symbol. "So it is."

"Like I told you, a pentagram doesn't always suggest Satanism." She reached up to touch the symbol. "Maybe Albert was a Freemason."

"Maybe." Father Gilbert was annoyed by the ambiguity of the symbol. But his instinct told him that it was there for no holy purpose.

Mary coughed slightly. "It's too oppressive in here. I've got to get some air." She moved back to the gate.

Father Gilbert continued to scrape at the moss until he'd cleared the remaining markers. The Challoners had deaths in 1901, 1910, three in 1919 from the Spanish Flu, and another in 1924. He scrutinized the area around the crypt from 1924, but couldn't find a way to get inside any of them without a sledgehammer.

A shadow moved across the wall. He turned, assuming Mary had returned. No one was there. He held still, listening. He heard a low rumble, as if a hard, strong wind moved through the unseen parts of the mausoleum. Craning his neck, he looked through the open doorway. The scattered trees within eyesight were perfectly still.

He turned back to the wall of vaults. The Challoners in repose. His eyes drifted to a column of names and dates from the nineteenth century. One name caught his eye. He moved closer. The craftsmanship on the marker looked newer than the others.

Richard Doyle Challoner
In The Arms of His Lord
14th December, 1872 – 3rd August, 1889

"Doyle," Father Gilbert said softly.

* * *

Father Gilbert emerged from the mausoleum and closed the gate behind him. "We can't do anything more without the family's permission."

"Or without a pneumatic drill." Mary stood a few feet away, gazing pensively at the cemetery. She puffed on a cigarette.

"You smoke?"

"Only on occasion," she said, then added, "You would have seen one of those occasions for yourself if you weren't such a prude."

He looked away.

She tossed the cigarette down. It hissed in the wet grass. She stamped it out. "It was silly to hope that we could open one of the vaults like a file drawer and find the sword just *lying* there."

"Clive Challoner will be buried here in a few days. We might get permission from the family then."

She sighed. "It's not here."

"How do you know?"

"I can feel it." She nudged the smashed cigarette with the toe of her shoe. "Call it intuition."

"Did your intuition also tell you that there's a relationship between the Challoner and Doyle families?"

She turned to him. "What relationship?"

He told her about the marker for Richard Doyle Challoner.

"Don't all of these local families have a shared gene pool?" she asked with a smirk.

Father Gilbert shrugged. "The connection may mean nothing, or…"

Mary wrapped her arms around herself as if suppressing a shiver. "Can we go? I'm going to be late for another appointment."

"With anyone I know?" Father Gilbert asked.

"DS Sanders. Maybe he suspects me, too." She shot him a sharp look, then walked away.

* * *

Mrs Mayhew frowned at Father Gilbert from her desk.

"Is there something wrong?" he asked.

She opened her mouth as if to reply, then closed it again. He knew she wanted to say something about Mary Aston. She was *bursting* to say something.

Instead, she adjusted the pens in the cup-like holder as if they were flowers in a vase. "Father Benson would like to see you," she eventually said.

Father Benson's office was little more than a closet with a metal desk, chairs, and bookshelves. The bookshelves were empty. Three unpacked boxes sat against the windowless wall.

"You left with Mary Aston," he said as he stood up behind his desk.

"That's correct."

"She also showed up at your house and you went to the pub together."

Better that than my bedroom, Father Gilbert almost said, but nodded instead.

"This morning you met her in your office, whereupon you *closed* the door."

"Also correct," Father Gilbert said.

"Then you left with her for over an hour."

"Correct again," Father Gilbert said. Rather than feeling annoyed or defensive, he was impressed that the young priest had the courage to speak up so directly.

"Isn't that rather reckless?"

"Is it?" He knew it was reckless, but wanted to see just how far Father Benson would go.

"She's a beautiful woman." Father Benson's cheeks flushed – not from anger, but embarrassment. "You know how often priests are accused of sexual harassment. If Mary decided to make a case against you, if she showed up somewhere right now with her hair messed up and her dress dishevelled and streaks of tears on her cheeks and suggested that you'd made unwanted advances, the evidence would be rather damning."

Father Gilbert stood for a moment, waiting to see if there was anything else the priest wanted to say. Benson held his ground, waiting. Father Gilbert inclined his head. "Point taken."

Benson nodded, then sat down again as if exhausted from the effort of being so honest. "I'm sorry. I hope that wasn't over the top."

"Not at all," Father Gilbert said, sitting down in the visitor's chair. The metal creaked. Not only did it creak, but it was hard and uncomfortable. "You are right to speak up. Perhaps you should chaperone us from now on."

Benson offered a non-committal chuckle, as if he wasn't sure whether Father Gilbert was joking or not. Father Gilbert wasn't sure himself.

"Mary and I drove to the Challoner mausoleum," Father Gilbert said. "We didn't find a sword. But, curiously, there was an engraving of a pentagram on Albert Challoner's marker."

"Another one."

Father Gilbert shifted in the chair. "I also found the marker for a young man named Richard *Doyle* Challoner."

"There's a relationship between the two families?" Benson asked.

"He died in early August, 1889."

Benson shook his head. "Is that significant?"

"That's the date on the letter from Francis Todd. The one addressed to *D*," Father Gilbert said.

"*D* for Doyle?"

It made sense. Father Gilbert drummed his fingers lightly on the chair arms. "We may be going about this the wrong way. We're looking for the sword. Maybe we should be looking for the skeleton."

* * *

In the reception area, Father Gilbert said, "Mrs Mayhew, will you go through the archives again to see if you can find any reference to that skeleton found in 1938?"

"What, specifically, am I hoping to find?" she asked.

"What became of it."

Mrs Mayhew wrote a note on her desk pad. "I would be surprised to find that information in our archives. I suppose the police will have files about it. The skeleton was removed by them, wasn't it?"

"Yes. Find out whatever you can, please."

"Of course."

"Oh – and phone Detective Sanders with anything you discover," he added. "He's looking into it from the police side."

"All right."

"Come on," Father Gilbert said to Benson, "we have just enough time to find that letter at David Todd's house before the noon service."

Benson returned to his office to grab his car keys.

Father Gilbert leaned on Mrs Mayhew's desk. "I know Mary Aston's not to be trusted," he said softly.

"It's not merely about trust, Father," Mrs Mayhew said. "I believe that woman is dangerous."

CHAPTER 23

David Todd's house was at the far end of a narrow lane bordered on both sides by walls of trees. Though the sun had broken through the clouds, the woods seemed particularly dark, even ominous. Father Benson had to weave the car left and right to avoid ruts in the road. It made Father Gilbert feel nauseous.

"What happened when you talked to David Todd?" Father Benson asked.

Father Gilbert summarized the experience, including Todd's psychotic behaviour. He left out the part about the video camera.

"What do you make of it?" Benson asked.

"He's in a battle," Father Gilbert said.

"With insanity?"

"With evil."

Benson glanced at him. "We're all in a battle with evil, aren't we?"

"We're fighting our fallen nature and the evil that wants to exploit it. I suspect he's fighting something more overt – a specific *force* of evil."

"You're going to have to explain that to me." Benson dodged another rut. "I don't know what you believe about evil. I suppose we should have talked about it before I took this job."

Father Gilbert conceded the oversight with a chuckle. "Do you know why I left Scotland Yard to become a priest?"

"I understood it was because your wife died."

"My wife's illness gave me the excuse I needed to leave my job, but it's not really why I left."

"Then, no, I don't know why."

Father Gilbert hesitated, his eyes going to the road ahead of them. He didn't want to sensationalize what had happened. Yet, he didn't want to understate it either. "I dealt with a particularly difficult case. Horrific, in fact. One that brought me face to face with something I could only describe as pure evil."

Benson was silent. "What kind of a case?" he finally asked.

"We were investigating what we thought was the kidnapping of a teenage girl. She had come from a respectable middle-class family. Unfortunately, the more we investigated, the more it began to look like she wasn't the victim of kidnapping, but had run away and got caught up in the drugs and porn industry of the Soho district." Father Gilbert looked down at his hands. His fingers were tightly threaded together.

"You found her," Benson said.

"Yes, we did." He cleared his throat. A taste like old nicotine lingered there. "But there were things about the case – the girl – that didn't line up."

"Like what?"

"She was sweet and innocent. She came from a loving, Christian family. Very straight-laced."

"How can you know for sure?"

"I dealt closely with the girl's parents. It was their faith that made an impression on me."

"Kids run away from good homes all the time," Benson said.

"Of course they do, but I believe this girl was *lured* away."

"By whom?"

"A force of evil."

"The devil."

"*A* devil," Father Gilbert said.

A thoughtful silence from Benson. "What became of her?"

"Officially, she committed suicide," he replied, remembering the report, seeing the colour of the folder, the lines and boxes on the police form. "But I believe she was murdered."

Benson looked at him, the obvious question in his expression.

"I saw her before she died. She was desperate to escape from where she was. But she was afraid. I tried to persuade her to come with me. She told me that 'he' wouldn't like it. 'He' would stop her."

"Who?"

Father Gilbert shrugged. "At the time, I assumed she was talking about a pimp, or whoever had coerced her into that life. Now I assume it was the demon."

Benson shook his head slowly.

"I very nearly took her by force," Father Gilbert continued. "I wish I had. But my sensibilities as a detective said she needed to come willingly, otherwise she'd run away again and wind up in the same sort of place. So I agreed to leave her, with the promise that she'd contact her parents."

"She didn't."

Father Gilbert looked down at his twisted fingers again. His knuckles hurt. But not as much as the pain in his heart. "I failed her because I didn't recognize true evil."

"You can't hold yourself responsible for her decision."

"No. But had I known then what I know now…" He wondered what he would do now. "She looked and sounded the way David Todd did this morning. There was a deep conflict going on, a struggle…" He stopped.

"So… what happened with the case?" Benson asked.

"My superiors thought I was cracking up, that I'd been too personally involved. They took me off the investigation. It was a suicide. There was nothing to pursue."

"That's when you quit?"

"Not long after. The experience had been an epiphany for me. I saw evil for what it truly was – a very personal and supernatural force. The world as I knew it had changed."

Father Gilbert knew how unpopular talk about Satan was within the Church of England. He imagined Benson going back to St Mark's and calling the Bishop to ask for a transfer to another parish.

"Some of us actively fight evil, as best we can, based on our limited understanding of it," Father Gilbert said. "We underestimate its power and make stupid mistakes out of weakness. Or we overestimate its power and make stupid mistakes out of fear. I suspect that Colin Doyle killed himself out of fear."

"Fear of what?" The question came in a flat tone. Father Gilbert wasn't sure how to read it.

"That medallion represented something terrible to him, something he didn't believe he could cope with," he replied.

"You and I both saw the medallion," Benson said. "We held it in our hands. I didn't feel anything significant about it."

"Neither did I. But Colin believed something about it that we don't know."

They were approaching David Todd's house. Father Gilbert felt relieved to have this conversation interrupted.

"Does David Todd know what that something is?" Father Benson asked.

"I don't know." Father Gilbert hadn't had time to think about it properly. "David may be like a lot of people who can't accept the idea of a supernatural evil, which makes him all the more susceptible to its persuasions. People like that are empty houses, just waiting to be broken into."

"But David's been going to St Mark's most of his life, hasn't he?" Benson's implication being that, as a Christian, Todd should know better or be spiritually protected somehow.

"I wouldn't want to judge him, but I've always suspected he attended as a cultural duty. He's English, so he goes to the Church of England. It's an activity that has brought him some sort of satisfaction."

"Like people who fight to preserve the language of the original Prayer Book but don't actually pray," Benson added.

Father Gilbert thought for a moment. "It's possible that his bitterness against Lord Haysham has interfered with his ability to grasp God's grace. Maybe that bitterness has led him to a darker place, where he's even more open to evil because of the power or glory or personal victory it might bring to him."

"So you believe that people can be possessed," Benson said.

Father Gilbert turned to Benson. "Yes."

Benson met his gaze. "Have you ever witnessed it first-hand?"

"Yes."

He paused. "Will you tell me about it?"

"Not now," Father Gilbert said. That story would take more time than they had.

Benson frowned. "Then... what are we doing here?"

"I believe that David Todd, in a lucid moment, was right. This isn't about land development or greed. If we follow the trail of evil, we'll find out what's *really* going on here."

They reached the turning for Todd's house.

CHAPTER 24

Davied Todd's driveway curved around to a modernized brick house of two storeys with leaded windows and decorative gables. Father Gilbert recalled that it was spacious, with a generous kitchen and dining area, a room Todd used as an office, a sitting room, four bedrooms upstairs, and a loft conversion above that. Ironically, the house had more actual living space for Todd than Haysham Manor afforded Lord and Lady Haysham.

A low whistle from Father Benson. "He lives here alone?"

"He does now," Father Gilbert said. "His wife let him buy her out after their divorce." Love reduced to contracts and negotiations.

"What killed their marriage?" asked Benson.

Father Gilbert thought about Todd's affair with Mary, but knew it was more than that. He shrugged. "It's as if they both gave up." He remembered reaching out to them, but both refused any offer of help. Father Gilbert's impression was that David Todd's drive and arrogance was a bad mix with Penelope Todd's sense of propriety. To overtly show too much initiative was simply not the English way. Todd wanted a wife who was a female version of himself. Instead, he married a woman who was pleasant enough, but aloof and distant, with a strong sense of privacy. Perhaps she used it as a disguise for her pride. Getting help for their marriage would have been an embarrassing indication of weakness and vulnerability.

"Kids?" Benson asked.

"Two grown boys – at university." Father Gilbert thought about Todd's sons. Jeremy, the older, had the looks and ambitions of his father. Joshua, the younger, favoured Penelope with a fair complexion and quiet stubbornness. Todd didn't talk about his sons much at all. Father Gilbert suspected they weren't in contact.

The driveway ended at a three-car garage on the side of the house. A dark-blue saloon and a bright-green police car sat by the open garage doors. A uniformed officer and a detective in a drab suit stood by the lawn. Each took a last drag on a cigarette, then tossed them onto the grass as if the newcomers were part of a no-smoking patrol.

"The police are already here?" Benson said.

Father Gilbert frowned as he climbed out of the car. "DI Wilton?" he asked the first man.

"Inside," the man replied in a low rumble of a voice. "Go through the garage. But don't touch anything."

They walked through the open garage door into the first bay, which was actually a half-bay filled with cardboard boxes, old newspapers and magazines, and shelves covered with gardening supplies.

A white Ford sat in the next bay to the left. A red Peugeot sat in the bay beyond it.

"Be sure to put on the foot covers," the detective called from behind them.

The foot covers were plastic coverings for their shoes, presumably to make sure they didn't track anything into the house, nor contaminate what was already there. A box sat just inside the door, in a room containing a washer and dryer, cleaning detergents, and shelves of food. One wall served as a coat rack. There were jackets, coats, and macs on hangers, and shoes and boots on the floor beneath. An umbrella stand sat off to the side with half a dozen handles sticking up.

After putting on the plastic footwear, Fathers Gilbert and Benson moved towards the next door, but DI Wilton came from the other direction. He was startled to see them. He was carrying green rubber boots.

"Boots?" Father Gilbert asked.

He held them up. His hands were covered with latex gloves. "A partial boot print was found near Lord Haysham's body on the path. Boots like these."

"I have a pair just like them," Father Gilbert said. "They're worn by a lot of people in the area."

"Maybe so. But not everyone wears the same size as the killer." He skirted past them and opened the door to the garage. A loud whistle, and the man in the suit ran over. Wilton handed the boots to him. "Put these with the rest."

The man nodded and retreated.

Wilton eyed the two priests and said, "I expected you to have been here and gone long before we showed up with the search warrant."

"We were delayed," Father Gilbert said without explaining why.

Wilton made a feigned noise of sympathy.

"Did you find the note David mentioned?" Father Gilbert asked.

"No," he said. "But I found something else. Come in."

They stepped through to a spacious kitchen with chrome appliances, white cabinetry, and quartz countertops. A few mugs and plates sat next to the sink. Father Gilbert smelled old grease and burnt toast.

"You know that Lord Haysham received a note like the one Todd described," Father Gilbert said.

"Probably written by Todd," Wilton said. He moved beyond the kitchen to a small breakfast area with a round table and four chairs. A sliding glass door sat behind it, the plain beige curtains pushed aside.

Father Gilbert glanced out at the green lawn that stretched back to a forest.

Wilton said, "We found a shopping list, a notepad with a few phone numbers scribbled on it, and this—"

He held up a clear plastic evidence bag with a single piece of A4 paper in it. From a few feet away, it looked like childish doodling – straight lines that formed triangles, and then violent cross-outs, as if the artist had become annoyed with his work.

"May I?" Father Gilbert asked.

Wilton handed the bag to him. "Help yourself."

Benson stepped next to Father Gilbert and they looked at the page together.

"Do you see that?" Benson asked, pointing to the page.

Father Gilbert nodded. The triangles formed a pentagram.

"See what?" Wilton asked.

Father Gilbert showed him the shape of the pentagram, then reminded him of its appearance on the church cellar wall and at Clive Challoner's house.

Wilton looked smug. "That reinforces my theory. David Todd put the symbols in those places for some sick reason. Maybe he's obsessed. Maybe he's lost his mind."

Benson pointed to the right-hand side of the paper. The words *servo vel intereo* and *aut ministrare aut mori* had been scrawled in a swooping cursive. "Do you know what that means?" he asked.

"'Serve or die'," said Father Gilbert. "Another variation on 'Take your place', I think."

"He's conning you with all his demon-possession rubbish," Wilton said.

"Maybe so." Father Gilbert handed the evidence bag back to him.

Father Gilbert's gaze went to the next room. Something beyond the doorway caught his eye. He moved towards it.

"Is there anything else you'd like to see? A tour of the house, perhaps?" Wilton asked sourly.

It was a sitting room, if he remembered correctly: a television, a couple of chairs and a sofa, maybe a drinks cabinet. But there was something about the wall that didn't seem right. "Have you looked in here?"

"Yes," Wilton said in an "Of course, do you think I'm an idiot?" tone.

"Weren't you curious about this wall?" Father Gilbert asked once he was inside and had confirmed what he'd seen.

"Family photos," Wilton said as he entered. "I saw them earlier. Old photos of his wife and kids when they were—"

He stopped, flinched, and moved away from the wall.

Benson moved in and looked. "That's curious."

The wall was made of plaster. Nails, meant to hold the family photos, were naked and exposed. The frames were on the floor, leaning against the skirting board. The photos faced away from the three men.

"When were you last in here?" Father Gilbert asked.

"Not ten minutes ago," Wilton replied. His tone had lost its confidence.

"No one else has been in here?" Father Gilbert said.

"No."

"Then how did the photos wind up on the floor?" Benson asked.

"They must've fallen," Wilton said.

"If they fell, you would have heard them," said Father Gilbert.

Wilton growled, trying to sound angry. "It's a joke. I'll get to the bottom of this." He marched out of the room and began to shout for the other officers.

Father Gilbert picked up a frame. The glass in front of the photo was intact. The photo itself was of the Todds on a seaside holiday somewhere, the two boys probably eight and ten years old. As Wilton said, they were all family photos, from various years in the family's life. Happier days, to be sure. The frames and glass were undamaged.

"If the photos had fallen, surely some of the glass would have cracked," Benson said.

Father Gilbert nodded.

"And they would have landed face down on the floor," Benson said. "These are leaning against the wall, facing the wrong way."

Father Gilbert nodded again.

"I don't get it."

Father Gilbert put the photo down where he'd found it. "In some cases of hauntings, the spirit or demon would turn family photos to the wall," Father Gilbert said.

"Why?"

"Because a united family is a representation of the love and unity of the Trinity," he said. "Demons despise it."

Father Gilbert moved to the centre of the room. It was as he'd remembered it, apart from a brightly coloured tapestry hanging on the wall behind the television. He lifted it up, just in case it was hiding something. It wasn't.

The leaded windows looked out onto the back garden. One of the detectives appeared to be examining the back of the house.

Benson moved in front of Father Gilbert. He looked pale, his eyes wide. "Are you suggesting this house is haunted?"

Father Gilbert smiled at him. "Don't be ridiculous. What priest in his right mind believes in haunted houses?"

* * *

If someone on Wilton's team had played a trick, he didn't own up to it. Wilton then adjusted his story to allow that the photos had already been taken off the wall and put on the floor when he walked in. He simply hadn't noticed.

Father Gilbert didn't believe a word of it. If that were true, then how did Wilton know they were family photos? But there was no point asking.

As they walked back through the garage, Father Gilbert saw that forensic detectives now surrounded the red Peugeot.

"We're checking for any evidence of Haysham," Wilton said when they assembled again on the driveway. "If we find Haysham's fingerprints inside that red vehicle, then your boy is a goner."

Father Gilbert said to Wilton, "He's not *my* boy. Like you, I want to find the truth. Providing that you *do* want to find the truth." He thought of the photos again.

Wilton scowled. "If you expect me to believe Todd is tormented by demons, I won't do it."

"Even if that's the truth?" asked Father Gilbert.

Wilton turned away.

* * *

As Father Benson drove them away from the house, Father Gilbert felt liberated, as if he'd escaped some sort of oppression.

"You felt it, too?" Father Benson asked. "It was like something was pushing against my chest, making me feel weighed down."

Father Gilbert restrained from adding that he had felt a distinct presence and a feeling as if he was being taunted or laughed at. He'd felt it in other places at other times.

He tugged at his collar. The sun had come out. The day was becoming hot and muggy. He wound down his window and breathed deeply. The fresh air was a comfort.

"It wouldn't surprise me if the Woodrich sword and ring were found hidden in that house somewhere," Benson said.

"Why do you say that?"

Benson shrugged. "Has the house been in the family long? It looked fairly modern."

"The section we were in was added to the original house several years ago," Father Gilbert said. "But other parts date back to the late 1800s. I believe the garage was originally a stable."

"Did Francis Todd live in that house?"

"He may have. But more than likely he lived in the vicarage."

They reached a junction. "Are we going back to the church?" Benson asked.

"No. Let's talk to Adrian Scott."

CHAPTER 25

Adrian Scott's bookshop in Stonebridge sat on a corner of the High Street and Darcy Lane, one of the many slivers of road that branched off from the town centre. The front of the shop looked as if it had been designed from drawings in a Charles Dickens novel – the kind of shop that ought to have "Ye Olde" in front of the name. Instead, the sign simply said *Scott's*.

The two bay windows sitting on both sides of the front door sported cluttered displays of rare and antique books. One on local shipbuilding, another covering the history of the world as it was known up to 1919. There was a uniform set of Graham Greene novels and a hodgepodge of G. A. Henty titles. A cat slept in the corner.

Beyond the displays, the shop was dark. A sign on the door announced in neat lettering that "The shop is closed out of respect for Lord Haysham and his untimely death."

A woman from a clothes shop next door was gazing at her front window display and giving directions to someone inside about how to rearrange the mannequins, when she saw Father Gilbert standing at the door. "He's at home," she said.

"Where does he live?" Benson asked.

Father Gilbert pointed up. "Above the shop. It's a flat. We can use the stairs around the back."

The rear of the shop faced a car park. There was a door for the shop itself on the ground level. A wooden staircase rose and dog-legged onto a wide balcony that covered the width of the building. In the middle of the wall was a door with the number "7" on it and a small button for a doorbell. Father Gilbert pushed the button.

The Dickensian look of the shop was explained when Mr Fezziwig himself opened the door.

"Hello," Adrian Scott said. He seemed a foot shorter than most adults, with a round face and a matching round body that he had marginally contained in a white shirt, a very tight waistcoat, and trousers that looked like riding breeches. He had a mop of long brown hair and side-whiskers that flared out like bird's wings. A pince-nez was perched on his bulbous nose.

Father Gilbert had to smile every time he saw Scott, which was once a week when he went to see what might be new or interesting on the shelves.

"Father Gilbert," he said, then turned to Benson. "You must be Father Benson. Lord Haysham – God rest his soul – said you'd be paying me a visit. Come in, come in."

The two priests stepped in and were transported to a home that Dickens himself would have described. Uncarpeted creaky floorboards and bare wooden walls and a scattering of furniture were centred mostly around a modest fireplace in the corner. The place was dominated by rows of open bookcases, with shelf after shelf of books from various epochs and in various conditions. Father Gilbert resisted the temptation to stop right then to look.

Another cat brushed against his leg. A third cat gave Father Benson a similar expression of welcome.

"Can you believe he's dead?" Scott asked. "I can't. It's more than I can bear. There are those you can imagine being murdered, but he isn't one of them. No, indeed. They think David Todd did it, and he might have, but it hardly seems possible. I never thought of Todd as the killing type. But, then again, I never thought of Lord Haysham as the being-murdered type."

"How well did you know Lord Haysham – I mean the father of the Lord Haysham who has just – er – passed away?" Benson asked.

"Not very well," he said. "He invited me to a Christmas party at his estate once. He shook my hand and said that he loved, absolutely *loved*, my bookshop. To my knowledge, he'd only set foot in it once and that was to buy his wife a Jane Austen. Not even a first edition, just a run-of-the-mill Nelson's. But he said he liked how I had organized the shop and wondered if I was as good with family documents and archives. I didn't know anything about archiving, but I thought I could learn as well as anyone. And I did. Would you like a cup of tea or coffee?" His eyes darted back and forth between the priests.

"Tea, thank you," said Father Gilbert.

Benson asked for the same.

Scott scurried off, disappearing around a corner. Benson put a hand to his mouth, as if he might laugh. Father Gilbert nodded.

"This way!" Scott called out.

They followed the sound of his voice and entered a kitchenette, enclosed with bookcases as walls. He stood at a small counter and busied himself with the kettle and mugs.

"Milk, sugar?" Scott called out.

"Both for me, please," Father Gilbert said.

"Neither for me." Benson stepped to one side and nearly toppled a stack of books on the floor.

Father Gilbert turned to a shelf behind him. He was faced with a row of novels from the middle of the twentieth century – replica first editions of brilliant authors who had led Western literature into angst, despair, and cynicism.

"We're investigating the Haysham family's relationship with the Todd family over the past 200 years," Father Gilbert said.

"That's easy. They didn't like each other," Scott stated.

"We know that much. But we'd hoped to get more specific about it."

"Well, that will be so much easier than it used to be." He turned with two mugs, thrusting one into Benson's hands and another into Father Gilbert's. He returned to the counter to retrieve his own mug and then went over to a table with a computer nearly hidden amongst piles of books. "I've spent the past few years organizing the Haysham family's letters and deeds and documents of all sorts. I've been scanning and cataloguing everything into the computer, even paintings and photos. It's an exhaustive database, but I haven't quite organized it yet."

"Then you can look up the Woodrich Set," Benson said.

Scott turned to him, his eyebrows dark clouds over a stormy expression. "Oh, we don't talk about that."

"Who doesn't?" asked Father Gilbert.

"Those of us who know about it."

"Why not?"

"The Woodrich Set is bad luck."

Benson looked surprised. "Seriously?"

Scott nodded with great fervour.

"But we have to talk about it," Father Gilbert said. "We believe it's connected to Lord Haysham's murder – and to everything else that's gone on around here since that body was found."

"The body. Yes, I know about that. Joshua Todd."

"They don't know for certain. Not until the DNA results come back."

"They've come back. It's Joshua Todd. No doubt about it, for those who had doubts. I didn't."

"How did you hear that?" Father Gilbert asked. It bothered him that he hadn't been told.

"I'm a resourceful fellow," said Scott with a wink.

Benson looked at Father Gilbert and frowned.

Scott tapped the computer screen. "It's all in here, only it's in bits and pieces for someone clever to put together."

"And you're clever enough to do that," Father Gilbert said.

"With what I have, yes. But there are a few boxes the Hayshams haven't let me catalogue."

"Why not?" Benson asked.

Scott looked thoughtful. "Maybe they're embarrassed. Or ashamed. Some families get like that. Very proud of their heritage and they want to keep up appearances. Other families don't care so much. They don't think the actions of their ancestors reflect poorly on them now. But they do, you know. It can't be helped. The sins of one generation will be carried to the next, and the next, and the next, until something breaks the chain – or curse."

Benson was about to drink his tea, but lowered it again. "What curse?"

"Are you talking in general, or about the Woodrich Set?" Father Gilbert asked Scott.

"Curses in general and the medallion in particular. It was found with the body under the bridge. And what happened next? Poor Colin Doyle offed himself because of it. He knew something."

"What did he know?" Father Gilbert pulled a wooden chair over and sat down to face Scott. He crossed his legs and rested his mug of tea on his knee.

Scott spoke slowly, as if speaking to an obtuse child: "That the sins of one generation get carried onto the next – to *his*."

"What sins?" Benson asked.

"Well, if I knew that, I wouldn't be wondering about it, would I?" said Scott impatiently. "Lord Haysham was upset about the medallion. I could hear it in his voice on the phone. He knew it had meaning, but he wasn't sure what that meaning was. Though he probably had his suspicions but didn't want to admit what they were."

Father Gilbert shook his head. "Can we go a few steps back in this conversation?"

"We can go further than a few steps," Scott said and turned to the computer. He fiddled with the mouse and the keyboard and then he turned the screen so Fathers Gilbert and Benson could see it. A black-and-white photo of a painting appeared. A plump-faced man in a white wig and a red uniform looked unpleasantly at them.

Father Gilbert froze. It was the man with the sword – the one he'd seen behind him in his bathroom.

"This is Samuel, the third Lord Haysham," Scott explained. "He lived from 1752 until 1804. He was born on a wintry night—"

Father Gilbert held up his hand. "Not to be rude, Adrian, but I'm not sure we want to go back *that* far. Can you stay with the relevant highlights?"

Scott looked disappointed. "I would if I knew what the relevant highlights were. I can't know without going through *everything*."

Father Gilbert took a sip of his tea and opted to be blunt. "Did the Hayshams cheat the Todds in business back then?"

Scott was unperturbed by the question. "Based on what I've read, yes. I would say so."

"Did *this* Lord Haysham – Samuel – murder Joshua Todd on the bridge and dump his body in the river?"

"Ah, now, that's a more difficult question to answer."

"Why?"

"Because there's no evidence that he did, but it was well within his personality to do it."

"He was a nasty man?" Benson asked.

"Ruthless," Scott said. "And he became rather volatile and short-tempered after returning from the war."

"Which war?" Father Gilbert asked.

"The American war for independence."

"He fought in that?" Benson asked. "For which side?"

"England, of course." Scott tapped at the computer keyboard. "It changed him."

"How?" asked Father Gilbert.

"Whereas he'd been an amiable sort of person, if a little eccentric, he turned into a bit of a monster. I tracked down a letter from a servant describing how horrible he'd become. It described him as storming around the mansion, shouting at no one in particular, and ranting about the glory that would come."

"Glory – because of the war?" Benson asked. "Was his battlefield experience that impressive?"

Father Gilbert wondered if he had meant some sort of spiritual glory.

A cat leapt on the table and sniffed at Scott's mug of tea. Scott didn't seem to mind. "I don't know how much battlefield experience he had. He served briefly with Cornwallis in New Jersey and Philadelphia. That was long before the Yorktown debacle."

"Then what was he talking about?" Father Gilbert asked.

Scott shrugged. "Two things happened while he was in the Colonies. First, his father died. He adored the man and the loss was hard on him. Second, he came down with a terrible illness – a fever of some sort – that rendered him incapable of any further military service. So he came home in 1778 to take charge of the estate and to recuperate. But he never really did. The consensus is that he wasn't the same man. He had become irrational, even egomaniacal. That's why, though there hasn't been any proof, it's easy to believe that he murdered Joshua Todd."

Staring at the face on the screen, Father Gilbert imagined that same face on the man in his bathroom. He saw the uniform and the sword held high. He thought he felt a cool movement of air on his neck as the blade swung past. He winced.

Father Benson looked at Father Gilbert with a quizzical expression.

Father Gilbert took a deep breath and turned his attention back to Scott. "We know that Joshua Todd had the Woodrich medallion around his neck, but did Samuel Haysham have the Woodrich sword and ring?"

"I can't confirm that," Scott said. "Persuade Lady Haysham to let me have a look at those other boxes, and I might be able to."

"Father Gilbert may be able to do that," Benson said.

"And tell David Todd, if he ever wants anyone to archive his family's documents, I'm the one to do the job." Scott nudged the cat and picked up his mug of tea.

"I'll mention it," said Father Gilbert. "Though he's a little preoccupied right now."

Scott tapped a finger alongside his nose. "Understood. And you might mention my archiving services to the Doyles, too. If they have need for them."

"Thanks for the tea." Father Gilbert stood up. "By the way, have you seen in any of the documents phrases like 'Serve or die' or 'Take your place' – in English or Latin?"

"I don't believe so." He thought about it. "No – it doesn't ring a bell."

"What about pentagrams? Have they shown up?"

"Pentagrams, yes – occasionally," said Scott. He hammered at the keyboard again. "Samuel and various Hayshams after him put the symbol in the corners of their letters, or under their signatures, like a seal."

"Do you know why?"

"No."

"When did they start? Using the symbol, I mean."

"After Samuel's return from America, I believe."

Father Gilbert couldn't think of any other questions. "Thank you for your time. We'll be in touch."

Benson drained his tea and put the mug on the table.

The three men walked back to the door.

"You're going to call back to say that I'm allowed access to those other boxes, right?" Scott asked. "Unless they've been moved, Lord Haysham kept them in a storage cupboard off his main study. You'll let me know soon, yes?"

Father Gilbert thought about the grieving family and couldn't imagine anything more absurd than asking for boxes of old papers.

CHAPTER 26

Father Benson drove Father Gilbert out to the Haysham estate in the middle of the afternoon. Father Gilbert didn't want to bother the grieving widow about mundane issues like the archives, but he conceded that they might yield information that would help the police investigation now rather than later.

Approaching the door, Father Gilbert thought about the manor – the generations that had suffered pain and loss, had come and gone within its walls. The manor was still there while its inhabitants had been relegated to painted portraits, old boxes of letters, framed photos, and whatever memories the living still held of them. The size of the house, the value of its contents, even the beauty of the grounds, suddenly seemed indifferent to the humanity that had built and maintained them all.

A young man answered the door – a younger version of the now-deceased Michael Haysham, complete with blond hair and fair complexion. Even the lips were turned down in the same way. His eyes were glassy and the tip of his nose was an angry red from too many tissues. He wore a sweatshirt with a logo Father Gilbert didn't recognize, and faded jeans. This was Philip, Lord Haysham's son.

"I'm very sorry about your father, Philip," Father Gilbert said as they shook hands.

A brief nod in return.

Father Gilbert introduced him to Father Benson.

"Come in," Philip said.

They stepped into the front hall, but no further.

"Look, Mum's in no condition to talk right now," Philip said. "The doctor's got her medicated. What can I do for you?"

"It's an odd time to ask," Father Gilbert said, "but Adrian Scott believes you have some boxes of documents he hasn't seen."

"Adrian Scott? The bookshop owner?"

"Your grandfather hired him to serve as the family archivist," Father Gilbert said.

Philip nodded. "Oh, yes. I remember something about that now. But why are you bothering about the archives?"

"Because we believe your family's history may be connected to your father's murder," Father Gilbert said.

His eyes widened. "Do you think Todd was motivated by something from the *past* to kill Dad?"

"We don't know that he killed your father," Father Gilbert said.

"Of course he did it!" the young man said. "He's hated my father for as long as I can remember. If it'll help make the case, then you're welcome to whatever we have. But I'm afraid I don't know where they are."

"Mr Scott said they're in a cupboard off the main study," Benson said.

"This way, then."

Philip led them down a long hallway to Haysham's office. It had the look of a well-worn study, with books shoved haphazardly on the shelves, a desk cluttered with papers and mail, and even a miniature indoor putting green near the window. A filing cabinet sat next to a door. Philip pulled the door open.

"It's a bit of a mess," he said as he turned on an inside light.

They crowded into the small room. There was little floor or wall space left thanks to the discarded office machines, unused furniture, and stacks of cardboard file boxes.

The three of them turned in different directions to scan the handwritten labels on the boxes. There were business files and correspondence from recent years, magazines, seasonal cards and decorations, keepsakes, but nothing indicating old archival material.

"Adrian Scott must have misunderstood," Philip said. "There are a dozen other places where those kinds of boxes might be, but I'd have to ask my Mum when she's able to think about it."

Father Gilbert noticed an old-fashioned trunk in the corner. "What about that?"

It took some work to get to it, pushing all the other clutter aside, but they eventually cleared enough room to pull it out. It was heavy –

wooden with leather straps, metal studs, and a tarnished brass latch. Philip struggled with the lid and finally got it open.

Father Gilbert mused on the childlike feeling old trunks brought out in him: an expectation of lost pirate treasure, jewels and bullion, or rare books, or a monumental discovery of documents or sketches by a famous artist. This trunk, however, was filled with notebooks, ledgers, boxes of letters in their envelopes, and coloured binders.

Philip dug through it all, as if to make sure he wasn't giving anything valuable away. Then he closed the lid. "You can take it," he said and helped them carry the trunk back to the front door.

At that moment Father Gilbert remembered that they were in Benson's Mini Cooper.

Benson thought of the same thing. "I'm afraid I don't have room in the boot or back seat for a trunk that size."

Philip didn't seem bothered. "It's easily taken care of. I'll have it sent over to Mr Scott right away."

"He's in number 7, above his shop," Father Gilbert said.

"He'll have it within the hour." Philip walked them to the door. "But I want to be the first to know if he finds anything incriminating."

"You're more likely to find any incriminating documents in the recent file boxes we looked past," Father Gilbert said.

Philip's expression lit up as if he'd been given a new purpose for being there. Grief, Father Gilbert knew, could be a huge black hole of waiting, of tedium. Endless cups of tea and merely sitting around fielding sympathy. That's why so many people filled it with busy-ness, as Lady Haysham had with the gardening.

"Perhaps I'll look," Philip said.

Father Gilbert doubted Philip would find anything, but hoped the young man would find a helpful distraction in the effort.

* * *

Mrs Mayhew was hunched over her desk, looking with great concentration at a piece of paper.

"Is everything all right?" Father Gilbert came close to the desk. Father Benson seemed to linger a few steps away.

She looked up at Father Gilbert, then at Father Benson, with tired eyes. "I've spent most of the afternoon searching the files for anything at all about that mysterious skeleton. Finally, after going through every drawer and box I could find, I found a single reference in a file that I had placed on my desk yesterday. It was right here under my nose."

"What's the reference?" asked Father Gilbert.

"It's an unsigned note to Reverend Ainsley in 1938, explaining that the 'unfortunate person' from the cellar would be honourably interred in Southaven at All Souls' Church. And 'Happy Christmas!'" She held up the note for them to see. A very masculine writing style, Father Gilbert thought. There were no other markings on the plain white sheet.

It was more than nothing. "Thank you, Mrs Mayhew."

She put the note down again. "That's not all," she said. "I rang DS Sanders, like you asked, and gave him this information. Because of the 'Happy Christmas', he looked up reports from December 1938. He found that the body was officially released to be buried on the 12th of December, 1938."

"Released to who?" Benson asked.

"Whom," she corrected him.

"Who picked it up?" Father Gilbert asked.

"The first name was unreadable. The last name was *Doyle*." She looked rather pleased with herself. "The skeleton was buried with the Doyle family."

CHAPTER 27

"But didn't you say Richard Doyle Challoner was in the Challoner mausoleum?" Benson asked as they drove into the car park for All Souls' Church.

"There's a marker there for him. But that doesn't mean he's there," said Father Gilbert.

"So the skeleton from the church cellar might not be his."

Reverend Desmond Singh came out of All Souls' Church to greet them. He wore a traditional priest's shirt and collar. He seemed relaxed and greeted both of the priests warmly, as if they were all old friends. Father Gilbert was all too aware of the weirdness of their last conversation. He hadn't told Father Benson about the implausible dreams they'd discussed. He hoped Reverend Singh wouldn't bring them up.

After Father Gilbert explained more fully why they'd come, Singh simply shook his head. "Do you think the events from the past 200 years will answer questions about poor Colin's suicide or the murder of Lord Haysham? Are you sure the two of you aren't getting carried away by this mystery – a bit of Indiana Jones thrown in with Agatha Christie – that sort of thing?"

"The lives of this generation have been impacted by things that happened in previous generations," Father Gilbert said. "So we're chasing every clue we can get."

"So, how can I help you?" Singh asked.

"Would your church records register a burial in the Doyle mausoleum – late in 1938?" asked Father Gilbert.

"That's an easy question to answer: no."

Father Gilbert was surprised to get such a fast answer. "Why not? Don't your records go back that far?"

"They do. But there's no record of the burial you're looking for."

"How do you know?" Benson asked, as puzzled as Father Gilbert was.

"I had to look up the answer to your question not an hour ago, for a detective from Stonebridge."

"Which detective?" Father Gilbert already knew the answer.

"Sanders." He pointed to a silver car sitting alone at the other end of the car park. "That's his car over there."

"He's still here?"

"I assume so. I didn't see him leave."

"Would you mind showing us to the Doyle mausoleum?" asked Father Gilbert.

"Not at all."

They walked down a stone path to a low iron gate. Reverend Singh opened it and they continued on into the vast graveyard. Father Gilbert glanced up at the sky. He wondered if they'd have more rain.

"Why don't your records say anything about the burial?" Benson asked Singh.

"*If* the body was buried there, then it may have been done surreptitiously, probably late at night without the vicar knowing about it."

"Or he knew and agreed not to record it," Benson said.

"It may have been a matter of great privacy, or scandal," said Singh.

"So Sanders talked to you about Richard Doyle Challoner?" Father Gilbert asked.

"He asked about the Doyles," Singh said. "No, I'm not familiar with any *Challoner*. Did he attend All Souls' recently?"

Father Gilbert shook his head. "He died in 1889."

"I thought we were talking about 1938," Singh said.

"We are," said Father Gilbert. He could appreciate how confusing this was becoming. "I suspect the skeleton found in the cellar of St Mark's Church in 1938 was actually Richard Doyle Challoner from 1889. He was belatedly buried here."

"What exactly is going on, Father Gilbert?"

Father Gilbert explained as simply as he could about the Woodrich Set, the Doyles and Challoners, and everything else they'd learned since Colin Doyle had died.

Singh took it all in his stride, nodding silently from time to time. "And you believe the sword was placed with that skeleton?" he asked at the finish.

"Possibly."

"Why put the sword in his vault – or *any* vault, for that matter?" Benson looked as if the question had been on his mind, too.

"If the vault is well kept and weatherproof, it's a fairly good place to hide durable treasures." Father Gilbert wasn't convinced by his own statement, but it was better than admitting he was working from gut instinct.

Benson said, "I've read how, in some ancient cultures, a warrior's weapons were buried with him so he would have protection in the afterlife. It was a matter of honour."

"That makes sense for an ancient culture, but is that how they were thinking in 1889 or 1938?" Singh asked.

Why should it be any different then? Father Gilbert wondered. The note Mrs Mayhew found in the files had mentioned the word "honourable". Why would putting the skeleton in this mausoleum be honourable – or more honourable than being buried in the Challoner mausoleum, or in the cellar of the church?

More questions for which he had no answers.

* * *

Singh stopped in front of a mausoleum made of a light-coloured sandstone. It was a plain square structure with an arched roof. An iron gate stood open at the front.

"Is this where Colin Doyle will be buried?" Father Gilbert asked.

"If Jack Doyle gives his permission," Reverend Singh said. "He hasn't confirmed what he wants to do."

"Surely Colin's wife has something to say about it," Benson said.

Singh looked at Benson with a thin smile. "You would think so, wouldn't you?"

The three men walked into the mausoleum. Father Gilbert guessed it was about thirty feet by thirty feet in size. Burial vaults were lined up like filing-cabinet drawers, much like the mausoleum containing the Challoners, except this one had individual rectangular tombs sitting on the floor itself. The afternoon light shone through the entrance, turning the very air a hazy yellow.

"What's that?" Singh asked and their eyes went to one of the markers. The stone had been bashed open and gaped like a black wound.

They moved closer to look. Father Gilbert knelt next to the hole. Reverend Singh crouched down next to him.

"Can you see inside?" Benson asked from behind them.

"It's too dark," Father Gilbert said.

"I have a light on my mobile phone," Benson said and dug into his pocket.

To make room, Father Gilbert stood up and took a few steps further into the mausoleum. His foot slid on something slick and he looked down. It was a puddle of rust-coloured water. He moved off it, wondering where the leak might be, his eye following the stream.

The liquid wasn't water – and it wasn't really rust-coloured – and it had come seeping from a shadow where a crypt met the stone wall.

"Bring that light over here," Father Gilbert said.

Benson approached, the mobile phone light bright enough to guide planes in for a safe landing. Father Gilbert pointed and the light followed.

DS Sanders was propped up against the wall, his eyes wide open and his mouth slack, as if he simply couldn't believe the amount of blood coming from beneath his blood-soaked shirt.

Chapter 28

The sun was on its descent, the headstones reaching out as long shadows. Father Gilbert watched the Southaven SOCO officers do their work, moving in and out of the Doyle mausoleum, the occasional flash of a camera inside – photos for evidence – and the meticulous effort to find anything that might help identify the cop-killer. They wanted Father Gilbert's shoes, just to match the bloody footprints he'd made. Maybe the soles had picked up evidence.

Reverend Singh had found a replacement pair in the church's charity box. They were tight, but would do.

Chief Constable Macaulay was there, pacing and fuming about the murder of one of his own men. He'd interrogated Father Gilbert as if he suspected the priest of being involved somehow.

And, of course, Father Gilbert *was* involved. Only, he still didn't know why.

"DS Sanders didn't pay you a visit *after* he died, did he?" the Chief Constable asked sarcastically.

Father Gilbert responded in kind. "The night is still young."

A bird called from a tree somewhere. In the distance, a lawnmower roared and rattled. Father Gilbert thought he smelled fresh-mown grass.

Nearby, Father Benson leaned against a tall cross-shaped headstone, looking as ill and bewildered as he had when they'd first seen the body. Father Gilbert assumed he was in shock. Reverend Singh walked over, placed a hand on his shoulder, and bent forward to say something privately. Benson nodded at whatever Singh was saying. Father Gilbert hoped he was speaking comfort to the poor curate. Then they both looked in the direction of Father Gilbert.

He felt a flash of guilt, as if he'd somehow caused DS Sanders' death. It was irrational, he knew, but the feeling was there anyway.

The obvious question was: why would anyone want to murder DS Sanders? Who would gain by it?

Mary Aston had been going to meet with DS Sanders. She'd said so. Was she the last to see him? Did they find the sword in a vault? Had she killed him for it?

Father Gilbert should tell the Chief Constable about it. But, for all he knew, Macaulay had also had an affair with Mary. He'd mention it to the investigating officer from Southaven.

He was so very tired of the secrets, the *not knowing*. He was weary of how motivations, rationalizations, justifications, and simple denial became the weapons that people used to destroy themselves – and others. His mind kept replaying Colin Doyle's suicide on the tower, but now, instead of the face of Colin he saw the grotesque death mask of Sanders.

What was Sanders' first name? Father Gilbert couldn't think of it.

Reverend Singh was at his side. "Are you all right?"

Steve. His name was Steve. Father Gilbert nodded.

"Father Benson is worried about Evensong."

"Mrs Mayhew is taking care of it," he said, glad he'd thought to phone her. He hadn't explained why he and Father Benson were delayed, but she'd assured him Reverend Walker, a local retired vicar, would fill in.

"Will they want formal statements?" Singh asked. All three of them had already answered *a lot* of questions.

"Tomorrow."

"Good. I don't think Father Benson is in any shape to do it now."

Father Gilbert glanced at Benson again. He hadn't moved. He leaned and stared. "He must be wondering what he's walked into by taking a job at St Mark's," said Father Gilbert.

Singh gave a practised smile – which wasn't a denial. He said, "One of the police radios said that Jack Doyle is at the Southaven station answering questions."

"Why?"

"He was here earlier today, to talk about his son's funeral." Singh's tone betrayed little. "He came to look at the mausoleum."

"Before or after DS Sanders arrived?"

"They may have overlapped."

Father Gilbert nodded, understanding. "They'll want to know if he saw anything unusual."

Or maybe Jack Doyle killed Sanders.

He had no idea *why* Jack Doyle would do such a thing. Maybe DS Sanders had annoyed Doyle. Or he'd once been on a taskforce to catch Doyle doing something illegal. Or Doyle was angry about his son and decided to take it out on the nearest person available. Or Doyle hadn't done anything at all. As insane as the last few days had been, anything seemed possible.

"Go home," Reverend Singh said. "Take Father Benson home."

Father Gilbert nodded. He walked over to Benson, put a hand under his arm, and guided him away. "Are you able to drive?"

"Where are we going now?" he asked, a slight whine to his voice. "I feel like I want nothing more than to curl up in bed and pull the covers over my head."

"I understand." Father Gilbert gently led him along, the tragedy falling behind them. "Can you drive?"

"Yes."

Father Gilbert wanted to assure him that they were going home. Their work, for this day, was done. He couldn't dare ask any more of his curate.

But there was a momentum building around this case and he didn't want to lose it.

This case, he thought. Was he investigating a case? Was it true that, while you could take a detective out of an investigation, you couldn't take the investigation out of the detective?

"Where are we going?" Benson asked again.

He looked at Benson and rebuked himself. He was a *pastor*, not a detective.

"I'll call a taxi."

Benson stopped and turned to him. "We don't have to go back to Stonebridge. I'm all right. Tell me where you want to go."

"You don't have to—"

"*Where do you want to go?*" Benson said, his voice raw emotion.

"Jack Doyle's. He's with the police."

They continued walking to the car. "If he's with the police—"

"Then I may be able to talk to his wife," Father Gilbert said.

"About what?"

"I'd like to hear why Colin and his father had a falling out. And we might get some information about the family history and how they're connected to the Hayshams and Todds," he said.

Benson pulled the car keys from his pocket. They jingled as they trembled in his hand.

CHAPTER 29

The Doyles lived in a surprisingly modest house, tucked away in an older section of Southaven. Colleen made them tea while they waited in the front room – a cosy space with a small fireplace, *faux* antique furniture, and paintings probably bought from a department store.

Father Gilbert was grateful to be proven right. Colleen had allowed them to come in, based on Father Gilbert name-dropping Reverend Singh. But she was quick to point out that her husband wasn't at home, the hint being that, should he arrive, they would have to leave.

Her willingness to invite them in gave Father Gilbert the impression that she was lonely. Where were her relatives and friends? Considering the fact that their family had just suffered a tragic death, the house seemed quiet.

Colleen was ginger-haired with expressive green eyes, a petite nose, and a perfectly shaped mouth. The lines around her eyes and mouth were complimentary, speaking of character rather than age. Father Gilbert wondered how Jack Doyle had wound up with such a wholesome-looking woman. She didn't have the clichéd look of a crime-boss's wife. On the contrary, she wore the expression of a woman who seemed mystified by her circumstances, as if she were stuck in the wrong place at the wrong time.

"When is this going to end?" she asked after they'd expressed their sympathy about the death of Colin. She was already aware of the death of DS Sanders in their mausoleum. She paced back and forth, wringing the life out of a handkerchief. "First, Colin. Then Lord Haysham. Now this," she said. "It's like a war."

A spiritual one, Father Gilbert thought.

"They don't think Jack had anything to do with the detective's death, do they?" she asked.

"Is there any reason they should?" Father Gilbert asked.

"No, of course not. But Jack and the police don't get on," she said.

She spoke in a weary matter-of-fact tone, as if they were discussing problems with teachers at school.

"I'm sure Colin's death must have you both deeply grieved," Father Gilbert said.

She looked at him with a sad look. "Jack doesn't grieve. He gets angry. All of his emotions wind up as anger."

What was the outlet for that anger? Father Gilbert wondered.

"Was it his anger that drove Colin away?" Father Benson asked.

Father Gilbert winced. The question was too direct. He shot a look at Benson, but the priest's eyes were on Colleen. Benson held his cup of tea tightly with both hands.

Colleen shook her head. "Colin grew up with his father's anger. He was long past allowing it to bother him."

"Then why were they estranged?" Benson asked.

Again, the question was too direct. Father Gilbert expected Colleen to retreat and shut down the conversation.

Instead, she sat down on the edge of the sofa. She leaned forward and clasped her hands together. "Colin is – *was* – like his father. They're both so stubborn. So it was a surprise when Colin said…" Her voice trailed off.

"Said what?" Father Gilbert asked gently.

She sighed deeply and looked at the floor. "He said he was done with being a Doyle. He stood in this very room and announced it. He had better options, he said. Well, you can guess how Jack felt about that. Family pride is very important to him. He expects everyone to take their place, play their part."

The phrase caught Benson's attention. He looked at Father Gilbert.

"Take their place? To do what?" Father Gilbert asked.

"To do his duty for the family, to take responsibility." She lifted her head. Her eyes were filling with tears. She fought them back with a frown. "I don't know why Colin would take his own life. None of us can work it out."

"I've wondered if it had something to do with the body they found on Haysham's estate," Father Gilbert said. "There was a medallion…"

"I've heard something about all that."

"The medallion doesn't mean anything to you?" Father Gilbert asked.

"Why should it?"

"No reason, really," Father Gilbert said. "Do you know the name Richard Doyle Challoner?"

She thought about it and then shook her head. "No. Is it one of our relatives?"

"From the past."

"I don't know much about the Doyle family's past."

"Do you have any family histories or records?"

"The Doyles go back a few centuries, Father. They're *Jack's* ancestors, not mine." She sat up straight. Father Gilbert anticipated that her good grace would end soon. "What does this have to do with anything?"

"Maybe nothing, maybe a lot," Father Gilbert said. "The discovery of that body – and the medallion – affected Colin for some reason. It may be connected with the family histories of the Hayshams, the Todds, and even the Doyles."

"I can't imagine how."

"That's why I'd hoped to look over any family archives you might have."

She thought for a moment. "Our solicitor keeps all our legal documents."

"I'm thinking of more informal records – diaries, letters…"

"Anything like that would be in Jack's office."

"May we look?"

She was on her feet. "Absolutely *not*. Jack would be furious if I let anyone snoop around in his office."

Father Gilbert stayed seated. He wasn't giving up easily. "Will *you* please look?"

She stared at him.

"Please. I wouldn't ask if it wasn't important," he said. "There's a link between the past and what's happening now. We're examining Lord Haysham's archives and hope to do the same with David Todd's."

He could tell she was trying to assess the risks. "I won't dig around in his files," she said.

"I'm talking about the *past*, Mrs Doyle, not anything from your husband's present." He hoped to reassure her that it wasn't a ruse to implicate Jack.

"I'll look," she said.

"Thank you."

"Now?" she asked.

"If you don't mind."

She went off. Father Gilbert and Father Benson looked at each other.

"You're getting some colour back into your cheeks," Father Gilbert said to Benson.

"I feel sick."

"That'll pass, too."

"This feels wrong. She's grieving over the loss of her son and we're…"

"Being ruthless?" Father Gilbert asked. He'd thought the same thing.

"I'm surprised she hasn't thrown us out," Benson said. His eye went to the hall, his voice lowered: "You don't think Jack is abusing her, do you?"

Father Gilbert didn't know how to answer. If the rumours about Jack Doyle were true, he was capable of anything.

Colleen's footsteps brushed the carpet as she returned to them. "Everything's gone. Jack must have got rid of the boxes. Or maybe Colin had them. I remember he went through a period where he was interested in our family history. Ask Amanda."

"Colin's wife," Father Gilbert confirmed.

She nodded. Remaining by the door, she waited.

Father Gilbert stood up, as did Father Benson. They thanked her for the tea and expressed their condolences again.

At the front door, she put a hand on Father Gilbert's arm. "Is there a chance Colin didn't kill himself?"

Father Gilbert often thought about the odd hope that came with such a question – as if her son being the victim of a murder was more tolerable than him wilfully taking his own life.

"I don't want to give you the wrong impression," Father Gilbert said gently. "The evidence shows that he did. *Why* he did it may never be known. Or, by the grace of God, we may discover what pushed him to do it."

"If you do, please let me know," she said. "Promise me that."

"I will," he said. But he doubted she would like whatever he found.

* * *

"No," Father Benson said when they were in the car.

Father Gilbert had been looking at his watch. It was after nine. "No – what?"

"I won't take you to Amanda Doyle's," he said. "I've had enough grief and death for one night."

"All right," Father Gilbert said. His mind had already moved beyond paying Colin's wife a visit anyway. "I'll phone Reverend Singh. If there are any family documents there, then he's the one to get them."

Benson looked at him. "Sometimes you're more like a detective than a priest."

Father Gilbert grimaced. "Yes, I know. I'm not sure that's a good thing."

CHAPTER 30

"There was a box in the garage, but it contained mostly legal documents," Reverend Singh said. He'd arrived at St Mark's unannounced late the next morning. Father Gilbert was surprised; he'd only left a voicemail about the Doyle family archives the night before.

"Thank you for checking so quickly," Father Gilbert said after they shook hands. They were in his office. He waved to the guest chair.

"I was going to see Amanda anyway," Singh said as he sat down. "She was confused, though. She was certain Colin had a second box of family papers, an older one."

"It's missing?"

"Burnt."

Father Gilbert frowned.

"There was a barrel in the back garden. I assumed it was for burning leaves. But there was part of a box inside – wooden – vintage-looking. It looked as if Colin had tried to burn the whole thing."

"Did anything survive?" Father Gilbert asked.

"There were bits of paper among the ashes, but nothing one could read."

He wondered what had been in those papers that had caused Colin to burn them. *Something terrible,* he thought. *So terrible that he killed himself?* "Then there's nothing left."

"There is this." Singh held up a book. It looked like a trade paperback. "This was in the box in the garage."

"What is it?"

"An aunt of Jack Doyle's spent years writing up a family history. She had it published – oh, twenty years ago – and sent it around to everyone in the family. She was very proud of it." He handed the book to Father Gilbert.

The cover was adorned with a family crest and was fancifully titled, *The Doyle Family: Larks, Legends, Gossip and Scandal.*

"I glanced through it," said Singh. "The first half is mostly about the Doyles of Ireland. The second half is about the branch in England."

Father Gilbert thumbed through the pages. Blocks and blocks of type, with a few family trees and diagrams.

"She wasn't much of a writer, but she was meticulous," said Singh. "There's even an index of names in the back."

"I wonder what Jack Doyle thought of this," mused Father Gilbert. He couldn't imagine Doyle appreciating anything dragging up his family's larks, legends, gossip, or scandal.

Singh smiled. "Amanda said he hated it. He didn't think it was anyone's business to dig up the past. In fact, he didn't want Colin to take it out of the house. He was afraid someone outside the family would read it. He thought it would give people a reason to laugh at them."

Family pride, Father Gilbert thought, then asked: "How is Colin's wife?"

"Not well," said Reverend Singh.

"Is she on good terms with Colleen Doyle?" Father Gilbert was thinking about Colleen, alone at home.

"I don't believe they are close. I don't believe Jack Doyle allows his wife to be close to anyone."

"That's what comes from keeping secrets," Father Gilbert said.

* * *

After the midday service, Father Gilbert and Father Benson went to The Mill House for lunch. They found a booth for privacy. Father Gilbert put on his glasses and opened the Doyle family book while Benson ordered their food.

"Well?" Benson asked after the waiter stepped away. "Anything useful?"

Father Gilbert took a drink and looked at the curate. "How did you sleep last night?"

"Fine," Benson said, "apart from the image of DS Sanders' face appearing over and over."

"I'm sorry you saw it." Father Gilbert returned to the book and began to summarize what he saw there. "Richard Challoner has a lengthy annotation in the Doyle canon. He was allegedly the illegitimate son of Martin Doyle and Jane Challoner – thus the middle name, given to him by Jane to assert his true lineage. Richard was an awkward lad who had a harelip and lost a front tooth in a fight."

"Margaret Clarke said that the skeleton from the church cellar was missing a front tooth."

"Right." Father Gilbert took another long drink. "As a young man, Richard Challoner went to the Doyles to claim his rightful place in their family. He was soundly rejected. Shortly thereafter, he disappeared from the area under suspicious circumstances. There were claims by the Challoners that the Reverend Francis Todd of Stonebridge was somehow involved, since Richard was last seen going into St Mark's Church – and was never seen again."

"Incredible," Benson said. "So the skeleton is his."

"Hold that thought," Father Gilbert said. "Jane, convinced that Richard had been murdered, insisted on a grave for him in the Challoner family vault, even though his body wasn't in it. Though she later married and had other children, it was said she bordered on the insane. And, according to this book, local legend claims that Richard's ghost wanders the fields between the Challoners' and Doyles' homes during full moons, looking for his lost honour."

"Is that really a local legend?"

"I'm not a local boy."

Benson eyed Father Gilbert. "Have *you* seen Richard's ghost?"

Father Gilbert laughed. "No."

"It wasn't an unreasonable question, all things considered."

"I'm curious about something else." Father Gilbert pointed to a page and read: "'Reverend Todd, who was rumoured to be a disreputable person and was later defrocked, denied ever seeing Richard Challoner, though several witnesses clearly saw the young man enter the church.'"

Benson looked surprised. "Todd was *defrocked*? I didn't think the Church of England ever defrocked anyone for anything—"

"—except being faithful to orthodox Christianity," Father Gilbert added wryly.

Benson shook a finger at him.

"What time is it?" Father Gilbert asked.

Benson glanced at his watch. "A little after one."

Father Gilbert dug into his pocket and pulled out his mobile phone.

"I know how to find the truth about the Reverend Francis Todd."

* * *

The diocesan library was located in a cold stone building in Lewes, as part of the small seminary established there by a nineteenth-century bishop.

A fastidious and bird-like woman named Vivian Littleton pretended to be put out by the priests' unscheduled arrival. It was now close to three o'clock. "We close at four, you know."

"Isn't that early?" Father Benson asked.

"We don't have the budget or the volunteers to stay open longer," she said. She looked at Father Gilbert. "I don't have time to run around finding you things in my last hour of work."

"You are a marvel to me, Vivian," Father Gilbert said.

She looked stern. "Stop flirting and tell me what you want."

"Whatever you've got on the Reverend Francis Todd. He was the vicar in Stonebridge around—"

"I know very well who he is. I haven't worked here all these years to stay ignorant of the diocese's history. And one doesn't easily forget the scandals."

"Todd was a scandal?"

She gave him an *oh-you-ignorant-man* look. "You'll see. Go and find yourself a table and don't make a lot of noise." She gave Father Benson an impatient look, as if she resented him for existing.

They sat down at the appointed table. Father Gilbert looked at the various shelves surrounding them – theological tomes, academic magazines, and a few displays.

Benson asked, "Did you often find the truth to be so evasive? When you were a detective, I mean. We seem to be bouncing back and forth all over the place – even in history – to find out what's going on now. Were most of your cases like that?"

Father Gilbert thought about it for a moment. "Most cases are simple. A man robs a corner shop to get money to buy drugs. That's easy. It's a basic transaction, an exchange of goods. Why he's addicted to drugs may be more complicated, but the law isn't concerned about his abusive father or enabling mother or whatever drove him to drugs – that's for the solicitors to argue over. For a detective, there was a robbery, the culprit was found and arrested."

"So, which cases were the most complicated? The ones where death was involved?" Benson asked. "A man robs a corner shop to get money to buy drugs but the cashier won't cooperate. The man, who may be strung out, gets angry and shoots the cashier."

"Even that's fairly straightforward," Father Gilbert said. His mind raced around a dozen other scenarios. A man finds his wife in bed with another man and, in a flash of rage, kills one or both of them. No, that wasn't very hard for the law to deal with. "Now, *premeditated* murder – for one man to take another man's life as a matter of intention – is where things get complicated. The *why* of the murder takes centre stage. And when a detective is going after the *why*, then he finds himself in a labyrinth of relationships and motivations and activities."

"So you start with the *why*?" Benson asked.

Father Gilbert nodded. "Why did Colin Doyle commit suicide? The discovery of that body and the medallion seemed to be a trigger. Why was it a trigger? What's the significance of the Woodrich Set to him, or anyone, to the degree that it has now impacted the lives of all who came near it over the past couple of hundred years? Why? Mere coincidence? I don't believe in coincidence. Something else is at work here, bringing a pattern to what looks like random events."

"That's the priest talking, not the detective," Benson suggested.

"As a detective, I didn't believe in Providence. Good and evil were the result of psychological or circumstantial factors. But I was still wary of calling anything a coincidence. When I was solving a case, there were often too many coincidences for them to *be* coincidences," he said, smiling.

"If you didn't believe in Providence, what would you have called that?"

He had to think about it for a moment. "The pull of some kind of Truth. As if nature and evolution and all the forces in the world were being pulled to a great magnet of Truth. The pieces were being pulled together to get us to Truth. Since then, I've come to a better understanding of God, of good and evil – and I know that coincidences, the pull of Truth, are all part of a providential conspiracy to get us to Him."

Vivian Littleton arrived, pushing a cart covered with neatly stacked files and documents. "This is what we have," she said. "It won't be enjoyable reading."

"Thank you."

"We're missing an item. I'll check to see what became of it." She walked away and Father Gilbert noticed that she waddled. He remembered Mrs Nelson, the librarian at his grammar school, waddling like that. Did librarians go to a special school to learn that walk?

"Divide and conquer." Father Gilbert gave half of the files to Benson.

* * *

Over the next hour – which took them past closing time and got them scowls from Vivian Littleton – they learned some disconcerting things about the Reverend Francis Todd. Sporadically, over his six years as the vicar of St Mark's, he received complaints from various parishioners. On the surface, the complaints were petty and haphazard – a flash of inappropriate anger from him, some unkind words, a small amount of missing money from the church funds, an inappropriate deference to the wealthy, flirtations with married women, excessive and sometimes expensive socializing, a conflict with members of his vestry over unauthorized work on the church – and were all explainable and easily defended. Little wonder the Bishop at the time didn't take any particular notice or action.

Then they reached paperwork for the more serious allegations that Francis Todd had something to do with Richard Challoner's disappearance. Richard had been seen by several villagers – the names were given – entering the church on the evening of 3 August, and was not seen leaving the church again. The Bishop was forced to take action. He launched an investigation lasting three months. In January 1890, he convened an ecclesiastical panel to review the allegations and evidence and to come to a conclusion.

The minutes of an ecclesiastical meeting were detailed in the file. Reverend Francis Todd insisted that Richard had come to see him about borrowing money. Todd gave him a token amount. Richard departed by a back door. Todd believed that Richard was an unhappy young man who wanted the money so he could leave the area. Todd assumed Richard did just that.

Jane Challoner insisted that Richard had been invited to the church at that specific time by Todd to discuss "a private matter regarding the Doyle family".

A woman who often cleaned the church, Edith Peters, claimed that Todd had not been alone when Richard had arrived, but that several others had entered the church by another means. She also claimed to hear noises coming from the crypt, though the door to that stairway was closed. She didn't go down to investigate, "as she was in a state of distress" due to the sounds. Todd's response was that the noises Edith Peters had heard were made by a couple of stray cats "in heat" that had found their way into the crypt. The cats, he said, had gone wild and knocked over various tins, bottles, and boxes that were stored there.

A second woman, Anna Rogers, a member of the Altar Guild, stated that she had discovered remnants of occultism – candles, unexplained stains on the stone floor, and matted fur. She alleged that demonic orgies were taking place in the church. In his defence, Todd provided evidence that Anna Rogers was mentally unstable, creating all sorts of sexual and violent fantasies in her mind.

There was a transcript of a closed-door testimony with a Stonebridge prostitute who admitted to being paid to participate in sexual activities with the Reverend Todd – once on a slab in the church. The experience frightened her too much to go back, though she'd been offered more money. Todd called the prostitute a liar, plain and simple, and rebuked the panel for listening to such a witness.

Then a constable from Southaven gave testimony. He spoke of a prostitute from the docks who had told an acquaintance how she was to be paid well for an evening with the vicar in Stonebridge. She went and never returned. No investigation was conducted, since prostitutes often appeared and disappeared – and the disappearance of a prostitute was not a priority for the overworked police force. The constable admitted that a conversation had been held with his superiors over concerns that a Jack the Ripper had appeared in the area but, since no murders had taken place, the concern went away.

At the ecclesiastical meeting, documents in defence of the Reverend Francis Todd came from Thaddeus Haysham, Lawrence Doyle, and Edward Challoner, all reputable men who carried great influence in the diocese.

"*Edward* Challoner?" Benson asked.

"The father of Jane. She had the affair with Martin Doyle, resulting in the birth of Richard Doyle Challoner."

Benson scribbled the information onto a pad.

The Bishop and the members of the panel had been undecided until an additional piece of evidence was presented – a book that a housekeeper had smuggled out of the vicarage. The minutes didn't say what the book was or why it had swayed the panel. Within an hour of deliberations, the panel determined that, while no legal charges could be brought against Todd, it was within their powers to recommend that he be removed from the priesthood. The Bishop agreed with the recommendation and Todd was defrocked on 11 February 1890.

"Shouldn't the book be here?" Benson asked, searching the tabletop and the cart for it.

"Maybe that's the missing item Miss Littleton mentioned," Father Gilbert suggested.

There was nothing else about Todd in the file, except a news clipping from 1907 reporting that he had died in London after a career as a spiritualist in the Chiswick area. He was known for his ability to communicate with the dead through séances.

"What do you make of it?" Benson asked.

Father Gilbert leaned back in his chair and closed his eyes, forming a bridge with his fingers in front of him. "Here's one hypothesis. Francis Todd was a Satanist who used St Mark's for black masses, the dark arts, and orgies. Maybe he had a group of participants."

"Haysham, Doyle, and Challoner?"

"Possibly. Then things got complicated in 1889 when Richard Doyle Challoner asserted his rights as a member of the Doyle family. He was a pest. He wouldn't go away. So Doyle turned to Todd to do something about it. Todd told the entire coven."

"Coven?"

"That's what they were," Father Gilbert said. Then he continued, "They lured Richard to the church to discuss the situation. He wouldn't be reasonable. They drugged him, or overpowered him, and took him into the crypt. They conducted a black mass and offered him as a sacrifice—"

"You're kidding."

He shrugged. "It's one hypothesis. Even if we forget any satanic activity, it's possible they murdered him. They got rid of the body by burying it in the cellar of the church."

"Do you really think Edward Challoner would agree to the murder of his grandson?"

"Maybe he didn't know, or wasn't there. Or maybe he was so committed to the others that he was willing to go along with it. It's possible he simply wanted him out of the way."

"If Jane knew the truth, it might explain why she became mentally unstable," Benson said. "That's a horrible thing to have to live with."

"For anyone with a conscience."

"What about the sword?" Benson asked.

"Maybe it was part of the satanic ritual. They buried it with the body in the cellar."

"Why would they bury something so valuable?"

"To get rid of the evidence?" Father Gilbert said. He thought about it further. "We're assuming the sword was placed with him at the same time he was buried. Todd may have buried it later when the accusations began."

Benson frowned; the lines around his eyes were pronounced. "We're talking about something that happened in our church."

Father Gilbert had never thought of St Mark's as the epitome of holiness, but never imagined that it might be a place of profanity.

Vivian Littleton waddled up to them.

"Father Gilbert, the Bishop wants to see you," she said.

"Did you tell on us?" Father Gilbert asked.

"I would have, had I known he was here," she said.

"How did he know we were here?"

She shook her head, as if there was no knowing how the Bishop knew all the things he knew. "You'll find him in his office."

Benson looked puzzled. "His office is in Tunbridge Wells, isn't it?"

"One of several. He has an office here for his visits." Father Gilbert addressed Vivian Littleton. "I know you've gone above and beyond the call of duty. But would you mind making copies of this material and sending it to St Mark's? We'll cover any costs."

"I'll send what there is," she said, hinting at something Father Gilbert didn't understand. His expression prompted an answer from her. "According to the inventory, there was a bound book that had been entered as evidence against Francis Todd. But it was taken out on the 6th of May, 1938."

"By whom?" Father Gilbert asked.

"The verger at St Mark's: Albert Challoner."

* * *

The Bishop's office was a perfunctory box situated on a corner of the top floor. The desktop was mostly barren, apart from a few items the Bishop had brought with him. The bookcases held innocuous ornaments and only a few books, possibly lifted from the library or the church-owned second-hand bookshop. A small sofa sat along one wall. A matching chair sat next to it. Old magazines littered the coffee table.

One of the two windows looked down on the car park. Father Gilbert could see Hugh Benson standing next to his Mini, arms folded, lost in his thoughts.

Bishop William Spalding strolled in, wiping his hands with a paper towel. "Oh, hello, Gilbert." He binned the towel and they shook hands. His hands were clammy. "Sit down," he said, gesturing to the chair.

"I didn't know you were here," Father Gilbert said as he sat down.

"Nor I you," the Bishop said. He sat on the end of the sofa closest to Father Gilbert, leaning back, putting his feet up on the table. Had he been wearing a tie, he might have loosened it. He closed his eyes. In repose, he had a feminine face, with soft pale skin, no discernible beard, pink lips, and eyebrows that might have been meticulously trimmed. But Father Gilbert knew not to confuse his look with any sort of weakness. The Bishop's eyes were sharp, fierce at times. The man was ruthless with church politics. "Endless meetings today. Tedious."

Father Gilbert was aware of the Bishop's propensity for play-acting. The informal posturing on the sofa could have been genuine, or it could have been a contrivance to communicate that they were just a couple of pals having a chat, to get Father Gilbert to relax.

"How are you?" the Bishop asked.

"All right," said Father Gilbert.

"I mean, how are you *really*? We were meant to have regular meetings after you returned from your sabbatical," he said.

"You've been busy."

"I'm sorry about that." The Bishop opened his eyes. He picked at a piece of lint on the front of his trousers. "Well?"

"Well?"

"How are you really doing? Have you spoken to your father much since your mother's death?"

"Actually, he's not my father," Father Gilbert said. "He's my real father's brother."

"Yes, of course. But it's awkward knowing how to refer to him."

Awkward indeed, thought Father Gilbert. "I call him Uncle George."

"Not 'Dad'?"

"He was never much of one. It was easy calling him my uncle once I learned the truth."

"An itinerant actor," the Bishop confirmed. "He travelled a lot."

"That's right."

208

"Your real father was a policeman, is that right?"

Father Gilbert nodded. "He was killed before I was born. I knew him as Uncle Louis. I was named after him, though I wasn't sure why until my mother's death. She married George to give me a stable family life. It was a mistake, since George found it impossible to stay at home for more than two weeks at a time."

"You're not in touch with *Uncle* George at all?"

"I get the occasional letter from him, usually filled with newspaper clippings reviewing his stage performances, but I haven't seen him in a while," Father Gilbert said. He was growing restless with this recap of his personal life. He didn't know what the Bishop was after, but didn't want to be disrespectful enough to ask directly.

"Tell me about your mother," the Bishop asked.

"She's still dead."

The Bishop shot him a look of disapproval. "You know what I mean."

Father Gilbert tipped his head as a concession. "I grieved in all the normal ways after her death. I think of her often – and miss her."

"And what about the mystery? The one that began after her death. That woman – your girlfriend—?"

"She was my *first* girlfriend when I was a teenager," Father Gilbert clarified. "Katherine Donovan – er, *Perry*."

"Married that vicar in Windsor—"

"Ascot." Father Gilbert fought off a feeling of impatience. "Kenneth Perry."

"He died of cancer – how long ago?"

"A few years."

"Are you in touch with her?"

"Katherine lives in Southaven. We've had coffee together once or twice."

"Any sparks? Any rekindling of the old flame?"

"No."

The Bishop eyed him. "I'd have thought that you might, you know, pursue the relationship because of…" His voice trailed off.

"Because of the daughter I didn't know I had," Father Gilbert said. It was beginning to sound like a bad television series.

"Katherine broke up with you because…?"

"I was accepted for police training. She didn't want to be married to a policeman."

"But she failed to tell you she was pregnant with your child."

Father Gilbert nodded.

"Katherine married this Kenneth fellow – the vicar. How did you feel about your daughter being raised by another man?"

"Since I didn't know she existed, I couldn't have any feelings about it."

"And now? How do you feel about – what's your daughter's name?"

"Clare. Clare Perry," Father Gilbert said.

"She was adopted by Perry."

Another nod from Father Gilbert.

"She doesn't know about you, does she?"

"No. Katherine made me promise never to contact her." The irony wasn't lost on him – having a father who wasn't really his father, and having a daughter who'd experienced the same thing, and still didn't know it.

"How do you feel about that?"

"I'm reconciled to the idea."

"Where is Clare now?"

"Married and living in America. Her husband is a computer specialist, or something like that."

The Bishop gave a thoughtful *hm*. Then he sat up and faced Father Gilbert again. "The loss of your mother, the discoveries about your family…" The Bishop shook his head slowly. "Very difficult. A great emotional strain."

"The sabbatical gave me time to sort it out," Father Gilbert said. *That's* what the Bishop was really wondering about. "It took a while, but I had to admit that your predecessor was wise to force me to take it."

"He told me to watch out for you," the Bishop said. "He said you have a strong inclination to get in the middle of things, to lose your way as a priest for the sake of solving a mystery."

Father Gilbert didn't say anything. The Bishop was finally getting to his point.

The Bishop said, "It's a nasty business, with Lord Haysham and now that policeman—"

"Steve Sanders."

"You're caught up in it."

"At the request of the police."

"Not to the degree of involvement you've taken on."

"They didn't give me specific parameters for what I had to do."

The Bishop stood up. Informality time was over. "Let the police do their jobs, Father Gilbert," the Bishop said. "Don't get in the way."

"I wasn't aware of being in their way," Father Gilbert said, also standing. "Has someone complained?"

"You paid a visit to Colleen Doyle – while her husband wasn't home."

"You know the Doyles?" Father Gilbert asked.

The Bishop let the question slide. "I don't want you to lose your way again. Visions, hallucinations, visitations. It's all so freakish. You're really too valuable to be put back in a monastery."

Was it a threat? Of course it was. But, giving the Bishop the benefit of the doubt, it was also a fair warning. Slipping into detective mode, chasing after the Woodrich Set, digging into the past… for what? The police were investigating the murders. What could Father Gilbert do that they couldn't? The past was done, little more than an intriguing backdrop.

Even if he wanted to defend himself, there was little he could say. The Bishop didn't strike him as a deeply spiritual man, certainly not one who'd be able to discern the supernatural events of the past few days. What insight or advice could he offer?

"I understand, Bishop," Father Gilbert said.

* * *

"What did the Bishop want?" Father Benson asked.

They were driving back to Stonebridge. An accident further ahead put them in a long tailback.

"Just inquiring after my well-being," he said. "And he wanted to make sure I was happy with you as my curate."

"Really?"

"No."

"So he didn't mention me at all?"

"No."

Benson looked relieved.

A half-hour later, when they pulled up in front of the vicarage, Father Gilbert opened the door but didn't get out. "Come inside for a cup of tea."

"I ought to go home."

"Come inside." Father Gilbert climbed out and walked up the stone path to the door. He heard Benson turn off the engine. Then the driver's door closed.

Father Gilbert made the tea while Benson hovered, clearly wondering why he was there.

"I want to make sure you aren't unduly stressed by everything that's happened," Father Gilbert said as he handed over a mug.

"What's to be stressed about?" Benson asked. "Two people have been murdered. I saw one of the victims – which was a first for me. My boss gets regular visitations from dead people. And I've discovered that the church where I work might have a history including occult practices and all kinds of depravity. Honestly, it's all in a day's work."

Father Gilbert smiled. "In the future, talk to me before you go to the Bishop. It's all right."

Benson froze with the mug positioned in front of his lips. He lowered it and trained his eyes on the floor.

"Did you write to him just the once, or are you sending regular reports?" Father Gilbert asked and then drank some of his own tea.

"The Bishop asked for regular reports," he replied. "He said you needed someone to keep an eye on you. For your own good."

Father Gilbert nodded.

"I'm sorry," Benson said.

"You're under his authority. It'd be wrong to do otherwise." Father Gilbert pointed to the laptop computer on the small worktable in the corner and said as a clear change of subject: "Let's go over the schedule for the next few days. Mrs Mayhew will be reassured to know things are covered. We can't depend on Reverend Walker forever."

Benson sat down at the laptop.

"The schedule is one of the icons on the screen," Father Gilbert said.

He went to the French windows that led to the back garden. He looked through a panel of glass at the green lawn and trees beyond. Then his eyes focused on his own reflection, the face looking back at him a distortion of his own. Perhaps that was the problem: he couldn't see himself clearly.

He looked over at Father Benson. He didn't feel betrayed by the young priest. More than anything, he was bothered that the Bishop would put his curate in such an awkward position.

He turned his gaze to the back garden again. In the panel of glass, another face entirely peered back at him.

Chapter 31

Father Gilbert gasped and stepped back. Hot tea splashed on the floor.

Father Benson was on his feet. "What's wrong?"

The face moved and the handles on the doors jiggled.

"It's David Todd," Father Gilbert said and unlocked the door.

Todd came in, his expression twisted up.

"You scared the living daylights out of me," Father Gilbert said, annoyed.

Todd put a finger to his lips and spun around to lock the doors again. He grabbed the curtains and pulled them closed.

"What are you doing?" Father Gilbert asked him as he went to the sink to get a towel to mop up the spilled tea.

Todd went to the window above the sink and drew those curtains closed.

"David—"

"Just in case," Todd said. His eyes were wide and his face ashen.

"It's good to see you out of jail," Father Gilbert said. He knelt to clean the spill.

"I didn't want to leave. They forced me to go."

From his mopping position on the floor, Father Gilbert looked up at Todd. "You didn't want to get out of jail?"

"No! They told me about DS Sanders as they were releasing me. I begged them to put me back in where it's safe. If they'll kill Lord Haysham *and* a copper, they'll kill me without batting an eye."

"They?"

"I can't go home. I won't go home. That's why I came here."

Benson looked worried. "Were you being followed?"

"I don't think so." He went to the window and moved the curtain slightly to look out.

Father Gilbert put a hand on his shoulder and pulled him back. "David, sit down. I'll make you a cup of tea. Or wring one out of this rag."

Todd sat down at the kitchen table and said in a small voice, "I don't know what's happening to me."

"You've been through a lot," said Benson.

"I've never been so afraid." Todd looked at the two priests, dark circles under his eyes. Then he searched his pockets. "I got another message in jail."

He pulled out a slip of paper. It was torn from a yellow notepad. "It was in the discharge envelope with my belongings. I told the police it wasn't there when they brought me in. They said it must have been, since no one is allowed to tamper with personal effects. Do you see?"

Father Gilbert was pouring the tea, so Benson took the paper.

Benson showed it to Father Gilbert. It said *Take Your Place*.

Father Gilbert nodded and asked, "Finish making the tea, will you?"

They traded places. Benson finished making Todd's tea while Father Gilbert took the note and walked over to an alcove next to his refrigerator. It was the kind of place where people put papers they don't know what to do with, or haven't organized yet. He rifled through the stack.

"I need help," Todd said as Benson gave him his tea. "I have to get out of here and go somewhere safe."

"You're out on bail, right?" Father Gilbert asked.

"Right."

"Then the police won't be very happy if you leave the area."

"But someone will kill me if I stay! You don't really think I got this bruise and bashed lip from falling, do you? I was attacked outside of my house the night Haysham was killed."

"By whom?" Benson asked.

"I don't know. He was in a disguise – a hood and robe. He came at me out of the shadows, beat me up, and took my car."

"Which car?" Father Gilbert asked. He'd found what he was looking for in the stack of papers.

"The red Peugeot."

"Can you prove that? You didn't mention it to the police," Father Gilbert said as he moved towards the table.

"I was too stunned – too afraid. He said not to tell anyone or I'd die. I believed him. He returned the car later. When the police came for me about Haysham's death, it was in the garage."

"You didn't tell the police then."

Todd shook his head. "I told Wilton. Or, rather, I *tried* to tell Wilton. He wouldn't listen."

Father Gilbert placed Todd's yellow note and a second piece of white paper on the table in front of him. "David, the note you got in jail is in your handwriting."

Todd looked confused. "It can't be."

Father Gilbert pointed to the note. "You wrote this to me during one of our committee meetings. It's the same handwriting."

"I didn't write it," Todd said and pushed both notes away. "Someone is forging my writing to make me look guilty – or crazy."

"Why would anyone do that?" Father Gilbert asked.

"Wilton!" Todd shouted. "He has it in for me. He's friends with Lord Haysham. All of the police are. He used to throw parties for them and won them over with his charming smile. Now Wilton wants to pin Haysham's murder on me."

Father Gilbert sat down opposite Todd. "That may be harder for him to do now. If DS Sanders was killed with the same weapon as Lord Haysham, then you're in the clear. You couldn't have killed Sanders while you were in jail. Unless you've made a deal with someone else to do the job."

"What kind of deal? What do you mean?" demanded Todd. "Are you suggesting I'm part of a conspiracy?"

"Nobody's saying anything, David. Calm down."

"I can't tell whose side you're on."

"This isn't a football match. We're not on sides. We're all trying to get at the truth."

"Of course," Todd said sheepishly. He sipped his tea with shaking hands. He seemed childlike now, vulnerable and confused. It was a far cry from the brash and aggressive man Father Gilbert had known for so long. He wondered if it was an act.

"This is the vicarage. It's a holy place, right?" Todd asked.

The question reminded Father Gilbert of Colin Doyle on the

tower, when he held out the medallion and expressed the hope that giving it to a holy man might change things.

"It's only as holy as I am," Father Gilbert said. "If you want sanctuary, then we should go to the church."

"No – not the church," Todd said. He leaned forward onto the table and grabbed Father Gilbert's arm. "May I hide here for the night?"

Father Gilbert looked up at Benson, who was standing by the kitchen counter. He shrugged.

"You can stay the night, David. But I'm going to want answers from you."

"What kinds of answers?"

"Well, we can start with what you know about your ancestor: Francis Todd."

* * *

The three men relocated to the living room, but only after Father Gilbert had made certain that all the curtains were closed and all the doors were locked. David Todd slouched in an armchair. Benson sat on the antique wooden chair with the tapestry cushion. Father Gilbert had inherited it from his mother.

"Francis Todd, then," Father Gilbert said as he sat down on the couch.

"Francis Todd was my great-great-grandfather's brother, I think. The black sheep of the family," Todd said. "Nobody talks about him."

"Why not?"

Todd looked at the ceiling and squinted. "He was defrocked and became a spiritualist medium in London. They say he knew Arthur Conan Doyle and once met Harry Houdini."

"Was it ever suggested that Francis was a member of a satanic cult while he was the vicar here in Stonebridge?"

A shadow fell across Todd's face. "Just rumours, mostly. But talk of a satanic cult in this area goes back before Francis."

"How far back?"

Todd rested his elbows on his knees and concentrated on a spot on the carpet. "Joshua Todd. He was in some sort of alliance with Samuel Haysham."

"I thought they were sworn enemies."

"They were. But something changed between them after Samuel came back from America. They weren't friends, but they connected over... I don't know."

"You do know."

He hesitated, then said as a reluctant admission: "Joshua Todd and Samuel Haysham were involved in witchcraft of some sort. Maybe satanic rites. I don't even know the difference. But I never really believed any of that. Our families hated each other, then and now."

"Enemies can unite over a common cause."

"Maybe, but I don't know what common cause would have brought Joshua and Samuel together." He shook his head sadly. "It's funny, but my mother used to say things like, 'Behave yourself, you don't want to turn into a Joshua.' It became a family catchphrase. Sometimes they'd use Francis as the example instead."

"To have that kind of legend in the family sometimes means there's an undercurrent of genuine fear," Benson said.

"Fear that I might turn into one of my ancestors? Is that what you're saying?" Todd was on his feet, suddenly on the verge of panic. "Am I supposed to take my place?"

"David—" Father Gilbert was on his feet, too. He raised his hand, trying to anticipate what might happen.

"What kind of priests are you? Am I predestined to behave a certain way just because a couple of my ancestors did?"

"I wasn't suggesting anything," Benson said, also standing. "You make your own choices."

"Serve or die, that's what you're saying. I've heard it before."

"Sit down, David!" said Father Gilbert forcefully.

Todd sat down. He glowered at them.

The two priests sat down again. Father Gilbert stayed on the edge of the sofa, just in case. "That phrase – what does it mean to you?" he asked.

"I don't know. I think I dreamed it."

"You scribbled it on a piece of paper," Father Gilbert said.

"I did?"

"It was written on a sheet of paper, in your kitchen."

"It was?" Todd asked, and his expression went from annoyance to alarm. "I don't remember that."

"Those specific words. 'Serve or Die.'"

Todd's eyes widened. "I've told you: someone is forging my handwriting. I'm being set up."

Father Gilbert stood up again. "You should rest. I'll show you to the guest room."

* * *

"I wouldn't want to sleep in the same house with him," Father Benson said softly. He was making his way to the front door. "Has he gone crazy?"

"He's terribly conflicted," Father Gilbert said.

"Do you think he's told us everything?"

"He's told us everything he's able to tell. But, no, he hasn't told us everything."

Father Gilbert listened to the water rush through the plumbing. Todd was having a bath.

Benson opened the door, then lingered a moment. "I am sorry about the reports to the Bishop. I won't write any more."

"You must, if he asks for them," Father Gilbert said. Though he now knew he had to be more careful with anything he said to Father Benson.

He paced the house while David Todd was in the bath. Finally he settled in the front room, sitting in an armchair with a glass of Scotch and a novel about a priest on Malta trying to save lives during World War II. He didn't open the book. Instead, he thought about Colin Doyle, Lord Haysham, their ancestors, the past and the present, family legacies, and whether the sins of one generation could be carried on down the line like a kind of DNA. If so, then where was free will? Or was mankind living in a mixed reality of predetermination and choice, coexisting with an ongoing tension between them both?

He thought about Mary Aston and DS Sanders and the possibility that they had been in the Doyle mausoleum together. He imagined Sanders falling for her charms, taking a sledgehammer, and smashing through the grave marker for Richard Challoner's bones and the Woodrich sword. Sanders took the sword out and politely gave it to an astonished and grateful Mary. She looked it over with an expression of wild-eyed greed – and then suddenly thrust the point through Sanders.

Where is Mary? Father Gilbert wondered.

She stood over him now, wearing nothing but lingerie, the sword in her hand. "It's magnificent," she said.

Startled, Father Gilbert opened his eyes.

David Todd stood in front of him, wearing a dressing gown the priest had lent him. It was too big, making him look diminutive. "Are you all right?"

Father Gilbert sat up. The book had fallen to the floor. He must have been asleep. "Yes, why?"

"You cried out," Todd said.

"I'm sorry if I disturbed you," Father Gilbert said. Todd looked better for having had a bath. He seemed more relaxed.

"Do you often have bad dreams?"

"Lately, yes." But Father Gilbert wasn't about to mention the other strange experiences he'd been having.

"What's happening to us?" Todd asked.

Father Gilbert shook his head. He looked at his glass. It was empty. "There are times in our lives when all of our speculation about good and evil comes up against real good and real evil."

"This is one of those times?"

"It would seem so."

Todd shivered, and wrapped his arms around himself. "I don't think I'll survive. I'm going to wind up like Lord Haysham or Sanders."

"There is protection…"

Todd snorted. "The police are useless."

"I'm not talking about the police."

CHAPTER 32

In spite of his morning prayers and Bible meditations, Father Gilbert fell into a melancholy mood. He felt as if he was spinning in circles around something that should be obvious to him, something that was proving to be elusive.

The phone rang. It was DI Wilton.

"The Southaven Police have said you could give your statement about Sanders' murder to me," he said. "Bring Father Benson."

"When?"

"As soon as you can," he said. His voice was raspy, tired. "One question, though."

"Go ahead."

"Why are some of you called 'Father' and some are called 'Reverend'?" he asked. "I'm making a mess of my reports trying to keep it straight."

"Ministers with more Protestant leanings call themselves 'Reverend'. Those with an Anglo-Catholic sensibility go by 'Father'."

"So that means you're rather cosy with the Pope?" he asked.

"We haven't had dinner lately, if that's what you're asking."

"Just wondering." He hung up.

The phone instantly rang again.

"How is your cellmate?" Father Benson asked.

"Sleeping," Father Gilbert said, having checked on him before going downstairs.

"I wish I'd been able to," the curate said. "My mind kept jumping around between mysterious medallions, missing swords and rings, finding DS Sanders, and playing detective with you. Is it insensitive to say that it's all quite exhilarating?"

"There's an energy that comes with the effort," Father Gilbert said, remembering the buzz that came with investigating crimes. But he also knew the very high price for the exhilaration was the deaths of Colin Doyle, Clive Challoner, Lord Michael Haysham, and DS Steven Sanders.

After a moment, Benson asked, "Is that why you find it so hard to give it up?"

"I might be able to give it up if I weren't dragged into these situations," Father Gilbert said, trying not to sound irritated. "It's not as if I'm actively looking for these mysteries."

More silence. Father Gilbert could guess what Benson was thinking, but knew the conversation would only darken his mood.

Changing the subject, he said: "DI Wilton would like us to give our statements about what happened yesterday. I'll meet you there."

"I can pick you up."

Father Gilbert looked out of the window. A sun-bathed morning. "The walk will do me good."

* * *

Father Gilbert waited by the main door to the police station. He watched as Father Benson navigated his car through the crowded car park, found a spot at the opposite end, and half-jogged over.

"Are they having a sale?" he asked as he came close.

"Be warned," Father Gilbert said. "There is a palpable edge at police stations after a policeman has been killed." He'd seen it more than he wanted to remember. The staff became mournful, angry, and determined, wrapped up in camaraderie and bravado. Behind it, though, was the awareness of their own mortality – the sudden recognition that, at any time, the job could be a matter of life and death.

Father Gilbert pulled open the door. "They want to get the killer, no matter what it takes or who gets trampled along the way."

"Thanks for the warning."

An officer at the reception desk stopped them, asked for ID, then pushed a clipboard at them. "Sign in, please," he said. "They're tightening security."

Benson stepped forward and signed the sheet.

The phone rang. The officer turned away.

Father Gilbert picked up a second clipboard and quickly flipped through it. It was the sign-out sheet for the officers and detectives. He found what he was looking for and put the clipboard down again.

"It's *this* one," Benson said.

Father Gilbert nodded and signed in.

The officer led them into the main office. DS Sanders' desk was covered in a black cloth, like a flag on a coffin.

DI Wilton, his face set in a scowl, had them sit at his desk. "We'll find who did this," Wilton said.

Father Gilbert nodded, aware that Wilton and Sanders hadn't got along very well.

Wilton sat at his computer and served as the stenographer, hammering away at the computer keyboard while Father Gilbert explained the details of what happened at the Doyle mausoleum, why they were there, and what they found.

Father Benson's statement repeated the same details.

"Are you aware that Mary Aston was scheduled to meet with DS Sanders?" Father Gilbert asked.

Wilton stopped typing and turned to him. "She met with Sanders yesterday morning."

"You've spoken to her?" Father Gilbert asked.

"Not since Sanders' murder. But I was part of their meeting. We discussed Lord Haysham and where she was at the time he was murdered."

"London, she told me," Father Gilbert said.

He nodded. "And that's where she is right now. She left after our meeting. She's still chasing after that Woodrich Set."

"Have you checked her alibi for the time when Lord Haysham was murdered?" Father Gilbert asked.

A condescending smile. "Leave it to us, Father."

"To who?" Father Gilbert asked. "Is this your case or Southaven's?"

"We're working it together," he replied.

"What was in the crypt?" Benson asked.

"What crypt?"

"The one that had been smashed into at the Doyle mausoleum."

"A skeleton," said Wilton. He fixed his gaze on the screen.

"Whose?" Father Gilbert asked.

"There's no knowing unless we bother with the DNA," Wilton said. "We're not sure it's worth the effort."

"Did you see the skeleton yourself?" asked Father Gilbert.

"The photos were in the police report." More typing from Wilton.

Father Gilbert was getting tired of feeling brushed off. "Was there anything *unusual* about it?"

"It was the normal collection of bones, assembled in the standard way." He looked at Father Gilbert with a *What's your point?* expression.

"Did it have all of its teeth?"

The question threw Wilton. "Teeth?" He thought for a moment, then grimaced and worked the computer. He pulled up the photos from Southaven's SOCO report.

Father Gilbert positioned himself to see the screen. Images flashed past of the mausoleum, his shoes, various shots of DS Sanders, and the crypt.

Wilton stopped on an image of the skull. He pointed. "It's missing a front tooth."

"Richard Challoner," Benson said to Father Gilbert.

Wilton looked blank.

"The skeleton found in the cellar of St Mark's in 1938," Father Gilbert explained.

"What about the sword?" Benson asked.

He shook his head. "No sword. Though we're assuming that, if a sword was used to murder Sanders, it was taken by the killer."

"Can you go back a few photos?" Father Gilbert asked. He'd seen something, but wasn't sure if he saw it correctly.

"Technically, you're not supposed to see these photos," Wilton said.

"Can we please dispense with the superiority routine?" Father Gilbert snapped. "There was something on the wall next to DS Sanders."

Wilton glared defiantly at Father Gilbert. Then he turned to the screen and, with exaggerated effort, used the mouse to reverse through the images.

"That one," Father Gilbert said.

Benson stood up to look, flinched, and sat down again so the photo was out of view.

It was a close-up of DS Sanders' face, from the neck up. He was still propped up against the wall of the mausoleum, as Father Gilbert had found him. Just over his right shoulder, scratched into the wall, was a pentagram.

Wilton was surprised. "I'm sure the Southaven detectives are aware of it."

"Is it old or new?" Father Gilbert asked.

Wilton switched the screen from the photo to the written reports. He scanned them, then said, "They found bits of concrete on Sanders' shoulder and sleeve."

"Someone knelt over his dead body to carve a pentagram in the wall?" Benson asked.

Chief Constable Macaulay came over to them. He had dark circles under his eyes. "Has DI Wilton told you the news?"

"What news?"

"I was just about to mention it," Wilton said. Father Gilbert didn't believe him.

The Chief Constable said, "The initial forensics report on the weapon that killed Sanders indicates it *wasn't* the same weapon that killed Haysham."

A different weapon. "What kind of weapon was it?"

"A sword, probably," Wilton said. "But not the same sword. There were traces of oxidation in Sanders' wound—"

"Suggesting that the weapon had rust on the blade," said Benson.

Father Gilbert sat up. "Oxidation would have formed on a sword being kept in a crypt. Whereas, if a new sword had killed Haysham…"

Wilton smiled. "We thought Todd was off the hook. He was still in here when DS Sanders was murdered. But now, it's still possible that he murdered Lord Haysham."

"Did you find any evidence in Todd's car?" Benson asked.

Macaulay leaned against the desk. "We didn't, because the car had been thoroughly cleaned. There weren't *any* fingerprints. Which, of course, raises more suspicions. Who would do a thing like that unless there was something to hide?"

Wilton turned to face the two priests. "Have either of you seen Todd since he was released?"

"We've talked," Father Gilbert said.

"Does he still believe someone's out to kill him?" Wilton asked.

"He's worried."

Macaulay asked, "And you believe him?"

A very good question. Did he? "I believe he's in some kind of danger."

Wilton slowly shook his head, then brightened up as if he'd just had a cheery thought. "Ironically, his being out and about could help us solve this case."

"What do you mean?" Benson asked.

"If he's telling the truth and *isn't* the killer, then he might draw the killer out."

Father Gilbert frowned. "You want to use him as bait?"

"We're not using him," Macaulay said. "It's a possible outcome."

"He said he wanted to stay in here," Benson said. He looked aghast.

Wilton spread his hands in concession. "His solicitor posted bail. What are we supposed to do? Besides, we're a police station, not a hotel."

"That's cruel," Father Gilbert said. He might have thought the same thing when he was a detective, but found it terribly cynical now.

"Now, now," Macaulay said and turned to Wilton. "Of course, Father Gilbert is right. We shouldn't say it, even as a joke."

"Right, Chief Constable," Wilton said with feigned contrition.

Father Gilbert noted the wink exchanged between the two men.

* * *

At ten o'clock, Father Gilbert sat down at his desk at the church. He had a homily to write, but his mind returned to all the scattered pieces of information around him. Rust on the weapon that had killed Sanders supported his suspicion that Sanders had found the Woodrich sword. Whoever was there used it to kill him. However, if a sword had been used to murder Haysham, it wasn't part of the Set. Maybe the killer used it to *suggest* a connection to the Woodrich sword. Otherwise, why else would the murderer use a sword at all? Was it a makeshift attempt to fulfil a ritual? *Or* it was still possible that two different swords meant there were two different murderers.

Agitated, he lightly thumped the side of his fist against the top of the desk. It seemed like the pieces were close to fitting together, but they were still slightly misshapen.

Father Benson stepped into the office. "Just when I thought I'd have a normal day doing normal Church of England things."

"What's wrong?"

"Adrian Scott called. He's found something and wants us to come over right away."

* * *

"I've been up all night with that trunk you had sent over from the Haysham estate," Scott said when he opened the rear door. The bookshop itself was still closed to the public.

He turned without inviting them in, moving back into the recesses of his home and warehouse. "Following on from your visit yesterday, I focused my search on the areas we discussed," he was saying as he went.

"Did you find anything interesting?" Father Gilbert asked.

Further inside, Scott moved about excitedly, pacing and waving his arms. "I should say so! There was a reference in some of the letters to the 'Woodrich Society', mentioned just once, then thereafter coded as the 'Body'. Not only in Haysham's correspondence, but in his private diaries – which are illegible and, for the most part, incomprehensible."

"Samuel Haysham's diaries, you mean," Benson said.

"Yes, of course," Scott said as if he hadn't expected an interruption so soon. "*Anyway*, that was a key to unlocking many doors. Not only in these documents, but the documents I already had. I'd often wondered what the 'Body' was referring to – I thought it might be the church, you know, since it is called that in the New Testament. But it wasn't the church. Far from it."

"Mr Scott, you're rambling," Father Gilbert said.

"Oh, right. I do that." He chuckled. "It looks as if Samuel Haysham started the Woodrich Society, or the Body, here after he returned from the American war. I told you how he had fallen ill – and I hope to learn more about that as I go through the rest of the documents – but here's one of the surprises. Are you ready?"

It looked as though he intended to wait until they said the magic word, so Father Gilbert obliged him: "Ready."

"Haysham met a member of the Woodrich family while he was in America."

Scott waited, apparently hoping for a big reaction.

Father Gilbert lifted an eyebrow. Father Benson offered a not-very-convincing gasp.

"Amazing, isn't it? After our conversation yesterday, I had to wonder why the Woodrich medallion, sword, and ring would have any importance to Samuel Haysham. Now I see the connection. Haysham learned of the importance of the Set directly from a Woodrich."

"But the Bishop at the time was a cousin of Haysham. Wouldn't he already know of its value?" asked Benson.

Scott wagged a finger at him. "I didn't say *value*, I said *importance*. The importance of the Woodrich Set wasn't in the money, but in its power."

"What kind of power?" asked Father Gilbert.

"That's the thing, isn't it? The Set has *special* power. Magic, enchantment, witchcraft – call it what you will."

"They're *cursed*, you mean." Benson shot a look at Father Gilbert.

"A curse for some, but power for the ones who know how to use the Set properly." Scott was in his element, pacing and lecturing.

Father Gilbert found an empty chair and sat down. His mind was whirling.

"You don't really believe this, do you?" Benson asked.

"Does it matter what I believe?" Scott challenged him. "It was enough that Haysham believed it, perhaps as a result of his illness. So he called together a group of like-minded men who also believed it."

Father Gilbert raised his hand like a student in a class. "Todd and Doyle."

"Yes!" Scott exclaimed. "Plus a few other unknowns from the time."

"But what was this Society or Body hoping to accomplish?" Benson asked.

Scott was beaming. "Exactly what you'd expect. They wanted to become wildly powerful, restore their ailing fortunes, cure wig dandruff – how am I supposed to know for certain?"

"I don't suppose they published a set of corporate goals," said Father Gilbert.

Benson laughed.

Scott didn't. "Actually, they might have."

One of the cats nudged up against Father Gilbert's leg. He scratched its head. "What do you mean?"

"There are references to a single document – a Chronicle – which I take to be some sort of history of their Society and its members, even the spells and incantations they used, maybe their rites for a black mass." Scott nudged the Haysham trunk with his foot. "It wasn't in here. And I haven't found any clues to where it is. Presumably one of the members had it for safekeeping."

"Or it's been lost, like everything else," Benson said.

Father Gilbert thought of the book mentioned in the ecclesiastical minutes – and the missing item from the archive's inventory.

Scott's pacing was infectious. Benson was now doing the same. "Though, the medallion has been found," he said. "And, for all we know, the sword was recovered from the Doyle crypt."

"Leaving the ring?" Scott asked.

"Which may already be in someone's possession," Father Gilbert said. "Mary Aston hasn't mentioned the ring much. She's been searching for the sword. Maybe that's because she knows where it is."

Scott stood between the two priests, looking aghast from one to the other. "Are you saying there's a chance the sword, medallion, and ring are together again? The Woodrich Set is complete for the first time in over 200 years?"

"Possibly," said Father Gilbert.

Scott shoved his hands into his pockets, which was no small feat, considering the belly that covered them. "It's like the fulfilment of a prophecy."

"I wouldn't go *that* far." Benson looked exasperated.

"Why not?" Scott asked.

"What are you saying? That bringing together a medallion, sword, and ring will change civilization as we know it? We're living out a Tolkien fantasy?" He gestured to Father Gilbert as if he should intercede somehow.

Father Gilbert wished Scott would offer them a cup of tea, that great panacea for conflict and confusion. "I believe that items can be blessed and used in sacred ways. Those blessings can include supernatural power. Evil mimics that power. That's why baptismal fonts had locked covers over them, and Catholic churches locked up the consecrated bread and wine. They were often stolen by Satanists who wanted to desecrate the elements in their black masses and even use the power within them."

"*If* things have God's power somehow, why would God allow them to be used that way?" Benson asked.

"Why would God stop them?" Father Gilbert countered. "If consecrated bread and wine are mystically the body and blood of Christ, do we assume they suddenly aren't the body and blood if placed in unworthy hands?"

Benson frowned, as if he wanted to answer but wasn't sure how.

Father Gilbert pressed on, "What if supernatural power is constant, like electricity or gravity? Think of the story in the Old Testament when the two men were struck dead for reaching out to keep the Ark of the Covenant from falling over. King David was furious with God. But David was messing with a power he didn't understand – a power that was put into place by God, but not one that could be turned off and on like a light switch."

Benson folded his arms. His expression betrayed his scepticism. "Then you believe the Woodrich Set has power."

"It *might* have power," Father Gilbert said.

"I don't care about the theological arguments," Scott said. "But the Woodrich Set can trigger bizarre behaviour in those who *do* believe in its power. You must keep a close eye on David Todd. If his family have been part of this Woodrich Society in the past, maybe someone is trying to pressure him into joining now."

"That's it. 'Take your place. Serve or die.'" Benson paced again.

"Perhaps Colin Doyle and Lord Haysham refused, which is why they're dead now," Father Gilbert said.

"But who is 'they'? Who is behind this?" Benson asked, his voice on edge. "Can we get out of the realm of superstition and back to some concrete facts?"

Scott tossed his hands up. "I'm doing the best I can! I need a *month* with this trunk, not a few hours."

"Keep digging," Father Gilbert said as he stood up. "Father Benson will help you."

"I will?" Benson asked. "What about your 'house guest'?"

"I'll keep an eye on him," Father Gilbert said. "Just to make sure some demon doesn't claim him."

This caught Scott's attention. "Is that a possibility? What kind of house guest do you have?"

"The troubled kind." Father Gilbert walked to the door.

CHAPTER 33

D avid Todd was sitting on the sofa staring at a mind-numbing daytime television talk show when Father Gilbert walked into the vicarage. Todd was still in the borrowed dressing gown. He hadn't shaved. He looked up at Father Gilbert with the red-rimmed eyes of a man who'd been oppressed by wrecked expectations.

"I don't want to stay here," he announced. "I want to go so you can get on with your business."

"Right now you are my business." Father Gilbert picked up the remote from the table and turned off the television. "Tell me about the Woodrich Society."

A sharp look. "I've never heard of it."

"For an estate agent, you're not much of a liar," said Father Gilbert. He sat down in the easy chair next to Todd.

Todd shrugged. "I'm exhausted, otherwise I'd be lying with the best of them. And, frankly, I'm sick of anything to do with the name 'Woodrich'."

"How about a 'Chronicle'?"

"What is it, a newspaper?"

"It's a written record of the Woodrich Society. Maybe it's buried in your family papers."

"It doesn't mean anything to me, but you're welcome to look." He stood up with great effort. "Come back to my house while I pack a few things."

Father Gilbert was suspicious – and must have looked it, because Todd narrowed his eyes. "I won't do a runner. We'll go into the house, get what we need, and leave again. I'm not interested in staying there any longer than is necessary. And I'm certainly not keen to be seen in public right now."

"We'll have to take a taxi."

A grin from Todd. "You still don't have a car?"

"It's in the—"

"Garage. Yeah. The whole town knows."

* * *

Todd used a code to open the garage door. Father Gilbert noticed that the red Peugeot was in the second bay, but the white car was gone.

"Where's your other car?" Father Gilbert asked.

"It must be at the police station," Todd said.

"The police let you drive to the station when they arrested you?"

"No," he said. "I had the mechanic from the garage pick it up for servicing. They do that all the time. You're not the only one with car troubles."

Father Gilbert knew he was lying, but decided not to press the issue.

They entered through the kitchen. It didn't look as if anything had changed since Father Gilbert had last been there.

"I'll run up to the attic. That's where I keep our family keepsakes." Todd started through the sitting room and stopped. He swore loudly.

"Something wrong?" Father Gilbert asked.

Todd was looking at the wall with the framed photos. Father Gilbert stepped into the room. The photos were now hanging up, but some were hanging upside down, some of the glass in the frames had spiderweb fractures, as if they'd been shot, and others were missing the photos they were supposed to contain. He glanced down at the floor and saw anthill-sized piles, with the tiniest bits of paper meticulously torn up.

More expletives from Todd. "Wilton and his gang of thugs," he said.

"I don't think so." Father Gilbert knelt to look at the piles. The edges of the remains of the photos were ragged. They hadn't been cut up with scissors. But he couldn't imagine how a pair of hands had torn them into such small pieces. "Does anyone else have a key to the house?"

"No," said Todd. He had gone pale, making the red in his eyes that much brighter.

"Why would anyone vandalize your family photos?"

With a shake of his head, Todd moved for the stairs. "A cup of tea wouldn't go amiss," he shouted over his shoulder.

Father Gilbert looked at the photos to see if any pattern emerged in how they were arranged or defaced. Nothing came to mind.

He heard footsteps in the kitchen, then the scrape of a chair on the floor.

"Hello?" he said as he walked in. The kitchen was bright and warm from the noonday light. No one was there. A single chair had been pulled away from the table.

There was something oppressive about the house. Father Gilbert felt it hang on him, like air saturated with a foul clamminess. More than that was the *presence*: a feeling of someone or something sneering at him from deep inside the upper-middle-class veneer.

As he put on the kettle, he looked out the window to the garden and woods beyond. A tyre-swing hung by a rope from a tall tree branch. It moved back and forth. But there was no hint of a breeze at all.

Father Gilbert froze. Just beyond the swing, a man in a long, dark coat stood among the trees. He was facing the priest, but the details of the face were shadowed. The arm lifted up, a black hand – maybe gloved – pointed at him.

A pane in the window cracked. A lightbulb just above his head exploded. Father Gilbert flinched and jumped to one side. The water in the kettle boiled over like a witch's cauldron. Pots and pans, hanging by hooks on a metal square above the counter, swayed and shook, banging one another. Then they stopped as if suddenly held still by an unseen hand.

Father Gilbert looked through the window. The man was gone.

He reached for the power switch on the wall and the water from the kettle splashed on his hand. The water was still cold. He flipped the switch. The kettle calmed down.

He stood for a moment, trying to think through what had just happened. He knew of these kinds of paranormal manifestations first-hand. Why here? Now he wondered about David Todd.

He went to the front hall. "David?" he called out.

No response.

He could feel fragments of lightbulb in his hair. He saw the door to a small bathroom and went in. The mirror above the basin was tilted to one side. The shards of the lightbulb peppered his hair and had alighted on his shoulders like dandruff. Using a hand towel, he carefully dusted himself off, trying to get the pieces into the rubbish bin.

A loud thump sounded above him. He went back to the hall and went to the foot of the stairs. "David! Are you all right?"

Again, no answer.

He crept up the stairs. They were covered in thick grey carpeting, padding his steps. He came to a landing and the staircase doubled back upwards. At the top, a hallway stretched in two directions. A door creaked down on the left. He listened, his muscles tight, ready. This was the moment in the movies when a cat suddenly leapt out from nowhere for no reason other than to scare the audience to death.

The creaking door was half open. As he reached for the handle, the door slammed in his face. From the other side of the door came the sound of something scraping along the wood. He grabbed the knob and pushed the door open. The room – a guest room with bed, dresser, and wardrobe – was empty. A window on the far wall was open.

"The wind," Father Gilbert said to himself, though he felt no air moving and couldn't account for the scraping noise.

Back in the hall, he listened again. He heard a skittering sound, like mice in the walls. The hair stood up on the back of his neck. He was sure he heard whispering.

"David?" he called out. His heart was pounding now. He felt silly being afraid.

The doors to three other rooms stood open, each one vacant and undisturbed. He made his way in the other direction, passing the stairs. He saw a closed door at the end of the hall and headed for it. Suddenly David Todd stepped in front of him, carrying a cardboard file box.

Both men cried out.

"You scared me," said Todd.

"Where did you come from?" Father Gilbert asked.

He tipped his head behind him. There was another staircase leading up. It had been a few inches out of Father Gilbert's field of vision.

"Were you talking to someone?" asked the priest.

"No. Why?"

"I thought I heard whispering."

Todd looked at him without surprise. "Just wind in the rafters," he said.

"What was that loud thump?"

Todd chuckled nervously. "I knocked over an old wardrobe. I was trying to see if anything was behind it. Then I heard you call." He looked at Father Gilbert's head. "What's in your hair?"

"Bits of lightbulb," he said. "You may want to check your electrics."

"Are you all right?"

"Shaken, that's all."

Todd offered the box to Father Gilbert. "If you'll take this downstairs, I'll grab the second one. Then we'll get out of here." He swung around and ascended the attic steps.

Father Gilbert carried the box down the stairs and had reached the landing when he heard a noise at the front door. He froze where he was and watched. A silhouette moved in the glass. Then the mail slot opened and a single piece of paper was pushed through. Then the silhouette disappeared.

He put the box down on the landing and leapt down the bottom flight of stairs.

The paper lay on the mat, the writing facing up.

Take your place, it said.

* * *

"David! Call the police!" Father Gilbert shouted up the stairs and yanked the front door open. No one was in sight. He raced out to the pavement and looked around. The sun hit his eyes. He shielded them and caught something in his peripheral vision. He snapped his head to the left in time to see a figure disappear around the side of the house. Instinctively he gave chase, slowing at the front corner of the house to make sure the culprit wouldn't surprise him. He peeked around. He saw bushes, an outstretched garden hose, the expanse of lawn, and nothing more. He ran into the back garden, giving the rear corner a wide berth. The back garden was empty. But the tyre was swinging back and forth on the rope.

He ran to the edge of the woods and a sudden realization made him stop at the swinging tyre. The mysterious stranger could be hiding behind any one of those trees, ready to run him through with the Woodrich sword.

He wasn't prepared to risk his life to identify the writer of that note.

Circling the house on the opposite side from which he'd come, he slowly turned, bracing himself for an attack. He passed the garage. The doors were closed, but there were enough windows for him to believe he was being watched. And laughed at.

He came to a side door. It was locked. He continued around the house to the front door, which was still open. He stepped in and looked down for the note. It was gone.

"David?" he shouted. Dead silence. Then he heard banging in the kitchen. He raced in. All of the cupboard doors had been thrown open.

Calling out for Todd again, he crept up the stairs and passed the file box sitting on the landing where Todd had put it down. He continued on. The upstairs hall was perfectly quiet. A cardboard file box sat at the bottom of the attic stairs, the lid hanging off at an angle as if it had been dropped.

"David!" he called up the stairs. "This is a bad time for hide and seek!"

A feeling of dread came over him. Then he heard a loud scraping sound from the attic. He made his way up the stairs, his nerves jumping at the creak of every floorboard. The door to the attic was open an inch. He pushed it open with his foot.

The attic was an unfinished loft conversion – as if Todd had started to turn the bare attic into a living space, but changed his mind. It was cluttered with boxes, junk, and old toys. Dust floated in the shaft of sunlight coming through the single skylight.

A wardrobe lay prone on the floor. It was huge – tall and wide – big enough to put a body in. Father Gilbert frowned and stepped over to it lightly. The mirrored door faced up. He took hold of the handle and pulled up, swinging the door over. The wardrobe was empty.

He ran his fingers through his hair, dislodging more lightbulb powder.

Is this what Todd had knocked over?

"David!" Father Gilbert shouted again.

A few feet from the top of the fallen wardrobe, a small wooden box sat between an old briefcase, a hat box, and three ornate keepsake boxes. The small box was plain and square. The wood was scratched up.

Father Gilbert wasn't sure why it had caught his eye, with so much clutter around. Somehow it looked as if it had been dropped, while everything around it seemed purposefully placed. He knelt down and looked at the top of the wardrobe. A panel in the woodwork had come open, presumably from the wardrobe being knocked over. The small wooden box would have fitted perfectly inside the panel.

Picking up the box, Father Gilbert stood up and took a closer look. A brass clasp held it closed. He had to fiddle with it to get it free. Then he lifted the lid. Inside, encased in felt, was a gold ring with a ruby in the centre.

Father Gilbert thought of the style of the medallion – and instantly knew he'd found the Woodrich ring. It had been hidden in the wardrobe.

He was about to call out for Todd again when he heard a low wolf-like growl behind him, pure animal and vicious. He spun around to look, just in time to see something large swinging towards his head. He threw his left arm up to deflect it, catching the brunt of its weight, but the force was enough to drive him to the right. He lost balance and fell into the collection of clutter. His head slammed against something. A bright supernova consumed his vision. Pain blasted through his head, swallowing the light and enveloping him in a numbing darkness.

Chapter 34

"Father Gilbert?"

A very blurry Father Benson was kneeling over him.

His head felt like someone had been tap-dancing on it.

"Help me sit up," he said. He lifted his left arm and a pain shot through his forearm. He withdrew it and offered his right arm instead.

With careful effort, Benson helped Father Gilbert into a sitting position.

He leaned back against the fallen wardrobe and gingerly touched his head. A knot, the size of a small knuckle, had grown there. "How long was I out?"

"I don't know. I got here only a few minutes ago."

He turned his head and felt a dull ache in his neck – probably a kind of whiplash from whatever he'd hit his head on. He looked to his right. A side table with a broken leg was toppled over nearby. "What happened?" Benson asked.

Father Gilbert shook his head. "I was hit with something heavy."

"By that, I assume." Benson pointed to a light-blue bowling bag sitting off to the side. "It's got a ten-pound bowling ball in it."

"That sounds about right. I put my arm up. Got knocked over. I must've hit my head on that table on the way down."

"Lucky for you the bowling ball was wrapped up."

"I wish the table had been, too." He touched his forearm, which was surely bruised. Then he felt the knock again. "Any blood?"

"No. But I'll take you to A&E. A blow hard enough to knock you down could cause all kinds of trouble."

"I'm all right," he said.

"Was it David Todd?"

"I don't know. I didn't see him. Though whoever did it gave an uncanny impersonation of a wolf's snarl before hitting me."

"Wolf?" Benson said. "We're dealing with werewolves now?"

Father Gilbert smiled. Benson looked serious.

Father Gilbert looked around him. "Do you see a small wooden box anywhere?"

Benson stepped back to look. "How small?"

"Jewellery-sized."

"In this mess? What's it have in it – silver bullets?"

"The Woodrich ring."

Benson's eyebrows shot up. "You saw it? Here?"

Father Gilbert nodded – and regretted moving his head at all.

"Is that why David Todd came back to the house?" Benson asked.

Father Gilbert tried a slight shrug. "Maybe. But why invite me along?"

Benson wrapped his arms around himself. "Maybe he's afraid of being here alone. There's something about this place…"

The priest struggled to his feet. He swayed with dizziness and grabbed a tall floor lamp to steady himself. The pain radiated from the side of his head to the back of his eyes. He blinked a few times, then searched around him for the ring.

Benson joined in the search.

Father Gilbert knew it was futile. The ring wasn't there. Whoever, or whatever, had hit him would have taken it.

He now wondered if it was possible that Todd hadn't known the ring was hidden in the small compartment on top of the wardrobe. Had it become dislodged when David knocked the wardrobe over – and he hadn't seen it?

Perhaps Father Gilbert had interrupted Todd's search. Or someone else had. He still had no idea if Todd had hit him and escaped, or if someone else had and taken Todd with him, or…?

"Let's look around the rest of the house," Father Gilbert said.

* * *

Searching the house yielded very little. No one was there. The feeling of oppression, even the noises, had stopped.

"Are the cars in the garage?" Benson asked as he swept up the broken bits of lightbulb from the kitchen floor.

"The red one," Father Gilbert said, having checked again. "The white car wasn't here when we arrived."

"Where is it?" Benson asked.

"I don't know." He now wished he had pressed the question of the white car with Todd.

Having completed their search, the two priests went to the front door, where Father Benson had put the two file boxes from the landing and the upper floor. Father Gilbert was relieved his assailant had left them. He stood by the front door while Benson squeezed the boxes into the back of his Mini.

Father Gilbert took a deep breath. The day was pleasant – sunshine, fresh spring air, and birds calling to one another from the trees. All the same, he couldn't get rid of a sense of impending darkness. Or his headache.

Benson was walking back across the front lawn when he suddenly looked up. "There's someone up there."

He bolted past Father Gilbert into the house and up the stairs.

Father Gilbert followed, faltering on the landing as a wave of nausea hit him. He waited there as Benson went from room to room, searching for whoever it was he'd seen.

"I know you're here!" Benson shouted.

Eventually he reappeared at the top of the stairs. He was winded. "I *know* I saw someone."

"What did he look like?"

"Long black coat. A fedora-type hat, I think. Black gloves."

"Did you see his face?"

He shook his head. "It was in a shadow."

Father Gilbert told him he'd seen the same figure in the woods behind the house. "I don't think it was a human."

Benson went pale. "We're leaving this house now," he said.

* * *

"Did Todd run away – or was he kidnapped?" Benson asked Father Gilbert as they drove back to Adrian Scott's bookshop.

"Kidnapped? You saw for yourself. There was no evidence of him being taken by force. A man in Todd's emotional condition would have fought. I'd have heard it."

"Could he have been nabbed when you ran outside?"

"I wasn't gone long enough for someone to knock Todd out and carry him down the stairs. And even if he'd been carried that far, how did they escape? There was no sound of a car."

"He could have been dragged behind a neighbour's house."

"Those houses are fifty yards away, maybe more. The obvious conclusion is that he hit me, took the ring, and ran off." Father Gilbert rubbed his eyes. The pain was receding. "Or…"

"Or?"

"He was under some kind of demonic influence."

"We should tell the police."

"We should," said Father Gilbert. "And do we tell them about the shadow-man?"

Benson pressed his lips together and didn't answer.

Father Gilbert's mobile phone rang. He fumbled retrieving it from his pocket and, with more fumbling, pushed the button. "This is Father Gilbert," he said.

"Gilbert? Macaulay here."

"Yes, Chief Constable?"

"Have you any idea where Mary Aston is?"

"I haven't spoken to her today. Why?"

"We got a partial of one of her fingerprints from a marble marker in the Doyle mausoleum." The Chief Constable sounded annoyed. "It was just above the crypt that had been broken into."

"So Mary was there with Sanders." He glanced at Benson. Benson shook his head, disappointed.

"What about David Todd?" Macaulay asked. "Have you seen him?"

Father Gilbert touched the knot on his head. "Funny you should ask."

CHAPTER 35

The two priests carried the file boxes up to Adrian Scott's flat.

Father Gilbert's mood had soured on the drive over, in spite of a stop at the chemist's for painkillers.

Macaulay believed the entire trip to Todd's house had been a set-up. Todd and an accomplice staged the whole thing. Why? To confuse, maybe to give credence to Todd's assertions that he was being stalked – or for the malicious fun of it. He was surprised that Father Gilbert had been duped so easily.

"Why did you let him stay at your house?" Macaulay asked by way of accusation.

"Compassion," Father Gilbert replied. "He's part of my flock."

Father Gilbert could imagine Macaulay shaking his head in pure disapproval.

"What about the mystery man?"

"How should I know?" Macaulay asked. "Probably an accomplice we haven't met yet. Or maybe he didn't exist at all."

"The over-workings of an overactive spiritual imagination?" Father Gilbert asked.

"Your words, not mine." Macaulay hung up.

And then there was Mary. After Macaulay's phone call, Father Gilbert realized he had still harboured some hope that she hadn't been at the Doyles' mausoleum. But the fingerprint placed her there, meaning she had witnessed the murder of Sanders, or had committed it.

Adrian Scott was leaning over a long library table, nearly unseen in a corner. It had been covered with books earlier, Father Gilbert remembered. Now it was covered with Haysham's documents. The old trunk sat open and empty on the floor next to it.

"I hope you're having a better day than I am," Father Gilbert said with more than a tinge of self-pity. He dropped the file box next to the trunk. Benson did the same.

"David Todd gave you these boxes?" Scott said as he straightened up, putting his hands on his hips as if his back ached.

"I don't want to talk about it," Father Gilbert said. "We have them. That's enough for now. I need a bag of ice for my head."

Scott waved a hand towards the kitchen. "Ice is in the freezer. And the kettle's on. Help yourselves."

"I'll do the honours," Benson said.

Father Gilbert was grateful. He didn't fancy going near a kettle after his mad-appliance experience at Todd's. He scooted a cat off an easy chair, the fabric stained and threadbare, and sat down. He put his head back and closed his eyes.

"Macaulay has put the entire constabulary on the watch for Todd and Mary Aston," Benson said from the kitchen area.

"Why Mary Aston?" Scott asked.

Benson explained about the Doyle mausoleum.

Afterward, Scott asked, "Why do you suppose the police have Mary Aston's fingerprints in their database? Has she been in trouble with the law before?"

Father Gilbert kept still, but said, "Routine procedure for someone assisting the police. She'd have gone through a security check."

"So she had a clean record, or they wouldn't have hired her," Benson said.

"Right."

"That's a relief," Benson said. "At least we haven't been hanging out with a known serial killer."

"That you know of," Scott said.

Father Gilbert lifted his head and asked Scott, "Have you had better success than I have?"

"As a matter of fact, I have."

Father Benson walked in with a small towel and handed it to Father Gilbert. It was wrapped around cubes of ice. The priest nodded and pressed the towel against the knot on his head. A sharp pain shot through his eyes. He endured it.

"I'll explain when we're settled," Scott said.

Benson went back to the kitchen, then returned a moment later carrying a tray with three mugs of tea. He handed them around. Then he found another chair and made himself comfortable.

Father Gilbert sipped the tea. He leaned forward, slouching in a way his headmaster would never have allowed. He felt the weight of the day on his shoulders – but mostly on his head.

Scott took centre stage and held up a tattered leather messenger bag. The stitching around the edges had snapped in places. The laces to secure the flap were frayed. "This belonged to Samuel Haysham. It was stuffed with financial records and other transactions for the shipbuilding business – and sundry other enterprises."

"And?" Father Gilbert asked.

"There was a substantial yearly payout to Joshua Todd," Scott said. "More than enough to keep the Todds from poverty. It might explain how the two families maintained some semblance of a relationship, if not actual friendship."

Father Gilbert slowly shook his head. It was bewildering that the Todds harboured such hatred and animosity when it seemed as if the Hayshams had made an attempt to help them.

Scott patted the leather pouch. "Tucked away in the back of this collection was an envelope with a letter inside. It's several pages long."

Father Gilbert groaned. "I can't read it right now. You'll have to summarize."

Scott smiled. "Samuel Haysham's penmanship wasn't very good anyway." He picked up the letter from the table. "We don't know to whom it was written. But there are references in the letter that cause me to think it was a business acquaintance. Samuel was trying to recruit him."

"Into business?"

"Into the Woodrich Society."

"Proselytizing," Father Gilbert said.

"Very quietly," Scott said. "They must have had a meal together and, at some point later, this gentleman asked for more details about the group. This is Samuel's reply."

"If it was supposed to be a big secret, why would he write a letter about it?" Benson asked.

"Haysham addresses that in the opening paragraph. He was

bedridden due to a recurrence of what he called his 'American affliction'. He didn't want to delay his acquaintance's decision about joining the Society, so he drafted this explanation. To ensure its safety, he gave a servant verbal instructions about where to deliver the letter, to wait while it was read, and then to bring the letter back again. The last paragraph indicates that Haysham intended to destroy the letter once it came back. For some reason, he didn't. It wound up in this packet."

"Does it detail the Society?" Father Gilbert asked. He was sitting up straighter now.

"Samuel Haysham's account boils down to this," Scott said, taking on the tone of a lecturer. "He was a commissioned officer in the King's army and went to America to fight in the War of Independence. He had always been a sickly man and his time stationed in Massachusetts exacerbated the worst of his health. He was seriously ill with a fever and a Dr Josiah Woodrich arrived to treat him. After conventional medicines failed, Dr Woodrich transported Samuel to his home near Salem."

Father Gilbert opened his mouth to ask.

"Yes, *that* Salem," Scott said. "One night, Dr Woodrich brought in some companions who practised spells of witchcraft on Samuel. His fever was gone the next day. Samuel was astonished and wanted to know more about Dr Woodrich and his friends and their practices."

"Are the friends named?" Father Gilbert asked.

"No." Scott gulped some tea, cleared his throat, and said, "At this point in the letter, Samuel begins to rant a bit about power and glory, and one could easily get the impression that he suffered mental as well as physical illness."

Father Gilbert thought of the cases he'd encountered where the quest for power – especially supernatural power – often led to madness.

"Regardless of all the noble phrases he used, it's obvious that Samuel was drawn into Woodrich's secret group and learned a lot about black magic and black masses. He brought all that knowledge with him back to Stonebridge, with the determination to start a society here."

"But I thought the Woodrich family were faithful Catholics," Father Benson said.

"Obviously not all of them."

"How do the medallion, sword, and ring fit into it all?" asked Father Gilbert.

"Dr Woodrich claimed that the 'three treasures', as he called them, were powerful tools. When Samuel learned that his cousin, the Bishop, had possession of them, he was determined to get them somehow. I'm speculating that Samuel secured a position for Joshua Todd to do the work in the Bishop's house in order to negotiate a purchase – or steal the items."

Father Gilbert suspected the latter.

"You won't be happy with this," Scott said. "For a few years, the Woodrich Society centred their black masses and rites around the medallion, sword, and ring. At St Mark's."

Father Gilbert expected it, but was still distressed to hear it confirmed. "Was the vicar in on it?"

Scott shrugged. "I don't know that they could have met in the church without the vicar's cooperation. He was either a member of the Society or was given an incentive to look the other way while they met."

"I don't know much about black masses," Benson admitted. "Just how bad did they get?"

Father Gilbert looked into his mug. The tea was gone. The bottom was stained black from years of tea leaves. "If they were true black masses, then they must have been bad."

"Orgies of sex or violence or both," Scott said with the happiness of a man all too pleased with knowing the answer. "In the letter, Samuel gets fairly graphic about the sex. Willing and unwilling virgins, servants, the occasional animal. No doubt he thought it would entice his candidate more."

Benson shuddered. "How bad was the violence? Did they beat one another with whips – or what?"

"Their normal black mass included self-abuse, or abuse of one another. Whips, rods, cat-o'-nine-tails, that sort of thing. An exceptional black mass, usually during a full moon, included the spilling of blood from a victim. The victim was a sacrifice to please Satan's appetite for 'new' blood."

"Is it a full moon tonight?" Benson asked, with a worried look.

"So the blood came from non-members," Father Gilbert said. He thought of the accounts he'd read in the ecclesiastical report.

Scott nodded. "It was all a grotesque mockery of the Catholic Mass. It's commonly known that one of the reasons churches had to lock up the bread, wine, and even holy water was to keep them out of the hands of the Satanists."

"They want consecrated items for their black masses, to make them more powerful," Father Gilbert added.

"Even the participants were a distortion of Catholic roles in the liturgy," Scott said. "You had the equivalent of a bishop or priest as the main celebrants, along with acolytes and servers."

"They did all this at St Mark's – in *our* church?" Benson asked Father Gilbert.

Father Gilbert nodded sadly.

"Should I verbally resign now or give you written notice tomorrow?"

"Tomorrow," Father Gilbert said. "I'll give it to the Bishop with mine."

"There is one important role to consider," Scott said. "The Society had a rather typical structure for any society, with a chosen leader and a secretary and officers—"

"Tea and scones with the Ladies' Auxiliary at the Guildhall? Sub-committee meetings and budget reports?" Father Gilbert asked.

Benson laughed. Scott gave Father Gilbert an indulgent smile. "*This* Society had an enforcer. What Samuel called an 'Avenging Angel'."

"Galling that they used the word 'angel', isn't it?" Benson said.

"Satan was a fallen angel, you'll recall," Scott retorted.

"What did this enforcer do?" Father Gilbert asked.

"It was the job of the 'Avenging Angel' to make sure the laws and very existence of the Society were maintained by its members. On pain of death."

Serve or die, Father Gilbert thought.

"Samuel makes it perfectly clear to his candidate what he'd be committing to, so there'd be no misunderstandings later."

"Does this mean that no member could ever leave the Society?" asked Benson.

"Oh, it's worse than that," Scott said. "Not only were the members committed, but their families as well."

Benson was on his feet. "Their wives? Their *children*?"

"The members took a blood oath, committing not only themselves, but their *sons* and their *sons' sons* to the Society."

Father Gilbert felt as if a cold hand had been placed on his shoulder. He leaned back in the chair. It groaned at him. Everything he'd heard and seen over the past couple of days raced through his mind.

"So that's the curse. It's not the sword or the medallion or the ring. It's the *promise* to do whatever the Society wanted," Benson said. "Is that why Joshua Todd was murdered? Did he try to get out of the Society, and Samuel Haysham killed him for it?"

Scott flipped through the pages of the letter. "I don't think Samuel was the Avenging Angel. This letter indicates it was someone else."

"Maybe they had a rotation schedule," Father Gilbert said sourly.

Scott put the letter down on the table again. "Frankly, I think Samuel himself was intimidated by their Avenging Angel."

"Who was it?"

Scott shook his head. "He doesn't say."

"At least we have a possible framework for what's happening now." Father Gilbert wasn't comforted by the idea, but it was better than what he'd had – which was very little.

"But who are the players?" Benson asked. He was pacing. "David Todd claims to be scared out of his wits and Lord Haysham is dead. Colin Doyle may have killed himself to keep from joining in."

"There's always Jack Doyle," Scott said. "He's nasty enough to keep a Society like this going."

"He had a solid alibi for Haysham's death," Father Gilbert replied.

"Why did the police ask him for an alibi? Was he a suspect?" Scott asked.

"He had business dealings with Lord Haysham. And there was

the connection with his son working on Haysham's property *and* receiving money from David Todd." Father Gilbert looked at his curate and the bookshop owner. "Do we really think Jack Doyle would have pushed the Society on his son?"

"Loyalty over affection," Scott said.

"Jack Doyle may not have expected Colin to commit suicide rather than join the club," Benson offered. "Or maybe he blamed Todd for Colin's death. Maybe *he* was writing the threatening notes."

Possibilities ricocheted around Father Gilbert's mind. What if Colin Doyle wasn't hired by David Todd to spy on Haysham because of the development scheme, but to watch out for the medallion? Todd knew somehow that the medallion had been lost there two centuries ago.

Benson continued to pace, wringing his hands. "What about the Challoners? Was Clive's heart attack connected to the resurrection of the Society?"

"Clive had no male children," Father Gilbert said.

"Maybe they've modernized," Scott said glibly. "Feminism has come to the covens."

Father Gilbert felt frustrated. He believed the answers were there somewhere, perhaps right in front of them – maybe in the boxes from Todd.

Scott was also looking at the boxes. They seemed to be thinking the same thing. He nodded at Father Gilbert and took the lids off the two boxes.

"What about that 'Chronicle' or whatever that document was called?" Benson asked.

"It's not in Haysham's belongings," Scott said. He began to rifle through Todd's file boxes. "It could be in here. But I would imagine a book of that nature being rather large. I'm not seeing any books or ledgers…"

Father Gilbert shoved to the edge of his seat. "The Chronicle was the book that went missing from the diocesan library. It was the piece of evidence that led the ecclesiastical court to its decision."

"And so it would, if it was a detailed report of the Society's activities," Scott said.

"It was signed out by Albert Challoner in 1938." Father Gilbert looked at Scott. "Was he part of the Society?"

"I don't know," Scott replied. "The Challoners once worked for Samuel Haysham – and had connections to that family, along with the Doyles, off and on for years. He might have participated in the Society. Though he wasn't a wealthy man. Certainly not in their class."

Father Gilbert frowned. How could they find out? Clive Challoner was dead and his daughter seemed oblivious. "Whether he was or he wasn't, Albert Challoner was the last to have that book. It could be somewhere in Clive Challoner's house, and Lynn Challoner would never know it."

* * *

Father Gilbert got Lynn Challoner's phone number from Mrs Mayhew. He reached her on her mobile phone and asked her to meet them at her father's house. She was puzzled, but agreed. They arrived within half an hour.

As they walked to the door, Benson asked, "If she doesn't know anything about the book, what do we do? We can't ask to ransack the house, can we?"

"We can try," Father Gilbert said. He smiled at Benson.

Lynn Challoner opened the door before they had a chance to knock. After a friendly exchange, Father Gilbert explained what they needed.

"A book? You mean, like a ledger of some sort?" she asked.

"A book, a packet of papers… we're not sure. Anything to do with something called the Woodrich Society."

"The Woodrich Society?" She looked surprised. "A detective came just an hour ago and asked about that."

"What detective?"

"Walters."

"Wilton?"

"That's it. I was concerned about having the police asking to look through my father's things. My father was a good man, law-abiding, straight as an arrow. But Detective Wilton assured me that he didn't believe my father had done anything wrong, but that the material might help with another case."

"Were you able to help him?"

"That's the remarkable thing. Yesterday I was looking through a cupboard that had china and cutlery in it. Under a stack of linens I found a box – the size of a big photo album. It had 'Woodrich' written on it. It was filled with old papers. I didn't pay much attention to it. Just one of those things I thought I'd look at later."

"Do you have it now?"

She shook her head. "I gave it to Detective Wilton."

"He's nothing if not thorough," Father Gilbert said and shot a look at Father Benson.

"Trustworthy, I hope. Especially since we're cousins," she said.

"How are you cousins?" Father Gilbert asked.

"I could never explain it. You'd have to ask him. But I'm supposed to meet up with his great-aunt. She's something of a family historian, I've heard."

"Margaret Clarke," Father Gilbert said. "We know her."

* * *

Margaret Clarke wasn't at home. And attempts to reach DI Alex Wilton went nowhere. Father Gilbert tried to figure out why Wilton was interested in the Woodrich book, or how he knew where to find it. A family connection to the Challoners was a surprise – and worrisome. Margaret Clarke hadn't told them everything at their little tea together, just as Mary Aston suspected.

With little else to do, they decided to return to Scott's. Later they would try to corner Wilton to find out how and when he got onto the historical side of this case.

Father Gilbert's mobile phone rang and he snatched it up, thinking it might be Wilton. Instead, Mrs Mayhew's voice was in his ear.

"I assume the two of you have forgotten your priestly duties," she was saying.

"What have we forgotten?" Father Gilbert asked.

"The hospital visitations," she said, then prompted with: "Joe Mumford?"

Father Gilbert frowned. "Joe Mumford," he said out loud for Father Benson's sake. Joe Mumford, ten years old, stage-four cancer.

"I'll go," Benson said. He looked anguished. "I saw him at church last Sunday and promised I'd come by. We both have an interest in online games."

Small drops of rain hit the windscreen. Dark clouds were rolling in from the south. Whatever was coming looked ominous.

"I'll drop you at Scott's," Benson said.

"Father Benson will take care of it," Father Gilbert said to Mrs Mayhew.

"I do hope you'll stop with playing detectives and think about the church again," she said sharply.

Father Gilbert didn't know how to tell her that he *was* thinking about the church. But if she knew what he was thinking, she might resign. He thanked her and ended the call.

"It was a dark and stormy night," Benson said. "Cue the thunder. Cue the shot of the full moon pushing through the clouds."

Father Gilbert nodded. Christopher Lee and Peter Cushing might show up after all.

CHAPTER 36

Father Gilbert was dropped off behind Scott's bookshop. The rain was cold. Getting in and out of the Mini seemed more arduous than usual combined with a headache.

As the Mini pulled away, Father Gilbert was about to climb the stairs when he was framed in the beams of white headlights. A white car in the car park faced him. The beams flashed. He thought it was David Todd's. Retreating under Scott's balcony to keep from getting soaked, he looked to see who was trying to get his attention. The windscreen was covered by the falling rain. He couldn't make out who was inside.

The car moved out of its space and pulled up alongside him. The driver's window slid down. Mary Aston beckoned him. "Get in! Please!"

Father Gilbert moved towards her. "What are you doing? The police are looking for you."

"I know, I know! Get in!"

The urgency in her voice and the panic on her face were so unlike anything he'd heard or seen from her before that he went to the passenger side to get in. He hadn't fully closed the door when she pulled away, the tyres screeching against the wet tarmac.

"If you're trying to keep a low profile, you're doing a pretty poor job," Father Gilbert said.

Her hair was pulled back, highlighting her face. She looked drawn. Her lips were pressed into a straight line. Her eyes had lost their luminosity.

"Is this David Todd's car?"

"He lent it to me." She fumbled with a lever until the windscreen wipers came on. At the High Street, she turned right – heading away from the town.

"When did he lend it to you?"

"I don't remember. The other day." She shook her head impatiently. "I didn't like the hire car the police gave me."

"Where are we going?" Father Gilbert asked.

"Stop asking so many questions!" she shouted. "I'm scared. I've been hiding ever since Sanders was murdered."

"The police found your fingerprints at the mausoleum."

She swore indelicately. Her hands kneaded the steering wheel like a lump of dough.

"If you turn left up ahead, we can double-back to the police station," Father Gilbert said.

"It's not what you think."

"What do I think? You said you were going to meet with DS Sanders and you did."

"I met him at the police station to talk about Lord Haysham. DI Wilton was there."

"Then how did you get from the police station to the mausoleum?"

"Sanders walked me to my car. He said he had his own suspicions about where the sword might be, but wanted to check further."

"He said this when DI Wilton wasn't around?"

"He didn't trust Wilton," she said, then took another turn a little too fast. Father Gilbert put his hand on the dashboard to brace himself. Another driver slammed on his car horn.

"You don't have to drive so fast," he said. "Especially since you don't know where you're going."

"Do you want to drive?" she demanded.

"Finish your story," he said and kept his eyes on her. If he watched the road, he would succumb to an anxiety attack.

"Sanders phoned me later," she said.

"For a date?"

She ignored him. "He'd been looking at the police records from 1938. Mrs Mayhew from the church called to ask about the skeleton from the church cellar. That led us to the Doyle mausoleum."

"Why 'us'? What made you two such fast friends?"

She shrugged. "He fancied me."

"Who doesn't?"

"*You* don't."

"Is flirting a defence mechanism or a contrivance?"

"It's a survival technique."

"Okay, so you charmed your way into Sanders' confidences and he phoned you about the Doyle mausoleum."

"I met him there."

"This car wasn't in the car park. Reverend Singh didn't mention you."

"I parked along the road on the other end of the graveyard. There's a gate there. It was unlocked. No one saw me enter."

"Why did you park there?"

"Instinct. I wasn't sure about being seen there with him. That may have saved my life."

"Go on."

"I met Sanders at the mausoleum and—"

"How did you know where the mausoleum was?"

"Are you going to listen or interrogate me?" she said in a shrill voice.

"I want to believe you, so I'm trying to fill in the gaps."

"After what happened at the Challoner mausoleum, I went online and downloaded whatever layouts I could find of cemeteries in the area. All Souls' had a detailed map. The Doyles' mausoleum was on it."

"Fair enough," Father Gilbert said.

"When Sanders and I arrived at the mausoleum, the grave had already been broken into. I was put out, to say the least. We were discussing who might have got there before us when…" She paused.

Father Gilbert watched her as her lower lip trembled. She pressed one hand over the other on the steering wheel and stabbed her fingernails into her flesh.

He tried a gentler tone. "What happened?"

"A man in a dark cloak or hood or – I don't know – came out of the corner of the mausoleum. It was like he spilled out from the shadows."

Father Gilbert thought of the figure in the woods behind Todd's house, the same figure described by Father Benson. He didn't know what to say.

She misinterpreted his silence. "I know. It sounds crazy. I'm not superstitious, but I thought it was a ghost."

"What did he look like?"

"I couldn't see his face. It was in darkness, like he was wearing a cowl. But I realized later that *he* was darkness. As if he stepped out of the shadows, but brought the shadows with him."

Another car horn. Father Gilbert looked and saw that she'd driven through a red light.

"I don't care if you believe it," she said, her voice growing shrill again. "Three days ago I wouldn't have believed it either. In my entire career of dealing with antiques and relics and artefacts and the most bizarre legends ever made up, I've never experienced anything like this."

"All right. So, this *thing* came up…"

"It was holding *the Woodrich sword.*" She was breathless. "Poor Sanders! He didn't know what he was dealing with. He stepped forward and said, 'Stop, I'm a police officer,' but that *thing* came at him, holding the sword up like a sentry. And then, faster than any man could move, it turned the sword and ran him through."

She was silent. Apparently the memory had stolen her words.

With squealing tyres, she steered to the left and into the car park of a pub. She drove to a far corner, empty of cars, and slammed on the brakes. It was all Father Gilbert could do not to fly into the dashboard.

"What are you doing?" Father Gilbert exclaimed.

She pulled on the handbrake and put her head down on the steering wheel. The wipers rubbed at the rain on the windscreen, smearing the view of a fence and an open field beyond.

Taking a deep breath, she said, "I was a coward. I screamed and ran."

"What else could you have done?" Father Gilbert asked. If her story was true, running was her only option.

"The cemetery was empty. And it was *dark*, like night," she said.

"The murder happened in daytime," Father Gilbert said.

"I *know*, but the light was… changed. The sky and colours were like early evening. I swear. It was like a dream." She paused, then gathered herself up again. "He – *it* – chased me."

"He ran?"

"He *moved*. Glided across the grass. Thank God I had parked where I did. The road was on the other side of a wood, at the edge of the cemetery. It wasn't very far from the mausoleum at all. I tore my clothes on a branch. But I was able to get to my car."

She looked around her, as if the car itself was some sort of guardian angel that had protected her.

"And then?"

"I saw him – it, whatever – standing among the trees as I drove off. It watched me as I drove away." She put a hand to her mouth and fought back a sob.

He thought about reaching over to her. His pastoral instinct said to give her a comforting hug, human contact to bring her back to the present and out of that nightmare. Instead he clasped his hands in his lap. He didn't trust her. He was afraid she might exploit the moment. If nothing else, he didn't want to be seen hugging a woman in a car sitting on the vacant end of a car park with the windows fogged up.

"Why didn't you go to the police?" Father Gilbert asked.

"I was afraid to."

"Why?"

"Because they're in on it."

"In on what?"

"The Woodrich Society."

He eyed her. "How do you know about that?"

"From London. I went up to investigate the Woodrich family. I read about its connections to the families around Stonebridge. I found an expert at the British Museum who explained it all to me." She reached down to the floor and pulled up her handbag. "I've got his card somewhere."

"Show me later," Father Gilbert said. "What did he tell you?"

She continued to dig in her handbag, then brought out a sheaf of papers. Father Gilbert saw typed pages, handwritten notations, and drawings. "For one thing, the sword, ring, and medallion weren't really a *gift* from Thomas Cromwell to Jeremy Woodrich."

"What were they?"

"An insult, more than anything. Cromwell was a rabid reformer who wanted a complete break from the Roman Catholic Church. Though Woodrich had recanted his Catholicism, he used his influence to keep some semblance of its practice alive in the emerging English Church. Cromwell despised Woodrich and gave him the Set, knowing that it was offensive, maybe even diabolical."

"What made it diabolical?"

She handed him a pen-and-ink drawing of an upside-down crucifix, like the one he'd seen on the medallion. "This, as a start. That image was meant to desecrate one of Rome's most venerated symbols."

"I suspected as much."

She handed him another page, this one with a rough copy of a photo. It was the symbols of the peacock and plumage. "Pride and vanity, which Cromwell ascribed to the Pope—"

"Also a description of Satan himself," Father Gilbert added.

"He thought the Pope was the Antichrist, the son of Satan." She pulled out another sheet. "The inscription about 'Lord of All' was also a snide reference to the Pope, or Satan. Even the ruby in the centre was meant to look like an evil eye. The ring also has a ruby and the inscription engraved around it. The whole Set was meant to be blasphemous – as nasty an insult as Cromwell could have given Woodrich."

"Did Cromwell create the Set or did it exist before him?"

"It definitely existed before him," she said.

"What better way for Cromwell to attack Woodrich than to give him something that might hurt him physically and spiritually?"

A lorry drove past, rumbling and spraying loudly.

Father Gilbert asked, "Did Woodrich know what Cromwell was doing?"

"Probably not. He was not an astute man," she said. "But he must've known it was an insult."

"Then why did he keep it?"

"Woodrich intended to show the Set to the King, to prove what a vile man Cromwell was. But events moved too quickly. The monarchy changed, the tug of war between Catholic and Protestant went on for years. The Woodrich family saw a rise and fall in their fortunes.

One of the Woodriches took the Set to America in the seventeenth century. You know about the Salem Witch Trials? It may have played a part in the witchcraft there."

"But there were no real witches."

She looked at him with something akin to pity. "There were witches. Sarah Woodrich became one of them. And she probably enticed her brother Daniel into it. Between the two of them, the seeds of the Woodrich Society were planted. And it was during this time that they discovered the Set had power."

"By 'power', you mean the alleged curse."

"They're one and the same to me," she said.

Father Gilbert wasn't decided on how much to tell her about the accounts in the Haysham material. Letting her talk seemed like the best option.

She glanced over at him. "I don't have the details, but one of the Woodriches made contact with Samuel Haysham somehow. He introduced Haysham to the Society and Haysham brought it back here."

"What do you know about Haysham's version of the Society?"

"What little I got from David Todd's archives," she said.

"The ones in the attic."

"Yes."

"Todd gave me the impression that he didn't know much, apart from family legends."

"Then he was being deceptive." She smiled scornfully as if she remembered something she wouldn't repeat. "The Society was engaged in all kinds of weird occultism. Black masses, orgies, probably murder. And then there was this thing called an Avenging Angel."

"An enforcer for the group," Father Gilbert said.

She nodded. "That's the part that frightened me the most. That's what I thought had killed Sanders and had come after me. I was sure it would kill me."

"But it didn't."

She reached over and took his hand. "Thank God," she said.

Thank God. He hoped she meant it.

"But the Woodrich Set is almost assembled again," she said.

"We know the medallion exists, and you saw the sword. But where is the ring?" He wondered if she knew where it was.

She looked at him, surprised. Her hand came away from his. "David Todd has the ring. He's had it all along. That's why he's been so afraid. He's expected to take his place back in the Society because the ring has been with his family for years. It's at his *house*."

"You saw it there?" Father Gilbert asked.

"I didn't see it, but I know that's another reason he was panicked. He'd had the ring, but never thought of it as anything other than some old family heirloom. It's buried somewhere in the house. He didn't know where, he said. He was lying."

Father Gilbert had to rethink what had happened with Todd. Was he really a frightened victim? Or perhaps he was playing them all. For all he knew, Mary was also playing him. And, admittedly, she was doing a good job of it.

"Have you seen David? Is he all right?" she asked.

"He was released by the police. He ran off," he said, staying with the short version.

"That idiot!" she cried. "With the three pieces of the Woodrich Set gathered together – we're all in danger."

He looked at her sceptically. "You think they'll try to take over the world?"

"Don't you believe in the power of evil?" she asked. "Haven't two people already died? There'll be more."

"We have to take all of this to the police," he said.

"DS Sanders *was* the police. It didn't help him at all."

"He should have told someone where he was going. It's basic procedure."

"Who should he have told?" she asked. "Not Alex Wilton. He's in on it somehow. Sanders was sure of it."

"Then we'll find someone else."

"How will we know who to trust? What if the Woodrich Society is like the Masons – with secret handshakes and secret identities? If we go to the police and they arrest me for Sanders' murder, I won't survive the night."

"David Todd suggested the same thing."

"And you don't know where he is right now, do you? He could be dead." She looked at him with eyes of fury. "Why aren't you taking this seriously? I thought you believed in the supernatural."

"It's not about what I believe," he said. "What do *you* believe?"

"I don't know how to explain any of this." She looked at her hand and rubbed the fingernail marks she'd made there. "There's something about the Woodrich Set that brings the worst out in people. It has its own kind of power."

* * *

They approached the town from the east. The rain fell harder against the windscreen. She sped past the turning for the police station and drove Father Gilbert back to Scott's.

"You're making a mistake," he said.

She was resolute in her silence. She pulled into the car park behind Scott's, returning him to where she'd picked him up. Father Gilbert considered his options. Should he try to physically restrain her somehow? Grab the keys?

He touched her shoulder. "Come into Scott's. Have a cup of tea. We'll sort out what to do."

"Do you trust Scott?" she asked.

"I have no reason not to," he said. "He's been a huge help. And he's found documents in Haysham's archives that will fill the gaps in what you told me."

This caught her interest. "I'll come in."

"Smart girl."

She pulled into a parking slot and turned off the engine. Father Gilbert waited until she had removed the keys, opened her door, and started to get out. He worried she might take off if he got out first. Together they ducked from the rain and ran up to Scott's flat.

Father Gilbert walked in without knocking and called out, "Adrian? Put some decent clothes on. I have a guest."

One of the cats cried from somewhere beyond the rows of books.

"Adrian?" They squeezed between the bookcases. His eyes went expectantly to the table where Scott had been working. The seat was empty and the table had been cleared of Haysham's archival material. The trunk was gone. David Todd's boxes were gone.

Mary stopped. "I don't like this."

Father Gilbert didn't either. He had that feeling in the pit of his stomach again. He held up a hand. "Then stay back."

The cat cried again, more of a howl.

After a few more steps, he saw a pair of legs stretched out on the floor from behind one of the bookcases that enclosed the kitchen. Mary gasped from behind him. Father Gilbert rushed forward. He saw the blood before he saw the rest of Scott's body. "Call emergency services!" he shouted.

Mary was backing away towards the door. "You see? You see?" she said over and over.

"Don't go," he said. "Call for help!" He navigated around the puddle, knelt down, and checked the pulse in Scott's neck. He was still warm, but definitely dead.

"I'm sorry." She spun on her heels and dashed out.

A cat brushed against Father Gilbert's leg and gave a spine-chilling cry. It then moved on to Adrian Scott's head, nudging it with a sniff.

Scott's head turned. It stared at the priest with an inquisitive look on its face.

CHAPTER 37

D
C Adams, whom Father Gilbert had met right after Colin Doyle's suicide, arrived on the scene. Then the SOCO team. Then Chief Constable Macaulay. And it was a blur of activity and questions and statements, official and otherwise. Macaulay was put out – not by the murder, but by the absence of his lead investigator. DI Wilton had disappeared.

"What's he playing at?!" the Chief Constable shouted at one of the uniforms. "Doesn't he remember what happened to Sanders?"

Father Gilbert went out to the balcony. He leaned on the handrail, the rain dripping past him from the slanted roof. The flashing coloured lights from the police cars and the ambulance reflected on the puddles in the car park and sprayed the surrounding walls.

The body count was up to three. Four, if one included Colin Doyle. Five, if one included Clive Challoner. Six, if one added the corpse of Joshua Todd.

And Mary Aston, David Todd, and DI Alex Wilton were now unaccounted for.

Dark clouds and the steady rain had swallowed up the afternoon. Father Gilbert wasn't sure how much of the darkness was the storm and how much was the approaching evening. The occasional thunderclap sounded from somewhere in the distance.

Father Benson ascended the stairs.

"What happened?" the curate asked.

Father Gilbert let out a long, deep sigh and wiped a hand across his eyes. "He was stabbed in the chest, just like Sanders."

Benson groaned.

"He was a good man," Father Gilbert said.

"Did he have family?"

"No. His wife died a few years ago. He had a son in the army, killed in the Middle East." He felt a pang of regret. He hadn't known

Scott well. Only as a customer in his shop. All of the *should haves* came rushing to mind.

They stood quietly for a moment. The noises from the police in the flat echoed out to them. Father Gilbert yearned for a cigarette, something he hadn't done in years.

"It occurs to me that Lord Haysham was struck in the head, like Joshua Todd," Benson observed. "But Sanders and Scott were stabbed in the chest. Two different weapons, two different killers?"

"Two different styles of execution," said Father Gilbert.

He looked down at the car park. Even in the downpour, a few people had gathered to see what the police were doing at Scott's. He scanned the faces beneath hats and hoods. He remembered from his police days how murderers often reappeared as part of a crowd. He almost expected to see the shadow-man standing there.

"Why Adrian Scott?" Benson asked.

"All of the archival material was stolen," Father Gilbert replied. "Maybe the killer hoped to find more information, or to keep us from finding it."

Benson shivered. "If I hadn't gone to the hospital, I would have been in there."

"How is Joe Mumford?" Father Gilbert asked.

"Braver than most people in the same circumstances," he said. A sideways glance at Father Gilbert. "Why weren't you in Scott's flat?"

"I was with Mary Aston."

Father Gilbert felt the change in Benson's posture.

"She picked me up right after you dropped me off," Father Gilbert explained. "She was upset."

"About what?"

Father Gilbert told him everything Mary had said.

Benson frowned. "You believe her?"

"As much as I believe David Todd." Meaning: he didn't know.

"So she could have murdered Sanders," Benson said. "Did she kill Adrian Scott?"

"I thought about that," Father Gilbert said. "She could have killed him before we arrived. But Adrian was still warm when I found him."

He saw himself, sitting there with the body, waiting for the police, trying to keep the cats from messing up the crime scene. He had watched Scott's face, thinking he might gasp or blink or suddenly snap back to life.

"How long were you and Mary gone?"

"Nearly an hour."

"The body would have been cold?"

"Not as warm as it was," Father Gilbert said. "The murder happened shortly before we arrived." He didn't add that the flow of blood had continued to trickle out of the body, though the heart had stopped.

"What does DI Wilton say?" Benson asked.

"He isn't here. He must be hidden away somewhere, reading the Chronicle he got from Lynn Challoner."

"Wilton might be part of the Society," Benson said. "He has family links to it."

The door to the flat opened behind them and Macaulay stepped out. He lit a cigarette and took a luxuriant drag. "Is the entire town going to be wiped out before we put an end to this?"

Father Gilbert shrugged sadly. He continued to watch the crowd in the car park below. A uniformed officer in a plastic mac held up his arms as if warning them off. The rain had subsided. Mostly, they stood still and talked amongst themselves. Then a woman crossed behind the crowd and headed for the bus stop at the far end. She didn't look at the crowd or the police cars or up at Scott's flat.

"Are we finished here?" Father Gilbert asked as he moved for the stairs.

Macaulay plucked a bit of tobacco from his lip. "For the time being. Why? Do you have a dinner date?"

"I might." Father Gilbert took the stairs two at a time.

"Father?" Benson called out.

The gathered crowd watched him as he ran, a stir of excitement that something dramatic seemed to be happening. He circled around them and intercepted the one person who didn't seem the least bit curious about what was happening at Adrian Scott's flat.

"Going home so soon?" Father Gilbert said as he touched her arm.

Margaret Clarke turned to him, a startled look on her face.

* * *

In the café light, Margaret looked as if someone had replaced her blood with chalk. Her eyes were anxious, her mouth set tight.

Father Benson brought over three cups of tea and placed them on the table. He sat down next to Father Gilbert, who faced the apprehensive woman.

"You haven't been completely honest with us," Father Gilbert said to her with a gentle smile. He felt genuine warmth for her. Not only did she remind him of his mother, but he was sure she didn't understand what she was up against.

She lowered her head. Father Gilbert thought it was a hint of contrition. Then he noticed she was trying to sneak a peek at her watch.

"Are you expecting someone?" he asked.

"No, no – not at all." She sat up straight. "Has something happened at Adrian Scott's?"

"You're interested now?" he chided her. "You weren't a few minutes ago."

She looked shaken. "I didn't want to miss my bus."

He told her about Adrian Scott, leaving out the gory details.

She closed her eyes for a moment. "That poor man. I often went in on a Saturday afternoon. He had a nice selection of Georgette Heyer novels."

"Where is Alex?" Father Gilbert asked, sliding a cup of tea in front of her.

She shook her head. "I don't know."

"Have you spoken with him today?"

A pause. She was working through the implications of her answer.

Father Gilbert said, "Margaret, this isn't a good time to hold anything back. We need to know what you know. His life may depend on it."

She looked as if she believed him. "Alex dropped by earlier this afternoon," she said.

"And?"

A small lift of her shoulders suggested the visit was merely incidental. "He wanted to talk."

"You have to be a little more cooperative," Father Gilbert said. "Otherwise, Father Benson will run back to Adrian Scott's flat and bring Chief Constable Macaulay here to talk to you."

Her eyes widened.

"Or he'll probably want to talk to you at the police station," Father Gilbert added. "Your nephew is being derelict in his duty as a policeman and the Chief Constable will want to know why."

She shook her head. "Please don't."

"What did you and Alex talk about?" Father Gilbert asked again.

She placed her hands around the cup of tea but didn't pick it up. The blue veins stood out like small rivers against her brown age spots. Her arthritic knuckles were swollen and white. "He wanted to know about that horrible skeleton in the church cellar," she finally said. "I told him what I told you."

Father Gilbert watched her. Her eyes found no fixed place to look on the table. "You know about the Woodrich Society," he said.

She slumped as if the effort of will holding her up had come undone. "Yes," she said. "We *all* knew about it, if only through whispers and rumours. It was what some might call an 'open secret'."

"What 'all'?"

"My family. Some of the people at the church. Many of the influential men around Stonebridge, I would imagine."

"Why didn't you tell us the other day?"

"Because of *her*," Mrs Clarke said, her tone contemptuous.

"Mary Aston."

"I would have told you, even Father Benson—"

"None taken," Benson said under his breath.

"But I didn't trust *her*."

"She's not here now," Father Gilbert said. "Were any of your family members of the Society?"

She reeled back, indignant. "Heavens, no!"

"Your ancestors?"

She picked up her teacup. It shook in her hands. She put the cup down again.

"Tell me what you know," Father Gilbert said.

Her eyes, blue but losing the vitality of the colour, fixed on Father Gilbert. "My father did what you're doing now. He investigated the Society. He wanted to know what really happened with the skeleton in the church cellar. It was the policeman in him. My mother was terribly upset. She was certain that something bad would happen to us."

"Why would something bad happen to you?"

She looked at him as if he hadn't been paying attention. "A demonic society? A *cursed* sword? She believed my father would get hurt." She shook her head slowly. "The police station burned down and the sword came into our house. Bad things happened. I've *told* you. That's why my mother demanded they take the sword out of our house."

"Did Albert Challoner help him?"

"Dear Uncle Albert," she said, her voice barely a whisper.

"He was your mother's brother, I assume," Father Gilbert said, to clarify. "Was he a member of the Society?"

"Oh no. Not *him*. If anything, he would have wanted the Society destroyed. I think he helped my father with the investigation. But – fear does strange things to people."

"He was afraid?"

"Everyone was. There was always a threat that something terrible would happen if you didn't look the other way."

"Why didn't the police arrest the members?" Father Gilbert asked.

"There was never enough evidence," she said. "But my Uncle Albert was shrewd. He made a deal."

"With the Society? What kind of a deal?"

"A deal to repair the past," she said slowly, as if repeating a well-practised phrase.

"What does that mean, exactly?"

"Uncle Albert had a deep love for his older brother. He couldn't bear what had happened to him."

Father Gilbert looked over at Father Benson, who was writing names on the back of a serviette – drawing lines to connect them. "What older brother?" he asked.

"Richard Challoner. He was Uncle Albert's half-brother. Surely you know that Richard was the son of Martin Doyle."

Father Gilbert nodded.

"Richard's murder devastated Uncle Albert. He hated the Doyles for it."

"Why the Doyles?"

"He was sure they'd arranged it. They wanted Richard killed."

"They arranged it with whom?"

"Francis Todd, of course." She worked her lips as if saying the name had put a bad taste in her mouth. "The man truly was evil."

"Evil enough to kill someone with whom he had no grievance?"

"Yes. We used to call it 'bloodlust' – maybe people still do."

Father Benson asked, "If Albert hated them, why would he arrange for the sword and the skeleton to be put in the Doyle mausoleum?"

She looked at him as if she hadn't realized he was there. "It was part of the deal," she said. "He wanted Richard buried properly, to be acknowledged as a son of the Doyles. I'm sure money changed hands, too, as recompense for Richard's death."

"And the deal was *what*? Your Uncle Albert would keep his mouth shut about the Society?" asked Father Gilbert.

"He persuaded my father not to investigate it any further." She sighed. "I believe that's how it happened. I was only able to piece it together much later. I've been haunted my entire life by the events of 1938 and I finally got my father to tell me what really happened shortly before he died."

"Did your Uncle Albert say anything about the book?" Father Benson asked.

"What book?"

"The Society's," Benson said. He tapped his pen against the napkin.

She thought for a moment, then said distastefully, "*That* book."

Father Gilbert explained, "Your Uncle Albert took it from the diocesan library around that time. Did he give it to them as part of the deal?"

"No. That was part of his protection." She nodded, as if remembering. "It was evidence. He threatened that if they went back on their agreement he'd make the book public. Everyone would know the truth in great detail. As far as I know, they left him alone."

Father Gilbert leaned back. His shoulders were stiff. His headache had returned. "Why didn't your uncle go public anyway – to stop the Society?"

"I assume he didn't want to destroy so many families," she said. "The scandal would have affected everyone, even the innocent people."

"Did Clive know about his father and the deal?"

"He was an eccentric fellow. Except for the occasional hello when he attended church, I rarely saw or spoke to him. We never compared notes on our family history." She looked concerned. "Has Clive's daughter said anything about it?"

"She found a box labelled 'Woodrich'."

"So it still exists." She pursed her lips, deep lines forming between her eyes. Then she said, "No one has mentioned the Society for over fifty years. It seemed to go away. I had prayed that it was finished."

"Clearly not."

"Have you seen the box? Did you look inside?" she asked.

"No. Because Alex picked it up earlier today."

"*Alex* has it?" She lowered her head again, shaking it back and forth. "Oh dear, oh dear. I *knew* I shouldn't have talked to him about the death of poor Clive Challoner."

"He gave me the impression he didn't know anything about this business."

"Why would he volunteer that kind of knowledge?" she asked. "He's known since he was a boy. He was always interested by it – as a sort of unsolved family mystery. At times I thought he was a little *too* interested. I tried to curb his interest. Oh, I hope he doesn't do anything foolish."

"What could he do?" Father Gilbert asked. He looked at the thin white hair covering the top of her head. Each strand seemed delicate, as if he could blow and scatter them all like dandelions.

She lifted her eyes to him. They were filled with tears.

CHAPTER 38

Father Gilbert walked Margaret Clarke to her door, then ran back to Benson's Mini. He got in and closed the door. The rain drummed its fingers on the small roof.

"If this is the kind of work we're going to do, I'll need a larger car," Benson said.

Father Gilbert, who'd done contortions to fit himself into the tiny back seat to accommodate the lift for Mrs Clarke, nodded. The front passenger seat suddenly seemed spacious comparatively.

Benson put the car into gear and pulled away.

Father Gilbert took out his mobile phone and rang Macaulay. A brief conversation, and he hung up with a groan.

"Well?" Benson asked. "What did he say?"

"Alex Wilton is still missing." Father Gilbert looked out at the wet night. The image of Sanders came back to his mind. "Though Wilton went to Professor Braddock to get the medallion."

Benson shot a look at him.

"He said he needed it for police business," Father Gilbert reported. "Braddock handed it over. Macaulay doesn't know what to make of it, since there's no official reason for Alex to need that medallion."

"What's he up to?"

Father Gilbert scratched at his chin. "He doesn't live far from here."

"Surely the police would have checked there."

"I assume so. But it's the only thing I can think of to do right now."

* * *

Wilton lived in a semi-detached house in what had once been a council estate. A low wall separated his tiny front garden from his neighbour's. A chipped garden gnome frowned at the rain as the two priests walked up to the front door. The curtains in the windows were closed. The front door was open an inch. A sliver of vertical yellow light highlighted the door frame.

Father Gilbert knocked and the door moved open another inch.

"Hello?" he called out. "Alex?"

A figure came towards them and yanked the door open. It was DC Adams.

"What are you doing here?" he asked.

"Probably the same thing as you – looking for DI Wilton."

"He's not here," Adams said, then retreated into the front hall, opening the door for them to enter. "The door was unlocked, so I let myself in."

"Friends, are you?" Father Gilbert asked.

"Close enough," Adams replied. "It's not like him to go missing. After what happened to Sanders, I was afraid he was in trouble."

"Have you found anything?" Father Gilbert asked.

Adams gestured for them to follow him. He led them down the hall, past a staircase and a front room on the left. Father Gilbert smelled the remnants of a fire in the air. They continued on to a second doorway on the right. The room was a makeshift office, a disorganized mess.

"Don't touch anything," Adams warned.

On the desk next to a computer sat an open square box. On the side were a crude drawing of a pentagram symbol and "Woodrich" penned in a handwriting style from another age.

Father Gilbert moved closer to the desk. Scattered over the surface were books about witchcraft, black masses, and charms. The books were both hardback and paperback, new editions. "These didn't come out of that box," Father Gilbert said.

"I don't see the Chronicle," said Benson, leaning in to look.

"Chronicle?" Adams asked.

Father Gilbert had an idea and left the office, returning to the front room. It was dark. He found the switch and a single light turned on overhead. On the opposite wall was a modest fireplace. Father Gilbert went over to it and kneeled down.

Adams came in behind him. "What are you doing?"

"Do you have evidence gloves?" he asked Adams.

Adams patted his pockets to show he didn't. "I didn't expect to be gathering evidence. I may have a box in the car."

"Never mind." Father Gilbert took a pen from his shirt pocket. He leaned into the grate. Charred fragments of yellowed papers were spread out among the ashes. He used the pen to lift the pages one at a time. They were handwritten letters. Each page had different handwriting. Early twentieth century, was Father Gilbert's guess.

"What do you see?" Benson asked.

"Letters." He spoke over his shoulder to the two waiting men. "This one is addressed to Albert Challoner. And I see... Haysham... and here's one from Doyle... and this is from Todd."

"If he was trying to get rid of evidence, he did a poor job," Adams said.

Benson asked, "Can you tell what they're about? Are they the negotiations for the deal?"

"Deal?" Adams asked impatiently. "What deal? What was Wilton investigating?"

"The same thing we are," Father Gilbert said, standing up. "Sanders was, too."

Adams looked annoyed. "This is connected to Sanders' death? Are you suggesting Wilton did it?"

"I'm suggesting that you get the SOCO team here," Father Gilbert said.

"Has a crime been committed?" Adams asked, bewildered.

Father Gilbert bent to look closely at the iron poker lying on the hearth. There was blood and hair on the spear-end. "It's possible."

* * *

They stood in the front hall of Wilton's house as Macaulay's SOCO team people moved in and out of the front room and the office.

"So what is Wilton doing?" Macaulay asked. "Should I be worried or annoyed?"

"Worried for now," Father Gilbert said. "Until we know if the blood and hair on the poker belong to Wilton, or someone Wilton struck."

Macaulay harrumphed and walked down the hall.

Benson stepped close to Father Gilbert. "Is Wilton playing detective or is he the Avenging Angel?"

Father Gilbert shook his head. "Either could be true."

"You think he could be the murderer?" Benson asked. He thought for a moment, then said: "But he was at the police station when Lord Haysham was killed."

"As it turns out, he wasn't," Father Gilbert said and nodded towards the Chief Constable. "According to Macaulay, Wilton signed out for dinner around the same time they think Haysham was murdered."

Benson was surprised. "Is that enough to make him a suspect?"

"It isn't enough evidence by itself," Father Gilbert said. "But it certainly makes him look suspicious." He stepped out into the small porch and held his hand out. The rain had stopped. "There's no point in standing around here." He moved down the path towards the road.

"Where are we going?" Benson asked from behind him.

"The church."

"Why there?"

"The church was the centre of the Woodrich Society's activities at various times over the past 200 years. Why not tonight?"

"Why tonight?" Benson asked.

Father Gilbert pointed up. Through a gash in the clouds, the white orb of a full moon shone down on them.

CHAPTER 39

When they arrived at St Mark's, Mr Urquhart was at the side door – the one they used to get directly to the offices.

"Is the church empty, Mr Urquhart?"

"Aye, Father." He hesitated. "You won't be needing to go into the crypt, will you?" he asked.

"No. Why?"

"I've got the pump going. The water's seeping in again," he said.

"Thank you, Mr Urquhart. We'll lock up behind us."

Inside, Father Benson walked straight to his office. Father Gilbert continued on.

"Where are you going?" Benson asked.

Father Gilbert nodded in the direction of the nave. "Give me a minute."

In one of his theological college classes, the teacher had surveyed the students and asked, "Where is your favourite place to encounter God?"

The answers were varied: in a deep forest, by the seashore, in a book-lined study, in a pub, while playing golf. Father Gilbert was the only student who'd answered, "In church." The instructor then spent the next hour criticizing the church for not being as attractive to people as a forest or a seashore or a golf course or a book-lined study or even a pub, and then he put forward the assertion that the Church of England needed to replace the liturgy and altars and music with more relevant enticers.

Father Gilbert was vocal in his disagreement – and was thereafter pegged as a boring traditionalist.

Most of his fellow students had only ever attended churches that had spent a lot of their time trying to be something other than a church. The liturgy was mere window dressing. The church structures had been abandoned for multi-purpose buildings that could be used for worship services one day and gymnastics the next. Worship itself had been relegated to a self-help effort – whatever had meaning for the individual. Just to be provocative, he would ask his fellow students if they believed God had a particular form of worship that He desired above all else. Of course not, they'd said.

Yet, in all of his readings of the Bible, he'd found very specific rules regarding the worship of God – dictated by God Himself – and at no point did the Creator ever ask, "Is this good for you?"

Stepping into the nave, there was no second-guessing where he was or what he'd come to do. This was a place to encounter God, to worship Him, to serve Him.

Electric candles in red glass holders hung discreetly above the pews, casting a reverent glow. The church was illuminated by small lights, angled to highlight the beauty of the altar, the screen, the marble floors, the dark wooden altar rail, the choir stalls, and the panelling that covered the walls.

Father Gilbert slipped into a pew, lowered a kneeler, and positioned himself for prayer. The silence would normally have brought him comfort and peace. This time it was thick with menace. He couldn't shake the knowledge that this church – *his* church – had once been used for the vilest purposes. He looked up at the altar and wondered if the abominations had taken place right there. Not on that same altar, since it had been replaced just before World War II. But the area itself had been desecrated. Had anyone ever bothered to re-consecrate the church? He didn't know.

He wondered why he hadn't felt the presence of evil. Then it struck him that his various encounters and apparitions might have been caused by the remnants of what had been done there. Perhaps, somehow and for some reason, he had a particular antenna for picking up signals from the spiritual realm.

He would ask the Bishop to lead a rite of reconsecration.

Doubling his efforts to pray, he tried to lose himself in time with God. But the present murders and the accounts from the past crowded in. A parade of the dead taunted him, shouting out and shattering the silence.

He held no illusions about the evil men were capable of doing, but he always held out hope that the mercy and grace of God would eventually prevail. Whoever had killed Lord Haysham, DS Sanders, and Adrian Scott would be found. Whatever had driven Colin Doyle to suicide would be exposed. One way or another, he was determined to solve this mystery.

He made his way back to his office. Father Benson was sitting at Mrs Mayhew's desk, typing away on her computer.

"Everything all right?" Benson asked.

Father Gilbert nodded. "You?"

"Just catching up on emails," he said. He looked up at Father Gilbert. "Why are we here?"

"I want to go through what we've learned, to see what I've missed."

"Why do you think we've missed anything?" Benson asked.

"Because we haven't caught the criminals," Father Gilbert said. "And they're not here."

"Who aren't here?"

"The Society. This is where they'll come – and they're not here."

"You could have said so before I agreed to bring you here," Benson said.

"Do you want to leave?"

Benson looked as if he might say yes. Then he shrugged. "Maybe it's too early. Midnight is the witching hour, right?"

"Or maybe they didn't like how we've redecorated since they were last in St Mark's," Father Gilbert said. From somewhere below, he heard the sound of the water pump in the crypt. "If they aren't going to meet here, then where are they?"

He turned and went into his office.

* * *

Father Benson made coffee. The two priests sat on opposite sides of Father Gilbert's desk and went through the documents they had, the facts they'd been told, even the information Benson had scribbled down on the napkin. They listed the cast of characters from the past and present and created a chart connecting them.

They returned to the murder of Joshua Todd, the tenure of Francis Todd at St Mark's in the nineteenth century, and the events surrounding the discovery of Richard Challoner's skeleton in 1938. Without question, the Woodrich Set seemed to be a source of corruption. The pattern of evil had been established by Samuel Haysham and carried on haphazardly after his death.

Three cups of coffee later, nothing new had emerged.

Father Gilbert glanced at the clock on the mantelpiece. It was almost 11:30.

"What if we're wrong?" Benson asked. "What if this whole thing isn't about the Society, but the value of the Woodrich Set? If it's worth a lot, then the murders may be more about greed than the occult."

"If that's true, then I'll be relieved."

"Why?"

"Basic greed is easier to deal with. I'm more worried about the restoration of an evil Society by evil people – or, equally dangerous, a group of people who may not know what they're doing."

"Are you thinking of anyone in particular?"

"Alex Wilton," he said. "He's not technically part of the Society's legacy, not as a direct descendant. But Margaret Clarke said he's been fascinated by its existence for years. What if it's been an unhealthy fascination? What if he's been seduced by a fantasy of demonic power and wants to 'earn his stripes' by playing the role of the Avenging Angel?"

"Is he the type of person to do that?"

"Who isn't that type of person?" Father Gilbert asked. "Which one of us, when tempted at the right time and in the right way, wouldn't give in?"

"Capability doesn't make it likely," Benson said.

"No, it doesn't," Father Gilbert agreed. He returned his attention to the copy of the file of Francis Todd's ecclesiastical trial, sent from the diocesan library by Mrs Littleton.

Benson took part of the file and looked over the pages.

Another few minutes passed, and Father Gilbert saw a small section he hadn't noticed before. "In the list of grievances against Francis Todd, it states that he'd had conflicts with his vestry over unauthorized work on the church."

"What kind of work? Does the record get specific?"

Father Gilbert checked the pages. "No."

"Do we have any records here?"

"Possibly." Father Gilbert grabbed his mobile and dialled Mrs Mayhew.

"It's almost midnight," Benson said.

"She's used to it." He punched the speaker button.

"Hello, Father. What's wrong?" Mrs Mayhew asked when she picked up. She sounded as fresh as she did at any other time of day.

"Where do we keep the files for any work done in the church?"

"What kind of work?"

"On the building. Changes, improvements, renovations, that sort of thing."

"Recent – or further back in time?"

"Further back. The Francis Todd period."

"Oh dear," she said. A rustling sound. Had she thrown the covers aside? "I'll come and get them," she said.

"No," he said firmly. "Just tell us where they are."

"There are three filing cabinets in the alcove to the left of Father Benson's office door. Look in the second cabinet, fourth drawer down."

"Can you be more specific? How many files back?" he asked.

She didn't get the joke. "I'm not sure, it may be—"

"Never mind, Mrs Mayhew. Sorry to awaken you. Come in late tomorrow." He hung up.

"You know she won't come in late," Benson said.

"I know."

They went to the filing cabinet and pulled out several files filled with musty papers.

"Does this church keep *everything*?" Benson asked.

Father Gilbert chuckled. "We've tried. Remember, Anglicans are mostly English bureaucrats in vestments."

The mantelpiece clock chimed midnight when they found a single piece of paper dated from 6 May 1886. It was a letter from the Reverend Francis Todd responding to the Mayor of Stonebridge. The Mayor had complained about the "disruptive" work going on at St Mark's. The work in question, Todd explained in his reply, was to allow proper drainage from the church, to alleviate the ongoing spring flooding in the crypt.

Father Gilbert fiddled with his pen.

"Is that significant?" Benson asked.

"I'm not aware of any particular drains going out from the crypt." Father Gilbert picked up his mobile. "I'll ring Mr Urquhart."

"It's *past* midnight," Benson reminded him.

"He's a Scot. They never sleep."

Benson pointed to Father Gilbert's empty mug to see about a refill. Father Gilbert nodded. Benson left with the two mugs in hand. Punching the speed-dial, Father Gilbert pushed the speaker button. Mr Urquhart picked up on the second ring.

"Yes, Father?" It sounded like the television was on in the background. "Don't tell me the pump has packed it in already."

Father Gilbert listened. The low rumble was gone. "Oh. Now that you mention it…"

"It's old," Mr Urquhart said.

Father Gilbert called out, "Father Benson, will you check the pump in the crypt, please?"

"Don't ask the poor man to do that," Mr Urquhart said. "It's a cantankerous machine. I'll be right over."

"We'll take care of it," Father Gilbert said and stood up. "But you can come with me."

"Eh?"

"The wonder of mobile phones. I'll carry you with me," he said. He came around his desk and out of the office. He looked over at the coffee machine, expecting to see Benson. A new pot was brewing but Benson was gone.

"Tell me about the drains going out of the crypt," Father Gilbert said as he walked down the hall. Small sconces – once gas, now electric – dotted the walls and cast a dim, pale light that didn't so much illuminate as emphasize the shadows.

"I don't know of any drains."

"Built by Francis Todd in the 1880s?"

"If the drains existed, we wouldn't be having so many water problems down there," Mr Urquhart said.

Father Gilbert was puzzled. "But they were done. I have the documentation."

Silence from Mr Urquhart. The sound of a television voice in the background. Finally, he said, "Unless they're plugged up."

"Where would they be?"

"The only place I can think is behind the old altar."

Old altar? Father Gilbert's heart rate quickened.

"The one from the nave," Mr Urquhart continued. "It was moved to the crypt after the new one was put in – right before Germany invaded Poland."

Father Gilbert reached the door to the crypt – an arched, wooden monstrosity that looked like it had come from the set of a Robin Hood movie. It was closed and locked.

The key was kept in a wooden lock-box to the left of the door. He took out his own set of keys, hoping he had the right key for the lock-box. A small skeleton key fitted perfectly. Retrieving the door key from the box, he then opened the door to the crypt. Considering its size and weight, it opened easily and quietly on greased hinges. "Well done, Mr Urquhart," he said.

"For what?" the Scot asked.

"Easy-opening doors," Father Gilbert said.

The first thing that hit him was the smell of damp, followed by the odour of burning candles. Then, to his surprise, he caught a hint of cool air. The damp made sense, the smell of both candles and cool air didn't.

The stone steps angled downward, curved around a supporting pillar, and disappeared to the left. He thought he saw a dull yellow glow.

"That's odd," he said.

Mr Urquhart said something in response, but the call broke up. Father Gilbert looked at the screen of his phone and saw the signal was gone.

He continued downward, thinking about the altar – was it the altar Francis Todd had used? – sitting in the crypt. It should have been destroyed years ago. Why hadn't he known it was there?

He felt the same feelings he'd had at Todd's house: an oppression, a mocking presence. He rounded the pillar and suddenly froze. What he saw caused him to back up, to retreat behind the pillar. Then he peered around again.

At the far end of the crypt was the old altar, a marble table with heavy wooden legs and gold embellishments. A prone body, its head covered with a cloth, lay on top. There were candles burning at both ends. Lit candles were also placed on the flat tops of the various tombs. A black-robed figure with his head covered and his back to Father Gilbert stepped up to the altar. His head was bowed as if in prayer.

A subtle movement to the right produced another black-robed figure from the shadows, carrying a large open book, holding it high like an acolyte presenting the Scriptures. The book was carefully placed on the altar, propped up against the prone body. There were low murmurings and whispers that Father Gilbert couldn't make out.

This was the black mass. And Father Gilbert wondered if this was some sort of vision – another vision like Colin Doyle on the tower, or the sword-bearer in the vicarage – of one of Francis Todd's Society rituals.

If it was real, then how did these three figures get into the church?

The candles flickered from a flow of cool air. He squinted and his gaze crossed to a far corner at the left of the altar. Normally a vertical column of three grave markers – similar to the ones he'd seen at the mausoleums – filled the wall. But now they were swung away, like the three panels of a door on a hinge. Instead of the graves in the wall, there was a passage leading into a cavern-like darkness. A light flickered somewhere in that darkness, with the consistency of an oil lamp or a candle.

He knew then that this was the work Francis Todd had done – the drains that weren't drains at all. And this was how the members of the Society could get into and out of the church. This was how Richard Challoner was seen going into the church but not seen coming out again.

Father Gilbert looked back at the altar. The second figure was out of his view. The one at the altar picked up a sword – it had to be the Woodrich sword – and held it up horizontally over the body on the table. An incantation was being said. A glint of candlelight caught the jewel of a ring on the forefinger of the right hand of the black-robed figure. The Woodrich ring, to be sure.

Father Gilbert saw it all clearly. The figure standing at the altar was playing the role of celebrant. The other was assisting. The body on the altar was being sacrificed.

If he was watching a scene from the past, then there was no guessing who the players were. If it was in the present, then he had to wonder whom he was looking at. Was it David Todd or Alex Wilton or Mary Aston? Or maybe it was another group of people he'd overlooked. One of the Hayshams? Macaulay? He'd seen enough double-crosses and betrayals in his life to know that the robed figures could be someone he knew – and trusted.

The robed celebrant turned the sword, grabbing it by the hilt. He lifted it high with the point directed at the body on the table.

Father Gilbert had to do something. He looked around and saw a shovel resting against the wall. He carefully picked it up and crept towards the altar.

He was only a few steps away, readying to take a swing, when he felt cold steel against the back of his neck.

"Drop it," a woman's voice said.

He dropped the shovel. It clanged loudly against the stone floor.

The black-robed figure at the altar turned around, the sword held up. The face under the cowl came into the light. It was David Todd. His eyes were wide, his face rigid, and Father Gilbert wondered what kind of drugs he'd been taking.

The barrel of the gun came away from his neck. Mary Aston carefully stepped around him as she pushed the monk's hood from her head.

"A black mass? Honestly?" Father Gilbert asked them as calmly as he could manage.

Todd said to Mary, "Make sure we're alone."

She turned just as Father Benson called out from the top of the stairs.

Father Gilbert opened his mouth to warn Benson. But Todd was fast, smashing the hilt of the sword against the side of Father Gilbert's head.

He stumbled and went down hard onto the concrete floor.

CHAPTER 40

Father Gilbert felt strong hands on his arm, helping him to sit up. He turned his head, trying to shake off the pain.

"Are you all right?" Benson asked, very close to Father Gilbert's ear.

"This is the second time you've had to help me up," he said. His voice sounded foreign to his own ears. The pain on the right side of his head was sharp. He felt a trickle of blood working down the side of his face. *At least he didn't hit me on the same side as my other wound,* he thought.

David Todd stood nearby, the sword held up, ready to stab. He looked at Mary, who had the gun trained on them. It was a .22 calibre pistol. Small but effective at this range.

Father Gilbert pressed his hand against a nearby pillar to stand up.

"It's better if you stay down," Todd said.

"I'd rather stand," Father Gilbert said, wondering if Todd would force him to his knees. He struggled to his feet with Benson's help. A raw ache worked through his hip. As he rose up, his eyes went to a pentagram scratched into the stone on the pillar.

"All right," Benson said sternly. "You've had your fun."

Father Gilbert wondered, absurdly, why people so often resorted to clichés in times of stress. *Too many TV detective shows,* he thought. He saw past David Todd to the body on the altar. The cloth had fallen from the head. It was DI Alex Wilton. His eyes were closed, but his chest rose and fell in a steady rhythm.

Father Gilbert turned to Mary. "So this was your plan – to get hold of the Woodrich Set."

She didn't answer, though her lips quivered. She shook with nervous energy.

"Did you seduce David – or was it the other way around? Who wanted what?" he asked.

"He's trying to solve the case," Todd said derisively. "Spare me!"

Father Gilbert kept his eyes on Mary. "You've been playing us all, haven't you?" He rubbed the side of his head. He felt the slick spread of blood on his face and fingers.

"Do I let him talk?" Mary asked Todd.

"It doesn't matter. The mass has been interrupted. We need to start again." Todd turned away from them and busied himself at the altar. He put the cloth over Wilton's face again. He appeared to be doing a reset of the stage.

"What was the motivation for you, David?" Father Gilbert asked. "Greed? Power? Love?"

Todd ignored him and continued his work at the altar. He flipped the pages in the book as if trying to find his place.

"What about Alex? Did you charm him specifically?" he asked Mary. "Or was it just a policeman you needed? Either Wilton or Sanders, right? Someone who could get what you needed – the medallion, access to the mausoleum to find the sword. I imagine you could have seduced either one of them."

She watched him, the .22 poised. "Are the police coming?" she asked.

Father Gilbert shrugged. "Does it matter?"

He realized that Benson's hand was still on his arm, holding tight. Benson was watching them all closely with a dangerous look in his eye. Father Gilbert wanted to tell him not to try anything, but didn't know how.

"We should stop, David," she said.

"No!" he snapped.

"I'm curious about the line between the truth and your lies," Father Gilbert said to Mary. "That whole business about the shadow -man – the one who killed Sanders."

She flinched. "What I told you was true."

"Then you're delusional," he said. "You killed Sanders after he found the sword."

"I didn't."

"It couldn't have been Todd, because he was still locked up. Unless it was Alex. But I can't believe he would kill a fellow police officer. Even for you."

"You'd be surprised to learn what some men will do for me. I'm very good at what I do for men." Her gaze was fixed on Father Gilbert. "You would have been very impressed."

"I'm glad I missed the chance," he said.

"Which one of you killed Haysham?" Father Gilbert asked in a "by the way" tone.

Mary frowned and her eyes went to Todd. "That wasn't part of my plan."

"You didn't have the sword then. What did you use?" Father Gilbert asked Todd.

Todd didn't answer.

"Another sword – to mimic the look of a so-called Avenging Angel?"

A grin from Todd. "One must improvise at times."

"And one of you killed Adrian Scott to get the archives," Father Gilbert said.

"Remember. I was with you," Mary said, her eyes darting to Todd again.

"So we have *two* plans at work here," Father Gilbert said. "Are you sure you're both on the same page?" He tried to sound confident, even cavalier, but he recognized that the situation was more dangerous than he'd thought. Mary Aston wanted the Woodrich Set and had created an elaborate scam to get it. Todd was operating from a different motivation altogether. "Was the Society part of the ruse to keep us distracted? The clues, the pentagrams…?"

"How did you manage to give Clive Challoner a heart attack?" Benson asked Mary, his voice a harsh rasp.

"That was a coincidence," Mary said.

"No it wasn't," Todd said over his shoulder.

"Challoner simply dropped in the front hall while we were talking," Mary added.

"Talking about what? Did you scare him with a lot of chatter about the evil Society and the book?" Father Gilbert asked. "Was he still alive when you left him? Could you have saved his life and didn't?"

She didn't answer – and he saw her in his mind's eye, watching

Challoner die, then scratching the pentagram in the doorpost and leaving.

Father Gilbert nodded to the altar. "What about Wilton? What does he get for bringing you the medallion and the Chronicle? Or is his reward the honour of being sacrificed?"

Mary's eyes shifted to Todd, then back again. She didn't speak.

"We're all going to be sacrificed," Benson said. His grip tightened on Father Gilbert's arm.

"That's what *they* think," Father Gilbert said. His attention went back to Mary. "That's right, isn't it?"

Creases gathered on her forehead. The gun trembled in her hands. "You shouldn't have come down here," she said softly. "Everything would have been all right if you hadn't come down."

"All right for who – Wilton?"

"It's all for show," she whispered. "David only wants to see what happens with the Set in the black mass, that's all."

Father Gilbert felt a veil of darkness cover them. It came with a thought, a recognition of their true situation – and whom they were dealing with. "Mary, you do know that David plans to be the only one to leave here alive?"

Her eyes widened, her mouth moved, but she didn't speak. She shook her head.

"You don't really believe he went along with this in order to put on some robes and do a little black mass for a few thrills, before you run off together?" Father Gilbert said. "The Woodrich Set is powerful beyond just the money. He's taking this seriously."

She tightened her grip on the pistol.

"I saw the look in his eyes at the police station – and at my house. I've seen it before. He was afraid at first, not sure of his role, but then he crossed the line." He turned to Todd, who was now facing them. "It was a struggle for you, wasn't it, David? You fought hard. But not hard enough."

Todd glared at him.

Father Gilbert pressed on. "You want to take your place in the Society. Perhaps start a new one. Is that why you recruited Colin Doyle? It wasn't about spying on Haysham. It was to befriend Doyle so you could get your hands on the medallion. You knew it would show up on Haysham's estate. But how?"

A slight twitch came to Todd's lips.

Father Gilbert came to another realization. "You struck a deal with Jack Doyle under the guise of corporate espionage and found out that Colin had the Doyle family papers. Was that it? And then you found the admission somewhere that it was a *Doyle* who had played the Avenging Angel and killed Joshua. Did you hope that the medallion was buried under the bridge with your ancestor?"

"The Doyles were fools to lose the medallion like that," Todd said with a sneer. "They still are."

"So Colin was after the medallion. But what happened? Had he read the papers? Did he decide he didn't want to take his place after all?"

"He was a coward," Todd said. "He was glad to have the money, but not the responsibility."

Mary exhaled sharply. "I had nothing to do with any of that," she said.

"How embarrassing. David was playing you while you were playing everyone else."

Todd chuckled, his face twisting. "I may cut your tongue out before we're finished, *Father*." His voice was low and seemed to come from somewhere other than his mouth.

A chill shot down Father Gilbert's spine. It wasn't Todd's voice, but one he'd heard a few years ago.

Shocked, Mary snapped her head around at Todd. "David?"

Todd's sneer twisted into a forced smile. "I'm sorry," he said. He still held the sword, but there was blood on it. "Let's continue."

Benson gasped and let go of Father Gilbert's arm.

Father Gilbert's mind raced with the various scenarios and contingencies of how to get them out of there alive.

Mary stepped forward. "David! What are you doing?"

"We need blood for the ceremony. Alex's will do. It's why he's here, after all."

Father Gilbert and Father Benson instinctively took a step towards the altar.

"Stop!" Mary shouted at them without conviction, her expression one of confusion. But she had the pistol and was still training it on the two priests.

They stopped.

"David, think about what you're doing," Father Gilbert said urgently.

"We need him *alive*, remember?" Mary said, her voice shrill. "The police won't believe he did all of this if he's *dead*."

Todd tipped his head to one side, the look of *you stupid woman* written on his face. "And what about these two? You think they want to play along?"

"What are you thinking: a couple of murders, ending with a suicide?" Father Gilbert asked. "Who gets to experience which?"

Todd gazed at Father Gilbert with a look of visceral hatred. Then he turned and raised the sword over Alex Wilton.

"It's not too late to choose," Father Gilbert said. "Whatever deal you think you made, you don't have to keep it."

"Shut up."

"You'll only be cheating the greatest liar of all liars," he said.

Todd muttered something, then brought the sword-point down, stabbing into Wilton's stomach. Mary shrieked, but kept the gun firmly trained on the two priests.

Father Gilbert's body tensed. The pain in his head intensified. Benson whimpered.

Todd lifted the sword again and began to whisper softly to himself.

A rivulet of blood flowed from Wilton, lined the edge of the altar, and dripped to the floor.

"Todd, stop!" Benson begged. "He'll bleed to death!"

"As priests, you must understand the importance of blood in the ceremony," Todd said as he brought the sword down again, near the place of the first wound.

Mary cried, "David!" The colour had gone from her face.

"We have to do something!" Benson said through clenched teeth.

Father Gilbert's eyes darted back and forth between Todd and Mary. Mary's finger was on the trigger. If he grabbed for it, she'd fire. And Todd would use the sword – with great skill, he suspected.

Todd turned around to face them. He held the sword in his left hand and moved towards the priest. The point hovered a few inches from Father Gilbert's chest.

Mary took a step back.

Todd reached out to her with his right hand. "Give me the gun," he said.

"Don't do it, Mary," Father Gilbert said. "Whatever plan you had is gone. Don't you see? If he doesn't kill you, you can be sure he's planted enough evidence to make it look as if you acted alone. He's thought it all through."

Mary let out a small sob.

The point of the sword touched Father Gilbert's shirt. "We know you well, Father. We'll delight in having our way with you."

Father Gilbert felt a wave of nausea at the sound. Again, the voice wasn't Todd's. "Tell me who you are," he said. His mind went to the Rite of Exorcism. "In the name of *Christ*, say your name."

"You know it already," Todd said. He said harshly, "Give me the gun, Mary."

"Don't," Father Gilbert said to her.

"*Shut up.*" Todd drew the sword back and then quickly thrust forward.

Father Gilbert acted instinctively, swinging his right forearm up to knock the blade aside. The edge was sharper than he'd imagined. It sliced the top of his arm through his clerical shirt. The metal rang out as the sword hit a nearby pillar.

Father Gilbert then brought his left fist around, punching Todd in the temple.

Todd staggered only a couple of steps while attempting a broad swipe with the sword.

Father Gilbert pushed Benson out of the way towards Mary and dodged the sword. The blade caught him in the right side. A slicing pain, followed by a cold sensation, raced through him. He clutched at his wound and fell back against the pillar.

Mary screamed. Benson shouted.

Todd regained his footing and brought the sword up to a more decisive position.

The pistol went off with a deafening explosion. All sound was instantly absorbed into a black hole of nothingness.

Todd's face contorted. He stumbled sideways.

Mary stood with an expression of surprise as if the pistol had gone off on its own.

Todd staggered, then spun, swinging the sword around towards Mary.

She fired again.

Father Gilbert imagined being hit by a stray bullet or stabbed by a wild swipe with the sword. He launched himself at Benson, hoping to knock them both to the floor. Benson fell towards the stairs. Father Gilbert hit the stone floor. Every nerve in his body screamed at him. His eyes went to Todd, who was now lurching to one side from the impact of the second bullet. The arc of the sword continued unabated, the blade slicing into Mary's hip.

She screamed and fell, pulling the trigger again and again and again.

Todd roared, though it was now a muffled sound amidst the high-pitched ringing in Father Gilbert's ears. There was a clatter as the sword fell to the floor. Then Todd was down.

Benson scrambled over to Father Gilbert. A cotton-wool voice kept asking if he was all right.

"Call for help," Father Gilbert said. The ringing was like a scream. Then he realized it was Mary. "Pressure – on her wound."

Benson pressed a cloth into Father Gilbert's hand, then moved to Mary.

Father Gilbert fumbled to find the wound. His arm was bleeding. So was his side. He was about to reach into his pocket for a handkerchief, but he saw he had another cloth in his hand.

The scene went into a spiral. *Shock,* he thought. He leaned back against the pillar, the stone cold against his upper back. He fought to stay conscious. He thought of the amount of blood now spilling all over Mr Urquhart's floor.

Alex. He had to help Alex.

He pushed himself to his feet. His legs wouldn't cooperate. Shifting his head, his gaze went to David Todd. Was he still alive?

There was no knowing how many of Mary's bullets had struck him. He was lying on his side, facing Father Gilbert. His eyes were closed.

Father Gilbert began to pray under his breath as he fought to stand up, but couldn't.

Suddenly Todd's eyes flew open. At first, they were unfixed and then they locked on Father Gilbert. He smiled. His teeth were red with blood. He licked his lips.

Legion, this demon had once called itself. Father Gilbert had encountered it more than he cared to remember. He continued to pray in a whisper.

With unexpected strength, Todd pushed himself up.

Father Gilbert wanted to warn Benson. He could hear the priest talking – over near Mary, who let out random cries of pain. He tried to shout a warning, but nothing came out.

Todd dragged himself up, his eyes darting from Father Gilbert to Benson and back again.

Father Gilbert said, "*Father—!*" but it was lost in one of Mary's screams.

Todd was on his feet now. He tilted his head at Father Gilbert, put a finger to his lips, and stumbled off towards the tunnel in the wall.

Father Gilbert couldn't bear to see Todd escape. With great effort, he got to his feet. His side throbbed, each pulse like being stabbed again and again. Taking a step, he realized his feet were bare. *Where are my shoes and socks?*

He turned his head to Father Benson. The curate was now at the altar, attending to Wilton. Mary still lay on the floor, holding a cloth to her hip.

He forced himself to the opening of the passage. He glanced back and caught sight of Wilton. The blood had soaked the shirt covering the man's stomach. Benson was now attempting to stop the flow of blood. He shouted into a mobile phone, which was pressed between his ear and hunched shoulder.

He must have a better service provider than I do, Father Gilbert thought.

A howl echoed down the tunnel. The priest chased after it.

CHAPTER 41

Father Gilbert half-staggered, half-ran through the tunnel in a painful slouch. The downward slant of it propelled him forward. His hands scraped against rough concrete and his bare feet kicked at puddles of water. Sharp stones stabbed into his soles.

A voice echoed from somewhere ahead – with blasphemous swearing and animal-like grunts.

He eventually came to an opening, with a square grate hanging open. It was covered with ivy. A step of about three feet led down to a section of Mr Urquhart's gardening. He jumped it, the jolt sending reverberations of pain to every nerve and synapse. He took a few steps forward and then fell into damp grass. He was so very tired. All he wanted to do was sleep. But he got onto all fours and began to crawl.

An upward slope brought him to the graveyard. He looked back at the church. The doorway to the tunnel was part of a cement decoration on the rear of the building. It looked like a memorial stone. Few would notice it.

He looked ahead. The full moon cast a blue light on the headstones and statues. A gentle breeze taunted the leaves and branches in the trees overhead. Shadows moved and all of his childhood fears rose up. The graveyard had come alive. Beasts waited behind every stone, hands were about to claw up through the dirt of each grave.

Courage. This is consecrated ground, he reminded himself and began to whisper, "Our Father, who art in heaven…"

One shadow took form, lurching from one grave to another, using the headstones as support. It fell to its knees at one point and raised its head up to the full moon and shrieked. Father Gilbert's blood turned to ice. Dogs barked in the distance. Then the shadow was on its feet and moving again, taking the shape of David Todd.

Father Gilbert pressed his hand against his side and it occurred to him now that he was either delirious or a fool for chasing Todd. Let the police find him later. How far could he get with so many bullet wounds? But he knew it wasn't Todd he was chasing. It was the thing inside Todd that had to be dealt with.

With more strength than he thought he had, he got up. He drove himself onward, the sound of his breathing in his ears. His head felt like he'd stuck it in a tumble dryer. He could feel his heart beating against his ribcage. The wound in his side seemed to be tearing apart.

A wrought-iron fence circled this part of the graveyard; the gate was at the far end to his right. He assumed Todd was heading for that. He fell to his knees again on the slick grass, scraping his forehead against the side of a headstone.

"God, help me," he whispered. He tried to remember where he'd left off with the Lord's Prayer.

An angry snarl sounded ahead of him. He moved for it.

Rounding a large crypt, Father Gilbert saw Todd struggling at the wrought-iron fence. It was six feet high, the top of each iron post shaped like the point of a spear. Todd was pulling himself up to climb over.

That's a stupid thing to do, Father Gilbert thought. Had Todd followed the fence in either direction, he could have easily found an escape. Todd knew that. But there he was, hoisting himself up.

"Todd!" Father Gilbert shouted.

Todd's head turned slightly, as if to confirm he'd heard a voice. Then he jerked himself up with greater determination. His upper body was poised over the fence. He kicked his feet, trying to catch them on something that would give him leverage. He reached for a branch from a tree, planted on the other side of the fence. Even if he had been in the best physical condition, he couldn't have succeeded in this effort.

Father Gilbert moved unsteadily towards him. He had no idea what he thought he'd do.

Todd grabbed the branch, but his weight caused it to swing back. He turned with it, facing Father Gilbert now, and then lost his grip. He fell onto the fence, the sharp points of the posts stabbing upwards through his upper arms and shoulders. He swore as he squirmed and thrashed. The weight of his body pulled him down, pushing the points further up. Then he stopped and simply hung there, like a puppet that had lost its strings. He looked at Father Gilbert. Then he laughed with a noise void of any humour, filled instead with a terrible brutality.

The pain in Father Gilbert's side intensified.

Todd swung his forearms playfully. "Well, now. Look at this."

Father Gilbert did.

"Remind you of anything?" he asked and laughed again as he stretched his forearms as wide as they could go. "Do you need a clue?" He went into a simpering voice: "Oh, *why* have you forsaken me?" He laughed again.

Father Gilbert prayed against the blasphemy.

Todd swung himself from side to side as if he might dislodge himself. He fumed, "Vile, weak bodies." A trickle of blood slipped from the side of his mouth to his chin.

"David—" Father Gilbert said and reached for him.

Todd swore with such violence that the priest stopped where he was. The voice was a harsh rasp of blood, spit, and dirt. "Todd is dead," he said.

Father Gilbert thought of the rules of exorcism. *Don't engage with the demon* was one of the first. He fell to his knees and said, "In the name of Jesus Christ, depart for the place appointed for you."

"I should have picked a more suitable partner. Todd was useless." The eyes went to Father Gilbert's. "*You* are meant to be mine. My *prize.*"

The horror felt like ice-cold claws wrapping around Gilbert's heart. He fell back against a tombstone. He whispered, "In the name of Christ—"

A gurgle came from the depths of Todd's throat. He coughed. "Just say the word, Gilbert. You can hardly imagine the wonderful things we could do together. Let me out of here so I can come to you."

Father Gilbert felt movement around him. He looked down. The grass came alive. Every blade had become a squirming maggot.

He was too weak to move. "No," he gasped.

"Not all temptations are lies," Todd said. "There can be delicious and satisfying pleasures. Think about it."

He saw in his mind Mary Aston, beautiful, coming to him for a naked embrace, her body perfection, and their unity explosive. He sobbed.

Todd licked his bloody lips and smiled. "I can give you whatever you desire, Gilbert. You know being a priest is a burden you weren't meant to bear. You're not even good at it. The corruption of your heart will always get in the way."

"God have mercy," Father Gilbert said as a plea.

"Listen to me!"

"Christ have mercy."

"Don't be stupid."

"God have mercy."

"You're meant for so much more!"

Father Gilbert couldn't think. He couldn't remember what to do. So he recited the only thing he could think of – his baptismal vows. "My friend, my Saviour, my God, Jesus Christ, stands at the threshold of my soul…"

"It's a waste of time. You're a second-rate priest, a third-rate Christian."

"I renounce Satan and all his works and all his pomp."

Todd lifted his head and shrieked, an inhuman noise.

"I believe that there is only one God, the Creator, Preserver, and Ruler of all things and the Father of all men."

Todd's shrieking seemed to fill every crevice and fracture in the graveyard. He squirmed, jerking wildly against his impaled arms.

"I believe that this our God and Father is a just judge, who rewards the good and punishes the wicked."

The shrieking stopped and Todd went still, his eyes on Father Gilbert. "I'll see you again," he said with a savage sneer. "Your wound will remind you."

The sneer remained as Todd's head drifted upwards, his eyes rolling back, the whites illuminated by the moon. He went limp and then his head slumped forward.

Father Gilbert fell over, his head falling gently on a cushion of grass.

He wondered if anyone would find him before he bled to death.

He was startled to feel a hand caressing his hair. He looked up. A young boy, maybe ten years old, with a pale face and jet-black hair, kneeled next to him. The boy smiled sadly, as if he understood the pain and confusion Father Gilbert was experiencing.

"Please, get help," Father Gilbert whispered.

The boy stood up, nodded, and walked away. His clothes were odd – a dark suit from some other time. Turning back, the boy held up his hand as if to say *wait*.

Father Gilbert closed his eyes.

Chapter 42

He was confused. He was aware of being jostled onto a stretcher and carried out of the crypt of the church. He didn't remember how he'd returned there. He wanted to ask, but an oxygen mask kept his mouth shut.

Four stretchers. One death.

Father Benson hovered over him in the ambulance. "Do you believe that in one God there are three Divine Persons – God the Father, God the Son, and God the Holy Ghost?"

"I do." Why was Father Benson going through the Last Rites?

"Do you believe that the Second Person of the Blessed Trinity, Jesus Christ, was made man, was conceived of the Holy Ghost, born of the Virgin Mary, suffered under Pontius Pilate, was crucified, died, and was buried, descended into hell, and on the third day rose again from the dead, ascended into heaven, sitteth at the right hand of God, the Father Almighty, and from thence He shall come to judge the living and the dead?"

"I do."

"Do you believe that the Third Person of the Blessed Trinity, God the Holy Ghost, enables us to live and accomplish what is right and just, and that without His grace no one can be saved?"

"I do."

"Do you believe in and openly profess the One, Holy, Catholic and Apostolic Church, the Communion of Saints, the forgiveness of sins, the resurrection of the body, and life everlasting?"

"I do."

"If you have firmly resolved to live in accordance with the holy doctrine of Christ, ever to remain faithful to His Church, to avoid sin, to love God with your whole heart, and your neighbour as yourself, declare now this your will, and promise in the presence of the All-seeing God…"

* * *

He heard a burst of static as a doctor was paged on an intercom system. The smell of disinfectant, an electronic beep, an ache in his right arm, and a soft touch on his left hand registered somewhere in his consciousness. Then he opened his eyes. Pale green walls and fluorescent lights came to him. He saw a soundless television – a talk show with a slick host and an overexcited audience. And then, as his gaze drifted down, there was Father Benson sitting in a chair, reading a magazine. He touched his dry tongue against his dry lips and winced at the metal taste in his mouth.

"Good morning," he croaked.

Father Benson looked up from the magazine in his lap with open-faced surprise. "Good *afternoon*," he said.

"Which afternoon?" he asked.

"The afternoon after the incident in the crypt."

"Everything happened last night?"

"Or earlier this morning, depending on how precise you want to be."

Father Gilbert surveyed his condition. He had an IV attached to the veins in the top of his left hand. His right arm was bandaged. A dull pain in his side made itself known. "Was the damage bad?"

"The doctor said the sword missed your major organs and got the fatty part of your waist. But they still had a fair amount of stitching to do. They're worried more about infection than anything else."

"When can I go home?"

"Maybe later today, or tomorrow morning. They want to make sure you're not bleeding internally. It could take a month or so before you're fully recovered." Benson spoke with a strained calm. He had more lines on his face than Father Gilbert had noticed before. Or it might have been the light.

He started to sit up, felt pleasantly light-headed, and lay back again. "Am I on heavy painkillers?"

"The best that the NHS can buy."

"Were you hurt?" Father Gilbert asked.

"I'm the only one who came out of the crypt undamaged." He leaned forward on his knees. "Thanks to you."

"I didn't do anything."

"You pushed me out of the way. There were bullet holes in the wall where I was standing."

"Alex Wilton?"

"He nearly bled to death, but the paramedics got there in time," Benson said. "He's down the hall. On the mend. He's got a nasty cut on the back of his head, too."

"Where David Todd hit him with the poker?"

A nod from Benson.

"Mary Aston?"

"A fractured pelvis, the muscles on that leg cut through, possible nerve damage. She'll probably walk with a limp for the rest of her life." Benson's gaze went up to the silent television. "I don't know how much walking they do in our prisons," he added.

Father Gilbert wanted to say something clever, but the words wouldn't come.

"I don't think she knew what she'd got herself into," Benson said.

"Everyone seemed motivated by different things." *Greed, power, lust, glory,* Father Gilbert thought. *Does the story ever change?* "David Todd?"

"Dead at the scene."

Father Gilbert saw the body hanging on the graveyard fence. He winced, then pushed the thought aside. "How did you find me? Was it the boy? Did he get help?" he asked.

Benson looked mystified. "What boy?"

"In the graveyard."

Benson thought for a moment, and then seemed to relax as if he understood something Father Gilbert didn't. "We don't have to talk about it all now."

"We don't have to talk about *what?*"

"The details. The doctor said it's better for you to put them out of your mind and rest."

Father Gilbert wanted to argue but, in his drug-induced state, couldn't be bothered. He thought everything would become clearer when he gave his statement to the police.

Benson looked uncomfortable. He was strangling the magazine he'd been reading.

"What's on your mind?" Father Gilbert asked.

"I want you to know before Mrs Mayhew mentions it," he said, then cleared his throat. "I've asked the Bishop to reassign me. I'm trained to be a minister, not a character in a horror movie."

Father Gilbert had seen it coming.

* * *

Father Gilbert was released the next morning. Mrs Mayhew drove him back to the vicarage, lecturing him the entire way about taking care of himself. When he tried to bring up what had happened at the church, she quickly changed the subject. Her only concession to the tragic events was that she'd been in touch with the Bishop about re-consecrating St Mark's.

He napped after she left. He slept deeply and dreamlessly and awakened feeling ready to get on with his life again. Then the painkillers wore off and the wound in his side persuaded him to take it easy for a while longer.

The local newspaper had a front-page article about the bizarre murders in Stonebridge. There was a picture of St Mark's and an old photo of David Todd and an official statement from Macaulay promising a full investigation. Father Gilbert later heard that the BBC had mentioned it in one of their news broadcasts, sandwiched between flooding in Leeds and a crime spree in Slough.

DC Adams arrived in the afternoon to get Father Gilbert's statement about the events. He went through all of the details as best he could, aware of how his slurred speech would sound on the digital recorder. When he began his account of what had happened in the graveyard, Adams' expression changed.

"Thank you," he said, turning off the recorder. "That's all we need for now."

Father Benson brought fish and chips for dinner. As they sat at the kitchen table finishing the cod, Father Gilbert asked directly, "Tell me what's going on."

"What do you mean?" the young priest asked.

"I mentioned the graveyard yesterday and you dodged the subject. DC Adams shut down the discussion completely. What don't I know?"

Benson busied himself with the bottles of sauces for the fish.

Father Gilbert watched him a moment, then asked, "Why don't you want to talk about it?"

"Because it didn't happen, Father."

"What didn't?"

"You weren't in the graveyard. You never left the crypt."

Father Gilbert winced. "What? But I chased after Todd."

"You didn't, because he never left the crypt either." Benson fiddled with a chip, looking at it as if he'd never seen one before. "He died right there from multiple bullet wounds. He was dead before he hit the ground."

Father Gilbert shook his head, the memories too vivid. "No, I chased him down the tunnel to the graveyard. He was impaled on the wrought-iron fence. And there was a boy…"

Benson shook his head.

Father Gilbert was stunned.

"It might've been like your experience with Colin Doyle," Benson offered. "Or you were delirious. You lost a lot of blood."

"No," he said softly, trying to comprehend that possibility. He wiggled his toes in his slippers. "How did I lose my shoes and socks?"

"I took off your shoes to get to your socks."

"Why?"

"To use as bandages," Benson replied. "I put one in your hand for you to hold against your side. Then you used the other as a tourniquet to stop the flow of blood from your arm."

Father Gilbert lightly touched his forehead. It was sore. "Then what is this?"

"A scrape."

Father Gilbert thought it through: the knot on his head he'd received in Todd's attic, the cut on the other side when Todd hit him with the hilt of the sword… but the scrape? He remembered how he had stumbled in the graveyard, scraping his head against a headstone.

He was going to say something to Benson, to argue about it. But the young curate's eyes begged him not to discuss it any further. So he didn't.

* * *

"It's not a big surprise that Mary Aston is talking only through her solicitor," Macaulay said to Father Gilbert the next day. "She maintains that she didn't kill Sanders. She ran for her life, she said."

"Any chance David Todd did it?"

"The timing of his release from jail – and when Sanders was murdered – makes it possible. But narrowly. Five or ten minutes could make all the difference."

They were sitting in the front room at the vicarage. Though he'd chosen the most worn armchair in the house, Macaulay somehow sat erect.

"She said as much to me," Father Gilbert said. He'd stopped taking the painkillers, for fear of becoming too dependent on them. Now he was aware of the stitches in his side.

"The Crown Prosecutor will go through all of the evidence and decide what, exactly, is indictable," Macaulay said.

"What do they have?" Father Gilbert asked.

"Mostly circumstantial stuff. The weight of the evidence goes against David Todd."

"That's convenient for her."

"Still, we'd like to convict her as an accomplice in the murders of Sanders and Scott."

Father Gilbert thought through the Chief Constable's difficulties. There was no evidence she was anywhere near Haysham at the time of his murder, nor that she had anything to do with Challoner's death. She was with Father Gilbert when Scott was murdered, though the timing of his death was still a matter of debate. Perhaps his and Father Benson's testimonies of what was said between Mary and David Todd in the crypt would be helpful. But that could also be dismissed as hearsay. In the end, everything would be pinned on David Todd.

"What about Colin Doyle and his connection with Todd?" Father Gilbert asked.

"Jack Doyle has gone on record with the Southaven police to say that their falling out was because of David Todd's influence over Colin. Jack felt that Todd was recruiting Colin for something."

"The Society?"

"Jack claims he knows nothing about the Woodrich Set or the Society. He thought David Todd was leading Colin into a business scam. So he blames Todd for his son's suicide." He hesitated, then said, "It was *Jack* who beat Todd up the night Haysham was murdered."

"*Not* an Avenging Angel," Father Gilbert said.

"Todd used everything that happened to add credibility to his story, to validate his sense of fear – and his position as a victim."

Father Gilbert wondered about David Todd. Catholics prayed for the souls of the dead. He sometimes wished Anglicans did the same.

"Mrs Clarke is terribly sorry about Alex's behaviour," Macaulay said. "She wants to apologize to you for your suffering and thank you for saving him."

Father Gilbert nodded, hoping he wouldn't have that conversation with her.

"She thinks his curiosity and ambition allowed him to get drawn into David Todd's scheme."

"David Todd's or Mary Aston's? I suspect she was the one who persuaded him to help."

"How he was drawn in makes no difference to me." Macaulay had the look of a man who was profoundly disappointed in a wayward son. "Had he been more conscientious as a detective, it wouldn't have happened."

"What will you do with him?"

"He's on probation from the force, pending a full inquiry into any illegalities in his actions."

"Spoken like a true police spokesperson," Father Gilbert chided him. "Have you had a chance to look at the Chronicle?"

"The Woodrich book? I'm not interested. It's locked up as evidence, and good riddance to it."

"It's the property of the diocese," Father Gilbert said. Admittedly, he'd rather watch it burn and bury the ashes somewhere than put it back in the diocesan library.

"Let them come and get it, then."

"And the Woodrich Set?"

"After it's no longer of use as evidence, Professor Braddock has arranged for it to go on display in London somewhere – with the Stonebridge Man."

Father Gilbert looked amused. "Is that what he's calling it? Not *Joshua Todd*?"

"Not sexy enough."

"Ah. The Stonebridge Man."

"They may make a tour of it."

* * *

"Father Gilbert…"

He was working at his desk at St Mark's. He looked up at Father Benson, who had made it a point to avoid any private conversations with him since the last one about the graveyard. "Yes, Hugh?"

"May I?" he gestured to the guest chair. Father Gilbert nodded and he sat down. "I want to ask you…" He picked up a paperweight and put it down again.

Father Gilbert waited.

"Do you believe David Todd was possessed?"

Father Gilbert rested his elbows on the desk and said, with careful diplomacy, "We may never know where the line was between Todd's wilful choices and an external force that drove him."

"I take that as a *yes*," Benson said.

"Why do you ask?"

"His behaviour in the crypt, the way he looked and talked…" Benson shook his head. Then he folded his arms as if he felt cold. He looked at Father Gilbert. "He said some very specific things to *you*. Not as David Todd, but as whatever it was inside of him."

Father Gilbert nodded slowly.

"You've met it before, haven't you?"

He gazed at Benson, trying to calculate the risks behind his answer. "We've met before. And I suspect we'll meet again."

"Why?"

"It wants to destroy me. Piece by piece."

Benson sighed deeply.

"I'm sorry. If I could have spared you from any of this…"

"I wish you could have," Benson said sadly.

CHAPTER 43

It was remarkable to Father Gilbert how the flow of life pressed on, regardless of the magnitude of its interruptions. Businesses have their opening and closing hours, newspapers are delivered, television follows its relentless schedule, kids go to school, men and women see to their jobs, pints are drawn at the pub, lovers argue, worshippers kneel, the dead are buried.

Even for those who were scarred by the events of those few days – and those who had to face justice for the roles they'd played – life pressed on. Mary Aston's solicitor was a master of delay and prevarication. Alex Wilton resigned from the police force. Father Gilbert finally returned to his full-time duties at St Mark's.

Adrian Scott's bookshop was put up for sale. Father Gilbert had some money put away and thought about buying it. He feared someone would turn it into a trendy pub or a mobile phone shop. But the latest rumours were that the owner of a second-hand bookshop in Southaven intended to grab it up.

It was three weeks before Father Gilbert ventured down to the crypt again. He'd asked Mr Urquhart to open the door to the tunnel for him. He had the impression that the Scot, who prided himself on knowing every inch of St Mark's, was embarrassed that the tunnel had existed without his knowledge. The plan was to use it as a proper drainage system, but to seal up any use it might have as a passageway.

Father Gilbert retraced his steps from the crypt to the graveyard. Everything was exactly as he remembered it – though it couldn't have been a memory, since it didn't actually happen. Yet, there was no explaining how he could know the details of the tunnel, or its entryway in the side of the church, when he'd never seen them before.

Astral projection, or what some people called "out of body" experiences, often accompanied near-death occurrences. Father Gilbert knew personally of a few cases. He could only guess that this was what he'd experienced with David Todd.

The tombstones were exactly as he knew them, if only from the many times he'd strolled through the graveyard. He came to the place in the iron fence where Todd had been impaled. Even in broad daylight, it was easy to imagine him hanging there.

He reflected that bona fide exorcists have recounted how the smallest and seemingly weakest possessed person can have extraordinary strength. Getting over that fence shouldn't have been hard for a demon. Unless the demon had been weakened by the consecrated ground. His formal theological training didn't allow him to come to a conclusion.

He sat down where he had collapsed that night and leaned his head against the same headstone. The ground was wet. He didn't care.

His side hurt – more than it had in several days.

Your wound will remind you, Todd had said.

He said a prayer for the souls of David Todd, Lord Haysham, Adrian Scott, Joshua Todd, Clive Challoner, and the nameless victims of the Society – regardless of Anglican teaching on the subject.

He lifted his head to the sunshine. It was a beautiful spring day. He yearned to take a long walk, to get lost in the woods.

He stood up, and his eye went to the name on the tombstone:

Adam Ainsley, 1926–1938, Beloved Son, Now In The Arms of His Saviour.

He remembered the name. It was the son of John Ainsley, the vicar at St Mark's whose boy had drowned in the pond while the Woodrich sword was kept at the vicarage.

Well, of course, Father Gilbert thought. He had no doubt that the boy had jet-black hair and had worn a dark suit of clothes.

CHAPTER 44

The reconsecration was a small event. For obvious reasons, Father Gilbert hadn't offered a general invitation to the parish. Bishop William Spalding officiated, though he did so nervously, as if he was participating in a superstitious ritual. Mrs Mayhew and Mr Urquhart were there. Father Benson attended as his last duty at St Mark's. He was to leave the next day for a parish near Nottingham.

The clergy were dressed in vestments – copes, chasubles, and stoles, with the Bishop wearing his mitre. Their colour was purple, to represent humility and penance.

Father Gilbert was disappointed to learn that the Church of England didn't have a set liturgy for the reconsecration of a church. He had assembled a rite from several liturgical traditions.

They began in the nave and slowly processed to every room of the church. The Bishop read the prayers and blessings.

They finished at the crypt door, which was closed. The Bishop read:

"Prevent us, O Lord, in all our doings with thy most gracious favour, and further us with thy continual help; that in all our works, begun, continued, and ended in thee, we may glorify thy holy Name, and finally by thy mercy obtain everlasting life; through Jesus Christ our Lord. Amen."

The Bishop lifted his pastoral staff and knocked three times on the door.

Father Gilbert resisted the sudden apprehension that someone – or something – might knock back.

"Open to me the gates of righteousness, that I may go into them and give thanks unto the Lord," the Bishop read.

Father Gilbert opened the door to the crypt.

The Bishop moved into the entrance and proclaimed:

"Peace be to this place where the bodies of thy people may rest in peace and be preserved from all indignities, whilst their souls are safely kept in the hands of their faithful Creator. Peace be to this place from God's Son who is our Peace and from the Holy Ghost, the Comforter."

He lifted his arms and staff, looking like Moses before the Red Sea. "Let us faithfully and devoutly beg God's blessing on this our undertaking." He then descended into the crypt.

One by one, they followed.

"O Lord, hear our prayer," he said.

"And let our cry come unto thee," they responded.

Father Gilbert thought about the black mass. Undoing it with the reconsecration filled him with a sense of holy purpose. The dark acts would be dispelled with light.

Mr Urquhart had rigged extra lighting along the walls, the shadows driven away by a warm glow.

The Bishop prayed:

"O Eternal God, mighty in power, of majesty incomprehensible, whom the heaven of heavens cannot contain, much less the walls of temples made with hands; vouchsafe, O Lord, to be present with us, who are now gathered together to reconsecrate this place, with all humility and readiness of heart, to the honour of thy great Name; separating it henceforth from all unhallowed, ordinary, and common uses; and dedicating it entirely to thy service."

"Amen."

The Bishop stepped forward to the centre of the crypt, very close to the altar where David Todd had performed his black mass. No one knew how many others had been conducted there. He took the staff and traced the sign of the Cross upon the floor. Beneath it, he traced the Greek symbols for the Alpha and the Omega. He spoke loudly, as if to make sure that everyone and everything could hear him. "I claim this place for Christ crucified, who is the First and the Last, and the Lord of all!"

"Amen."

"One Lord, one Faith, one Baptism!"

"One God and Father of all," they said.

There was a moment of silence and Father Gilbert strained to listen, sure that the screams of escaping demons would be heard. Instead, the wound at his side burned.

"And now, by virtue of the sacred office committed to us in the Church, I do declare to be reconsecrated and set apart from all profane and common uses this House of God. In the Name of the Father, and of the Son, and of the Holy Spirit. Amen."

"Amen."

"Glory be to the Father, and to the Son, and to the Holy Ghost; as it was in the beginning, is now, and ever shall be, world without end."

"Amen."

"Now unto the King eternal, immortal, invisible, the only wise God, be honour and glory, for ever and ever."

"Amen."

* * *

That night, the small group celebrated with a bonfire in an open space at the far corner of the graveyard. Those sections of the profaned altar that could be burned went up in bright flames and sparks like fireflies. Later, it was decided, Mr Urquhart would smash the marble from the top and use the pieces as paving stones in the graveyard.

"I hope this puts an end to it," Mrs Mayhew said as they walked to their cars.

Father Gilbert didn't tell her about the figure in the dark cloak who'd been watching them from the other side of the iron fence.

If you loved

THE BODY UNDER THE BRIDGE

don't miss…

THE BABYLON CONTINGENCY

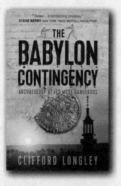

"This is a gem of a read, tense and fulfilling with a tantalizing premise."

STEVE BERRY, *NEW YORK TIMES*
BESTSELLING AUTHOR

"With no warning he slipped his gun off his shoulder, levelled it, and fired. The noise was devastating. We could see the muzzle flashes, like a jet of fire. Bullets sprayed in a semicircle as if from a hose."

Investigating a break-in at an English country house, DCI Robbie Peele comes face to face with armed burglars seeking some of the strangest objects in world archaeology, ancient clay disks inscribed with an unknown alphabet.

A Middle Eastern terrorist cell is determined to steal them. Why? And why are Mossad involved?

The vital clue is a long-abandoned Muslim village in Crete, where terrible things happened, witnessed by a Victorian explorer who left coded diaries. But Crete poses as many puzzles as it solves.

What do the disks really say, in what language, and who made them? And why is the answer stirring up the Middle East? This is archaeology at its most intriguing – and most dangerous.

CLIFFORD LONGLEY is an author, broadcaster, and journalist specializing in British and international affairs. For twenty years he wrote a weekly column in *The Times*.

ISBN: 978-1-78264-120-9 | e-ISBN: 978-1-78264-121-6

UK £7.99 | US $14.99

THE HERETIC

"Quite magnificent... moments of astonishing power... a work of importance... the capacity to become a cult book."

PENELOPE WILCOCK

1536: all is change in England. Strange ideas intrude, new lands are discovered, and Henry's dissolution of the monasteries overturns the certainties of centuries. In this new world order, spies abound. Who can be trusted?

Brother Pacificus hopes the rural isolation of the Abbey of St Benets in Norfolk will prove a sanctuary. But he hopes in vain: this last Benedictine house is mired in murder and intrigue. Pacificus is implicated, dark pasts are brought to light... and the body count keeps rising.

Three local children are torn from their parents and find protection from a mysterious leper, a Dutch eel catcher, and this errant monk. But soon they will discover that neither parents nor protectors are quite what they seem. The three youngsters are forced to grow up very, very fast.

Based closely on historical events, this post-medieval mystery is laced with romance, fuelled by greed, and decorated with bouts of feasting, smuggling, and jailbreak.

HENRY VYNER-BROOKS is a landscape architect by training. He lives in the Lake District, with his wife Ruth and five children.

ISBN: 978-1-78264-096-7 | e-ISBN: 978-1-78264-095-0

UK £7.99 | US $14.99